THE RELUCTANT VIRGIN

Also by Doug Taylor

Lilies of the Covenant

The trials and joys of five generations of the Taylor family in eighteenth-century England, nineteenth-century Newfoundland, and twentieth-century Toronto.

Citadel on the Hill

A history of a church community in Toronto in the first decade of the twentieth century, chronicling the trials and successes of the congregation as it progresses into the modern era.

The Pathway of Duty

An immigrant family from England arrives in Canada in 1907 and struggles to survive in the harsh conditions of Toronto's Earlscourt District. The sinking of the *Empress of Ireland* in 1914 in the icy waters of the St. Lawrence River dramatically changes their lives forever.

There Never Was a Better Time

Two young brothers immigrate to Canada. This is a humorous and intimate glimpse into their family life in bustling Toronto during the 1920s, as well as the adventures of their brothers, parents, and rascal of a grandfather.

The Villages Within

An irreverent history of Toronto and a respectful guide to the old St. Andrew's Market, Kings West District, colourful Kensington Market, and delightfully tacky Queen Street West.

Arse Over Teakettle: Toronto Trilogy, Book One

An intriguing tale of growing up in Toronto during the days of the Second World War and the immediate post-war era. Tom Hudson and his mischievous friend, Shorty, find adventure in their seemingly quiet neighbourhood as they yearn to discover the secrets of the older boys.

THE RELUCTANT VIRGIN

Murder in 1950s Toronto

◆

TORONTO TRILOGY, BOOK TWO

DOUG TAYLOR

iUniverse, Inc.
Bloomington

The Reluctant Virgin
Murder in 1950s Toronto
Toronto Trilogy, Book Two

Copyright © 2011 by Doug Taylor

All rights reserved. No part of this book may be used or reproduced by any means, graphic, electronic, or mechanical, including photocopying, recording, taping or by any information storage retrieval system without the written permission of the publisher except in the case of brief quotations embodied in critical articles and reviews.

This is a work of fiction. All of the characters, names, incidents, organizations, and dialogue in this novel are either the products of the author's imagination or are used fictitiously.

iUniverse books may be ordered through booksellers or by contacting:

iUniverse
1663 Liberty Drive
Bloomington, IN 47403
www.iuniverse.com
1-800-Authors (1-800-288-4677)

Because of the dynamic nature of the Internet, any web addresses or links contained in this book may have changed since publication and may no longer be valid. The views expressed in this work are solely those of the author and do not necessarily reflect the views of the publisher, and the publisher hereby disclaims any responsibility for them.

Any people depicted in stock imagery provided by Thinkstock are models, and such images are being used for illustrative purposes only.

Certain stock imagery © Thinkstock.

ISBN: 978-1-4620-4645-4 (sc)
ISBN: 978-1-4620-4646-1 (hc)
ISBN: 978-1-4620-4647-8 (e)

Library of Congress Control Number: 2011914632

Printed in the United States of America

iUniverse rev. date: 11/07/2011

Regardless of how long we live,
in certain situations and on some
occasions, we are all virgins.

This book is a work of fiction. Names of places in Toronto are real, as are the streets, buildings, and shops. However, other than the historical personages, the characters and incidents are the author's imagination, or the author has employed them fictitiously. Any resemblance to real events or to persons living or dead is coincidental.

Preface

In every decade, deeds are committed in dark places that are unknown to those who tread life's well-lit paths. This was true as the 1950s dawned in Toronto. The city's residents viewed their insular world as relatively staid and secure, even though they knew that crime existed and it was a part of daily life. However, no one suspected that a serial killer was soon to roam the quiet residential avenues and forested river valleys of Toronto. Crimes of this scope did not happen in "Toronto the Good."

Torontonians thought of their city as a place that embraced and maintained traditional values, even though they were mindful of the shifting morals and new attitudes that were creeping into their neighbourhoods after the war years. Despite this, they remained blissfully unaware that the changes would sweep away the last vestiges of the city's innocence, and that by the end of the decade, Toronto would be a vastly different city.

Every author's journey into the past, whether fictional or scholarly, includes truth, delusions, and exaggerations. This story is no exception. It unfolds in a decade when a well-connected businessman carried a gold-tipped fountain pen in the breast pocket of his pinstripe suit, rather than a Blackberry or cell phone. If men and women wished to be successful and enjoy the respect of their neighbours, their life needed to reflect the values espoused by the local churches or synagogues. Despite the increasing number of immigrants from non-English-speaking countries, respect for the traditional Canadian way of life, allegiance toward Britain, and loyalty to the royal family were important. This was the reality of Toronto in the year our tale begins.

Yonge Street in 1951

The photograph of Yonge Street in 1951 gazes northward from near Gould Street. On the west (left-hand) side of the photo, Elm Street intersects with Yonge. Steele's Tavern at 394 Yonge Street, where Gordon Lightfoot sang in the following decade, is in the foreground on the right-hand side of the picture.

The main characters of our tale are young Tom Hudson and his friends. They did not know about Steele's Tavern, but the Yonge Street in the photo was familiar to them. It was the main thoroughfare of what was then Canada's second largest city. The street they knew remains somewhat intact today. Many of the low-rise buildings flanking the street are still there, their signage as garish and intrusive as in yesteryear.

However, in 1951 there was less automobile and pedestrian traffic. Because there were fewer cars, the city allowed street parking on its main thoroughfares. In the photo, on the west (left-hand) side of the street, near the southbound streetcar, we see empty parking spaces. There was no subway. The square-shaped Peter Witt streetcars trundled noisily along the roadway on ribbons of steel. Despite the hustle and bustle of the nighttime bars and clubs, Yonge Street was quieter, calmer, and less hurried than today. However, the principal characters in our story visited Yonge Street only occasionally. Their daily lives centred more on the quiet community where they lived.

Although the next photo is not the neighbourhood of our story, Tom Hudson and his friends would have felt at home on this tree-lined avenue. The street was akin to a small village. For decades, families purchased homes and raised children, and after their offspring had departed, remained in the same dwellings. Up and down the avenue, people recognized each other, either by name or by sight. They warmly greeted those they passed on the street and conversed with those they knew more intimately. On Halloween, excited children knocked at their doors. At yuletide, they heartily wished each other a "very merry Christmas."

The corner store in the picture is typical of the type that the Hudson family patronized. In the photograph, a boy Tom's age stands on the sidewalk beside his bicycle, gazing at the quiet roadway. Coca Cola advertises its refreshing beverage, the price a mere seven cents. It was indeed a different world than that of today.

Though larger supermarkets were increasingly common, plazas had not yet appeared on the urban scene. The daily needs of the Hudson family were met by a corner store such as this. It was where neighbours gossiped and shared life's tribulations and joys.

It was a decade when homes lacked air-conditioning. Along with their neighbours, the Hudsons relaxed on their sheltered veranda on humid summer evenings to escape the heat inside the house and observe the passing street scene. In winter, they chatted with their neighbours as they shovelled the blowing drifts of snow from their sidewalks.

When compared to our modern world, the street seems to represent a less harried way of life, but despite the slower pace, Tom's parents did not always view it in that manner. The Second World War had ended just six years before, and the wounds had not healed. Although industry had converted to peacetime production, unemployment remained a threat.

Adding to their difficulties, as previously mentioned, it was increasingly evident that change was in the air, and they viewed it with apprehension. As in any generation, teenagers and young adults were the first to adapt to the changing times. It was evident in their music, slang, dress code, and behaviour. This too was a worry for the adults.

A corner store on a quiet street in 1950s Toronto

As the narrative begins, Tom Hudson realizes that his own life is drastically changing. In former years, he attended elementary school, played baseball, and learned about the sexual secrets of the "big boys" on a street such as the one in the picture. In the laneways behind the houses, he also discovered many of life's other lessons. In the local store, Tom overheard adults discuss important events of the day, and it was where he learned to be wary of the vicious local gossip, the formidable Mrs. Martha Klacker.

x

Then, on Labour Day weekend in 1951, as he is about to begin high school, a brutal murder occurs. In the days ahead, the murder intrudes into his formerly secure life. For Tom, nothing would ever be the same. In every decade, there are deeds committed in dark places that are unknown to those who tread life's well-lit paths. The "dark places" are about to enter Tom's world.

Chapter One

Storm clouds were gathering in the west as the amber glow of twilight hovered over the secluded Humber Valley. It had been a sweltering, humid day, and despite the sun's declining rays, the air remained oppressive. Trees were motionless, the wind withholding its breath, denying a weary landscape the relief it so richly deserved.

On a forested nature trail hugging the west bank of the Humber River, a young woman, who had entered the valley near Scarlett Road and Eglinton Avenue, was walking northward on the trail beside the river. At the north end of the trail, choosing a location where the thick foliage hid her from view, the woman paused to observe at a two-storey frame home on Raymore Drive, where builders had constructed houses on the floodplain of the valley.

Ten minutes later, after seeing eight or nine visitors enter the house, she commenced walking again. Clearly upset, her steps were now unsteady, and she stumbled repeatedly. She continued northward on the trail, exited the valley, and crossed over to the east side of the river via the bridge on Lawrence Avenue. An elderly man passed her on the bridge, and realizing that she was clearly upset, he smiled sympathetically. Later, he remembered her, as she was young and quite attractive.

In a state of confusion, the woman appeared to wander aimlessly on the wooded trail on the river's east bank. Then she turned and retraced her steps across the bridge. She descended again into the solitude of the valley and in a daze meandered along the embankment on the west side of the river. By now, the last traces of twilight had dissolved into the impenetrable darkness of the night. A slight breeze gently swayed the upper branches of the trees as the approaching rain clouds from the west drifted closer. Within a few moments, they ominously obscured the moon.

The woman's pace was slow. Several times, she stopped to wipe away tears. Oblivious to her surroundings, she was unaware that someone was following her. She continued along the forested trail, the intense darkness having closed the valley against the outside world.

The stalker required no light to perceive the victim, her image burned forever into memory—shoulder-length blonde hair, attractive features, and a shapely body. The stalker cared nothing about her beauty. She was a threat.

Familiar with the contours of the landscape, the stalker walked briskly on an alternate trail to a position on the path ahead of her and waited, hidden among the pitch-black foliage, knowing that the woman would shortly pass by.

Eyes misted with tears, the woman was stunned when a sinister shadow became human and sprang to life from the gloom surrounding her. She froze in her tracks as she stared at the apparition. The terrifying shape possessed eyes that glowed with hate. She recognized the eyes, which increased her shock. She was unable to react as fear paralyzed her.

With only a moment's hesitation, the stalker smashed a fist-sized rock against the young woman's head. She collapsed. As she lay unconscious, the murder weapon was thrown into the river. Next, the stalker lifted the helpless victim, carried her away from the path beside the river, and dumped her into the thick undergrowth.

In the darkness amid the secluded bushes, the stalker sexually violated her, and when finished, executed a strange course of action. An observer might have mistaken it for a ritual.

The stalker's face displayed no emotion while patiently waiting for the victim's breathing to cease. When certain she was dead, the murderer slipped away into the impenetrable darkness, thinking no more of the corpse in the valley than if it had been a sack of garbage.

Surrounding the body, the seasonal sounds of Toronto's Humber

Valley continued, oblivious to the human drama that just unfolded. An old bullfrog, partially submerged in a shallow eddy beside the river, continued his deep croaking, even though the mating season was long since spent.

The rumble of thunder rolled across the valley, and the patter of the first raindrops splashed on the parched foliage. Insects, oblivious to nature's endless cycles, infused the night air with their ritualistic buzzing, unaware that in the days ahead, the cruel frosts of autumn would either force them into eternal silence or deliver them into the slumbering depths of winter's lifeless hibernation.

Tom Hudson was not aware of the brutal murder in the valley. However, at thirteen years of age, he was cognizant that from this time forward, his life would be vastly different. He had arrived at a pivotal point in his journey toward manhood.

It was the final day of August, the beginning of the Labour Day weekend in 1951, and although the sun had already dipped below the horizon, the slow burn of a late-summer heat wave continued to scorch the tree-lined streets and darkened laneways of Toronto. Distant thunder echoed from the west, but the moisture falling over the Humber Valley had not yet reached Lauder Avenue. People remained out on their verandas, seeking relief from the stifling air inside their homes. Among them were Tom and his brother, Ken, who was two years older than he was. Their grandparents sat outside as well, the boys' parents inside the home listening to a murder mystery on the radio in the living room.

Having nothing else to do, Tom and his brother quietly observed the street scene. It was too late to go anywhere and too early to go to bed. They sipped on an ice-cold glass of strawberry Freshie, a powdered drink mix their mom had made earlier in the evening.

In the darkness, Ken leaned closer to Tom and whispered in a conspiratorial voice, "Hell, man, when I returned from the park this evening, I saw Old Shit-Bag Klacker sitting on her veranda. She's like a bitch watchin' a fire hydrant, always lookin' for an excuse to piss on someone."

Tom chuckled at his older brother's choice of swear words. He knew that Mrs. Klacker, an elderly neighbour, was a vicious gossip and troublemaker, and he admired his brother's mature vocabulary, although he was reluctant to add any cuss words of his own, as his mother had reprimanded him the previous week for saying the word "shit."

Instead, he said quietly to Ken, "Klacker really is a dog. She barks at anyone who steps near her precious lawn. I bet she has fleas!"

Ken grinned mischievously as he continued his rant. "On a hot night like this, I bet the old bitch is panting like hell from the heat. Dogs can't sweat. I'd like to give the old bag a swift kick in the ass and really give her something to pant over."

"Yeah, and I'd like to kick her water bowl off her veranda."

They both laughed quietly, enjoying the cleverness of their wit, grateful that their grandparents were unable to hear the reason for their muffled laughter.

Tom's grandparents had lived with the Hudson family for the past six years. Ken and Tom referred to their grandmother as Nan and their grandfather as Gramps. In some respects, their grandparents were a matched pair. Both were in their seventies, about five-foot five, their round faces lined from many years of toil. Age had peppered Nan's hair with gray, and she wore it pulled back in a bun. Gramps' remaining fringe of hair and his thin moustache were also gray. Despite being alike in many ways, their personalities were quite different.

Nan was fond of saying, "Life's a serious business."

Gramps always smiled when she uttered this remark and invariably added, "Yes! Damn monkey business." The irreverent comment always earned Gramps a rebuke from Nan.

Tom's relationship with Gramps had always been close. When Tom was younger, he told Gramps about his secret adventures, intimate thoughts, and daily problems. Gramps enjoyed upsetting the household by telling risqué stories and offering mischievous remarks. Whenever Gramps told a humorous tale, his ample belly shook and invariably, he rubbed his hand over his bald head as he chuckled. Though Tom was now a teenager, he would never have dared to utter comments like Gramps made, at least not within earshot of his parents.

Gramps was Tom's idea of a perfect grandfather, as he was a rascal who had survived the perils of life on the seas. When Gramps had been a young man, he had cooked for the crew aboard a schooner on the Grand Banks of Newfoundland. Now he was enjoying his retirement years in Toronto. His colourful language and desire to tease and provoke had not lessened with the passing years.

The previous day, Tom had heard Nan reprimand Gramps for saying, "The biblical tale of the whale swallowing Jonah is a ridiculous story. If Jonah had swallowed the whale then it would have been worth mentioning."

"Hold your jaw shut, you old goat," Nan had said in rebuke. "One of these days, you'll trip over that vile tongue of yours."

Gramps winked at Tom and grinned.

On this humid summer night on the veranda, as Tom and Ken continued observing the passing scene, Tom was unaware that his grandfather was watching him. Noticing the serious look on Tom's face, he suspected his grandson's thoughts. The previous week, Tom had told him that he was dreading Tuesday morning, when he would be entering grade nine at York Collegiate Institute.

Gramps gazed over at Tom and asked, "Are you still worried about goin' back at school?" When Tom offered no reply, he added, "Don't let yer loss of freedom bother you. I lost me freedom when I married your grandmother. I survived."

He chuckled after he completed the final statement, and despite the darkness, Tom saw him wink at him. Then Gramps gazed at Nan, hoping that he had provoked a reaction.

Nan took the bait.

"There wasn't much freedom for me after I married you. Raising seven boys and keeping house kept me as busy as an old workhorse."

"Having seven sons wasn't my fault. You couldn't find your shut-off valve."

"Never mind me valve. I should've tied a knot in that old rope of yours. I might've had more free time," she said in rebuke.

Almost as soon as she had spoken, Nan regretted it. She fell silent, hoping the conversation would end. Many times Tom had heard Nan say, "Raising a large family is a *serious* matter and not a subject for silly remarks."

Tom sometimes thought that "serious" was Nan's favourite word.

"If you had tied a knot in me rope," Gramps continued, "I'd still have found a way to slip me dory into the harbour."

Nan frowned in disgust. She had suffered enough of Gramps' asinine teasing.

"Hush. This conversation is unsuitable for the boys' ears. Give your tongue a rest."

"My tongue is always at rest. That's why it stays out of trouble."

Tom smiled at his grandfather's claim, appreciating the irony of the statement.

Gramps grinned in satisfaction, thinking he had uttered the final word. He adored Nan, but he also adored teasing her. Nan had once jokingly told Ken and Tom, "When I married your grandfather, instead of getting a silk purse, I got a bag of skin stretched over a supply of hot air and silliness." Then she added, "Love makes you overlook many things."

Within a few minutes, Nan decided to return inside the house. As she opened the screen door, she gazed at her grandsons and said, "When I married your grandfather, I thought I had found gold, but now I realize that I married a brass farthing."

Having delivered her final line, she departed the stage.

Tom's parents had christened him Thomas, after his father, but the family always referred to him as Tom. The previous June, he had graduated from

D. B. Hood Public School, which he had attended for all eight years of his elementary education. Throughout the years, he had never been at the top of his class academically, but through hard work, he had always managed to achieve decent grades. His family lived on Lauder Avenue in the Township of York, a suburb of Toronto. The family homestead was near Rogers Road and Oakwood Avenue.

Tom was slender and although not muscular, he possessed a wiry build. His legs were strong and well muscled from many long hours riding his bicycle. Brown hair, dark eyes, and clear skin gave him a wholesome appearance, not exactly attractive, but "pleasant to the eye," as some adults said. Others referred to him as "a nice looking lad," but it was rare for anyone to say he was handsome. Shy by nature, within the family he lived in the shadow of his older brother, and outside the home, his two best friends, Shorty and Harry, invariably dominated him. Though independent in his thinking, in his actions, he was more of a follower than an instigator.

On this evening, in the hazy glow of the streetlights, Tom noticed that Shorty was crossing the street and approaching the house. Shorty was a nickname that the guys had given him when he was younger, as in those years he had been several inches shorter than the other boys. During those years, his complexion had been pimply and the neighbours had referred to him as being homely. However, time had been kind to him. Each year, like a vintage wine, he seemed to improve.

The previous year, the pimples on his face disappeared, and he had grown several inches. Shorty was now as tall as his friends, and it appeared that if his growth continued, he would soon be taller than they were. He had always possessed a muscular build, and anyone who observed him walking knew he was athletic. His fine features and dark hair were appealing, but his most striking feature was his shiny turquoise eyes, which seemed to dart in every direction at once.

During the previous year, the girls had begun to notice him, but they remained wary of his mischievous ways. Adults sometimes said that when he was older, he might have movie-star looks. The girls that were his age remained doubtful. They viewed Shorty as a "wait-and-see" kind of guy.

Tom had known Shorty since he had had been in grade two at D. B.

Hood. At times, Shorty could be outrageous, a trait that endeared him to Tom. Shorty was also the only one of Tom's friends who was Jewish. Tom had never really thought much about his friend's religion, as it was a topic that boys his age rarely discussed. When Shorty was younger, the older boys teased him about his lack of height, and his being Jewish compounded the cruel remarks. When confronted by his tormentors, Shorty had always been able to defend himself, both verbally and with his fists. His tormentors soon learned to be wary of him.

As Shorty arrived on the veranda of the Hudson home, he greeted Ken and Tom. Then he said to Gramps, "Hi, Mr. Hudson." Gramps sleepily grunted an unintelligible acknowledgement. Shorty sat down beside his two friends.

"Hot as hell tonight," he said quietly to Tom and Ken, wiping the sweat from his brow in an exaggerated manner.

"Yeah! Shit man, it's bloody hot," Ken replied. "I'm too dry to spit."

"I went to Carol's house tonight," Shorty informed them.

The boys had also known Carol since they had been small kids. Shorty had harboured a humongous crush on her since he had first met her, but throughout the years, she had ignored his attentions, as she considered him an incorrigible rascal. Now older, Shorty longed to be her boyfriend. Carol admitted that Shorty was "sort of" attractive, but she never showed any interest in him romantically. She viewed him as a friend of long standing, almost a brother—a mischievous one at that.

Shorty continued. "I thought I'd sit with Carol on her veranda, but she said she was goin' up the street to visit Sophie. I asked her if I could walk with her. She said it was okay. On the way, we passed Old Shit-Faced Klacker's house."

At the mention of Klacker's name, the Hudson brothers perked up their ears. Mrs. Martha Klacker, whom they had been joking about earlier, had recently moved into their neighbourhood. On this evening, Shorty told Ken and Tom about his encounter with the dreaded woman.

"The old witch was sitting on her veranda and saw Carol and me walking by. It was dark and we didn't know she was there, 'til her voice cut the air like a wet fart during a synagogue prayer."

The boys laughed conspiratorially.

"She told us to shove off. She said she didn't want anyone hangin' around in front of her house, especially kids 'like the two of us,' whatever the hell that means. I felt like telling her to fly away on her broom and drop her shit somewhere else, but before I could say anything, Carol put her hand on my arm, warning me to keep quiet. I did as she told me."

At this point in the conversation, he sighed. Tom and Ken knew the reason. Shorty always obeyed Carol's wishes, but she never responded by accepting his invitations to go to the movies with him. Whenever he was with her, all the other kids were invariably tagging along.

Shorty continued. "We kept on walking up the street, and when Carol joined Sophie on her veranda, I came over here. I'm tellin' you, one of these days, I swear, I'll get even with Old Crap-Face Klacker. She's a real pain in the ass." Then, as an afterthought, he added, "Man, I wish Carol would understand how much I like her. Know my meanin'?"

While Shorty had been telling about his encounter with Old Klacker, the boys had assumed that Gramps was asleep, but he had been listening. He had encountered the odious Klacker many times, and similar to the boys, intensely disliked her.

Klacker was twice the size of Gramps. He enjoyed saying, "Whenever I see her, I feel like a harbour tugboat beside an ocean liner, even though she's more like a *tramp* steamer."

Indeed, Klacker was an imposing woman. Not fat. Simply large. She was only an inch short of six foot, big boned, and broad shouldered. When she had been a teenager, her neighbours had whispered that when she played basketball at the high school, it was on the boys' team. Now an older woman, Klacker's masculine oxford-style shoes and severe outfits added to her masculine appearance. It did not help that she sported a slight moustache on her upper lip.

Tom's parents had known Klacker since the days when they had lived at Dufferin Street and Eglinton Avenue. She had been the terror of their former neighbourhood. The previous month, Tom's mom and dad had been incredulous when they discovered that Klacker had moved to Lauder Avenue. Neighbours already referred to her as Mouthy Martha.

After listening to Shorty's tale of verbal abuse, Gramps decided "to shove his own oar into the water," as he liked to say. Nan was nowhere in sight, so he saw no reason to be careful with his choice of words.

"That Klacker woman has a face like a bucket of hen's arseholes," he mumbled in disgust.

Tom grinned, remembering that a few days ago he had heard Gramps say the same thing about Mrs. Klacker, and recalled that Nan had demanded that he retract his remark.

"Okay," he said, "I'll half take it back. Her face is like a half-bucket of hen's arseholes."

Nan had walked away in disgust, while Tom had suppressed his muffled laughter.

On this evening, the boys laughed aloud, thoroughly enjoying Gramps' colourful language, pleased that Nan was not present to censure it. About fifteen minutes later, Shorty departed. The air had not cooled, but the hour was late, so Ken and Tom retreated inside the house.

As midnight approached, the boys climbed the stairs to their bedroom. The gentle patter of rain was beginning. The storm that had commenced earlier over the Humber Valley was now moving eastward across the city. When the drops on the roof became heavy, Ken reluctantly closed the bedroom window, shutting out the cool air as well as the rain.

Outside, unheard and unseen by the boys, a car passed on the street, its tires hissing on the wet asphalt, its headlights reflecting off the glistening roadway. The rain held the promise that perhaps the following day the temperatures would be more comfortable.

Although it was past midnight, the stalker remained awake, sitting in the kitchen, staring at the trophy extracted from the victim. The raindrops beating on the windowpanes drowned out the dripping of the leaky faucet in the sink, but being absorbed in thought, the stalker heard neither sound. In the stalker's mind, the killing had been necessary.

Then, the stalker's childhood years flooded back—a quiet evening in the family homestead, and later, the anticipation of the bedroom door opening and knowledge of what was certain to occur. It was as if it had been preordained and beyond anyone's control.

On this humid August evening, the stalker finally retired. Wearily entering the bedroom, an hour later, sleep eventually delivered peace. As the early hours of the morning crept across the city, the rain ceased and silence fell across the city.

On Saturday morning, the sky was clear as the blood-red sun broke above the horizon. The air had not cooled, despite the overnight rain. It was to be another scorcher. In a modest two-storey house on Scarlett Road, in the west end of the city, nine-year-old Arnold Mason was awake. Arnold's brother, David, three years his junior, slept on a rollaway bed on the opposite side of the room.

The summer weather had taken its toll on the surroundings of the Mason home. The petunias in the flowerbed at the front of the house had wilted and collapsed against the baked soil. The lawn had many ugly yellow patches, the recent rain being too little, too late.

Across the road, the narrow strip of parkland that hugged the west bank of the Humber Valley dropped precipitously to the river that lazily wound its way southward toward Lake Ontario. The valley was the boys' playground in all seasons, but in summer, when the heat of a humid day descended, they particularly enjoyed its environs, as it always remained cooler than the asphalt-covered streets surrounding it. Because their family was unable to afford a cottage, the valley was the only retreat available to them.

Arnold was looking forward to the day, as it meant another excursion into the valley to splash through the river's shallow water, his blue overalls thrown over a low-hanging tree limb and his well-worn running shoes discarded under a chokecherry bush. He imagined himself to be Huck Finn exploring the wild banks of the mighty Mississippi, and his best friend, Mario, as a reincarnation of Tom Sawyer.

On this morning, the sunshine awakened Arnold shortly after daybreak. It was the final weekend before school opened. He disliked the confinement of the classroom. The only subject he enjoyed was science. Living beside the Humber Valley, he knew the world of nature intimately. He was familiar with the places where the salamanders scurried beneath the flat rocks, the grassy knolls where the garter snakes bathed in the sun, and the ponds where the biggest chub swam in schools.

Arnold's mom had forbidden him to get out of bed before she rose, a rule he felt that only an adult could concoct. He had often surreptitiously told his younger brother, "Adults' brains turn to mush on a hot summer day. They sit in the shade suckin' on a beer bottle. That stuff smells like cold piss!"

David giggled whenever he heard his brother cuss.

When Arnold heard his mother descending the stairs to the kitchen, he knew it was okay for him to toss back the bedsheet and scamper down the stairs. David observed Arnold rise, and within seconds, he was trailing behind him.

After the boys had wolfed down their Nabisco shredded wheat, they heard the voice of Mario hollering outside the backdoor. Mario also lived on Scarlett Road, five doors to the north of them. Mario was the same age as Arnold, but he was taller and stockier in build. His curly black hair and olive complexion spoke to his Italian heritage. His voice, calling for his friends to join him outside in nature's glorious sunshine, was worthy of the finest renditions of Enrico Caruso, even if it was the shortest aria ever written.

"Oh, Arnold!" he chorused with enthusiasm.

Impatiently, Mario waited at the backdoor of the Mason home for any signs of life within. In his hand he held an empty old plastic bucket. Its handles were long gone and replaced with a rope tied to new holes that his dad had drilled. He never filled the bucket above halfway, as the weight of the water would split the plastic where the rope was attached. The bucket could hold sufficient water to contain many minnows and chub. They always placed the captured specimens in an old washing machine stored in the Mason's garage. Mr. Mason had plugged the hole in the tub's bottom, after he had removed the bulky thrasher. It was a perfect aquarium, and they spent many hours in the garage observing the fish they collected. It was their personal "Sea World."

Breakfast finished, Arnold ignored his mother's warnings not to bang the screen door, as he and David crashed out the backdoor, the slamming noise drowning out her words. Arnold and Mario, with little David tagging along, set forth on this sun-filled Saturday morning in hopes of snaring the large chub that inhabited the pool where a small stream entered the river from the west. They had secretly nicknamed the fish the "big bastard," but never told anyone for fear their parents might punish them for using a swear word. They never understood why, as they constantly overheard adults cussing when they were angry and thought that no kids were around.

On this morning, although Mario was clearly the leader, Arnold walked beside him, while David trudged along behind. The older boys would have preferred to be on their own, but Arnold's mother had insisted that they allow David to accompany them. Anyone who observed Arnold and David knew they were brothers, as their slender builds, light brown hair, blue eyes, and fine features were similar.

The three adventurous musketeers crossed Scarlett Road and entered the valley about a half mile north of Eglinton Avenue. As it was a holiday weekend, vehicle traffic was sparse. Within minutes, they were traipsing along the trail among the bushes. Before they reached their intended destination, a foul odour assaulted their nostrils.

"Geez, damn, hell," Mario spat. "I think one of the big kids had a shit down here last night." Mario enjoyed cussing, secure that in the private world of the valley no adult could hear him.

"It smells more like a fuckin' dead dog to me," little David added from behind them, trying to compete with the older boy's use of bad language.

Arnold and Mario glanced disapprovingly at David. They considered the art of cussing to be their domain and resented the competition, not understanding that David felt that cussing was one of the few ways that he could be the equal of his older companions.

"I think he's right," Mario chimed in. "It does smell more like a fuckin' dead dog."

"More like a hundred fuckin' dead dogs," little David chimed in again, a satisfied grin on his face, proud that Mario had confirmed his diagnosis.

Ignoring David, Mario said, "I wonder if it's old man Jeffery's dog? That snarling bitch deserves to die." In disgust, he spit on the grass beside the trail.

"Let's look and see," Arnold said.

Holding his nose, Mario parted the bushes.

The boys gazed in shock. It was a human body, lying on its back, its face partially obscured by flies. Insects buzzed noisily, millions of them, while millions of others seemed to be gathering from everywhere to join the feast.

Mario dropped his bucket and fled, holding his nose, not daring to take a breath. The other two boys shrieked wildly as they raced behind him.

When the boys came crashing in the backdoor of the Mason home, Mr. Mason was relaxing in his favourite chair reading the Saturday newspaper. He listened only half-heartedly to their excited voices, seeing no reason to take their concerns seriously. It was not the first time they had raced home from the valley in a panic. He thought of the time his sons had sworn that there was a wild bear roaming the bushes, and it had turned out to be a tramp in a black coat. Then he smiled as he remembered the time an old woman had convinced David that she had found a cow's egg. She gave it to the boy, and he had lugged the damn rock home. He recalled that when David had arrived in the house, he had told his mom, "I want you to hatch a baby cow. I want you to sit on it. That's what moms do."

Mr. Mason had chuckled, as he said to his wife, "I agree with David, dear. His request seems reasonable."

She swatted him with the *Life* magazine she had been reading. "I know a few things *you* can sit on," she had teased in retaliation.

David had not understood his parents' mirth. He told them that the egg was getting cold, and they were simply joking around. For months, he sulked because he never got a baby cow for a pet.

Mr. Mason's thoughts now returned to the present. Mario was insisting that it was not a dead dog or any other animal. It was a dead body!

Finally, Mr. Mason reluctantly placed the sport's section of the weekend edition of the *Telegram* newspaper on the coffee table and pulled on his hiking boots.

Within fifteen minutes, he returned to the house, grabbed the phone, and twenty minutes later, two police officers came to the house.

By noon, police were swarming the Humber Valley.

Detective Ernie Miller, a senior detective with the Etobicoke Police, was a tall lanky man in his early forties. His thick hair had turned white prematurely, the worry lines on his face testament to the long hours he had spent solving crimes.

As the officer in charge of the murder scene in the Humber Valley, after viewing the body and surveying its surroundings, Miller phoned his superior, the newly appointed Etobicoke police chief, William Hastings. Township officials had recently lured Hastings from an inner city precinct. After listening to the details, Hastings informed Miller he would ask for the opinion of two detectives whom he had worked with when he was stationed downtown. Chief Hastings considered the detectives experts in solving difficult cases and informed Miller that he would contact his friend, Chief of Detectives Arnold Peckerman, at his former precinct, and request their assistance.

The worry lines on Miller's face deepened with annoyance as he listened. To seek help from outside the jurisdictional police force was a highly unorthodox procedure, and Miller resented the intrusion into his turf. He was not a man who tolerated interference easily, but he knew enough to say nothing when a superior officer gave an order.

The first of the downtown detectives to arrive on the scene was Detective Sergeant Gerry Thomson. A man in his midforties, Gerry had always struggled with a weight problem, and his short stature magnified his girth, which had slowly expanded during the previous few years. His colleagues often teased him, but he was impervious to their remarks. He possessed a round boyish face, free of wrinkles or lines. His easygoing nature had allowed him to shrug off the stresses that his job presented. His neatly trimmed, thick moustache and full head of hair were dark brown, with just a hint of gray. Gerry Thomson was the stereotype image of a father. Much to the puzzlement of other men, women found him attractive, even those younger than he was. He ignored their attention. Being a family man, he was as loyal to his wife, Ruth, as a cocker spaniel. Because of his casual approach during investigations, those he interviewed thought him nonthreatening. This trait had served him well, often putting nervous suspects at ease. As a result, Thomson sometimes retrieved information that would have eluded others.

When Gerry Thomson arrived in the Humber Valley, he was not in his usual happy mood. The phone call from his boss had unceremoniously disrupted his holiday weekend with his family. Besides, he felt uncomfortable intruding into the jurisdiction of another police force. Setting aside his feelings and grumbling quietly to himself, he proceeded to examine the body, while he awaited the arrival of his partner, as well as someone from the coroner's office.

A half hour later, Thomson's partner arrived at the scene. Jim Peersen was thirty-one years of age. His blond hair, kept well-trimmed, and fair complexion betrayed his Nordic heritage. An inch over six-foot, he was athletically proportioned—narrow waist, broad shoulders, flat stomach, well-muscled arms. Whenever time permitted, he worked out in a gym and was an avid jogger.

Despite Peersen's imposing stature, most people first noticed his deep-blue eyes. He was one of those men who simply had great eyes. The other feature that immediately attracted attention was his clear skin. A female colleague had once declared that his skin resembled porcelain, adding that any women would envy it. Though Peersen was ruggedly handsome, he was no mere pretty boy, but a highly intelligent and shrewd detective.

By the time Jim Peersen arrived at the scene, Thomson had already completed a cursory inspection of the body, careful not to touch anything for fear of disturbing evidence. He was presently examining the area surrounding the corpse. Judging by the lack of broken branches and disturbed vegetation near the body, Thomson was certain that the attack had not occurred at this location. It was a body-dump. The lack of blood at the scene confirmed his theory.

Thomson gazed up at Peersen. "She's dressed in a casual walking outfit, which perhaps explains why she was in the valley. I don't see any purse, and there's very little blood. She wasn't murdered at this site."

Peersen knew what Thomson was indirectly telling him. "I know, I know!" he mumbled. "Get my butt into the surrounding bushes and find where she was first attacked."

"Good thinking, boy wonder," Gerry replied, mimicking the famous quip that the comic book hero Batman employed to encourage his sidekick Robin. "While you're at it, look for the murder weapon. And if you come across a dog turd, don't step in it."

"Any turds I find, I'll bag as evidence and give to you."

"Great, as if I don't get enough crap thrown my way."

Jim Peersen disappeared into the bushes. Despite the killer's attempts to disguise the relocating of the body, the young detective was able to follow the path the murderer had used to transport the body to the dumpsite where Arnold, David, and Mario had discovered it.

Examining the primary crime scene on the pathway beside the river, Peersen noticed an absence of blood at this location as well. *Where did the victim bleed out?* he thought.

Rejoining Gerry, Jim informed his partner. "Even at the primary crime site, there's not much blood. There's damn little blood anywhere. Where did the blood go?"

"Think we're dealing with a vampire?"

"Good thinking, old man wonder," Jim Peersen replied, twisting the famous Batman quip to suit his purposes. "I think you've lost a little of the blood in your head. Have a late night?"

"Yeah! Ruth keeps inviting guests over to the house, and like vampires, they drain my bar and don't leave until the sun's rays force them back to their coffins."

"You married guys live a tough life."

"Well, at least we don't prowl the city looking for action."

"No, you prowl the house and get no action, other than late-night guests."

The arrival of Samuel Mann, the assistant coroner, interrupted their banter. Samuel Mann was overly proud of his position within the coroner's office, and resented anyone referring to him as "Sam." He was young, too young in Thomson's opinion. His red hair and freckles caused him to stand out in a crowd, and on this occasion, his dark-green suit, lime-green shirt, and bowtie with its bright yellow and red polka dots added to the effect. Because of Sam's weird taste in attire and condescending attitude, Gerry found it difficult to take him seriously. Peersen had once said that he found Sam's annoying verbosity almost as annoying as his "butterfly" outfits.

"The chief coroner is at his cottage near Huntsville and has no telephone," Mann informed them. Then, puffing with pomposity, he added, "I'm in charge this weekend. I'll perform the preliminary investigation and then you can transport the body to the downtown morgue. Have no fear. I will leave no stone unturned."

Thomson eyed the young man impatiently, knowing that he was wet behind the ears.

"Sam, give us as much information as possible," Gerry told him, trying not to show his irritation. Mann ignored Gerry, referring to him as "Sam."

Twenty minutes later, the self-proclaimed expert from the coroner's department commenced lecturing in a professorial voice. "This is a preliminary report. Nothing is gospel until after the autopsy."

"Tell us as much as possible," Thomson urged, feigning politeness. He was well aware that Mann never voiced an opinion in ten words if he was able to employ fifty.

"I don't think the victim was attacked where they discovered her body, but she died here. There's almost no blood. Strange! Have you found another site?"

"Leave that to us, Sam. Get on with it," Thomson insisted impatiently.

Mann continued, his irritation with Thomson clearly evident. "The severe lacerations on the right side, at the front of the woman's skull, indicate that the killer struck her with a blunt instrument, likely a rock, as the gashes are jagged. It was a severe blow, struck very forcibly. It suggests extreme anger, perhaps rage. Have you found the murder weapon?"

"For God's sake keep going," Thomson replied, his annoyance increasing.

"The cause of death was likely severe head trauma, but not necessarily, as the whites of the eyes reveal significant reddening, which may suggest asphyxia. The autopsy will determine the exact cause of death. There are no signs of a struggle, no defensive wounds, and no marks on the body to indicate that the killer tied her up. I found no extraneous material under her fingernails. At the morgue, I'll scrape under her fingernails and examine the contents microscopically. I believe that she either knew her attacker or it happened too fast for her to defend herself."

"Was she raped?"

"There are severe lacerations around the vagina. The sex act was extremely violent. The sex most likely occurred after she was unconscious. With the injuries that are evident, for her sake, I certainly hope so." Samuel continued. "It's difficult to determine the exact time of death as the heat and lack of movement of air in the underbrush have accelerated the decomposition. The rain also destroyed evidence. That's all I can tell you until I, and the chief coroner, perform the autopsy."

Thomson and Peersen ignored Mann's egocentric grammar and gazed silently at Samuel Mann as he strutted from the scene, adjusting his colourful bowtie as he departed.

Recovering, Peersen said, "Great! It'll be a damn difficult case to solve—a body found in an isolated location and no witnesses."

Thomson shook his head in frustration as he turned to Peersen. "Take me to the primary crime scene."

On the trail by the river, Peersen showed his partner where the killer had hidden in the bushes, and how the killer had tidied up the crime scene to conceal what had occurred. Fifteen minutes later, having discovered no trace of evidence, Gerry suggested, "Let's return to the precinct and leave the lab guys and patrolmen to search the area. For now, there's nothing more we can do here."

When the two detectives arrived at the downtown police station, Thomson telephoned Chief of Detectives Arnold Peckerman, who was at home with his family. Peckerman listened to the details of their investigation.

"You and Peersen remain with the case," he ordered, "or at least until you identify the victim. It's not within our jurisdiction, so keep the Etobicoke police force in the loop. Work through Detective Ernie Miller. He's the troublesome type. Pacify him as best as you can. Understand?"

Thomson felt they should immediately hand the case over to Miller and allow the truculent detective to sort out the case. However, orders were orders.

After he hung up the phone, he said to Sergeant Malloy, "Get some off-duty officers down here to help us contact precincts throughout the city for their missing persons' reports. We'll see if any descriptions match the deceased. Identifying the victim is our first priority."

As it was a Saturday, and as they were unable to do anything more, the frustrated detectives departed.

At the morgue, the corpse was now in a refrigerated wooden locker. The autopsy had to wait until Tuesday morning.

Early on Saturday, Tom Hudson decided to bicycle to the Humber River Valley to escape the heat of the neighbourhood. He phoned Shorty and asked him to join him, and then he contacted his two other close friends, Patrick and Harry. Shorty phoned Carol, who then asked Sophie to tag along. Sophie was an attractive, dark-haired Italian girl, another member of the close-knit group.

When they had all gathered, Tom told them, "I must get back by four o'clock to deliver my newspapers. Let's get going. It's almost eleven o'clock. It'll take a while to cycle there."

"No problem," Shorty replied. "I can pedal my bike faster than Old Klacker can shovel shit."

They all laughed, and in a lighthearted mood, they set off. Cycling west along Eglinton Avenue, and north on Weston Road, they then travelled west on Buttonwood Avenue. They left their bikes under the trees on the park-like grounds of the Western Sanatorium. Overhead, mature shade trees swayed gently in the summer breezes as they descended on foot into the lush greenery of the valley, feeling the air cool slightly as they neared the river. They knew a place where the water was of sufficient depth for swimming.

Hopping over the flat stones that littered the valley floor, their progress was slow as Harry paused frequently to examine rocks. He was an amateur paleontologist, knowledgeable about fossils, and possessed a small collection. Over his shoulder, he carried a knapsack to hold specimens and a small pickaxe to chip fossils from rocks that were too large to lift or carry away. At one location, he stopped to retrieve a fossil that erosion had exposed in the sedimentary rock.

"Wow," Harry exclaimed, "a trilobite." Then he glanced up and explained.

"A trilobite's a small marine creature from ancient times. They're common in the valley. Look! I've found another one in this rock." The rock in his hand was about the size of a Neilson's Four-Flavour chocolate bar.

"Thanks, professor, for the lecture," Shorty and Tom chorused.

Harry ignored them as he placed the specimen in his knapsack. Then the others sat under a shade tree and watched Harry while he continued to overturn rocks that appeared promising.

Harry's family had emigrated from Germany shortly before the war to escape the Nazi violence descending over their troubled nation. When his parents had first arrived in Toronto, they lived in the downtown area, but when Harry was thirteen, they purchased a house on Northcliffe Boulevard, one street west of Lauder Avenue. That year Tom was in Miss Bunker's grade-six class. Tom still remembered the day the principal, Mr. MacDonald, brought Harry to his classroom.

When Harry strolled down the aisle between the desks, the first thing Tom noticed was that Harry was older than the other students were. Because Harry's birthday was in September, he had started school almost a year behind those who had been born earlier in the year. As he spoke little English when he first arrived in Canada, the school had held him back a grade.

As a teenager, Harry had a wide range of interests. His grades in school were excellent and teachers adored him. The girls also loved him. He was now almost sixteen, as tall as an adult, possessed straw-blond hair, and fair skin that easily bronzed under the summer sun.

Other than Shorty, Harry was Tom's closest friend. The previous June, when they were graduating from grade eight, Harry had confessed to Shorty and Tom something personal that they had never suspected. On this hot summer day, they did not worry about it, although it did cross their minds that it might cause problems for Harry in the future.

The strong rays of the midday sun beat tirelessly on the teenagers as they sat out in the open, the gurgling sounds of the river surrounding them. Harry called to them. "I've found another fossil. It's a super one."

The others gathered around and examined it, but as fossils were of little interest to them, they soon wandered off, except for Shorty, who decided to assist Harry. During the following ten minutes, the only thing Shorty found was a woman's old, black dress shoe, which he tossed into the river. He also spotted several used condoms, which everyone referred to as "safes" or "rubbers."

Shorty drew Carol and Sophie's attention to them by shouting, "Hey, come over here. Want to see some secondhand safes?"

The girls ignored him.

Shorty quietly whispered to Tom, "Technically, they're not secondhand, but second-dick! Get my drift?"

Tom grinned and nodded, thankful that the girls had not heard Shorty's remark. He knew that Shorty's antics and vocabulary were the reasons that Carol never took him seriously.

Shorty continued scouring the valley floor as he sang aloud a verse from an irreverent song he knew, "Don't let your dingle dangle in the dust …"

Shorty often warbled silly songs that were unfit to sing when girls were around. He had acquired his repertoire of dirty ditties from the old man who had lived on the first floor of the house during the days when his mother had rented the upstairs flat. All the kids called the old man Grumpy. At the time, Shorty's mom had been a single mother.

Shorty and Grumpy eventually became close friends. Grumpy shared his books with Shorty, as well as a few cigars, an occasional small alcoholic drink, naughty stories, and songs he had learned while serving in the trenches during the First World War. One of them was a parody of a favourite American song: "Yank my doodle it's a dandy, just as big as Uncle Sam's …"

When Grumpy died, by then Shorty's mom had remarried. His new dad purchased the house in which they had previously rented the upstairs flat, the three of them now living there, not far from Tom's house.

The group of friends in the valley continued to explore.

Five minutes later, Carol yelled out, "I've found something wedged between these two rocks beside the water." Prying it loose, she continued. "It's a key chain, with a yellow stone attached, a key on it, and the initial 'M' on the leather fob."

They all now examined it. The stone was a translucent brownish-yellow, and in the centre of it was a small preserved insect. On close examination, they realized it was a tiny fly.

Harry explained. "It's a piece of amber. The fly was stuck in the sticky resin from a tree in ancient times. Over the centuries, the resin hardened. The trapped fly is real."

Carol remembered that her grandmother had often employed the expression, "That's as rich as amber." She wanted to keep it, but wanting to please Harry more, and because he collected such things, Carol said, "Here, Harry. You can have the amber."

In the mud beside the shallow water, near the shore, Carol next found two coins. After examining them, she exclaimed, "They're Edward VII quarters, minted in 1925. They're likely from someone's collection, because even though they've been in the muddy water, they're still shiny from being polished. I bet they were lost just yesterday."

Carol pocketed them to take home, as she had a modest collection of Canadian coins. Then she added, "Quarters from 1925 are not common, even though they're not all that old."

Sophie picked up a small metal ring with a red piece of glass in it. She placed it on her pinkie finger and pretended to admire it.

"It's junk," she finally declared, and as she tossed it in the river she added, "I think it was a prize from a box of Cracker Jacks."

Patrick found a rusted ice pick, which he similarly discarded.

The swimming hole that they intended to enter was near the bridge where Lawrence Avenue crossed the river. As they were preparing to continue walking, they noticed several police officers on the opposite side of the river. They had appeared from the tall grass by the water's edge and were searching along the west bank. Then the teenagers noticed that a dozen or more police were searching the tall grass and thick bushes further up the embankment.

Shorty gasped in awe. "Holy crap! What do you think happened? Look! They're using long sticks to search through the grass. They're lifting up the bushes and looking under them." Pausing, he added, "Wouldn't ya know it? A nosy crowd has gathered. The police have roped off the area so they can't get near. Oh well, let's be nosy too, and sit down and watch."

They had seen sufficient movies to realize that the cops were likely scouring a crime scene.

Carol said, "Do you think a woman has been robbed and the police are searching for her purse?"

Sophie replied, "Perhaps someone's missing and they're searching for a body."

"Geez, holy crap and more crap," Shorty gushed. "A body? That gives me goose bumps on my ass."

Though amused by Shorty's words, the group now became serious, submerging their desire to swim beneath the depths of their curiosity.

By three o'clock, tired of watching, as nothing was happening, they returned to where their bikes were located and cycled home.

When Tom entered the kitchen of his house, he related the afternoon's happening to his parents. They too suggested theories to account for the police search.

"Whatever happened," he told his mom, "it's not every day that a guy sees a police investigation."

That evening, the Hudson family heard the ten o'clock news on the radio. Tom listened intently for any details about the police search in the Humber Valley.

Nothing!

✧ ✧ ✧

Late on Saturday night, the stalker gazed out the kitchen window and scanned the darkened street. The day had ended, and the city's pace was slowing. Grasping a cup of hot tea and sipping slowly, the stalker thought of the victim. Her death had been fascinating, particularly the flow of blood from her neck.

The stalker wondered if the police had identified the remains and thought, *"Remains" is an excellent word—meaningless and impersonal. It reduces a human life to the inanimate, like the transformation of something essential into an object to discard.*

Relocating the body would have delayed the identification of the remains, but not for long. On the other hand, the police would have no clue who committed the murder, as the stalker was certain that no evidence had been left behind.

It was the stalker's second murder and quite different from the first.

Toronto was an enormous metropolis, the stalker thought. *Perhaps I can find other fascinating victims.*

✧ ✧ ✧

At the police station on Sunday morning, Thomson and Peersen stood near the coffee machine, in their hands steaming mugs of the worst java in Toronto.

"This stuff would rot the knackers off a brass monkey," Thomson complained.

"At my age, I don't worry too much about such things," Peersen retorted. "My knackers are impervious to rough treatment, thank you."

"Says you, my young friend."

A moment later, Gerry walked over to his desk, pulled out his chair, and sat down heavily. "I'm pooped," he began as he scanned the missing persons' reports.

Continuing, he said, "After I returned from the crime scene last night, friends dropped over and remained until the wee hours of the morning. My tired old rear end is badly in need of a little tender care."

"Well, don't look at me." Thomson's remark about his family life caused Peersen to be thankful that he was unmarried.

Silence now fell between the two men. They had not yet identified the body, and the crime scene had so far revealed no clues. As well, no one had discovered the murder weapon. As they continued examining the missing persons' reports, they quietly suffered the indignity the coffee inflicted upon them.

A half hour later, Gerry was sipping on his third cup of the devil's brew. A few drops had dribbled onto his gray suit, and he cursed under his breath; it was his favourite suit, the one he wore to work every day. Some of the men at the precinct had teased that it was his only suit of clothes, and that he had likely purchased it at "Edward's of Bloor Street" (Honest Ed's). Actually, he owned two other suits, but he preferred the one he was presently wearing, even though it was well worn. It was comfortable and familiar. His black oxford shoes, which he had resoled many times, were also well worn. He had purchased them before the war, some of his colleagues claiming it had been prior to the First World War.

Thomson's lack of attention to fashion contrasted with that of his partner. On this Sunday, he was wearing a made-to-measure navy blue suit. Jim Peersen's clothes closet contained an array of stylish suits, along with carefully selected ties and shirts to match. Each day he wore a different outfit to work. Peersen dabbled in the Toronto Stock Exchange, and he had been modestly successful. Though he was particular about his clothes, he was not vane. He neither preened nor strutted. His clothes were simply a part of his daily existence.

There was another aspect of Jim's wardrobe that separated him from his colleagues at the precinct, apart from his well-tailored suits. While all the other men preferred sturdy black oxford shoes, Peersen enjoyed the casual comfort of loafers. When he was overtired, he slicked his feet as he walked, in contrast to his usual athletic gait.

Though Thomson and Peersen appeared to be a study in contrast, they functioned efficiently as a team. They had no need to play the good cop/bad cop routine. Their methods complemented and reinforced each other.

Because of their difference in height, some of the men at the precinct referred to them as Mutt and Jeff. The women among the office staff jokingly called them "the sex pot and the meat pot." In reference to the latter remark, one young female clerk had giggled as she inquired, "Which one is which?"

✧ ✧ ✧

On Labour Day, Monday, 3 September, Tom arranged for a friend who lived on Glenholme Avenue to deliver his newspapers. Tom earned pocket money by delivering the *Star* newspapers to sixty-eight customers on Lauder Avenue.

As Tom was now free for the entire day, he and Shorty departed early for the Canadian National Exhibition (CNE), travelling on a crowded Bathurst streetcar to the eastern gate. It was the seventy-second edition of the annual fair. General George C. Marshall, the American secretary of state, had officially opened the Ex on 24 August.

Tom and Shorty enjoyed a wonderful day at the Ex, and as darkness settled over the grounds, not wishing their adventure to end, Tom suggested that they visit the midway again to ride the Ferris wheel. Ten minutes later, they were gazing down from its heights. Tom exclaimed, "Geez! I have a bird's-eye view of all over the bloody place." Then, as the wheel swooped down toward the ground, Shorty cried out, "Holy crap. There's that turd Kramer."

Kramer was the leader of a gang of bullies that through the years had often appeared out of nowhere and picked on Tom and his friends. Kramer was a nasty individual. Tall for his age, he was not heavily built. Though handy with his fists, he mostly relied on his gang of bullies to maintain his superiority over others.

Shorty and Kramer had been longtime enemies, and Kramer had a constant reminder of Shorty's enmity. His crooked nose was the result of a fight with Shorty many years before. Though recently there had been a truce between Tom's friends and the Kramer gang, Tom knew that Shorty was unlikely to resist a chance to annoy the bully.

Shorty watched as the Ferris wheel continued to dip toward the ground. "Kramer stinks like a wet turd," he uttered with disgust.

Within seconds, the Ferris wheel swept upward, continued its cycle, and slowly descended once more. It was then that Tom and Shorty noticed Kramer was strolling closer to the base of the Ferris wheel. Tom had not seen Kramer during the summer months, but at this close-up distance, he noticed that the bully looked different.

"Kramer's not wearing his dirty red cap," Tom told Shorty. "His head's bare, and he's actually combed his hair. Do you suppose he's discovered Lustre Cream Shampoo and Brylcreem?"

Shorty quickly reached into his bag and retrieved a Plaster of Paris egg he had pilfered from a refrigerator on display in the Electrical Building. Unseen by Kramer, he fired it at Kramer with great precision. Within seconds, the Ferris wheel swept Shorty and Tom upward and out of sight. Peering backward over the edge of his seat to catch a glimpse of Kramer, Shorty kept his head low. He chuckled as he said, "I hit Kramer in the back. Look, he's thumping the kid standing behind him. He thinks he did it. The kid is really upset. He's shouting back at Kramer."

Shorty and Tom laughed, pleased to see Kramer behaving like a fool.

"Look, man!" Shorty declared with glee. "Stupid Kramer has no idea where the blow came from. Good thing he didn't look up and see us, or notice the Plaster of Paris egg rolling on the ground."

When they were at the top position of the Ferris wheel again, Shorty shouted to Tom, "Quick! Pass me the egg that you have in your bag."

As the Ferris wheel again descended near the ground, Shorty fired it and amazingly achieved similar results. Kramer lashed out again and struck the same kid. Shorty was delighted. "Look! This time, the kid's defending himself. Wow!"

As the Ferris wheel rotated upward again, Shorty continued. "Holy craps, Kramer and the other kid are in a fistfight, and the rest of Kramer's gang is goading them on to keep the fighting going."

By the time Tom and Shorty exited from the ride, they saw Kramer chasing the kid he had belted as they ran toward the Coliseum, the rest of the gang following the action. Shorty and Tom laughed as they slipped away, wisely retreating in the opposite direction.

Twenty minutes later, when they passed the Food Building, in a newspaper box beside the entrance was a single copy of the late edition of the *Telegram*. They examined it, but found nothing about the event they had witnessed in the Humber Valley.

After arriving at the eastern gate, they commenced their streetcar ride home. Their final fling before the rigors of the new school year had ended.

The Ferris wheels and the CNE midway at night during the 1950s.

✧ ✧ ✧

Shortly before noon on Monday, a distraught Miss Bettina Taylor arrived at the police station to report that her roommate was missing.

"When did you last see her?" Desk Sergeant Patrick Malloy inquired as he reached for a pencil from a ceramic cup on his desk.

"She left the apartment early on Friday evening," Miss Taylor replied. "She said that she was going to visit her fiancé at his cottage in Muskoka. She said she would return to Toronto on Sunday afternoon. I phoned the police after midnight on Sunday and reported her missing, but they said I must wait twenty-four hours. I feared that something had happened, as she is always punctual. I admit that I thought it was possible that she had missed the bus. But it's now Monday. She still hasn't returned. I'm worried sick."

Sergeant Malloy asked for a description of the missing woman. After he recorded the information, he called for Thomson and Peersen.

Thomson requested that the distressed Miss Taylor accompany him to an interview room.

✧ ✧ ✧

Gerry Thomson had been married for over twenty years. He had completed only four years of high school (junior matriculation), because his education was disrupted when he enlisted in the army during the Second World War. Many believed that though Thomson might eventually become the chief of detectives, due to his age and lack of academic qualifications, he would never become the chief of police. He was not worried about not attaining the top position. His ambitions lay elsewhere. Gerry's highest priority in life was being a good father and husband.

Although Gerry lacked a formal education, he was a graduate of the "school of life" and possessed a high degree of street smarts. He was intelligent and knew how to read people. His most often repeated phrase, said in response to a questionable answer from a suspect was, "Now then, we'll just see about that."

By contrast, Peersen had graduated from the University of Toronto with a master's degree in sociology. After university, he entered the police academy and placed fifth among the sixty cadets in his class. He would have placed first, but he had received a reprimand and several demerits after an instructor inquired what he thought of his opinions. Peersen had replied, "Bullshit, sir!"

Next, he attended the FBI Academy, where he graduated with honours. He had learned to be more abstemious in the use of the word "bullshit." After joining the Toronto force, he was a constable for only six years before they promoted him to sergeant, and then to the rank of detective.

The men at the precinct respected Jim Peersen but not with any degree of affection. Some of the men thought that within a few years, Peersen might acquire the rank of detective sergeant, and some considered it a distinct possibility that eventually he might become the chief of police. Others thought that Peersen's independent attitude might alienate a superior, bringing his career to a dead end. He was well known for having a low tolerance for hubris, which he still referred to as bullshit. When listening to superiors, Jim usually kept his thoughts to himself, but his mannerisms often betrayed him. Jim believed that a man should earn respect, not automatically engender it through his position in life. As a result, Peersen saw no reason to cozy up to "the brass," even if it meant they would deny him promotion.

✧ ✧ ✧

On this day, Constable Paul Masters enviously observed Peersen walking toward the front desk in response to Sergeant Malloy's summons. Masters disliked Peersen. He knew that women found Peersen attractive and resented that he had not been born so fortunate. Though Masters was only in his midthirties, he looked much older. He was short and stocky with massive shoulders that hid his neck. His round face, with its jowls and small eyes, created the appearance of a bulldog. Indeed, most of the officers referred to him as "Bulldog" Masters. A few referred to him as "Wild Dog" Masters.

Masters, who felt that Peersen had merely been lucky, envied Peersen's success within the department. Given half a chance, Masters believed he would be a greater asset to the force. He did not realize that Peersen had achieved his success through intelligence and hard work. Besides, he thought that Peersen dressed too well for a man on a detective's salary and wondered if he was accepting bribes or engaging in some other illicit activity. On this occasion, Masters said nothing as he observed Peersen escorting the woman who had appeared at the front desk, toward an interview room.

✧ ✧ ✧

Inside the room, Thomson smiled sympathetically and pulled out a chair for Miss Taylor. Thomson listened as she explained why she had come forward. She repeated the description of her roommate. On the information sheet, Sergeant Malloy had recorded that Miss Taylor and her roommate taught at York Collegiate Institute. *This could be a high profile case*, Thomson thought.

Though Thomson was anxious to identify the victim, he was reluctant to allow the woman to look at the body at this time, as it had not been prepared for viewing. However, about twenty minutes into the interview, Thomson changed his mind. It was a hell of a risk. Allowing a witness to see a corpse before the coroner had prepared it was against procedure. On this occasion, necessity won out over prudence. If they could establish the identity of the victim, they might be able to hand the investigation back to the local police force. Peersen inquired if Miss Taylor was willing to visit the morgue. Hesitantly, she agreed.

Thomson phoned the morgue and informed Samuel Mann, the assistant coroner, that they wished to view the body.

"I'm unable to allow it," he replied firmly.

There was silence as Thomson considered his dilemma. Identifying the body was imperative, but he was aware that his request was irregular.

"The victim was wearing a ring. Correct?"

"Yes, there's a gold ring with a small sapphire in it, on her right hand. But I'm unable to remove it from her finger."

"Can you allow us to see the body and tell Dicer, if he asks, that we only viewed the victim's ring? An identification will enable us to proceed with the investigation. This is a decision that you can make on your own, as you are someone with superior authority. Dicer never need know that we saw the body."

Thomson was appealing directly to Mann's ego. After a few moments hesitation, Mann replied pompously, "I believe I can justify such a course of action."

"Fine. We'll be at the premises within thirty minutes."

Thomson was well aware that Doctor Theodore Dicer, the chief coroner, would not approve of sidestepping the long-established procedures at the morgue. Dicer was a demanding and cantankerous man, but a true professional. Anyone who interfered with his work received the brunt of his wrath. Samuel Mann, his assistant, might wear off a guy's balls with his boring lectures, but Dicer's specialty was cutting the balls from those who annoyed him. Even Thomson stepped lightly around the chief coroner.

The morgue for the city of Toronto was at 86 Lombard Street, a short street located between Jarvis and Church Streets, one block south of Richmond Street. The morgue, with its granite trimmed windows and impressive main door, had served the needs of the city since 1911. When Thomson and Peersen arrived with Miss Taylor, the afternoon sun was splashing across the red-brick façade, creating a cheery appearance that belied the gruesome tasks performed within.

Inside the building, while they waited for Mann to bring out the body, they stood in the small anteroom outside the autopsy room. Soon, a set of heavy doors opened, and Mann wheeled out the corpse on a stretcher. Thomson stepped forward and gently removed an appropriate portion of the white sheet.

Miss Taylor stared in shock at the lifeless corpse. Drained of blood, the body was chalky white. Then Miss Taylor gazed at the ring of her friend. It was the final proof that it was her friend. She nodded her head and clutched Gerry's arm to steady herself.

Thomson assisted Miss Taylor to leave the room.

As Peersen followed them out, though he said not a word, he felt deeply for Miss Taylor. Her friend had been young, in the prime of life, and a brutal killer had deprived her of the years to which she was entitled. The murder of the young woman caused memories of the tragic death of Peersen's older brother to surface. He recalled the pain and remembered how the death had devastated his parents.

After a constable arrived to drive Miss Taylor home, Thomson gazed at his partner and sighed in resignation. "A policeman's lot is not a happy one," he said, parroting a line from a song in *The Pirates of Penzance.*

Jim pushed his personal thoughts from the past from his mind and replied, "This murder is within the jurisdiction of the Etobicoke Township Police, not our precinct, but I fear Peckerman will likely insist that we remain on the case. Damn it! The death of a young teacher is going to be a high-profile case, and Peckerman loves publicity."

Thomson nodded his head in agreement. Long days were ahead.

✧ ✧ ✧

Tuesday, 4 September, Tom, Tim, Patrick, Harry, and Shorty chatted quietly as they walked south on Lauder Avenue toward Rogers Road. The morning air was crisp and fresh. Tom's brother Ken had departed earlier, as he preferred to be with friends his own age.

As the boys proceeded along the street, the previous weekend's activities dominated their discussions. Tom avoided the topic that was uppermost in his thoughts—the unknown and new world he was facing at York Collegiate Institute, better known as YCI.

When they arrived at school, Tom gazed up at the imposing structure. Constructed in the 1920s, it was in the ornate Gothic style, ornamented with carved-stone scrollwork over the main doorway. High above the doorway was a fancy turret topped with pinnacles. It was an intimidating building, readily portraying the serious activities that occurred within its confines. Tom's stomach knotted as he opened the door of the building.

Inside, Tom and Shorty approached an older student who was in charge of the information table.

Shorty inquired, "Where do we register?"

The student replied with a sneer, "Worms like you should crawl into the gymnasium."

Tom was surprised when Shorty ignored the put-down, but the remark reinforced his feeling that he was entering dangerous territory. They followed the senior student's instructions and proceeded down the hallway, passing several teachers that were huddled together quietly talking. Tom noticed that they seemed deeply concerned about something. He found it odd that they were ignoring the confusion created by the hordes of students in the hallway. The atmosphere did not conform to his idea of an educational institution. Under his breath he muttered, "If I'm going to be thrown into a jailhouse, I'd prefer one that's better managed."

Arriving in the gym, noise and confusion continued to reign. Against the far wall, Tom saw a row of tables with signs on them indicating that students should locate the one that displayed the first letter of their surname. As Tom was walking toward the table displaying the letter H, he spotted Kramer, the bully whom Shorty had pelted with the "egg" from the heights of the Ferris wheel at the CNE. He was conversing with two teenage guys and did not see Tom.

Tom was relieved.

Similar to when Tom had seen Kramer at the CNE, he was not wearing his dirty red cap, and he had neatly combed his hair. Tom noticed other changes that had occurred since he had seen him the previous June. Before his teeth had been crooked, but now there were braces on them. This was unusual, as very few families could afford them. Tom also noticed that Kramer's teeth were whiter than he had ever seen them, the yellow stains having almost disappeared.

Tom told Shorty, "Look at that creep Kramer. I think he's discovered the worlds of Colgate toothpaste, Lustre Cream Shampoo, and Brylcreem. His skin still has acne blotches, but the worst of the red pimples have disappeared. I wonder if Kramer's dad won money in a poker game from a dentist and a dermatologist? Kramer's put on a little weight. He always had muscles but was skinny. Man, he'll now be harder to beat in a fight."

Shorty listened to Tom's assessment but did not comment. He did not care. If he fought Kramer, he was still confident that he could trash him.

Tom resumed the search for the table displaying the letter "H." Locating it, he approached a grade-thirteen student who was tending the table. The older student searched in a box of envelopes for the one with "Tom Hudson" written on it. Inside it, Tom found a sheet that contained his class schedule and discovered he was in form 9L. "I hope it won't become 9-hell," he mumbled quietly. Then, bible of information in hand, Tom walked over to Shorty. After comparing information sheets, Tom exclaimed, "Hey, we're in the same homeroom class. This is unreal. We've been in the same class since grade four."

In their envelopes was the list of subjects they were to study, locations of the classrooms, and names of the teachers. There was also a list of the required books. They were responsible for their cost. There were no classes the first day, allowing them time to visit a bookstore.

After registration, Tom, Shorty, Harry, and Patrick had agreed to meet near the flagpole, located on the front lawn. Before exiting the school, Tom went to the washroom. In one of the cubicles, he noticed some graffiti. This was his first experience with the literary finesse of the washroom writers of Toronto's high schools. Someone had written: "Baldy sucks in French."

"Who was Baldy? Doesn't everyone suck when French kissing?" Tom said quietly to himself. Then he noticed that another person had written: "Leck my bane."

He repeated the words aloud and added, "What does that mean?"

An older student standing at a urinal heard him and started laughing.

Slinking away, when Tom met up with his friends, he did not mention his cubicle readings or his recitation.

As they walked home, they discussed the morning's experiences. Tom did not share his first impressions of the world of York Collegiate and pretended that he was comfortable with his new educational environment. The guys were surprised to learn that Shorty and Tom were both in 9L. They discovered that Patrick was on his own, as were Carol and Sophie. Shorty had hoped to be in the same class as Carol, but it had not happened.

At the corner of Rogers Road and Oakwood Avenue, they passed a variety store with a newspaper box outside. Tom generally ignored newspapers, as later in the day, when he delivered the *Star*, he would scan the front page.

Shorty glanced at the bold letters of the headline of the *Toronto Tribune* and abruptly stopped in his tracks. "Holy shit!" he exclaimed.

Retrieving a copy of the newspaper, he read the headline aloud: "Woman's Body in Humber Valley." Within seconds, Tom, Harry, and Shorty were reading the front-page article written by the reporter Frank Gnomes.

Gruesome Valley Murder

The body of a young woman was discovered in the Humber Valley on Sunday morning. The cause of death appears to have been a severe injury to the head. The police have confirmed that it was a homicide. They have not yet released the time of death.

On Monday, Miss Bettina Taylor identified the body as belonging to her roommate, thirty-year-old Miss Elaine Stritch, an English teacher, who taught at York Collegiate, near Oakwood Avenue and Rogers Road, in the Township of York. It would have been her eighth year at the school. She was the fiancée of William Matheson, a science teacher at the same institution. The victim's mother resides in Hamilton, Ontario, where Miss Stritch was born and raised.

Mr. Matheson had been staying at his cottage on Pine Lake in Muskoka for a week, and Miss Stritch had not accompanied him due to family obligations. Mr. Matheson did not learn of his fiancée's demise until he returned to the city late Monday evening and the police contacted him. Authorities released news of the tragedy to the press this morning.

Miss Bettina Taylor stated that she had last seen her roommate early on Friday evening.

Miss Taylor also teaches at York Collegiate. The victim was her colleague and close friend …

The newspaper article momentarily stunned everyone into silence. Shorty, rarely lost for words, declared, "Geez man! We were there."

Tom added, "Imagine! If a killer had not murdered Miss Stritch, she might have been one of our teachers. I've never been this close to knowing someone who was murdered. I wonder if Miss Taylor will be one of our teachers?"

✧ ✧ ✧

The stalker stared blankly at the newspaper report about the murder. *The police are clueless,* the stalker thought. *The plan worked perfectly. Hiding the body delayed its discovery for twenty-four hours, and during the night, the heat accelerated the decomposition. The next few weeks will be interesting.*

A knock on the door interrupted the stalker's thoughts. Opening the door, a teenage boy requested the week's payment for the newspapers he had delivered. The stalker smiled ingratiatingly at the lad and handed him the correct amount, plus a ten-cent tip. The pleasantry was easy to fake. A simple "hello" and a ready smile hid a myriad of sins. No one who met the stalker had ever detected the murderous intent behind the smile.

The stalker thought that teenagers were less threatening than adults. It was easier to mislead them, as they were mentally passive. If you were eccentric or exhibited strange behaviour, they simply passed it off as typical, "old fogy" behaviour. They considered every age group weird, except their own.

✧ ✧ ✧

Tom and Shorty had agreed to meet with Patrick at eleven o'clock to travel downtown to the Coles Book Store at 726 Yonge Street, a block south of Bloor, to purchase their school texts for the coming year. Tom's mom insisted that he pay for his books and supplies from the profits from his paper route.

After selecting the books, Shorty gave the cashier a ten-dollar bill, and received $1.70 in change. He told Tom, "The face of George VI on the ten-dollar bill gave a fart grin as it disappeared into the cash register drawer."

Tom replied, "I thought fart grins were your specialty."

"True, but the king borrows a few of my better habits occasionally."

Patrick listened but said nothing. The expression on his face clearly told them that he thought they were both crazy.

Later, during the supper hour, when Tom's family sat around the kitchen table, they listened to the news on CFRB. The newscaster, Jim Hunter, mentioned the Stritch murder but provided no information that Tom did not already know.

✧ ✧ ✧

A view of Yonge Street looking south toward College Street, where the Eaton's College Street Store (now College Park) is visible in the distance. The famous Peter Witt streetcars line the street. The streetcar in the foreground has a trailer car attached, as does the one in front of it. Tom and his friends rode a streetcar similar to these when they journeyed downtown to purchase their schoolbooks. However, they travelled only as far south as Bloor Street.

Many reporters throughout the city were pursuing the Stritch murder investigation. The famous or infamous Frank Gnomes—depending on one's viewpoint—was one of them. He had been on the staff of the *Toronto Tribune* since graduating from university. Having started with the *Trib* as a cub reporter, he had quickly risen to become the paper's chief investigative crime reporter. The newspaper had become his life. Even though he was fond of gorgeous women with oversized busts, the gals in his life were subservient to his career.

Frank's first and second marriages had failed, and he was now on his third. For a man only thirty-two years of age, this was an astounding record. It was a decade when people considered one divorce scandalous. Two divorces labelled a man as a marital miscreant beyond redemption. Thus, though Frank was quite attractive, he was a leper to the female staff members at the *Tribune*—an untouchable.

Sally-Lou, his present spouse, was stunningly attractive, with long blonde hair courtesy of the local drug store. Her figure, augmented by the mandatory full bosom, men adored and women envied. Wearing too much makeup, she was the type that attracted men, but when overexposed to her too obvious charms, their interest waned. Frank had made the mistake of marrying her. The gossip at the *Trib* was that another divorce was pending.

Frank wore no wedding band, a practice that was common during the 1950s, although double-ring ceremonies were becoming more popular. The women in the office sneered as they whispered, "Frank wears no ring as he views matrimony as impermanent territory."

However, despite Frank's devilish ways and condescending attitude toward the opposite sex, it was apparent why he had never remained a single man for long. His good looks often outweighed his faults, especially with the women he met in bars and nightclubs. He was developing a slight paunch, which some women thought was sexy. He often used his boyish grin to his advantage, and he was capable of being exceedingly charming. Because of his dogged devotion to his work, he frequently ignored his friends. However, this quality made him an excellent reporter.

One female colleague at the newspaper had once reluctantly admitted,

"Frank's the type of bad boy that some women are unable to resist. Scarlett O'Hara was never able to resist the charms of Rhett Butler." This was not a fair comparison, as Rhett Butler possessed a noble side that Frank lacked.

Frank feared having free time on his hands. As he often said to his colleagues, "For me, freedom means nosing around in other people's business, not sweating my balls on a Florida beach or toasting my ass under a palm tree while the world passes me by."

The Stritch murder intrigued him. He was certain that the cops knew more than they were telling, and he was good at being nosy, both personally and professionally. He was determined to discover the missing details.

He thought, *I'll phone my snitch on the police force and arrange a meeting. A copy of the coroner's report would also be nice, but it might take a while for them to complete it, so I'll settle for the preliminary report. It will give me an angle to begin my investigation. The death of a young woman always sells extra papers, especially if there's a sex angle. People love a scandal.*

✧ ✧ ✧

Frank called Officer Snitch, as he referred to his informant, and arranged a meeting at Fran's Coffee Shop on St. Clair Avenue, west of Yonge Street.

That evening, Frank slipped into a booth at the restaurant, and shortly after, Officer Snitch arrived, his coat collar turned up against the cold and a wool cap pulled low, hiding his round beefy face. He slid into the booth and without any pleasantries, gazed in contempt at his benefactor.

Frank fired his questions about the Stritch murder like bullets from a revolver.

"What was the cause of death?"

"It's early in the investigation. The official autopsy report has not been received, but they think it was a blow to the head."

"What was the time of death?"

"It was likely sometime between 6:00 p.m. and midnight, on the Friday before the holiday weekend."

"Did she die where the body was found?"

"They think she was attacked on the walking trail, and then pulled into the bushes. They interviewed an elderly man who saw her going cross the bridge on Lawrence Avenue and then enter the valley on the east side of the river. They think that she was originally on the west bank of the Humber River, crossed over to the east side, and then retraced her steps."

"Get any other information from the old guy who saw her on the bridge?"

"He said she was crying and that she was beautiful."

"Had she been screwed?"

Officer Snitch, whose real name was Constable Paul Masters, better known as "Bulldog Masters," smiled. He loved reporting details involving sex. He did not feel guilty about being a snitch. His wages as a patrol officer were far from generous, and he considered his relationship with Frank a simple necessity. Besides, he believed that dollars should always govern one's scruples and knew that many other cops also held their noses if they wanted to live a decent life. Peersen, he was certain, was one of them.

"I asked had she been screwed." Frank repeated, clearly irritated at the delayed response.

"She was screwed royally. She was a good-looking broad. But an early morning thundershower soaked her clothing and destroyed any vaginal secretions. However, there were cuts and traces of blood around the vagina."

"Post-mortem?"

"No."

"Any defensive wounds?"

"No."

"So she knew her attacker."

"Likely."

"Did they find any clues in the surrounding area?"

"They're still searching."

"Have they found the murder weapon?"

"No."

"Anything else?"

"There was another puzzling aspect to the case. The victim's body contained very little blood, and there was no blood at the primary death scene or at the dump site."

"Almost no blood?"

"That's what I said."

"That *is* interesting. Anything else?"

Paul Masters paused, as if he were thinking about the case, and after several moments replied, "That's all at this point."

There were a few more puzzling facts, but he did not intend to reveal them. The victim's fiancé had said that Miss Stritch had not joined him at the cottage as she had family obligations, but her roommate had stated that Miss Stritch had said that she was driving north to visit Mr. Matheson.

Masters has no intentions of doing Frank's job. He thought that the damn reporter should dig up his own bloody suspects. Why should he do all his work? Besides, if he told too much, it would be obvious that Frank had an inside source at the precinct.

✧ ✧ ✧

Shortly after four o'clock on Tuesday afternoon, detectives Thomson and Peersen arrived at the morgue on Lombard Street and walked down the long hallway to the domain of Dr. Theodore Dicer, whom the men disrespectfully referred to as "Doc Slicer."

Dicer had been Toronto's chief coroner for fifteen years. Over six-foot in height, his ruddy complexion and bulbous nose betrayed his fondness for whiskey and rum. He was as familiar with booze bottles as with the chemical jars that lined the shelves of the autopsy room. His full head of hair, rarely combed, gave him the appearance of a comic-book style, mad scientist. In some respects, his appearance suited his personality. Theodore called the autopsy room "his lounge," and the corpses as "his silent beauties."

The harried coroner glanced up at Peersen and Thomson as they entered the autopsy room. Dicer nodded to acknowledge their presence and continued working. He had been busy since daybreak.

"What've you got?" Thomson inquired, breaking the silence within the room.

"I've got a hangover."

"Sure, Doc. Now tell us what you got from your examination."

"A pain in the ass as well as my neck."

"Sure, Doc."

Thomson and Peersen were relieved that the coroner did not mention that they had previously viewed the body before the morgue had properly examined it. After an awkward pause, Dicer began. "This beauty's cause of death was hypovolemic shock."

"English, Doc," Gerry said.

"She bled out—exsanguinated through the carotid artery, here, in the neck, where the artery is quite large. The artery leads directly from the aorta of the heart, so the slightest puncture and the victim would have bled copiously."

The coroner turned the victim's head to the side and pointed to a small hole, halfway down the neck, well below the jaw line.

Continuing, he added, "She hemorrhaged through the small cut, likely made with an ice pick or a very small narrow knife. I'd estimate that within a short period of time, almost half of the blood drained from her body. Shit, there must have been a hell of a lot of blood at the scene."

Thomson winced at the coroner's choice of words. "Actually, there was almost none, Doc," he replied, ignoring the Dicer's street-language vocabulary.

"Then I think your vampire friends have visited this beauty," Dicer quipped. Earlier, at the crime scene, Thomson had made a similar comment and now realized how insensitive the remark sounded.

"It might have been a ritual killing," Doc Dicer suggested.

"It's true that we don't know where the blood went, Doc, but I doubt it was either vampires or a ritual killing. It's a sex crime, and God knows what else is involved. We're working on it. Oh, another thing, your assistant mentioned the redness of the whites of the eyes, which suggested a possibility of asphyxia?"

"That clown Sam doesn't know asphyxia from his asshole. My guess is that she likely had been crying and rubbing her eyes, which caused the redness. I'd say that the victim was very upset during the last half hour or so before she was killed."

"But she *was* struck on the head."

"Yes, by a blunt object. Perhaps a rock. It rendered her unconscious. The head wound is deep, suggesting extreme rage, but was not the cause of death."

"What can you tell us about the lacerations around the vagina?"

"The sex wasn't consensual, as the wounds around the vagina are too deep, and they too display evidence of extreme rage. I hope the sex occurred after she was unconscious, as otherwise, she would have suffered greatly." Sam Mann had expressed similar sentiments.

"Any semen?"

"None. Because of the delay in finding the body, and the rain shower, any traces of seminal fluid have disappeared. It's also possible that a condom was used."

"What are we dealing with here, Doc?"

"I'd say it was a sadistic psychopath, not a crazy drooling lunatic, but a psychopath nonetheless. The head wound was a random strike, but the body wounds indicate that despite the rage, the cuts were carefully inflicted. I'd even go so far as to say preplanned."

"Thanks, Doc. If you discover anything else that's pertinent, you know where we are."

"Yeah, and you know where I am too. Stuck here with my silent beauties."

Thomson and Peersen were glum as they departed from the autopsy room. Gerry told his partner, "We'll begin by interviewing Stritch's family. However, I fear that the killer is among the teachers on the staff where she was employed."

✧ ✧ ✧

The first day of classes, Wednesday, 5 September, Shorty and Tom located their homeroom and selected desks near the rear of the room. Piling their books on the top of their desks, they waited for their homeroom teacher to arrive. They knew from the information sheet that his name was Mr. Rogers.

Mr. Rogers was a slender, middle-aged man with wire-rimmed glasses and slicked-back dark hair graying at the temples. He possessed high cheekbones and eyes that he never seemed to open fully. His voice was clear and precise, his diction similar to an actor. The room fell silent as he spoke.

A few moments later, crackling sounds came over the PA system, and everyone stood for "God Save the King" and the "Lord's Prayer."

Next, the voice of Mr. Tyrone Evanson, the principal, boomed over the speaker. He welcomed everyone to a new school year and stated the rules of proper decorum: "No improper or vulgar language, no fistic maneuvers, and no expectorating."

Tom whispered to Shorty, "No swearing, no fighting, and no spitting—same as elementary school."

"Yeah!" Shorty replied. "No screwing around."

Evanson continued. "Slacks are not considered proper attire for young ladies at this academic institution. All skirts and dresses must reach below the knees."

Shorty was unable to resist whispering to Tom. "How's a guy get to see a little leg or panty if the skirts drag on the ground?" Then he added, "A guy Evanson's age thinks that exotic sex is changing hands."

Tom stifled his laughter for fear that Mr. Rogers might hear.

Evanson continued. "There will be an emergency staff meeting after the last period of the day," and then pompously added, "I, Mr. Evanson, your principal, wish you a harmonious day."

Despite his farewell words, no one broke into song.

Tom heard Shorty mutter under his breath. "The only music that old geezer makes is when he farts over the toilet bowl."

Mr. Guido Tyrone Evanson's close friends called him Gus. To the staff and teachers, he was Mr. Tyrone Evanson. He preferred the name Tyrone, as he believed it possessed the sound of authority. When he was a teenager, he had been a gifted student, and as he enjoyed history, he became a history teacher. He was highly regarded as an educator, and they quickly promoted him, becoming the youngest man they had ever appointed in Toronto as a high school principal. Since the early 1930s, he had ruled supremely from his office throne.

The opening exercises having ended, Mr. Rogers called aloud the names of the students and checked them against his class list. Then he distributed the locks, which cost two dollars each, and assigned the lockers. Several of the kids glanced at Shorty when they heard his surname, as they recognized the name Bernstein as being Jewish. Shorty's full name was Forester Horatio Hornblower Bernstein, and he was grateful that the other students did not know his full name. Several students smiled when they heard that Shorty's real first name was Forester.

As Mr. Rogers continued to read aloud the names, Tom realized almost half the class likely shared Shorty's religious heritage. Tom Hudson was too ordinary a name to attract any attention or ridicule, and he was grateful.

Next, Mr. Rogers explained, "You will have more class periods with me than any of the other teachers. In addition to being your homeroom teacher, I will be instructing you in history, English composition—that includes grammar—and English literature, including poetry."

Then he inquired, "Has everyone purchased copies of the book, *Words Are Important?* We will be employing it in vocabulary development for your prose writing. You will look up the listed words in a dictionary, record their meanings, and memorize them. You will be tested each week."

Tom glanced at Shorty, and they both rolled their eyes as they inwardly groaned.

In earlier years, Shorty had received language enrichment from Grumpy, the old man who had lived on the first-floor level of his house. As a result, Shorty knew more swear words and could place them in more creative contexts than any other kid on the street. Tom knew it was doubtful that the new textbook would add much to his friend's street-language vocabulary, but it might increase the number of words he could use in polite company.

Next, Mr. Rogers inquired, "Does everyone have a copy of the poetry and prose book, *Peddler's Pack?* Also, all students must purchase *Working with English*, the grammar text. A copy of Shakespeare's *Merchant of Venice* is mandatory as well."

✧ ✧ ✧

The first period ended at 9:45, and then they departed for Mr. Bowler's room. He taught history and geography. In a monotone voice, containing an upper-class English accent, he informed them, "We will study the geography of Europe, Australia, and Africa. Be prepared to travel to foreign climes. You may even learn to ride a kangaroo or a camel."

Then, although he did not smile, he paused and gazed around the room Jack Benny style, as if he had cracked a joke. The students remained as expressionless as he was.

Bowler was a short, rotund man, with a narrow fringe of hair, grown long on one side and pulled over the skin on his baldhead. As he continued to speak, he remained stone-faced, employing no facial muscles when he spoke, similar to a ventriloquist. Mr. Bowler would have been perfect for the role of the butler in a murder drama.

Shorty whispered to Tom, "I think we should call old Bowler, 'the Hat.' He's as interesting as a bowler hat—useful but boring."

"Yeah, I admit he's weird."

✧ ✧ ✧

At third period they met Mr. Baldwin, their French teacher. A slender man, tall like an ostrich, he strutted among the rows of desks, his head bobbing as he walked. The girl sitting behind Tom whispered, "Boy, he's a smart dresser. He's kind of cute." Tom was later to learn that many of the girls considered Mr. Baldwin attractive.

However, Tom whispered back to the girl sitting beside him, "I guess he does have great clothes, but I think he looks weird."

When Baldwin turned to write on the blackboard, Shorty quietly told her, "Even though he has lots of hair, I hear that the older students call him Baldy Baldwin."

Tom now understood the meaning of the washroom graffiti, "Baldy sucks in French."

There was a small gap between two of Baldwin's upper front teeth.

When pronouncing certain sounds, he emitted a tiny whistling sound, and he spoke with a slight lisp. Tom knew he would have difficulties learning a foreign language when the teacher was unable to enunciate clearly. He feared that French would not be one of his best subjects.

Later, Tom learned that Shorty felt the same, and similar to the other kids in the school, they fell into the habit of referring to Mr. Baldwin as Baldy.

✧ ✧ ✧

In fourth period, the girls went to the girls' gym, where Miss Manson was to instruct them in PT (physical training). Earlier in the day, Tom and Shorty had seen her in the hallway, and they both had thought she was pretty.

The boys departed for the boys' gymnasium, where they met their own PT teacher, Mr. Millford. He was young and good looking with an athletic build. His thick dark hair and handsome face, well tanned by the summer sun, presented the perfect image of Mr. Joe Jock.

Millford already had a nickname, "Coach," so the boys did not attempt to invent another. One boy suggested they call him "Milly." Everyone ignored his proposal.

Tom found the enormous gym and military-style teacher intimidating. He had attended a public school with no PT classes, and to him, the gym was a new and strange world. Coach lectured the students on his expectations, while the class stood in straight rows and listened attentively.

"My classes will be rigorous and everyone must always put their best foot forward. Every student must follow instructions instantly and carefully. You will wear gym uniforms at all times and they must be sparkling clean. At the end of each period, you must return all gym equipment to its proper place. Military precision is required. Look smart, act smart, and be smart!" he barked. "Do you understand?" he added in a commandant's voice.

The boys chorused, "Yes, sir."

As they stood at attention, he added a warning. "A gym is a place where boys are easily injured."

Most of the guys shifted uneasily in embarrassment when he held up a jockstrap, which he referred to as an "athletic supporter" and explained its use. Shorty smirked as he listened to the information.

"Buy one and wear it. It's for your own safety," the coach said as he finished his lecture.

Shorty whispered to Tom, "The balls you save could be your own."

Later in the day, Shorty gleefully told Patrick about the episode. Patrick had fair skin, and when embarrassed turned beet red. His discomfort increased as Shorty exaggerated the jockstrap episode in the gym.

Tom felt sorry for Patrick, but in all honesty, he failed to understand his reaction to silly jokes about a guy's balls.

✧ ✧ ✧

The first day, though Tom had only a single period for lunch, he had told his mom that he would run home for a quick sandwich. When he opened the door, he heard the music of a soap opera on the radio. The tortures of the soaps were dear to her heart. Tom had often said to Ken, "I think the misery of the characters makes her grateful for her own happy life."

When Tom entered the kitchen, a grilled cheese sandwich was on the table and vegetable soup simmering on the gas stove.

Tom's mother, Mrs. Hudson, had been born in Newfoundland, in the small community of Epworth, on the rocky shores of the island's southeast coast, which jutted into the turbulent Atlantic. The traditions of the Methodist faith dominated the village of her birth. Methodism was a faith that frowned on alcohol, dancing, and playing card games. Because of these restrictions, Mrs. Hudson celebrated life in her own way and was freethinking in her religious views. She instilled this attitude in Tom and Ken. Her sense of humour was rarely missing from the home, as she possessed the ability to see life's humorous side, even during depressing times.

After lunch, the door slammed behind Tom as he quickly departed to return to school. It was important that he be on time. Failing to be punctual meant receiving a detention. This meant signing into the detention room by 3:10 p.m. and remaining there for forty minutes. He could not allow this to occur, as he would be late delivering his newspapers.

The first period in the afternoon was science, taught by Mr. William Matheson, whom the students had read about in the newspapers. He was absent, due to the death of his fiancée, and a supply teacher was present. He told everyone to read the science text or do other homework. They sensed that they could do whatever they wished, as long as they did not bother him.

✧ ✧ ✧

The next class of the afternoon was art. It was merely an introductory session, so it was only a single period. Normally, it would be a double period to allow sufficient time for drawing or painting instructions, a work session, and cleanup.

The art room was on the second floor, and as Shorty and Tom walked toward the classroom, they saw the vice-principal, Mr. Dinkman, patrolling the hallway. The students referred to him as "Dickhead."

Ken had told Tom and Shorty, "The upper hallway is Dickhead's domain, because old Evanson is too fat to climb the stairs. When Dickhead's alone in the upper hallways, I've seen him slam guys into the wall. He's bloody dangerous."

They also overheard a grade-twelve student say to a friend, "You remember how old Dickhead drooled over Miss Stritch? I think he had a boner for her."

On this particular day, as Tom and Shorty passed the vice-principal in the upper hallway, they eyed him suspiciously. When they entered the art room, they caught their first glimpse of their teacher, Miss Hitch. Their mouths dropped in surprise. After everyone settled in their seats, they gazed at her expectantly. She in turn stared at them, resembling a spider observing her prey. When she finally spoke, her voice was soft but husky, as if she were breathing intimate details to a lover. She held the class spellbound.

"All students who enter my art room must be well equipped," she purred.

Shorty whispered to Tom, "I have a feeling she isn't referring to paint tubes and brushes."

Miss Hitch was a remarkable sight. She wore a tight, bright-green skirt. Beneath her flimsy green blouse, the students could see her black bra, the outfit revealing more than any grade-nine boy should ever perceive. Numerous green bracelets dangled on her long arms, rattling and clanking as she wrote the list of art supplies on the blackboard. When she wished to emphasize a point, she took a deep breath, heaving her large breasts upward, almost hitting the ceiling. A few of the immature kids giggled. Shorty and Tom ignored them. They preferred Sophie's breasts.

Miss Hitch wore her brunette hair swept up at the back of her neck, forming a large bun on the top of her head, the hair held in place with several jewelled combs. Tom wondered if she might have been sort of attractive, but he really could not tell. She wore far too much lipstick, thick mascara, and rouge. The oddest thing about the makeup was that everything was some tone of green. She looked like something that had escaped from the Garden of Eden, after Adam and Eve had fled the scene. Perhaps she had been frolicking with Adam's notorious snake.

When they departed the art room, Miss Hitch looked at Shorty and in a silky voice said, "For the next class, be certain to bring all your equipment."

Outside the classroom, Shorty grinned as he told Tom, "Wow! Did you hear the way she said 'all your equipment?' Horny Hitchy is quite a broad. I bet she could gobble a guy for breakfast, two for lunch, and three or more for supper."

"I doubt it. She's an older woman. She must be thirty-five."

Neither Tom nor Shorty had ever before encountered anything like her.

◇ ◇ ◇

The final period of the afternoon was with Miss Taylor, their mathematics teacher. They had assumed that she might be absent as her friend, Miss

Stritch, had recently been murdered. Tom whispered to Shorty as they entered the room, "She has dark circles under her eyes. I guess she hasn't slept well. She looks pale, and without makeup, her skin looks gray."

Miss Taylor was in her early thirties. On this day, she wore no jewellery. Her short-sleeve dress was a drab olive colour. She was not a woman most men would say was beautiful, but there was something attractive about her. Her smooth skin, coffee-coloured eyes, and brown hair, pulled back severely from her face, created a wholesome appearance. Her strong personality was evident when she spoke to the students and told them what she expected of them.

"I tolerate no nonsense in my classes," she declared authoritatively.

As she was tall and well muscled, the students had no reason to doubt the veracity of her statement.

Then she added, "Mathematics is a serious subject. Come prepared to work hard."

Math was not one of Tom's better subjects, and he feared the classes ahead. She doled out two exercises from the text as homework on the first day. Tom inwardly groaned as he gazed at the assignment.

✧ ✧ ✧

At 3:00 p.m., following Miss Taylor's class, the school day ended. Tom walked home with Harry, Patrick, and Shorty. Shorty smirked as he said, "If Miss Stritch's killer had met Miss Taylor in the Humber Valley instead of her roommate, Taylor would have creamed the guy."

Then they discussed their other teachers. Shorty and Tom did most of the talking, with Harry offering a few comments. Patrick, as usual, said nothing beyond a simple yes or no reply.

Shorty informed them, "After the final period, I saw Kramer at his locker. It's at the far end of the same row as ours." Then he added, "I strolled past the jerk while he was bending over, searching for some crap in the bottom of the locker." Shorty chuckled as he confessed, "I was tempted to give him a goose that would send him flying headfirst into his locker. I didn't do it, as I would prefer to goose him when he knows who delivered the thrusting finger."

"Yeah, you're a real angel," Tom told him with a mocking grin.

Shorty smirked mischievously and dramatically fluttered his eyelids, as he knew the last thing anyone would call him was an angel. Tom realized that in the days ahead, it would require restraint on Shorty's part to avoid open conflict with Kramer. Shorty informed the guys that he had caught a glimpse of Kramer's classroom schedule taped to the inside of the door of his locker and noted that his name was listed as Horace Kramer. None of them had ever known Kramer's first name before. Everyone had simply referred to him as Kramer.

As Shorty continued to complain about Kramer, Tom noticed that Harry remained quiet. Tom sensed that he was concerned about the hatred between Shorty and Kramer. It had begun one Halloween evening, when they had been much younger. While they were shelling out, Kramer had mistakenly thought Shorty was an easy victim because of his lack of stature and tried to steal his bag of treats. Though he was small, Shorty had been muscular. He bloodied Kramer's nose, humiliating the taller boy.

In the months ahead, Kramer constantly sought revenge. As the years passed, the enmity between them grew. Actually, at one time or another, everyone had received a beating from Kramer's gang and had their pockets emptied of the few coins that they carried.

Now, Tom and his friends were older and in high school, but the antagonism from former days remained alive.

❖ ❖ ❖

After Horace Kramer arrived home after his first day of high school, he stood beside the sink in the bathroom and gazed into the mirror as he reflected on his situation. For weeks after Shorty had thrashed him in the alley the previous June, he had been bitter. His gang members did not attend York Collegiate, but he now realized that not having them around him was not so bad. He was managing okay on his own.

He felt good about the teenager reflected in the glass. Passing his comb through his thick dark hair, he gave a satisfied grin. He couldn't believe the changes that had occurred in his life since he had graduated from public school, just two months earlier.

He still missed his mom, who had died the previous March. In June, his dad, a hulking aggressive man and a bully by nature, had wed a petite attractive woman ten years younger than he was. Kramer had originally resented that his father had remarried with such undue haste, but now realized that it had worked out for the best.

Mr. Kramer had believed that his new wife would be gentle and compliant, like a pet monkey. Shortly after their marriage, he learned to his dismay that she was a King Kong in disguise. Though she did not break chains or pound on her chest while atop a New York skyscraper, she could swing a frying pan with deadly accuracy. She soon ruled the house as if it were her jungle domain. She would not tolerate his rude and bullying ways.

Unlike Kramer's birth mom, his stepmother protected him from his dad's abuse. She liked Horace, and her liking had quickly turned into motherly love. She cooked him proper meals, insisted that he bathe regularly, forced him to brush his teeth, and purchased Clearasil to control the pimples on his face.

Finally, she took him to a dentist and demanded that his dad pay for braces on Kramer's teeth. His dad had objected, but his stepmom's threat to employ her "frying pan therapy" quickly cured him of any delusions of resisting. His new mom also insisted that Kramer stop smoking. She did the "sniff test" several times each day to be certain that he was obeying her edict. Kramer had told a friend, "My new mom can smell a fart in a windstorm at forty paces." Cigarettes disappeared from his life.

Kramer had always been skinny, and though he still lacked the build of a Charles Atlas, the famous bodybuilder, he had put on a little weight and developed more muscles. Girls had always ignored him, but now they took notice. Not certain how to react when they flirted with him, he either stammered or was speechless. Surprisingly, instead of being annoyed, they considered his reaction "cute."

However, whenever he saw Shorty, Kramer knew exactly how to

behave. He hated Shorty, always had and always would. Revenge was an emotion Kramer understood well. His physical appearance might have changed, but the bully-of-old smouldered within him.

✧ ✧ ✧

Carol thought over her first day at YCI. There had been so many cute guys in the hallways that she had not known where to cast her gaze. Secretly she had eyed them all, particularly a hunk in her homeroom. He was tall and good looking, but she considered him nothing compared to Harry.

Then she wondered what Harry had thought about all the girls at the high school. Unlike when he was at D. B. Hood, Harry now had many attractive girls around him. To make matters worse, she was sure that the girls in grades twelve and thirteen would be attracted to him, as he looked mature enough to be in the upper grades.

This worried her.

Carol was confident that she was attractive and was certain that her breasts were larger than most of the other girls in grade nine. Her bust had developed later than Sophie's had, but they were now of a size that other girls envied her. She knew that in her homeroom, several of the boys leered whenever she walked down the aisle to take her seat. But they were only in grade nine. To keep Harry, she had to compete with the girls in the upper grades.

She considered changing her hairstyle again and wearing tighter sweaters. Harry was a guy and guys always liked well-filled sweaters.

Shorty's feelings for her never entered her mind. He was a friend, a great friend, but not a dreamboat like Harry.

✧ ✧ ✧

After Tom arrived home, he picked up the newspapers for his paper route. He saw that another picture of Miss Stritch was on the front page, and again, he noticed that she had been a beautiful woman. Her long blonde hair fell over her shoulders, framing her attractive face. There was also information about Mr. Matheson. It read:

> Mr. William Matheson, thirty-four years of age, born in Bath, England, immigrated to Canada with his family when he was a young boy. He attended Oakwood Collegiate and later received a Bachelor of Science degree from the University of Western Ontario. Having graduated from the Ontario College of Education, his first teaching assignment was at Scarborough Collegiate, and he has been teaching science at York Collegiate Institute for the past five years. He is deeply saddened at the sudden death of his fiancée and does not expect to return to his teaching position for another week …"

Tom read the remainder of the article, but there was no information about the murder that he did not already know.

✧ ✧ ✧

Despite having the inside information from Paul Masters, Frank Gnomes' progress had been agonizingly slow. He had a reputation for scooping the other Toronto dailies, and a few times, he had solved crimes ahead of the police. One of his trademarks as a columnist was to coin a catchy name for each crime: the Scarborough Slasher, the Main Street Mutilator, the Thornhill Thrasher. He had yet to invent a catchy title to hang on the murder in the Humber Valley. "The Valley Murderer" had no ring to it. Then, recalling the information he had received from his snitch, he remembered that the victim's blood had disappeared. He grinned as he said aloud, "The Valley Vampire—a great name for the killer."

He was aware that some of his colleagues considered him unprofessional, as he wrote in a sensationalized style, badgered and bribed witnesses to receive intimate details, and often employed sensational gossip, some of it unsubstantiated. What did he care? His editor supported him as his column boosted sales and attracted advertisers.

I do my job well, he thought. *To hell with those who cannot compete.*

He knew that this case was growing cold and he needed to write something sensational to stir the pot. He thought: *The Valley Vampire will serve me well as a gimmick. Besides, everyone seems to think Stritch was a choirgirl, but I bet she sang a few naughty songs. I need to find these indiscretions. A little exaggerated dirt can often open up a can of worms. Time to go fishing.*

✧ ✧ ✧

In Tom's home, later in the evening, the news on the radio rehashed the details of the Stritch murder, but Tom heard nothing new. Included in the broadcast was a recording of a recent speech of Prime Minister St. Laurent's, talking about the increase in the cost of living.

The PM declared at the end of his speech, "Price controls are no answer to high prices, as it is not wartime. I assure Canadians that my government will act, if necessary, to protect the public."

Tom's dad shook his head as he said, "St. Laurent is sounding more like Mackenzie King every day. I still remember King saying during the war, 'Conscription if necessary, but not necessarily conscription.'"

Thomas Hudson had been born in Burin Bay, Newfoundland, a small village a mile across the water from where Tom's mom had lived. They had not known each other when children, as his dad was seven years older than his mom. They had met and married in Toronto.

When his dad was a young man in Newfoundland, he had endured the harsh realities of fishing for a living, hauling heavy nets from a small boat, known as a skiff. Stormy seas, dangerous shoals, and a rocky shoreline often led to tragedies. In 1921, he and his brother Fred immigrated to Toronto, in the days before Newfoundland joined Canada.

When Ken and Tom had been younger, their mom had not allowed them to listen to their dad's jokes. The few that they had overheard, they had not always understood. However, they had been anxious to listen, as they were certain that they were naughty. If their dad began to tell a joke when they were near, their mom shushed him.

Now being older, they understood his stories, but their mom still did not approve of them listening to them. Similar to earlier years, this did not prevent them from overhearing a few. The previous week, Tom had heard his dad tell a joke about an elderly Newfoundland woman.

He had said, "She was over ninety years of age and had a fatal disease. Her doctor told her that the only cure was to have sex five times a week. She informed the doctor that she was unable to reduce her sex life to that infrequent."

Their dad chuckled as he finished the story. Gramps laughed heartily, and then proceeded to tell about another elderly woman with the same odd disease. "She too," Gramps had said, "was also told by her doctor to have sex five times a week. When she told her husband what the doctor had said, the old man told his wife to put him down for one."

When Ken and Tom had been younger, they had loved trying to overhear their dad's naughty stories. Shushing times were always interesting in their home. Tom now heard off-colour jokes regularly, as they were a normal part of high school life. Shorty, of course, was a major source.

Chapter Two

From their preliminary investigations, Thomson and Peersen had learned that since moving to Toronto, Elaine Stritch's social life had centred on the teachers of YCI. She was the staff advisor for the drama club and spent many hours working on the two annual school plays. Miss Stritch was close to her students and spent much time with them after school and sometimes during evenings. When it became close to performance time, rehearsals often involved weekends. The detectives thought it odd that Miss Stritch, being young and attractive with an outgoing personality, had made no friends other than those among the students and staff at the high school.

On Thursday morning, Thomson and Peersen visited Hamilton, the hometown of Elaine Stritch and her family. Her father had passed away several years before. They interviewed the mother, as well as any high school friends that remained in "the steel city." By the end of the day, they had received no information that was helpful.

So far, everything seemed to reinforce Thomson's theory that the murderer was a member of the staff at YCI, especially since it appeared that Stritch had known her killer. Before beginning their interrogations at the school, they reviewed the police reports they had received on the teachers, two of whom had criminal records.

When William Matheson, Stritch's fiancé, had been twenty years of age, the police had caught him having sex with a young woman in a car in High Park. In broad daylight, he and the girl had climbed into the back seat of an automobile, only a blanket preventing people passing by in the parking lot from viewing Matheson's bobbing ass. When a patrolman confronted them, the girl had said that Matheson threatened her and forced her to have sex. Matheson denied her accusation. Unable to substantiate either story, the police officer charged them both with an indecent act in a public place.

The records also revealed that Sam Millford, the boys' PT teacher, had been involved in an altercation with a young woman in the rear section of the balcony of the Imperial Theatre on Yonge Street. The woman sitting next to Millford claimed that he had tried to "feel her up" in the dark, but a friend of Millford, who was also in the theatre, confirmed Millford's claim that nothing had happened. The police were unable to substantiate the girl's story. The case went to court, but the judge dismissed it.

Thomson and Peersen thought it strange that two individuals, on the same staff, had criminal records, yet Mr. Dinkman had hired them.

✧ ✧ ✧

It was now time to interview the teachers of York Collegiate Institute. Chief of Detectives Arnold Peckerman's warning rang in their ears as they drove to the school. He had forcefully declared, "The staff members are highly respected in the community and know how to vocalize their complaints to the press. I want no adverse publicity."

As they parked the police car in the parking lot of York Collegiate, they knew that they were facing a daunting task. With 650 students, the school had thirty-five members of staff.

The vice-principal made available two rooms in the guidance office and supplied them with the classroom timetables for each teacher. In an attempt to be as unobtrusive as possible, they interviewed the staff members as they became available.

It was quickly evident that the staff resented the intrusion, as they were busy with the myriad of tasks that the beginning of every new term entailed. Thomson and Peersen conducted their inquiries, ignoring the objections. The teachers were aware of their suspicions, causing a heavy cloud to descend over the school.

While the interviews proceeded, the students observed the constant intrusion of the police into the day's routines. To assist the school programs, supply teachers were on hand to babysit the classes while teachers were with the police. It was not long before students were discussing the turn of events, feeling that the cops suspected one of the teachers.

The comments spread like multiple ripples in a pool. Soon the students were looking at their teachers through different eyes.

✧ ✧ ✧

After school, as Tom, Patrick, Shorty, and Harry trekked homeward, they discussed the turn of events. "The police must think that one of the teachers could be the murderer," Shorty oozed. "Geez, we could be sitting in a classroom watching a teacher write on the blackboard with the same hand that killed Miss Stritch."

"Come off it, Shorty. You're letting your imagination run wild," Tom replied.

Harry said, "Well, it would explain the constant parade of teachers going to the guidance office. On the other hand, it might simply be that the police are covering every possible angle and are trying to learn about the background of Miss Stritch. They'll want to know about her friends, and who she hung around with at the school."

"Well, I don't think the butler did this murder, but Miss Stritch was engaged to Mr. Matheson, and the husband or lover is always the best suspect."

"I think you've been reading too many detective novels," Patrick interjected.

"Patrick's right," Harry responded. "I doubt that Matheson is a murderer."

"You never know what evil lurks in the minds of men," Shorty replied, quoting the line from the radio program *The Shadow*.

The conversation ended when they arrived at the corner of Amherst and Lauder avenues, and they separated to go to their individual homes. However, they were unable to erase from their minds the thought that one of their teachers might be a murderer.

✧ ✧ ✧

By the end of the week, the two detectives had completed their preliminary interviews with the staff. Jim's patience was wearing thin. "The teachers who knew Stritch the best all have alibis that are tighter than a camel's ass after a hundred-mile trek in the desert," he told Gerry. The flippant comment ably expressed the frustration that they were feeling. Thomson had also conducted many unrewarding interviews.

"What're the chances that all these teachers can account for their whereabouts on a particular evening, and that most of the alibis overlap, each one confirming the others'?" Peersen added.

Gerry simply nodded his head in agreement and replied, "Now then, we'll just see about that."

Peersen continued. "No teacher is above suspicion, but those who associated with Stritch during after-school hours are the ones that merit further investigation."

"True! And they're the ones with the ironclad alibis."

"Bill Matheson is a prime suspect as he knew her best, being engaged to her."

"Bettina Taylor, her roommate is another."

"Gregory Baldwin, the French teacher knew her well."

"Then there's Elizabeth Hitch, the art teacher."

"And Sam Millford, boys' PT instructor."

"What about Jim Rogers, who teaches English, and the geography/history teacher, Anthony Bowler?"

"They seem squeaky clean, but who knows?"

"I think we should reinterview Gayle Manson, the girls' PT teacher, and Mary Allyson, the librarian. Though they're likely not the murderer, they knew the victim well and might know something, even if they are unaware that they know it. In some investigations, we have a lack of suspects, but in this case, we have too many," Thomson said as they departed for the day.

Adding to their difficulties, they were aware that Arnold Peckerman was anxious to hold a press conference to brag about the progress of the police investigation.

✧ ✧ ✧

On Thursday, 13 September, Mr. Evanson ended the classes at noon to allow teachers to attend the funeral of Miss Stritch. The family had postponed the funeral for over a week, as the coroner's office had delayed releasing the body.

After the funeral, the investigation continued. Tension among the students increased. It was evident in the hallways as students rotated between class periods. Despite the many interviews and the disruptions they caused, by the end of the following week, Thomson and Peersen had learned little new information.

Peersen again complained. "All the teachers that knew Miss Stritch the best have consistently repeated their alibis, over and over. They never change a word. Half of them can't remember what they did yesterday, but they sure as hell remember every minute detail of their behaviour the night Stritch was murdered. I'm more convinced than ever that they have closed ranks and rehearsed their stories."

Thomson agreed and added, "I've reread my notes from the earlier interviews. Among the teachers of the 'inner group,' whenever they tell me anything about Miss Stritch, they employ almost the exact same wording. Whenever I ask them to describe Miss Stritch, they all tell me that she was a hard-working teacher who loved her job, and that she had lived an exemplary life. They all used the word exemplary. As well, they all claim there was no friction among any of the staff members."

"I don't think we'll ever get them to change their tune," Jim concluded.

"Now then, we'll just see about that," Gerry replied.

Meanwhile, tension among the students increased as the days passed, and the police arrested no one for the murder.

✧ ✧ ✧

Unlike their years at D. B. Hood Public School, Tom and his friends now had a different teacher for each subject. Because classroom periods were only forty minutes long, they did not develop the same rapport they had experienced with their elementary school teachers. Adding to the stress was the knowledge that one of their high-school teachers might be a murderer.

The second week of school, Tom and Shorty finally had a class period with Miss Allyson, the school librarian. She was close to retirement age, and the students referred to her as "Ancient Alice." Throughout the fall term, they were to have one class a week with "Alice."

Alice was even more difficult to approach than the other teachers. Mousy in attire and manner, she gazed at the students through her thick glasses, a confused expression on her wrinkled face. Her straight brown hair, parted in the middle, drooped close to her shoulders. A gray skirt and brown blouse, which they were to learn was her constant daily attire, added to her mousy appearance.

Shorty whispered to Tom. "I doubt she's ever seen a penis in her entire life. If she did see one, she'd likely think it was for stirring her tea."

A boy sitting beside Tom added, "Unlike a sidewalk or railway tracks, she's never been laid."

Tom noticed that when a male student stood too close to Alice, she blushed crimson and hastily stepped back. When talking to students, she rarely looked them in the eye and stammered badly while attempting to answer their questions. It was as if she were only comfortable when immersed in her world of books, wrapped within their secure covers.

During the first library class, she stood at the front of the class, a thick book in her hand, gazing at it intently. It was as if the students did not exist. She only glanced up periodically as she informed everyone about the library rules, gave instructions for locating books, and told how to sign them out. Alice ignored any raised hands. When her soliloquy ended, she turned the students loose in her fiefdom, eyeing them warily as they perused the shelves to examine the various sections in an attempt to understand the intimidating Dewey Decimal System.

Miss Allyson noticed Shorty examining books that she was certain were not within his reading level. Walking over to him, she observed that he was returning to the shelf a copy of Nathaniel Hawthorne's *The House of the Seven Gables*. She glanced at him suspiciously, and condescendingly said, "You're wise to place that book back in its place, young man. I doubt you'd understand it."

"I read that book three years ago," Shorty replied. "I find Hawthorne too verbose, and his Gothic stories depressing. *The Scarlet Letter* was interesting, but it too was depressing. Edgar Allan Poe's tales of horror are also too wordy, and man, are they weird."

Miss Allyson eyes widened in surprise, and against her better judgment, for the first time she looked closely at Shorty. Gazing up, he peered directly into her eyes, submerged behind her thick lenses, and grinned amiably. This increased Alice's discomfort as she had rarely confronted a student who knew anything about books, never mind one that gave her a friendly smile.

Remaining leery, she told him, "You might wish to examine the books of a more up-to-date author, such as F. Scott Fitzgerald."

"I've already read *The Great Gatsby*. Besides, a story published in 1925 is hardly up-to-date. Even *Tender is the Night* was published in 1934," he told her. Then he added, "However, I admit that in *The Great Gatsby,* the character Daisy was hot."

Miss Allyson was now thoroughly confused. She considered a grade-nine student who had read anything beyond a comic book or the poems on the school's washroom walls, a rarity. Without realizing it, she inadvertently smiled at him. Shorty noticed her reaction and decided that despite the rude comments he had heard from the other students, Alice was an okay gal.

Even when Shorty was younger, adults had not intimidated him. His parents had separated when he had been a toddler. Before his mother had remarried, she worked two jobs to survive financially, and thus was rarely at home. When Shorty misbehaved, the neighbours were unable to complain to her, so they had attempted to chastise Shorty themselves. He quickly learned to defend himself verbally. Because he spent so much time alone, he read profusely.

Now, as a teenager, he was unafraid to express his opinions with adults.

Tom often wished that he had Shorty's confidence.

During the days ahead, the students continued to ridicule Miss Allyson. One day in library period, someone tied a brassiere, pilfered from his sister's bedroom, on the back of Miss Allyson's chair. The prankster had strategically placed two apples inside the cups. When Alice saw them, she burst into tears. Shorty felt sorry for her and quickly removed the bra and the offending objects from the chair. As long as Tom had known Shorty, he had defended the kids that the bullies picked on. At the end of the school day, Shorty confronted the bra thief.

The jerk said with a smirk, "I'll torment old Alice whenever I feel like it."

The smug look disappeared when Shorty overpowered him, pinned his hands behind his back, and with the purloined bra, secured him to his locker door.

As Shorty sauntered away, the guy screamed, "Untie me you piece of shit."

Shorty turned around, walked back, and shoved one of the guy's sweaty gym socks into his mouth.

After this incident, nobody in class 9L dared disrespect Alice.

Carol heard about the incident and teased Shorty. "I hear that today you rescued a fair damsel in distress, even if Miss Allyson does not really fit the description of a fair damsel."

The word damsel reminded Tom of a story that his dad loved to tell.

"A little kid in school had learned that the word frugal meant to save, to be saving. The teacher asked the kid to show that he understood the word.

"He thought for several moments and then said, 'A fair damsel was tied to a tree. She screamed, 'frugal me, frugal me.' A handsome knight heard her cry, dismounted from his horse, and frugalled her."

✧ ✧ ✧

Frank Gnomes held in his hand a purloined copy of the Stritch autopsy. He had applied considerable pressure on Masters to steal it and had paid extra bucks, but he knew it was worth it. It gave him an advantage over every other reporter in Toronto.

Frank noticed that as usual Masters was reluctant to hand over the report and grumbled about the risks he had taken. However, he noticed that an extra ten dollars eased Master's fears and he departed with a satisfied grin on his face.

What a creep, Frank thought.

Paul Masters was indeed happy with the money, but unknown to Gnomes, one of the reasons for this was because he had again withheld information. He had omitted to inform Frank about the plaster casts of the bicycle tire tracks that the police had made at the crime scene. They had found an area under the bushes, protected from the rain. Despite the shielded location, the soil was damp, the tires leaving clear impressions.

Scanning the report, Gnomes quickly extracted the essential data.

Stritch's death had not been from blunt-force trauma to the head. She had bled out. The coroner had confirmed that the time of death was somewhere between 6:00 p.m. and 12:00 a.m. on Friday, 31 August. He scanned the other details and carefully read the information about the absence of blood at the scene.

Frank mumbled under his breath, "It's a juicy detail that I've already used to my advantage." Then, as an afterthought, he muttered, "I wonder what occurred between the killer and the victim to inspire the rage that's evident in the coroner's report?"

◇ ◇ ◇

On the third week of school, Mr. William Matheson returned to the classroom. The only reason the students were aware of his first name was the articles that had appeared in the newspapers. Matheson was tall with a slim athletic build, handsome features, and surprisingly thick, light brown hair, considering that he had a small bald spot at the back. He appeared younger than his thirty-four years, the age the newspapers had given. The girls in Tom's classroom adored him on first sight, and because of the death of his fiancée, they considered him a tragic figure, akin to a suffering hero in a romantic novel. Shorty said that he believed they referred to it as a *Wuthering Heights* complex.

Shorty soon learned to be leery of Matheson, as he was condescending, sarcastic, and ignored the boys in the class. During the first class, for no apparent reason, Matheson told Shorty, "Your head resembles the top of a test tube—round and empty."

Shorty resented the insult. This was the beginning of the tension between Mr. Matheson and Shorty. During the following days, Mr. Matheson continued to lavish attention on the girls, while he ignored the guys. Tom felt that his teaching skills were not as well groomed as his mop of hair. He disliked the way he treated Shorty.

They soon learned that "Wild Bill" Matheson also ridiculed Kramer. It seemed strange that the brunt of Matheson's enmity was two students who were bitter enemies. None of the boys in his classes received any kindness, but Shorty and Kramer were the butt of his cruelest remarks.

Shorty expressed the opinion that if Matheson was as deadly with his fists as he was with his tongue, he might have murdered his fiancée.

"After all," he explained, "as I said before, the husband or lover is always a prime suspect."

✧ ✧ ✧

When Kramer was working on an assignment in the classroom, he was aware that Matheson was observing him, like a cat watching a mouse. Day after day, the close scrutiny and sarcastic comments continued, but unlike Shorty, Kramer suspected the reason for Matheson's hatred toward him.

Matheson thinks I might tell the police what I know. He doesn't realize that I wouldn't blab. I am not that stupid. It would be too dangerous.

Kramer had heard that Shorty was also the brunt of Matheson's enmity and wondered if Shorty also knew something. Perhaps he was unaware that he knew. Kramer hated Shorty, so whatever cruelty Wild Bill Matheson inflicted on Shorty, it was fine with him.

Perhaps he could drop the two of them in a vat of sulphuric acid, he thought. *It would be a fitting fate for a science jerk and an all-around everyday jerk.*

Ever since the day Kramer's stepmother had entered his home, his life had improved. The bullying of his father had been contained, and lately he had felt less inclined to bully others. Matheson's cruel remarks caused his aggressive habits to surface once more.

I can't get back at Matheson, but there's always my old pal Shorty to torture. Humiliating him will be a pleasure.

✧ ✧ ✧

As September progressed, the bright foliage of summer slowly dissolved into the softer hues of autumn, as Toronto descended into the harvest season. The mornings were chilly as Tom and his friends walked to school, but at day's end, the warm afternoon sunshine erased any fears of the impending frosts. A new indication of the fall season was the tryouts for the school football team.

It did not surprise Tom that Harry and Shorty were among those competing for a position. They were both successful, and it was rumoured that Harry might be the quarterback. Most doubted it was true, because Harry was only a freshie, as they referred to grade niners, but anyone watching him perform on the field realized that he had the skills to lead the team. Tom envied Harry, thinking that he had a charmed life, as well as good looks and great athletic abilities. Tom had always looked up to Harry.

Shorty and Tom were best friends, but Tom accepted that Shorty considered Harry to be a brother. Most days, Tom did not walk home from school with them as they remained late for football practice. The previous June, Harry had confided in Tom and Shorty a dark secret, and at the time, it had bothered Tom. Now, in the golden days of late September, it no longer seemed important.

Tom was tired of delivering newspapers, as it restricted his routines. Besides, he felt he was too mature to be a newspaper delivery boy. Each day, when he retrieved his bundles of newspapers, he glanced over the front pages, noticing that more articles were appearing about the forthcoming royal tour of Princess Elizabeth and Prince Philip. As the heir apparent, when Elizabeth ascended the throne, she would become the seventh sovereign queen of England. Her mother, Queen Elizabeth, was the queen consort to the King George VI and not a sovereign monarch. The princess's tour of Canada was generating much excitement. The immense affection that her parents had engendered by their steadfast devotion to the war effort included their daughter.

Though Hollywood's stars captivated much interest, people viewed the royal couple as having star qualities more glamorous than the world of Hollywood. They were young, attractive, and possessed the mystique engendered by the pomp and pageantry of royalty. Living fairytale lives, people avidly read about their activities, which transcended the royals into realms of fantasy that embraced the poetic tales of courtly knights. In the minds of Canadians, the 1951 royal tour was to be a spectacular event.

✧ ✧ ✧

It was now past 4:00 p.m. on Friday, 28 September, and as Frank Gnomes sat at his desk at the *Trib*, he thought about the article he had just finished editing and typing for the Saturday edition. He had again stressed the vampire angle.

Despite having inside knowledge of the police investigation, too many questions remained unanswered. The victim's residence had been close to the high school, near Rogers Road and Oakwood Avenue. Why had Stritch been in the west end of the city in the Humber Valley? It was highly unlikely that such an attractive young woman was strolling simply for exercise along secluded valley trails on a Friday night. Had she arranged to meet someone?

Miss Bettina Taylor had refused him an interview. He was certain that she had intimate knowledge of Stritch's male friends. He must find a way to loosen her tongue.

Were there problems between the victim and her fiancé, William Matheson? What was the real reason Stritch and Matheson had not been together on the Labour Day weekend? Again, Bettina Taylor might know the answer.

Frank thought, *The teachers all insist that Miss Stritch was a Goody Two-Shoes who wouldn't say shit if her mouth were full of it. I don't believe it. Stritch's neighbours say they saw students entering and leaving her flat during the late evening hours. Tutoring? Sure, but in what subject? I doubt that the principal, old fat boy Evanson, will allow me to interview the grade-thirteen students. I suppose I'll have to follow them home after school to get their addresses.*

Before Frank placed the cover over his typewriter for the day, he added the final touches to the article he had written for the following day's edition. He added another sentence to the opening paragraph, inserting the word "vampire" another time. He knew it was "bloody overkill" and smiled smugly at the crude pun.

◆ ◆ ◆

The stalker scanned the front page of the Saturday edition of the *Trib* and again noticed the word "vampire" in the article on the front page. For the stalker, the word embodied a sense of power. The creatures of the night were immortal and invincible. Blood was the source of their power.

The stalker needed another victim. However, for now, patience was required while the police chased their own tails.

◆ ◆ ◆

On Friday, 5 October, Tom attended his first football rally in the school auditorium. All the morning periods had been shortened by ten minutes, which allowed forty minutes for the rally. Mr. Evanson strutted on stage, his rotund belly preceding him as he stepped to the microphone.

Peering through his thick glasses, which pinched his generous nose, he intoned in a monotone voice, "The long tradition and excellent standards of the athletes of York Collegiate are unchallenged throughout the city. We support our athletes."

Tom smiled, as he was familiar with the corny joke, "We will be *athletic supporters—real jocks.*"

After Evanson had finished his speech, coach Millford gave a pep talk, ending with the words, "Let's all cheer for our heroes." Then he introduced the members of the team. Tom felt proud when the students applauded wildly for Harry and Shorty, his best friends.

Next, the cheerleaders came on stage and led everyone in rousing cheers as they did cartwheels and somersaults, their short skirts flipping upside down as they jumped and performed. The sight of girls' panties was sufficient to convince the students that they should all be true "athletic supporters." If it had been possible, those wearing testicle containers would have tossed them in the air. The cheerleaders led the assembly in shouting:

Victory, victory is our cry.
V- I- C- T- O- R- Y
Are we champions? Well, I guess,
Can we beat them? Yes! Yes! Yes!

The display of skirts, panties, and lusty cheering caused an arousing experience. After sustained applause, the students entered into a full-throated rendition of the school song.

To dear old York we'll e'er be true,
Colours red and green and blue.
We'll fight for thee, and never fail,
When e'er we seek the Holy Grail,
Keeping high York's flag of fame,
Bringing honour to its name.

As they sang the dear old song of York Collegiate, everyone was high with enthusiasm. The boisterous singing rattled the roof of the auditorium. The "Hallelujah Chorus" from Handel's *Messiah* could not have brought more students to their feet. Tom felt an electric tingle race up and down his spine. He had never attended a hockey or baseball game, and his previous experience with mass hysteria had been when he was a kid and Roy Rogers had galloped across the purple sage in a black and white film at the Grant Theatre. With a single shot from his pearl-handled six-shooters, the cowboy hero had decimated five guys wearing black hats. In this decade, the Indians conveniently lined up along the tops of the hills to provide better targets, and the hero quickly demolished them as well.

The high school football rally generated far more noise than a mere band of wild cowboys assaulting the lair of a gang of bad guys. To win the football game was surely a divine quest, blessed by the god of sports. Before Mr. Evanson dismissed the students from the assembly, he reminded them that he expected "first-class sportsmanship at all times."

In the afternoon, the school cancelled the final period of the day to allow the students to attend the football game against Vaughan Road Collegiate. YCI lost the game six to twelve, Harry scoring the only touchdown for his team. He missed the conversion, although the two extra points would not have altered the outcome of the game. Despite the loss, Harry was the hero of the moment as he had put the team on the scoreboard.

Tom did not have a chance to talk to Harry and Shorty after the game. Because they were now school heroes, Tom wondered if they would treat him the same as ever. He feared that they might forget about him, as they were now a part of the school's "in" crowd. Tom was pleased that they had acquired new friends on the team, but he wished to remain their close buddy.

After the football game, Tom walked home with Patrick. Patrick had grown into a good-looking teenager—clear skin, blue eyes, and golden-blond hair that flopped over his forehead. Somehow, there was something fragile about him. His walk and mannerisms were almost graceful. He attracted the attention of the girls but seemed unaware.

On this afternoon, Patrick told Tom, "The football game was great. It's one of the few things about high school that I like. I really miss my Catholic elementary school. I was happy back there. I still enjoyed attending church and singing in the choir, but attending high school is …" He stopped talking.

After a long pause, he continued. "Yesterday, when I was in the boys' washroom, some older guys …" He paused again. Tom waited, but Patrick never said anything more. As they walked along in silence, Tom wondered what had happened to Patrick in the washroom at school.

Patrick's closest friend remained Sophie Cellini, who had attended the Catholic elementary school with him. Attending a public high school was a new experience for them both, so they continued to hang around together. Some thought they were girlfriend and boyfriend. Tom did not know if Patrick harboured romantic feelings for Sophie, as he had never said anything.

✧ ✧ ✧

While Tom and Patrick were returning home after the football game, Thomson and Peersen were discussing the interviews they had conducted with the teachers.

"We've still been unable to find any discrepancies in the alibis of those who interest us the most," Thomson lamented.

"True," Peersen agreed. "Bill Matheson, her fiancé, and Miss Taylor, Stritch's roommate, are the most obvious suspects."

"I doubt that a woman would commit such a violent killing. However, a dispute between the two women might have escalated into violence. On the other hand, why would Taylor kill her roommate in the valley? It would be easier for her to do it on a street close to home."

"True! But killing her at a remote location creates less suspicion to fall on her."

"That's true. I suppose we should not rule out a woman being the killer. It doesn't take great strength to cave in a skull with a rock or heavy object, especially if a person is enraged. On one point, we agree. The killer's most likely one of the staff members."

Peersen said, "I'm going to examine the articles in the evidence box one more time. It contains the objects they found near the body and on the pathway where the attack occurred. It also has the junk discovered within a reasonable circumference of the crime scene. Most of it's garbage. Anyone could have deposited it during the two days prior to the murder. The park officials for the Township of Etobicoke have confirmed that they cleared the litter from the park on the previous Thursday, and we did not discover the body until Saturday."

"Yeah, I saw the pile of crap," Gerry reiterated. "Gum and chocolate bar wrappers, apple cores, a sweater, a running shoe, a leather belt, tissues galore, several Cracker Jack boxes, a discarded flashlight, and numerous other pieces of crap, including quite a few condoms."

Peersen added, "I examined a tube of lipstick that they found on the pathway, and I wondered if the colour might be matched to a member of the YCI staff. There were no fingerprints on it. Even if there were, it would be circumstantial evidence."

Then Jim picked up a small plastic evidence bag containing two five-cent coins and one twenty-five-cent piece. "They found the two five-cent coins near the crime scene, on the pathway, and the quarter they discovered on the path about fifty feet to the north. The coins are shiny, as if they had been polished."

As he examined them, turning them over in his hand, he said, "I just noticed that all three coins were minted the same year—1925."

Picking up the phone, Peersen called a friend who was a coin collector. The friend consulted a numismatic book.

"They minted only 201,921 nickels in 1925," he said. "By contrast, in 1924, over three million nickels were cast. Although the 1925 coins are not particularly valuable, they are not common."

After ending the phone call, Peersen informed Thomson, "The three coins were found within close proximity, and in all probability were dropped by the same person, likely a coin collector. It's strange that a person would collect the coins with such care and place them in a pocket with a hole in it, if in fact that is how the coins were lost. I wonder if any of the staff members at the high school are coin collectors. If there are any, then similar to the lipstick tube, it would be circumstantial evidence. However, it might point the investigation in the right direction. Even a small lead is better than none."

✧ ✧ ✧

On 9 October, while Tom was busy in the classroom, a BOAC Stratocruiser was nearing Montreal's Dorval Airport. The royals touched down in Canada's largest city after a sixteen-hour journey, including a two-hour stopover in Gander, Newfoundland. For much of the trip, the plane had been on automatic pilot, which the crew referred to as George. At 11:45 a.m., Princess Elizabeth alighted from the plane and set foot on Canadian soil. The royal tour of Canada had officially commenced.

Toronto's Malton Airport in the early 1950s

Four days after their arrival in Canada, the royal aircraft landed at Toronto's Malton Airport. People lined the observation deck on the airport's roof, many having arrived the previous day to reserve a viewing spot.

The airport staff did not have to remove thousands of condoms from the airport roof, as people were more sedate in this decade. They confined their outdoor sex to automobiles in the drive-in movie theatres, affectionately referred to as *passion pits,* and on hot summer evenings, the bushes in High Park. As well, there was no nude beach in the city.

Following the usual official greetings, the royals departed for Union Station in a convertible limousine and proceeded to a reception at

Toronto's City Hall where a half-million people greeted them. Later, they reported that while the crowds had lined the viewing areas on Bay Street, a man had pretended to faint, and when bystanders assisted him, a woman accomplice picked their pockets. Fortunately, they arrested the thieves and returned the $4.50 in loot to its rightful owners. They ignored that the financial community on Bay Street also picked the pockets of Canadians, and never returned the gains of their illicit activities to the rightful owners.

During the days ahead, the meals served in the dining car were from the provisions the staff had purchased from the stalls at the St. Lawrence Market. They did not record if the chefs visited the basement and bought kosher dills.

Saturday, 13 October, was a day for the couple to view the city and for thousands of Torontonians to catch a glimpse of their future queen. It was an event-filled day. At 6:20 p.m., they returned to the train and prepared for a state dinner at the Royal York Hotel. After the glittering affair, they returned to the York Street railway siding.

Finally, the royals departed for Niagara Falls, their visit to Toronto having ended. Their trip had generated much enthusiasm. The values of the war years remained firm, the majority of Canadians maintaining unquestioning loyalty toward members of the royal family.

✧ ✧ ✧

During November, Tom finally discovered the meaning of the graffiti he had seen on the washroom walls on the first day of school, which had said, "Leck my bane." It meant the same as a crude English phrase that sounded similar. No further explanation is necessary.

One afternoon, class 9L was forced to vacate Mr. Matheson's classroom as someone had dropped garlic buds into the air vents. The odour soon permeated the entire school, but it was the worst in the science room, as it was the source of the garlic.

In the hallway, Mr. Matheson was in a rage, and between gritted teeth, several of the students heard him proclaim to a couple of teachers, "That damn Bernstein kid did this. I saw him loitering around my classroom during the first lunch period. I'd like to kill the son of a bitch."

Miss Taylor told him, "Calm down and be careful of your language in front of the students."

Tom had been with Shorty during the lunch hour, so he knew that he was not to blame.

When Shorty heard about Matheson's accusation, he told Tom, "If I ever shoved anything into Wild Bill's classroom air vent, it would be a dog turd, not a hunk of garlic."

The uproar ended, as Mr. Matheson was unable to provide proof. The incident further poisoned the relationship between them.

The following day, Tom heard a kid in the hallway say, "Kramer put the garlic in the radiator, and then he told Matheson that it was Shorty."

✧ ✧ ✧

Saturday, 9 November, was Sadie Hawkins Day. Throughout the city, schools held dances, but unlike other dances, the girls invited the boys of their choice. Harry was swamped with invitations, being the star football player of the school. He accepted Carol's invitation to accompany her to the dance. Her invite was a great compliment to Harry. Many other boys at school had noticed Carol. Her willowy body, shoulder-length hair, clear blue eyes, and attractive features had even attracted the attention of guys in grades eleven and twelve. It was obvious that she would soon be one of the most sought-after girls at YCI.

A cute girl named Delores, whom they called Delly, asked Tom to the dance. She had long black hair and a nice figure. Tom had spoken to her in the hallways at school and liked her personality and sense of humour. He felt honoured that she had invited him.

✧ ✧ ✧

The stalker was to celebrate Sadie Hawkins Day quite differently than the students at YCI. After making a phone call, the stalker placed a razor blade in a Chiclets box and departed into the night. Arriving at the edge of the Humber Valley, near the bridge at Lawrence Avenue, the stalker entered the valley, hidden among the shadows of the blackened trees, which the November winds had stripped bare. In the distance, a dim light in the kitchen window of a house on Raymore Drive glowed in the inky darkness. It was the last house in the row, adjacent to the bushes and trees of the valley. It was possible to approach it without the other residents of the street being aware. Slowly, the stalker crept toward the rear door of the dwelling and rapped gently. A shaft of light cut the darkness as an attractive man cautiously opened the door. Recognizing the stalker, he smiled and motioned the visitor to enter.

Inside, the stalker descended the cellar stairs to a room in the basement. A black leather couch was against the west wall, and a similar one on the opposite wall. The owner of the house had covered the walls with mahogany wallboard to keep out the dampness, and a small electric heater glowed beside the door, ensuring that the room was cozy and warm. A small lamp on a walnut table provided minimum light, deep shadows enfolding the corners of the room. Waiting impatiently, the stalker paced back and forth, unable to sit down. In the rooms above, the stalker could hear the excited voices of numerous people as they engaged in their own nefarious activities.

Twenty minutes later, a woman quietly entered the basement room. Though she was only thirty-one years of age, she looked older. In earlier years, she had been beautiful, but her blonde hair and skin tone had lost their luster. She had maintained her slim figure, and her breasts remained firm. The dim light within the room failed to mask the dark shadows under her eyes. Recognizing the stalker, she smiled and commenced removing her skirt and blouse. The familiarity between them erased any awkwardness.

Standing in front of the stalker, she watched as the stalker removed her panties. Then the stalker took the razor blade from its container. Slowly, with careful precision, the stalker cut several shallow incisions at the top of her left leg, below her vagina. Within seconds, the blood trickled down her leg. Two more small cuts added to the flow. The right leg was not available, as the wounds from the previous encounter had not yet fully healed.

The stalker was now fully aroused.

When the session ended, the woman removed several bandages from her purse, pulled the small incisions closed, and taped them to stem the flow of blood. The participants said nothing, finding the anonymity of silence mutually agreeable. Within a few moments, after an exchange of money, the woman dressed and departed as silently as she had arrived.

Good, but not sufficient, the stalker thought. *I need another kill.*

✧ ✧ ✧

The following Monday, Remembrance Day, the schools were closed. On the way to school on Tuesday morning, Tom and his friends discussed the events that had occurred at the Sadie Hawkins dance.

Shorty said, "Some of the older students hid small bottles of vodka in their pockets. I think several guys were pissed. When the teachers discovered the bottles, all hell broke loose. Shit! It was crazy."

Sophie ignored Shorty's comments and oozed eloquently about the music at the dance. "My favourite songs were 'Red Sails in the Sunset' and 'Unforgettable.' I adore anything Nat King Cole sings."

Carol replied, "I loved 'Kisses Sweeter than Wine' and 'You're Just in Love.' Perry Como is a dreamboat." Then she asked Sophie, "What did you think of the hunks who were there?"

At this point, Shorty, Harry, and Tom tuned out.

However, Carol forced Tom back into the conversation when she asked him, "Did you have a dreamy time, Tom?"

"I really enjoyed dancing close with Delly."

He instantly regretted saying the word close.

Carol smirked and teasingly said, "So Tom Hudson's found a sexy gal! Sexy, sexy, belly Delly!"

Tom blushed with embarrassment.

✧ ✧ ✧

Early on Tuesday, 27 November, a half hour before the first period of the day, Peersen and Thomson arrived in the YCI office and informed Mrs.

Applecrust that they wished to see her boss. Though the police had been in the school many times during the preceding months, she was surprised that they had returned. She feared that it might mean trouble.

Most people thought that Mrs. Abigail Applecrust was more "crust" than "apple." A matronly gray-haired woman in her late fifties, she had raised five sons and survived to tell the tale. Her parents had been staunch Methodists, and Abigail reflected their high moral standards. However, her sons had knocked much of the prim and proper out of her. Her husband, Herbert, whom she affectionately referred to as Bert, was the one of the few who knew that her tough exterior was a hangover from the days when her sons had been boys, and she had felt duty-bound to provide a staunch example of proper behaviour.

Abigail Applecrust, whom Bert called Abby, was now a grandmother. She was a voracious knitter, and during the war years, she had provided more socks and mitts for the troops overseas than any other woman in the community. She was an excellent cook, addicted to the soaps on the radio, a member of the Orange Lodge and the Women's Prayer League—and a poker shark.

Bert Applecrust had once jokingly told his buddies that if they ever player strip poker with his wife, she would denude them faster than a dog could wolf down a bowl of chow. However, he added, for any player that lost his clothes, she would knit a set of wool underwear to allow him to depart from the game without his participle dangling in the breeze. Bert chuckled every time he told the story.

On this dismal November, in deference to the detectives' request, Mrs. Applecrust knocked on the principal's office door and informed Mr. Evanson, "Sir, two policemen are here to see you."

Tyrone Evanson made no effort to hide his displeasure. "Don't these men know they're interrupting my busy morning?" he grunted. Then, resigning to the inevitable, he told Mrs. Applecrust, "Tell the gentlemen they may enter."

✧ ✧ ✧

Mr. Tyrone Evanson sat down behind his large oak desk, his protruding potbelly pushing against the drawer. He was a "beer and beef" man, and his rotund waist was testament to his inability to control his diet. He peered at the world through thick, round glasses, the type of eyewear that in the following decade would be associated with the hippies in Yorkville.

However, YCI's principal was hardly the hippie type. He was a serious man, who took himself serious and considered education serious business. His mother was Italian, and she had added generous helpings of Italian pasta and bread to complement his father's British preference for beef and potatoes. Mr. Evanson's father had earned his living as a butter-and-egg retailer, owning a small shop in the Junction area, which centred on Keele and Dundas Streets.

Tyrone had been a slim and athletic boy, but as the years passed, the heavy intake of food had added considerably to his weight. By the time he was in his twenties, his most strenuous activity was pushing his chair away from the dinner table.

Now in his early fifties, Evanson's doctor had warned him that he was in danger of a stroke or heart attack. Tyrone finally took the doctor's concerns seriously and commenced a regimented walking program. Though he lost a considerable number of pounds, he remained overweight. Finally, he purchased a bicycle that could fit into the trunk of his Oldsmobile. Before riding his bike, he drove to a neighbourhood a considerable distance from his house, as he considered it undignified for the neighbours to see the principal of the local high school pedaling around the district like a teenager. Sometimes he journeyed as far west as the Humber Valley.

✧ ✧ ✧

Detective Peersen gazed around Mr. Evanson's inner sanctum. He noticed that on the window ledge, and on several of the bookshelves, were elephant figurines in every size, shape, and material, one of them carved from pure ivory. After the usual greetings, Thomson asked Mr. Evanson if anything new had occurred to him since their previous interviews. Gus shook his head to indicate that he had nothing to add, his jowls shaking to emphasize his statement.

"Sir, can we go over a few details again?" Thomson asked. Evanson winced at the detective's incorrect use of the word "can" and slowly nodded.

"How would you describe Miss Stritch's teaching style? Did she relate well with her students?"

The principal motioned Thomson and Peersen to sit down. His irritation melted, and the pompous expression that habitually masked his face slowly disappeared. Thomson thought that Evanson's eyes had moistened slightly.

The old windbag is not as awesome as he likes to appear. Beneath the façade, he's an old softy, Peersen thought.

"Miss Stritch was an exemplary member of staff," Evanson began.

There's that word "exemplary" again, Peersen thought.

"She taught at my school," Evanson continued, "while she was a student teacher. When she graduated from the Ontario College of Education, I personally hired her. For the past eight years, she excited her classes about English literature, and last year, her students performed in a production of *Hamlet*. Miss Stritch was a valuable member of this staff. In some respects, I almost looked upon her as a daughter."

When Mr. Evanson finished speaking, he removed his thick glasses and placed them on the desk. He sat motionless for a few moments, as if reflecting on his words. Then he perched his glasses back on his nose and reached for a book on the shelf behind his desk. He flipped through its pages. It was a yearbook. He handed it to Thomson. Evanson had opened it to the staff pictures. Although Thomson had already examined the book, he accepted it and gazed again at the young innocent face of the murder victim.

Unlike the photograph taken in the morgue, Miss Stritch's smile beamed from the picture, portraying a vibrant young woman with movie-star looks. Her long blonde hair fell gracefully to her shoulders, and her skin appeared clear and smooth. Her eyes seemed to sparkle, something that the mortuary photo was incapable of capturing. Thomson knew that she had been thirty years old at the time of her death, but she appeared more like eighteen. No wonder she related so well to her students; she looked like one of them.

Thomson passed the book to his partner, who scanned the photograph. Similarly, the eyes drew his attention. He was not so much fascinated by their beauty, as he was by the intelligence that he thought they portrayed, an intelligence that belied her young years. He liked smart women, and somehow he felt that Miss Stritch had been very bright. He also knew that her face would haunt him until he caught her killer.

Gerry Thomson now revealed to Mr. Evanson the true reason for their visit. Mr. Evanson listened and complied with his request.

✧ ✧ ✧

Before the morning announcements on the PA system, Mr. Evanson requested, "Any students who were in the Humber Valley during the Labour Day weekend, kindly indicate this to your teachers and report to the office."

Shorty and Tom raised their hands and Mr. Rogers excused them. Arriving at the office, they saw Vice-Principal Dinkman standing in the doorway. He motioned for Shorty and Tom to go inside the office. Carol, Patrick, and Harry were already present. Detective Sergeant Gerald Thomson introduced himself and showed them his badge.

"We need your help," he explained. "The police reported seeing teenagers in the valley on the day we discovered the body of Miss Stritch. This is why we are visiting all the high schools in and near York Township. We are anxious to talk to anyone who was in the valley. We're hoping they might have seen something."

The detectives now requested that the students wait in the outer office while one of the secretaries notified their parents that they wanted to interview them. Twenty minutes later, the detectives commenced the interviews. Peersen ushered Tom into the vice-principal's office. During the interview, Tom confirmed that he had been in the valley. Detective Peersen then asked Tom several questions, and he answered them as best as he was able, all the time doubting that he was being very helpful. When the interview ended, Peersen told Tom to return to the classroom.

When all the interviews had been completed, Thomson and Peersen compared notes.

"Another bloody waste of time," Thomson said, the disappointment heavy in his voice.

✧ ✧ ✧

Later in the day, Tom and his friends compared interviews. They had all told the police that they had seen nothing suspicious, and this was true. Their stories were the same. The teenagers lamented that they had not seen more, as if they had been able to supply information, perhaps their names would have appeared in the police report and eventually in the newspapers.

Fame had eluded them.

On the following day, Wednesday, before the last period in the afternoon, one of the younger school secretaries approached them in the hallway.

"Are you willing to speak to a newspaper reporter?" she inquired.

They all said, "Sure!"

She told them, "The reporter is waiting for you on the sidewalk, outside the school. The reporter says that if you are agreeable, he'd like to meet you there after the final period of the day."

When period eight ended, after going to their lockers, Shorty, Patrick, Harry, and Tom walked outside, their homework books tucked under their arms. They identified themselves to the reporter, who told them his name was Frank Gnomes. They agreed to an interview.

Tom gazed carefully at the reporter. He had curly brown hair that fell over his forehead, and he had a handsome face. His dark eyes were penetrating and never seemed to blink. The suit he wore was not new, but it was neatly pressed. His shoes were carefully shined, and as Gramps might have said, "They had likely been around since Adam was bounced from the Garden of Eden." After the usual introductions, for several moments the reporter said nothing but simply stared at them. Tom found this unnerving.

Finally, he said, "I won't beat around the bush. Have any of you recalled any details since you talked with the police?"

They shook their heads to indicate that they had not.

"Look, kids, I know that the police interviewed you because you were in the valley the day they discovered the body of Miss Stritch. Did you know that the victim, at one point, was also on the river's east bank?"

Again, they shook their heads. It was news to them. There had been nothing in the newspapers about it. Tom wondered how Mr. Gnomes had found out. In addition, how had he discovered that they had been in the valley? They were unaware that he knew the young secretary intimately.

"Did you see or notice anything? Think back. Something trivial might be important."

They shook their heads once more. They wanted to be helpful, so their names would be in the newspaper, but they had seen nothing.

"Let me try another angle," he continued. "They never discovered the victim's purse. Did you see it? Perhaps her attacker dropped something. Find anything? The four of you were on the scene on the east side of the river before the police scoured the area. See anything at all?"

Again, they shook their heads. The things they had found were too trivial to mention. They thought that to tell about them would make them look stupid.

"Thanks," Gnomes said with a sigh. Then he added sarcastically, "You're certainly not a talkative bunch, but you're all great at shaking your heads."

Tom resisted the temptation to shake his head in agreement.

Gnomes told them to call him at the *Trib* if they thought of anything. As he departed, they heard him mutter, "Bloody teenagers. They can spot a tit at fifty miles, but never see a damn thing that's under their noses."

Their hopes of having their names mentioned in the newspapers had evaporated again.

Tom said to the others, "I guess we're not destined to be celebrities."

As they strolled homeward, Harry said, "Do you think we should have mentioned the coins that Carol found?"

Shorty shrugged. "Can't see how they're important. It would have been dumb to mention them."

After a slight pause, he added, "But you know, old Baldy Baldwin has a coin collection. He sometimes uses the coins to teach the numbers in French classes. Do you think he was in the valley?"

"I doubt if he would drop anything, especially coins. He won't even allow us to drop a syllable in a word," Harry responded.

They all nodded their heads. Then Harry added, "You know, Mr. Millford has a coin collection too. I often see him in the cafeteria checking his change after he buys a coffee. He's always looking for old coins."

"I doubt that either Millford or Baldwin would have been in the valley," Shorty asserted.

"What about the keychain Carol found, with the initial M on the fob? That's Wild Bill Matheson's initial," Tom said.

"Now you're really letting your imagination go wild," Shorty teased. "I suppose you think they might be interested in the fossils too. Maybe we should have told the police about the used safes."

Even Patrick smiled.

As they walked away, they were no longer certain that the objects they had found in the valley were not important. However, none of them intended to phone the reporter. It would be too embarrassing to admit that they had withheld information.

The reporter's newspaper column the following day mentioned the Humber Valley "vampire" murder, but their names did not appear.

During the coming weeks, news of the murder dwindled in the *Trib*, as well as in the other daily newspapers.

✧ ✧ ✧

On Friday, 30 November, the football season concluded. York did not win the championship, but the team had performed well and coach Millford was pleased. The students heard that Mr. Evanson was also happy with the team's effort.

On Saturday, the first day of December, Tom and the guys attended the Grant Theatre, their local movie house, near the corner of Vaughan Road and Oakwood Avenue. Following the movie, they visited a restaurant on Oakwood Avenue, sat on the stools at the soda fountain, and for the grand price of ten cents, enjoyed a tall glass of Cherry Coke. Shorty slipped an aspirin into his drink, as he had heard that the combination could make a person drunk. He was sadly disappointed.

In the newspapers, a new comic strip in the *Toronto Star* attracted Tom's attention—*Flash Gordon*. Should you be wondering, Flash Gordon did not run around naked covered only with an overcoat, which he flashed open on appropriate occasions. Created by Dan Barry, it was the story of a hero who commuted each day in a rocket from Long Island, New York, to Manhattan. His exploits fighting crime were an instant hit with the public. Tom was no exception.

At supper times, when Jim Hunter read the news, conversation ceased around the table, as Tom's dad listened to the events of the day. Despite the passage of time since the Stritch murder, Tom always listened for any new developments. Nothing!

✧ ✧ ✧

During December, temperatures dropped and freezing north winds lashed the city. Tom and his friends walked to school in the brisk winter air, their breath forming vapour clouds as they proceeded gingerly along the icy sidewalks. Signs of the yuletide season were appearing in the shop windows throughout the city. The newspapers were crammed with ads for the approaching shopping season.

Whenever Tom journeyed downtown, he had often passed the Brown Derby Tavern at Yonge and Dundas Streets. Many devotees of the brew lamented that the Liquor Licensing Board had suspended the license of the famous watering hole for two weeks. This was a severe hardship for both patrons and management, as the festive season was in high gear. The reason for the suspension was that an entertainer at the tavern had told a few jokes that were, as the newspaper reporter stated, "Offensive to all decent morals."

Toronto's famous Brown Derby during the 1950s, located on the northeast corner of Yonge and Dundas Streets.

In one of the routines the comedian had said, "A man who had been severely chastised for farting near the queen apologized and said, 'I'm sorry. I didn't know it was her majesty's turn.'"

Most people considered it a very disrespectful joke—an insult to the royal family.

The Christmas movie scene continued to unfold across the city. At the Victoria, Runnymede, and Palace theatres, the National Film Board's full-length feature *The Royal Journey* chronicled the recent royal tour. The second feature was *The Wooden Horse*, which some unkind souls thought was the life story of Prime Minister Louis St. Laurent.

The University Theatre was showing *Double Dynamite*, starring Jane Russell. Shorty said, "I think the 'double dynamite' refers to Jane Russell's bra."

Gordon MacRae was on stage at the Casino. Shorty smirked as he said, "I hope MacRae is singing, not removing his clothes like the strippers who are usually on stage there."

Patrick shrugged and said, "I'm more worried about the Christmas exams. It'll be my first time writing them."

Harry and Carol said that they had begun preparing several weeks earlier.

Shorty interjected. "I'll cram the night before the tests, and like the strippers facing a rowdy crowd at the Casino, hope for the best."

Patrick gazed at Shorty but was not amused. He was obviously worried.

Tom? He knew that he was in trouble, as he had not done any extra studying and was poor at last minute cramming.

Somehow, however, they all managed to survive the exams. They would not receive the results until after the holidays.

On Tuesday, 18 December, Toronto was smacked with the second biggest snowstorm of the season. Traffic was snarled and drivers cussed as they maneuvered the hazardous streets. Young children howled with delight, knowing that a white Christmas was assured.

Friday, 21 December, was the final day of school for the term. Christmas was fast approaching.

✧ ✧ ✧

Following Christmas and Boxing Day, Mr. Marlton's store reopened. Neighbours were anxious to purchase fresh bread and milk, enjoy a little gossip, and exchange stories about the Christmas activities.

Marlton's Grocery Store was next door to the Hudson house, and although Tom's mom shopped once a week for most of their requirements at the Dominion Store at Oakwood and Amherst avenues, the Marlton's shop supplied their daily needs. On either side of the store's central doorway, large glass windows displayed flyers and signs advertising various products. Marlton's resembled a typical corner grocery store, such as those found in almost every neighbourhood throughout the city.

The proprietors were Mr. George Marlton and his brother Harry. George handled the till (cash register), and Harry worked behind the meat counter. Because Harry never emerged from behind the counter, during past years, women in the neighbourhood had jokingly spread the rumour that he did not wear pants.

Tom had heard these remarks when he was a small kid, and many times he had tried to peek behind the counter to see if Harry *was* naked below the waist. When he grew older, he realized that there was another reason that the women said that Harry did not keep his pants on—his nickname was Romeo Marlton.

The previous July, Harry Marlton had married. The couple's first child was born three month later. The neighbours had smiled knowingly and said, "We now know for certain that Harry Marlton has trouble keeping his pants on. If his wardrobe difficulties continue, he'll have the largest family in Toronto."

On the day after Boxing Day, in Marlton's Store, Mrs. Leyer was chatting with Harry the butcher, while he trimmed a small blade roast for her. Mrs. Leyer was a neighbour whom Tom had known since he was a young boy. At one time, she had been Tom's enemy, but he had eventually come to view her as a friend.

"I've had enough turkey to last a lifetime," Mrs. Leyer commented. "I need a good chewy piece of beef to sink my teeth into."

Harry Marlton muttered under his breath that all his roasts were tender. After slicing off another piece of fat, he glanced up and saw Mrs. Martha Klacker approaching the counter. *Now there's a tough ton of meat,* he thought. *If she's rude to me today, I'll take the cleaver and trim her down to size.*

Mrs. Leyer saw Old Klacker nearing the counter. She refused to greet Klacker openly but nodded and smiled half-heartedly. Having no desire to be rude to the old windbag, the last thing in the world Mrs. Leyer wanted was to encourage any conversation. Then she noticed Tom's grandfather walk through the door. She feared that the gathering had the potential to be explosive. She decided she would depart as soon as she received her roast, as she did not want it burnt from the flames that were sure to ignite during the pending incendiary verbal battle.

Mrs. Leyer remained silent, and Gramps kept his mouth zippered. Harry continued trimming the meat, his cleaver banging noisily on the butcher's block. When there was a lull in the pounding, old Mouthy Martha commenced an unsolicited soliloquy.

To no one in particular, she bragged, "My Percy said that my Christmas turkey dinner was the best ever served in the history of Toronto. Of course, I bought the bird at the St. Lawrence Market. Theirs are always the best."

Silence!

Realizing they were ignoring her, she continued. "My Percy says I'm such an important customer that the butcher at the St. Lawrence Market always gives me the finest turkey he has in his stall."

"I'd like to give you the best 'goose' you've ever had," Gramps replied, "right up the arse with a broom handle."

Gramps knew that Nan would skin him alive for saying such a thing, but he had been unable to resist. Harry suppressed a grin as he loudly hit the butcher block again, and Mrs. Leyer covered her mouth with her hand as she invented a coughing spell.

"Old man," Klacker exploded, "if I had my broom with me, I'd swat you across your ugly face."

"Woman, if you had your broom, you could fly out of here and get the hell on home."

Martha Klacker, unable to muster a stinging reply, retreated in a huff.

Gramps now fired his parting shot. "The reason you enjoy flying on your broom is so you can throw your crap from a little higher up."

Mrs. Leyer's cough disappeared. She cackled so loudly that poor Harry thought she had laid an egg.

The incident never reached the ears of Nan. Gramps was grateful, as he knew that she would box his ears if she ever learned about his bad manners. She would have insisted that when attacked, he should have "turned the other cheek."

He felt that the only cheeks he wanted turned were the ones on Klacker's rear end, so he could swat them with a broom.

◇ ◇ ◇

Tom enjoyed the Christmas holidays. He was grateful that the TTC work strike had not materialized, as streetcars were his only means of travelling downtown to attend the movies. The workers' union and management were twenty cents apart in the negotiations, and the city was hoping that they could avoid a strike. The deadline was the following Saturday.

Harry was pleased that the Toronto Maple Leafs were in second place in the National League. "They're tied with Montreal, each with thirty-eight points," he declared. "Detroit's in first place. In the American League, Pittsburgh's in first place, but I won't be interested in that league until the regular season is over."

Listening to Foster Hewitt narrate the games on the radio was a cherished Canadian tradition. Perched in the Gondola, high above the Garden's ice surface, he provided the play-by-play narration of the games that hockey fans across the nation so eagerly sought. The following Saturday's game would feature the Leafs versus Chicago.

Harry ended the hockey conversation by saying, "I hope the Leafs win on Saturday and Montreal loses. Then Toronto will be in first place. I really want the Leafs to make it to the Stanley Cup finals."

Every day or two, Tom scanned the pages of the newspapers to see if there was anything about the Stritch murder investigation. Nothing.

At least the holiday had provided him with an opportunity to be away from the school, where the possibility of having a murderer on the staff created a latent but ever-present degree of tension.

◇ ◇ ◇

Frank Gnomes had not enjoyed the days after Christmas. As usual, meaningful activity had ground to a standstill at the *Tribune*. Unless a big story broke, everyone was treading water, trying to make it appear as though they were working, when in truth, they were recovering from indulging in too much food and drink over the holiday. Until after the New Year, a rehash of old events would appear alongside reprints from other newspapers.

He thought, *That turd Masters has revealed nothing useful and despite my best efforts to interview Bettina Taylor, nothing. I'm sure Matheson is hiding something. This case is like trying to grope a broad in a sleeping bag, when you can't find the zipper. I need a small opening. I'll lean heavier on my old friend Masters.*

As he raised himself from the couch to saunter up to bed, he heard his wife, Sally-Lou, yell from the upstairs hallway.

"Frank! Get your ass up here. It's about time you slipped me another Christmas present."

"Shit," he mumbled. "I wish I were Henry VIII and could simply behead her and then go out and find a fourth wife."

In truth, no woman would ever be to his liking. The newspaper was his perfect mate—demanding, sexy, and always interesting.

✧ ✧ ✧

New Year's Eve was approaching, and the stalker was restless. Nothing had appeared in the newspapers about the "Valley Vampire" for a few weeks now. Though publicity increased the stalker's sense of self-importance, it also necessitated that greater caution be exercised.

The stalker had again visited the house on Raymore Drive during the second week of December, but rather than create a sense of fulfillment, it had increased the desire for another kill.

On Saturday, 29 December, the stalker set forth into the night.

Alighting from the Bloor Streetcar at Broadview Avenue and walking eastward along the Danforth, the stalker carried a backpack. Finding an unfamiliar tavern, the stalker entered. In its beverage room, the pungent odour of cigarettes, stale beer, and a hint of sweat assaulted the senses. The noise level in the room indicated that the patrons were well on their way to inebriation and far too busy to notice anything beyond the clutter of LCBO-approved draft beer glasses on the tables. Despite this, as a precaution, the stalker pulled the wool cap lower over the head, obscuring the upper portion of the face.

Within a few moments, the stalker had found a victim. She was sitting in a secluded corner of the room, the cigarette smoke and dim lighting isolating her from the other patrons of the tavern.

The woman was not young, perhaps in her midforties, slightly on the plump side, with invitingly large breasts. Most of the patrons were young, and to them a middle-aged woman was invisible. *She is not unattractive*, the stalker thought. *Her face is pleasant. But her most attractive feature is her ruddy complexion. She has an abundance of rich red blood.*

The stalker approached her. The woman, whose name was Susan Holden, smiled. Her eyes betrayed that she would not find conversation with the stranger objectionable. The stalker was not certain if it were a result of the desire for money, loneliness, or mere curiosity. The stalker smiled and motioned toward the empty chair at her table, asking permission to join her. A nod and a greedy smile indicated that she was agreeable.

A half hour later, they departed by the back door, supposedly to visit the woman's hotel room. In the darkness of the parking lot, the stalker guided her to the far corner of the lot, where Susan Holden assumed her companion had a parked car. Between two of the automobiles, where there was a sewer drain, the stalker gently but forcibly pushed her into the side of the car. As she fell, her head hit against the door handle with a crunching thud. Knocked unconscious, the stalker sexually assaulted her. When finished, the stalker cut a small hole into the side of her neck and allowed the pulsating blood from the puncture to flow freely into a large glass jar. When the jar was full, the remainder of the blood was allowed to run into the drain beside her.

After the flow of blood ended, her heart stopped and her breathing ceased. The stalker gently pinched the small hole in the neck closed and cleaned the blood from the area around the wound. The stalker then placed over the small opening a Band-Aid, which had been soiled by attaching it to an orange and rolling it over the kitchen floor. Because it appeared as if it were several days old, the stalker hoped that the police would assume that the victim had placed it over the tiny cut several days earlier. The stalker also hoped that the police would think that she had hemorrhaged from the gash on her head, not the cut on her neck, and that all the blood had disappeared down the drain. To add to the deception, the stalker poured a small amount of blood from the jar to draw more attention to the small stream of the rich red liquid, which led from her head to the drain.

Two hours later, when the owner of one of the autos entered the parking lot, he discovered Susan Holden's body. During the police questioning, no one remembered seeing her in the tavern. It was supposed that she had left the establishment with someone unknown, slipped in the parking lot, and bled to death between the two cars. Tests indicated that she had a high degree of alcohol in her blood. Samuel Mann, the pompous assistant coroner, authoritatively stated that she had bled out, the blood disappearing down the water drain into the sewer. There were no marks on the body to indicate that someone had pushed her, and the tiny cut on the side of her neck, covered by a soiled Band-Aid, drew only a cursory examination from Sam. If it had not been for the lacerations and bleeding around her vagina, the assistant coroner would have ruled the death "accidental."

Thomson and Peersen were unaware that the "Valley Vampire" had claimed another victim.

✧ ✧ ✧

On New Year's Eve, Tom's family celebrated in its customary style. They remained within the home and listened to the radio. When Johnny Ray's latest hit "Cry" began to play, Tom's dad tuned to another station. It was playing "Because of You," by Tony Bennett. Tom and Ken continued to listen to the old folks' music until midnight, when their mom presented the small glasses of Bright's Dry Sherry, sugar code number four.

Moments later, they heard the shouts outside on the street as neighbours welcomed the new year of 1952. Tom's dad went outside and banged two pot lids together, while others employed pots and pans to create as much noise as possible. The raucous lasted only a few minutes, before the cold drove everyone inside to the warmth of their home.

On New Year's Day, Tom's dad mentioned that the Empire State Building in New York City, at the corner of Fifth Avenue and Thirty-Fourth Street, had been purchased by a Detroit syndicate for fifty-four million dollars, the biggest real estate deal in history.

Tom told his dad, "I can't imagine a 102-storeyed skyscraper, and the sale price is too fantastic to be real."

His dad replied, "Your mom and I paid $3,300 for our house in 1942, hardly a major transaction in comparison."

✧ ✧ ✧

The Christmas holidays were soon over and the New Year's celebrations were again tucked into memory.

At breakfast on New Year's Day, Tom heard Gramps say, "Now we face the thumb-sucking cold days of January."

When Tom returned to school on the first school day, his hopes were high for a successful term. The first thing he heard in the locker room was a grade-thirteen girl saying, "I'll be glad to graduate from this place. Having a murderer among the staff gives me the creeps."

✧ ✧ ✧

Chapter Three

On 3 January 1952, the hallways of YCI were bustling with conversation. Students were pleased to see their friends again and relate their exploits during the Christmas break. Tom noticed that everyone seemed to have more to tell than he did.

In the evening, sitting around the supper table, Tom's father told his mom, "I see that Allan Lamport has been elected as the new mayor. He's asked the provincial government to help the city financially to avoid a big increase in property taxes. Toronto is over thirty million dollars short in its budget."

In the days ahead Torontonians learned that the response from Queen's Park was again the same—silence.

Lamport, whose name adorns a stadium on King Street West, became a colourful and controversial political figure. He often uttered convoluted statements that created unintended meanings, and sometimes no meaning at all. The press referred to his malapropisms as Lamportism.

On one occasion he said, "Canada's greatest nation is this country." In another speech he declared, "I spent a week in Montreal last weekend," and "Let's jump off that bridge when we come to it."

The press loved it when he said, "I am a man of sound prejudice," and "We've got to act wisely and other-wisely." In referring to the marvels of the decade, he said, "All this progress is wonderful—now if it would only stop."

Some people referred to Lamport as Metro's Golden Mayor, as he had spearheaded the plebiscite to allow Sunday sports. Four years before, he had worked with George Drew's provincial government to permit cocktail bars to open on Sunday if a city possessed a population of over a hundred thousand. As chairman of the TTC, he won approval for the building of the Bloor Subway. During the following decade, many applauded his efforts to rid Yorkville of the hippies. He was indeed an influential public figure.

Shorty once told Tom that if Mayor Lamport were referring to Charles Dickens' book *The Tale of Two Cities*, he would likely have called it *The Sale of Two Titties*.

✧ ✧ ✧

The final week of January, the police arrested Horace Kramer. Two grade-thirteen girls observed the police escorting him out of Mr. Evanson's office.

One of them breathlessly told her classmates, "I saw them take him away in a cruiser." Then she gasped, without any attempt to disguise her delight, "Gosh, do you think he's the murderer?"

As the police car drove away from the school, Thomson and Peersen sat in the back seat on either side of Kramer, a young officer at the wheel. The passenger seat beside the driver was empty. Peersen had read that confining a suspect was an effective psychological technique, particularly useful with young offenders. It physically reinforced the idea that they were trapped and that they had best be cooperative.

Thomson thought the idea was nonsense, but went along with it to allow his younger partner some leeway. In truth, he would have preferred to sit in the front seat, in comfort.

At the precinct, they escorted Horace Kramer into an interview room. Because he was a minor, they phoned his parents. His father said, "I don't give a damn what you do with him. Lock his ass up for a hundred years."

Through the phone receiver, Peersen heard a loud clunk, as if someone had hit the man with something. Then his mother came on the line. "I'll leave immediately and be at the station within the hour."

Inside the interview room, Horace sat staring at the puke-green walls and cursing his bad luck. Sweat trickled from his hairline, dampening his forehead. He wiped it away with the sleeve of his shirt.

Finally, the door opened and his stepmom entered the room. She hugged him and sat down beside him. "I'm so glad I got here," she told him. Then, without stopping to take a breath, she inquired, "Why are you here?"

"I don't know. Really, I don't."

While he was reinforcing his claims of bewilderment, the two detectives entered the room.

They seated themselves opposite Horace and for almost a minute, stared silently at him. After the awkward pause had ended, Thomson began questioning Kramer in a calm fatherly voice. His kindly expression was almost reassuring.

Despite this, Kramer continued to sweat and wring his hands.

"Son, begin by telling us why you were in the Humber Valley on the evening that Miss Stritch was murdered."

"I wasn't there."

"Now then, we'll just see about that."

Thomson gave Kramer a casual smile. Kramer shifted uneasily in his chair.

"We have proof that you were there. Lying to us will make it harder for you. Why were you there?"

"I wasn't there," he repeated.

Kramer looked warily at Thomson and then at Peersen.

Thomson gave a slight grin and continued. "Son, we found bicycle tracks on the trail, not far from the body. They were in a place where the overhanging limbs had protected them from the rain. We have plaster casts of them. Our forensics boys noticed a tiny flaw in the tread of the rubber on one of the wheels. We examined all the bikes in the racks at your school and found the same exact flaw in the rear tire of your bike."

The evidence proves that Kramer was in the valley, but it doesn't establish that he was there the night of the murder. However, Kramer doesn't know that we don't have conclusive evidence, and that what we have is at best circumstantial, Peersen thought.

Peersen continued staring intensely at Kramer and then reinforced Thomson's assertion. "We know you were there."

Peersen now dramatically tossed the photographs of the plaster tire treads on the table.

"Now, tell us why you were there," he said, his voice rising in volume.

Kramer gazed intently at Peersen, unable to take his eyes away from the young detective.

After several long moments, Kramer caved in, dropped his head toward his lap, and terminated eye contact with his accusers.

"I often go to the valley to ride my bike on the trails," he confessed hesitantly. "So, what?" he added, trying to muster more courage. "Besides, on the day of the murder, I was in the valley in the afternoon, not at night. I lied about being there because of the murder. I didn't want to be involved."

His voice was barely audible above the noise of the cracking and groaning from the ancient hot water radiators. Outside, they heard the siren of a police cruiser rushing away from the station. A car backfired, and Kramer jumped nervously.

"Why journey all the way over to the Humber Valley? There're plenty of places nearer your home, like the Cedarville Ravine."

"I like the trails there better."

"Now then, we'll just see about that," Thomson said calmly.

Peersen was less patient.

"Bull shit!" he snarled as he banged his fist on the metal table. "Why you were there?"

Kramer's stepmother, having observed the proceedings without saying a word, now intervened. "I resent your language and your bullying," she proclaimed forcefully. Warming to her protest, after pausing momentarily, she gazed directly at Peersen and added, "I'm warning you, young man. Mind your tongue! My son deserves respect."

She clutched Kramer's arm protectively. Peersen knew he had overstepped the boundaries and retreated slightly. "Sorry for the outburst, Mrs. Kramer, but it's really important that your son tell us everything he knows."

The interview lasted another half hour, but Kramer refused to change his statement or reveal more details. Frustrated and realizing they were getting nowhere, Thomson finally nodded toward the door. Peersen raised himself slowly from his chair and opened it.

"For now, the interrogation is over," Peersen said.

Kramer's stepmother glared at him. "I told you that my son knew nothing about the murder." Then she angrily stomped out of the room, still gripping Kramer by the arm.

As Kramer departed, he thought, *Hell will freeze over before I'll tell them what I saw.*

When they were out of sight, Thomson said, "He knows something. I'll bet my grandmother's knickers on it. By the way, did you think his reaction to you was strange to say the least?"

Peersen nodded, but said nothing. Indeed, the teenager had reacted to him in an odd way. His stare had been unnerving. He was used to unnerving a witness, not the other way around. What did it mean? In addition, he was certain that his partner was correct. Kramer had not been honest about his reason for being in the Humber Valley.

This teenager will bear close watching, he thought.

✧ ✧ ✧

On Wednesday, 6 February, Tom trudged to school under dismal skies, sullen clouds scuttling over the frozen landscape. Arriving in Mr. Roger's classroom, his homeroom, within minutes he heard the static noise on the PA system at the front of the room and waited for the booming voice of Mr. Tyrone Evanson. Each morning he instructed the students to stand for the playing of "God Save the King."

On this morning, Tom heard only buzzing sounds on the PA—no voice. Everyone gazed up at the loudspeaker, wondering what had happened to dear old Gus.

Shorty whispered to Tom, "I bet his stomach swallowed him."

After twenty or thirty seconds, they heard Mr. Dinkman say, "Please remain in your seats. Mr. Evanson has an important announcement for the student body."

Another four or five-second delay ensued. Then Dinkman said reverently, "Here is your principal."

"Staff and students," Gus began, in a voice dripping with self-importance, "it is with the greatest regret that I make the following announcement. At six o'clock this morning, Toronto time, his majesty King George VI, sovereign of Great Britain, the Commonwealth and the Empire, passed away quietly in his sleep."

Mr. Evanson paused again, the silence in the classroom almost overwhelming.

"The school flag has been lowered," he continued. "It is now at half-mast in respect for our beloved sovereign who reigned over our Dominion for fifteen years and one month. He was a good king, but more importantly, a noble person.

"For those of us who served during the war years, we will always remember his words on September 3, 1939, when the conflict commenced, 'Stand fast and have faith,'" he said.

"We would do well to embrace his words in our hearts today. We expect all members of York Collegiate Institute to conduct themselves today with dignity and decorum. The Privy Council, constitutional advisers to British monarchs, has formally accepted Elizabeth II as queen.

"Please stand as we listen to the anthem 'God Save the Queen.'"

✧ ✧ ✧

Tom realized that the death of the king had deeply moved Mr. Evanson, but he knew nothing about Mr. Evanson's background. Tom was unaware that the principal's father was British, and he had raised his son in a home that revered the traditions of the monarchy. Being a monarchist like his father, the death of King George VI had profoundly shaken him.

For Tom, the words "God Save the Queen" sounded strange and unnatural. All throughout his days of elementary school, the word "king" had seemed an eternal part of the national anthem.

A new age was dawning, but Tom had no way of knowing that during the years following the ascension of Queen Elizabeth, great changes would occur in the daily life of Canadians.

✧ ✧ ✧

On this morning in February of 1952, when the playing of the anthem ended, silence prevailed. Nobody was certain how to react. Throughout the morning at school, the hallways were quiet as students rotated between classes. No teacher cracked a joke. They remained serious and businesslike. Tom understood something of the sorrow and finality of death, as he had observed people grieve at the annual Remembrance Day services. The war had ended only seven years earlier and wounds remained unhealed. He had witnessed powerful emotions among those who had survived and the terrible pain the losses had inflicted. When he had been six years old, his uncle Will had passed away, and he remembered how it had devastated his family, especially his grandmother.

How would the death of the king affect Canadians? One thing was certain. The events pushed any thoughts of the Stritch murder from the minds of Tom and his friends.

✧ ✧ ✧

In downtown Toronto, the bells of St. James Cathedral on King Street tolled throughout the morning hours. The church had hastily arranged a Service of Intercession, which they would hold at 12:30 p.m.

Long before the noon hour, mourners commenced filling the pews under the high-vaulted ceiling of the nineteenth century Anglican cathedral. The CBC cancelled all commercial programming and instead broadcast only the news and music, classical and sacred, including favourite hymns of King George VI. In the evening, the Toronto Symphony Orchestra would perform a special program of tribute. The New York–Toronto hockey game at Maple Leaf Gardens was cancelled.

On Yonge Street, merchants draped shop windows with black crepe, and in prominent positions in the display areas, they placed large photos of the king. In the downtown, shoppers and the business crowds were subdued, and though people had been unable to adjust their choice of clothing, most planned to dress more appropriately the following day. Ottawa had stated that wearing black was not necessary; severe dress was the most suitable attire.

✧ ✧ ✧

At noon, as Tom walked home for lunch, he noticed that in the parlour windows of several of the homes on Lauder Avenue, the occupants had placed pictures of the king, the photographs trimmed with black cloth. People conversed quietly as they swept the dusting of snow from their porches and verandas.

When he entered the back door of his home, he saw that his mom had placed his lunch on the kitchen table. From the dining room, he could hear the radio. His mom was listening to the news. As he joined her, sandwich in hand, he stopped in the doorway and listened to the broadcast, a repeat of an earlier transmission. He now learned the details of the death of the monarch.

The early morning BBC announcement was repeated: "It is with the greatest regret that I make the following announcement …"

Tom recognized the words. They were the same ones that Gus had employed on the PA system at the start of the school day. It crossed Tom's mind that Gus had likely plagiarized them.

Then the announcer continued. "The king, fifty-six years of age, died in his sleep at Sandringham. He was discovered by his valet at 7:30 a.m., having died in the same house in which he had been born on 14 December in 1895. The valet immediately summoned the queen to his bedside. Later, the staff reported that she had not wept, but that her face was wracked with grief.

"She gently kissed his forehead, and after several minutes silence said, 'We must tell,' and she hesitated, 'must tell the queen.'

"The king had had surgery the previous September, and a part of one lung had been removed. They had reported that he had been recovering nicely. He had gone hunting the day before his death and retired early in the evening. The cause of death was reported to be coronary thrombosis, a blood clot."

The CBC newscast ended with the statement, "Radio Moscow announced the death of the king in four short words: George the Sixth died."

After school, Tom delivered his newspapers. He observed the quiet and respectful manner in which people scanned the front pages. He remembered the reactions of his customers when they had glanced at the front-page pictures of the *Noronic* in flames, when the ship had burnt in 1949 in Toronto harbour. On that occasion, their silence had portrayed shock and dismay. The news of the death of the king produced quiet acceptance and sadness at the passing of someone whom they had admired.

George VI was the monarch who had delivered guidance and hope through the horrific years of the Second World War. People remembered his resolution not to abandon London and retreat to the safety of the countryside. When Buckingham Palace had been bombed, he had declared that he now shared the sorrow of loss with others who had suffered during the blitz. As people scanned the articles on the front page and saw the peaceful regal photo of their late king, they knew that the scepter of a generation had been passed to another's hand.

✧ ✧ ✧

In Toronto, on the day of the funeral, it was as if an almighty hand had silenced the humble residential streets and grand avenues—Rosedale was as silent as Cabbagetown. The pulse of the great metropolis ceased to throb. Factory whistles were silent, automobiles' horns remained untouched, and the noisy clatter of the streetcars on Yonge Street appeared strangely out of place. Shops lacked customers. Restaurants were nearly empty. Many residents attended one of the numerous funeral services, the largest being in Maple Leaf Gardens.

In the evening, bars and restaurants were quiet, some having closed their doors to all customers. The CBC broadcast Gabriel Faure's celebrated "Requiem." It was more than the death of the king that had stunned the city into immobility. His passing severed an important link with the past—the war years. Despite the horrors of battle, people remained proud that the Empire and the English-speaking peoples had stood together against insurmountable odds. They cherished the victory, and the king had played a major role in the outcome.

Though it had been only seven years since the war had ended, the experiences of the conflict had already mellowed in memory into a golden time, when the camaraderie and pride in the accomplishments overshadowed the wounds of battle. The valiant struggles of the king and the trust the nation had placed in him during the war years were being fondly remembered.

✧ ✧ ✧

When the mourning for the passing of the British monarch ended, life returned to the exploits of lesser kings. The estranged wife of Clark Gable, the King of Hollywood, was suing a Toronto lawyer who had been vacationing in Nassau. The lawyer had been involved in a traffic accident with her car, and Gable's wife claimed that the man had been negligent in his driving. She had suffered a broken ankle.

Meanwhile, at YCI, Carol was ready to sue Harry. "He's the king of my heart," she lamented to Sophie, "but he's neglected me. I invited him to the Sadie Hawkins dance in November, and he invited me to the Christmas dance. I've rarely seen him since." Then Carol asked Sophie, "Do you think I did something to offend him?"

Sophie replied, "Don't wait around. You've had plenty of offers for dates from other boys, so why not play the field? Besides, it might bring him to his senses if he sees you on the arm of another guy."

"Would you play the field if Patrick ignored you?"

Sophie said nothing in reply.

✧ ✧ ✧

During February, Carol rarely saw Harry, except in the hallways at school. Tom recalled that during the Christmas holidays, he had attended the movies with Shorty, Patrick, and him, and gone skating with them several times.

Tom told Carol, "Other than at school. I've not seen much of him either. He's likely studying. He's serious about his schoolwork. Basketball also absorbs much of his time. Don't be offended."

Although Carol listened to Tom's words, she was not comforted. She had deep feelings for him and was hurt.

Tom quietly sympathized, but said nothing more.

✧ ✧ ✧

Patrick, Carol, and Tom were walking home from school on a cold February day when they saw the reporter from the *Trib*, Frank Gnomes, approaching them. Curious, they eyed him expectantly. His ingratiating smile warned them that he wanted something.

"Can we go over the details of your afternoon in the valley on the day they discovered the body of Miss Stritch?"

"Geez, it's been many months. We don't remember anything new. We've already told you everything," Tom told him.

Patrick nodded in agreement. None of them wanted to mention the dumb things they had found in the valley.

"What exactly are you trying to find out?" Carol asked, taking the initiative in the questioning away from the reporter.

Frank Gnomes paused and gazed intently at Carol. Tom wondered if he was ogling her breasts.

After a few moments, he continued. "Did you see anyone else in the valley? Did you see anything that looked out of place? Did you notice anything that someone had thrown away or left in the valley? Look, help me here. If you think you saw a dinosaur laying an egg, tell me. Tell me anything at all. Speak to me!"

To their surprise, Patrick spoke up, breaking their silent agreement.

"We saw no dinosaur laying an egg," he said impatiently, "but Harry found a few fossils. Carol found a key chain and a few coins. As we said, we didn't see or find anything useful."

Frank looked at them gloomily and seeing no importance in the objects they had found, gave up and said, "Thanks for your help anyway."

The teenagers heard him mutter under his breath as he walked away,

"Kids picking up junk, like I pick up dumb women. Damn, I need a break in this case. A decent break with the fairer sex would be all right as well."

After the reporter departed, within a few minutes Tom and his friends were talking about the school basketball team.

Carol said with an impish grin, "The guys are really cute in their short shorts and T-shirts. I can see their bodies real well."

Despite their lighthearted manner, it occurred to Tom that until the reporter had appeared no one had mentioned the Stritch murder for several weeks. Perhaps the fear of having a murderer for a teacher had died away to some degree.

✧ ✧ ✧

Harry and Shorty were both on the school basketball team, and by the end of February, competition within the league was increasing. YCI's team was doing well. Harry's height and coordination made him a natural, but Shorty was the star. Whenever the ball touched his fingers, he scored. His accuracy was amazing. Unfortunately, Kramer was also on the basketball team. Although they had been at YCI for six months, Shorty had experienced no problems with Horace Kramer.

The calm was not to last.

One afternoon after basketball practice, Shorty was showering, thick steam billowing around him as he washed away the sweat from his exertions in the gym. He was lustily singing, "I'm going to wash that gal right out of my hair." Judging by his raspy voice, a *South Pacific* star he was not.

It had been a particularly difficult session, the coach having driven the team hard as they had lost the previous week's game against Oakwood Collegiate by eight points. Shorty enjoyed the warmth of the water because it relaxed his muscles.

Continuing to warble, a stinging sensation on the left cheek of his rear end interrupted his shower performance. Startled, he turned to discover the source of the hurt when a second blow struck his other cheek. Within seconds, it was as if a swarm of angry hornets had surrounded him, his body receiving smarting blows from every direction. He was defenseless as the steam continued to create sheets of mist, hiding his attackers from view.

Kramer had convinced a group of players on the team to give Shorty a "towelling," as they referred to it. A towel was wrapped into a coil and snapped against a person's bare buttocks, inducing a stinging sensation on the exposed skin.

Kramer had said, "It's a great prank. Shorty deserves a towelling. He knows he let us down in the last game."

What the other players did not know was that Kramer had inserted numerous thumbtacks into his towel, and every time they struck Shorty, they inflicted small pinpricks. As the hits were repeated in rapid succession, they drew blood. Shorty yelled loudly, but the guys thought that he was purposefully overreacting to the swats of the towels to join in the fun. They laughed as they increased the intensity of the blows. The clouds of steam hid the attackers as well as the effects of the Kramer's towel. Blood was not visible because the water washed it away as fast as it was created.

Finally, the pranksters grew tired and disappeared toward the locker room. Shorty turned off the shower, and when the vapour dissolved in the cooling air, he noticed the blood running down his stomach and legs. He was unable to view his back and rear end, so was unaware that they bled more than his front. Shorty turned on the cold water and allowed the frigid shower to rinse away the blood and assist it to congeal.

When he finally entered the locker room, the guys laughed and hooted. They were unaware of Kramer's cruel prank and had participated in the hazing as a joke, with no intent to cause injury.

Then they noticed the pinpricks on his flesh. Puzzled but unfazed, one of the team members asked, "Did you receive a rash from the girl you got lucky with last night?"

They remained unaware that anything amiss had occurred in the shower room. Shorty noticed that Kramer had already departed the scene, taking his towel with him. His absence alerted Shorty that perhaps his old nemesis had played a devious role in the attack.

There was another incident in the shower that same week. The guys noticed that Patrick always avoided the showers after gym classes. As a prank, before he could change out of his gym clothes, they dragged him into the shower room. Thoroughly drenched, he had to remove his gym shorts and underwear to wring them out before he dressed.

Tim Wilkinson, a big hairy guy whom everyone called Wilkie, caught sight of Patrick's bare bum and decided to taunt him.

"Your white ass is as smooth as a girl's. Bring it over here," he sneered. "You're almost as good looking as any broad in this school."

Patrick was so stunned that he dropped his towel, which gave the appearance that he was complying. The raunchy laughter in the locker room was humiliating for Patrick. He fled in terror.

The school bullies had found a new victim.

In the days ahead, their girlfriends heard the story and embellished it in the retelling. As the rumours spread, they became crueler.

Someone said, "Patrick was on his knees in the shower, doing the unthinkable to Wilkie."

Others simply said, "We always suspected Patrick was a pansy."

Tom heard the remarks. He admitted that he had wondered about Patrick, who was slim, had a girl's build, and was soft-spoken. Now that he thought about it, he did walk sort of funny. A person never truly knew another guy's secrets. Tom had learned this when Harry had told Shorty and him his secret. It was the knowledge of Harry's secret that now compounded Tom's confusion.

He and Shorty had found out about it shortly before they graduated from grade eight. One afternoon, they were playing a kissing game on Sophie's veranda. Carol had grabbed Harry and French-kissed him. The kiss almost sucked his socks out through his teeth.

Harry quickly fled the game and went home. Later, Shorty and Tom walked over to his house. Harry was sitting on his veranda, and it was obvious that he was upset.

Harry told them, "I feel that something is wrong with me. I don't enjoy kissing girls. In fact," he confessed, "I don't feel about girls the way other boys my age do."

Shorty and Tom had been puzzled, but after a brief pause, Shorty replied, "Your feelings will change. But regardless of what happens, Tom and I will always be your friend."

Tom had nodded in agreement and now wondered if Harry's attitude had changed since last June. Did he now like girls in the special way that the other guys did? If he did not like girls, did he like boys?

Judging by the reaction when the guys in the shower thought that Patrick was a pansy, Tom shuddered to think about the uproar that would occur if they discovered that Harry was one too. Hardly anyone paid much attention to Patrick, but Harry had been the captain of the football team and was now a key member of the basketball team. He was "Joe Jock." Guys could easily accept that someone effeminate like Patrick was queer, but for a guy as masculine as Harry to be a pansy would threaten their entire world. Shower-room nudity, slapping team members on the rear end to encourage them in a football games, and the hugging when they won would all become questionable.

Then Tom had a selfish thought. He was a close friend of Patrick's, and a good friend of Harry's. Would they think he was queer too?

What a dilemma.

✧ ✧ ✧

The conversation around the Hudson supper table often centred on the latest entertainment news. Ken and Tom were keenly interested in the new television programs, but their family remained without a TV set. They hoped that mentioning the programs available might help persuade their parents to purchase one. A twenty-inch Admiral now cost $499, and a seventeen-inch was $399. Both models were available with a down payment and monthly installments. They knew that their parents were unable to afford a TV if the merchant required a single payment.

The shows that they mentioned were: *Wild Bill Hickock, The Cisco Kid, Hopalong Cassidy, Sagebrush Trail, Gabby Hayes, Roy Rogers, Kit Carson, Perry Como, Dinah Shore, Name That Tune, Charades, Gary Moore, I Love Lucy, The Goldbergs,* and *Fireside Theatre.* As an afterthought, they added, "Educational programs are also on TV: *Museum of Science* and *The Nature of Things.*"

Gazing directly at his mom, Ken declared, "The soap opera *Search for Tomorrow* is broadcast each weekday at 12:15 p.m."

Ken knew how much his mom enjoyed the soaps. However, she showed no interest in his remark and offered no comment. Soon he and Tom were immersed in the magic of radio and forgot about television and its visual world of ever-expanding programming. Although it was the new age medium, they contented themselves with their self-created images of the faithful characters of the airwaves.

On the radio news, their dad was interested in hearing how the Robert Simpson and T. Eaton companies had stated that the Yonge Street strip, north of College Street, was deteriorating. They suggested that a cluster of stores would serve their customers better, and so the retailers were proposing to build a new suburban shopping mall near Dufferin Street and Lawrence Avenue. Local residents were worried that 50 percent of the mall space was to be warehouses, meaning that only half of the space would be retail stores and parking lots.

Conflicting interests eventually compromised, and the city approved the Yorkdale Shopping Mall. It was to be Canada's first enclosed mall, where shoppers would be impervious to the vagaries of the Canadian climate.

✧ ✧ ✧

March was unusually cold, even for Toronto. The stalker was restless, having remained indoors most evenings to avoid the freezing temperatures. By the final week of the month, it was as if a volcano was bubbling within. On the last Friday, the weather turned milder. Shortly after 11:30 p.m., the stalker ventured out in search of a kill.

Arriving at a bar on Yonge Street, the stalker surveyed the room carefully. It was not a popular drinking spot with the younger crowd but rather an establishment where women of indeterminate ages sought the companionship of older men in exchange for a predetermined fee. As it was a mild night and the beginning of the weekend, the barroom was crowded.

As the midnight hour approached, a degree of desperation was in the air, almost as palpable as cigarette smoke and the lingering odour of stale beer.

Women who earlier in the evening had appeared unattractive without a price attached were now deemed more appealing, even with the expected fee. Such was the nightly ritual in the downtown bars where hookers plied their trade.

The stalker slipped silently among the tables, appreciating the anonymity that the late hour and the type of establishment offered. The stalker noticed a lone female sitting at a table in the far corner, near the door. She was carefully observing the men in the room, seeking any body language or eye contact that might denote a buyer for the wares she was selling. Slim, with long brunette hair, she was attractive, even though her lifestyle had left dark circles under her eyes and more lines on her face than was normal for her age. She was only twenty-eight but looked a decade older.

Her name was Moira Peters. Life had been difficult for her, even as a child. Abandoned by her mother, an aunt had raised her. The aunt had resented the responsibility and displayed little kindness toward her unwanted niece. When sixteen, Moira ran away, and she had lived on the street ever since.

Moira took notice of the patron who sat down at a table near her. Sensing no danger, she smiled, and five minutes later, Moira moved over and seated herself at the stranger's table. It was obvious to her that a liaison was pending. Though she sensed that something was not quite right, money was money, and it had been a difficult month. A hooker could not always be choosy.

Shortly after midnight, Moira and her client slipped out of the bar. Ten minutes later, they entered the rear entrance of a rundown hotel in the Jarvis/Sherbourne area of the city. Inside the hotel, the scent of disinfectant and urine permeated the hallways. Moira led the stalker to a secluded room on the west side of the building, which overlooked the wrought-iron fire escape and alley below.

Moira rented the room in the establishment on a weekly basis, and a few of her personal items sat on a night table beside the bed. The stalker noticed a cheap metal frame containing a faded photograph of a smiling boy, perhaps eight or nine years old. The cupboard door was ajar, and several dresses, a nightgown, and a faded-green coat were hanging from the well-worn wooden hangers. The room spoke of Moira's sparse life, reflected her past and the few memories she treasured. She was unaware that her memories were to fade into oblivion on this fateful night.

Offering to share a needle with her client, Moira wrapped a thick rubber elastic around her left arm and injected herself with the right, allowing half of the needle's content to enter her body. Smiling, she offered the other half to the stalker, who nodded to refuse her offer and gave a slight grin while slowly pushing the needle's plunger to the empty position so that Moira could enjoy its full contents. Within minutes, her body went limp.

The stalker then sexually assaulted her.

Afterward, employing a Swiss Army knife, which had been wiped clean of fingerprints, the stalker placed Moira's right hand around the knife handle. Then the stalker manipulated her arm to slice repeated wounds in her neck. Blood from the smaller wounds trickled down over her skin, but from the puncture into the left carotid artery, the blood pulsed freely. Two jars were employed to contain the flow, and when they were full, the remainder of the blood spilled onto the urine-stained mattress. As the stalker screwed the lids on the jars, the victim's heart ceased to beat. The young woman known as Moira was a lifeless corpse.

Before departing the room, the stalker opened the hotel room door and placed the "Do Not Disturb" sign on the outside doorknob. Then, before leaving the hotel room via the fire escape, the stalker gazed back at the bed. Sufficient blood had soaked into the mattress that there was no reason for the police to suspect that it did not contain all the blood that had departed from the victim's body.

It would appear as if she had taken drugs, and after someone raped her, in a state of suicidal depression, she had slashed her neck, one of the wounds ending her life.

◇ ◇ ◇

Good Friday was 10 April, the beginning of the Easter school break. The weather was sunny and warm with the threat of afternoon thundershowers. Although thousands flocked to the boardwalk at Sunnyside to enjoy the first holiday of the season, more and more Canadians were taking to the highways. The 1950s was witnessing an explosion in car ownership, and officials expected chaos on the roads during the holiday weekend. There were now ten thousand miles of highways in Ontario, and ninety-nine thousand road signs to assist drivers.

Being too young to travel beyond the city, Tom and Shorty opted to see a few movies. They decided not to go downtown, as the Yonge streetcars remained rerouted due to subway construction. They attended the Grant Theatre and saw *Abbott and Costello Meet the Invisible Man*. The second feature was *Rawhide*, with Susan Hayward and Tyrone Power.

Shorty made silly comments about the movie: "*Rawhide* is a story of a woman who's not wearing panties, and the movie we saw last week, *Cheyenne*, was about a woman wearing three pair of panties."

Tom laughed at the corny pun on Cheyenne (Shy Ann) and told him. "You're too concerned with women's panties."

"Man, that's true."

✧ ✧ ✧

After Easter departed, teachers at YCI hastily completed the remaining course material and then commenced reviewing. Mr. Rogers reminded the class, "The end of the year is approaching. Everyone should be preparing for exams." Despite his warnings, most students failed to spend more time at their studies. Tom was one of them, reasoning that the exams remained in the distant future.

The basketball finals began the last week of April, and the pressure on the YCI team increased. Harry and Shorty attended practices every weekday morning before school, as well as two hours at the end of the day and Saturday mornings. Coach Millford was determined to have the best team possible.

During practices, the coals of enmity between Shorty and Kramer smoldered beneath the surface. Shorty continued to suspect that Kramer had played a role in the towelling in the showers. Each day, Tom heard Harry and Shorty discuss the team's chances of success and bemoan Kramer's lack of basketball skills. Tom had watched Kramer perform during games and had to admit that he was actually quite a good player, although he suffered in comparison to Harry and Shorty, who rarely passed the ball to Kramer. Everyone hoped that the basketball season and the school year would end without an incident, as the coach had warned all players that he would not tolerate any infraction of the no-fighting rule.

The rows of lockers were adjacent to the cafeteria in the basement of the school. Anyone sitting at the tables in the eating area possessed a view of the guys changing after gym classes. Tom thought this was an odd arrangement, as the women who served the food had a clear view of the boys as they dried themselves after showering and getting dressed. The serving woman never seemed to pay any attention, but Tom was certain that a few of the old gals sneaked an occasional peek.

Shorty and Tom had heard one of the women whisper to a workmate, "I saw a huge dill pickle during the first lunch period." Their raunchy giggles alerted them to the hidden meaning contained in her statement.

Shorty quietly said, "I don't think dill pickles are that funny. I think they mean dill peckers."

✧ ✧ ✧

An incident occurred between Kramer and Shorty on a dreary day in mid-May. The rain had poured since the early morning hours, and everyone was in a foul mood. Tom had decided to remain at school for lunch and sat at a table in the lunchroom eating a salmon sandwich, while sipping on a bottle of Sunkist orange soda. Shorty and Harry joined him. Kramer was seated at a table behind them. None of them acknowledged his presence.

An egg salad sandwich and a drink were on Shorty's tray. He had purchased them at the cafeteria. Harry had brought his own lunch. They chatted about the morning's activities, and chuckled as they recalled an incident in Baldy Baldwin's class. A student had pronounced a French word incorrectly, and Baldy had thrown a blackboard brush at him. The boy had picked it up and shot it back. Baldwin dragged the student to the office to see Vice-Principal Dickman.

Shorty was laughing as he bit into his sandwich. Then there was a crunching sound. Shorty gagged and spit the mouthful of sandwich onto the plate in front of him. Glancing down, he noticed to his horror the remains of a dead cockroach, the pieces of its dark body starkly contrasted against the white bread.

Shorty was sitting opposite Tom and had a clear view of Kramer. The instant the small mound of food had landed on the plate, he noticed a malicious smile flicker across Kramer's face. Certain that Kramer had known about the cockroach before he had bitten into the sandwich, Shorty lunged at Kramer, literally flying over the table, sending Tom's bottle of Sunkist crashing to the floor. Shorty's roar, as he grabbed Kramer, muffled the sound of breaking glass.

Harry reacted immediately. He restrained Shorty in a bear hug to prevent him from throttling Kramer, who had instantly jumped to his feet. Taking advantage of Shorty's confinement, Kramer jabbed a forceful blow to Shorty's face. This was too much for Harry to tolerate.

Harry placed the dazed Shorty on the closest bench and grabbed Kramer. Harry lifted Kramer off his feet, his legs dangling in the air. This was no small feat, as Kramer was heavy. Kramer's teeth rattled as Harry shook him like a rag doll. When he released him, the bully fell to the floor, his face as white as a bedsheet. Meanwhile, the women in the cafeteria had sent for Mr. Dinkman, who within minutes appeared on the scene. He escorted the three pugilists to the office. Later, they called Tom to the office as a witness.

There was no doubt that Harry had grabbed Kramer, but he had not actually struck him. The action that had caused him to intervene had not been seen by the women in the cafeteria. The situation required a decision, so Dickhead Dinkman decided to defer to Gus and delivered them into the elephant den of the ever-sagacious Judge Evanson.

When Gus heard the details, he asked how Shorty knew that Kramer had inserted the cockroach into the sandwich. Harry and Tom were certain that Kramer had done it, but they were unable to prove it. It disgusted them to watch Kramer play the role of an innocent victim and assert that Shorty's attack had been unprovoked. Unknown to Evanson, Kramer had an accomplice who had placed the beetle inside Shorty's sandwich while he was paying the cashier.

Gus relished his role as King Solomon, scowling fiercely as he adjudicated. After several moments of deliberation, he told Kramer, "You are free to leave."

Tom saw arrows of hate dart from Shorty's eyes, his enemy smiling at him as he calmly waltzed out the door. Next, Judge Gus demanded that Harry Heinz and Forrester Bernstein wait in the outer office while he decided their fate. Evanson dismissed Tom, who resented his expulsion from the courtroom before Gus had delivered his verdict. He was frustrated, as he knew that his testimony had provided little to aid in the defense of his friends.

Harry and Shorty remained in the office all afternoon. When Tom passed by the office at the end of the sixth period, he saw them sitting on the straight-back chairs, two condemned criminals in the holding pen.

Shortly after four o'clock, Judge Tyrone Evanson instructed Vice-Principal Dinkman, "Deliver the miscreants into my chambers." Then he pronounced his sentence in an authoritative voice that was worthy of a supreme court judge: "Forrester Bernstein, I'm suspending you from the basketball team for the duration of the season. If you intend to be on the team next year, you must first make an application to my office."

Turning to Harry, he said, "Harry Heinz, even though you did not strike any blows, you manhandled another student. I will allow you to remain on the team, but you will serve two weeks' detention. This will limit your attendance at basketball practices, Mr. Heinz, but it is the price you must pay for choosing your friends unwisely and becoming involved in an unwarranted fistic maneuver."

Pausing for effect, he then added, "You are both dismissed."

Tom waited outside the school for them. For once, his newspaper customers would receive their papers later than usual. He knew it had gone badly when he saw the expressions on their faces as they descended the front steps of the school. Harry explained the details to him.

Tom mumbled under his breath, "Gus has a reputation for being fair, but not this time."

Kramer had escaped punishment by being sneaky and dishonest. Perhaps Shorty had overreacted, but Tom felt he had been justified. Harry, who had tried to prevent the fight, was now a severely disadvantaged member of the basketball team. As William Bendix might say on *The Life of Riley* radio program, "What a revoltin' development this [was]."

For Shorty, the season had ended.

✧ ✧ ✧

Three days passed before the police discovered Moira's body and summoned the forensic team to the scene. Because the victim was a female drug addict living in a seedy hotel, it did not warrant more than a cursory examination. The police quickly determined that someone had raped the woman, and in despair, accentuated by the drugs, she had stabbed herself. They found no fingerprints on the knife other than that of the victim. The yellow mattress, stained from many years' use and caked with dried blood, caused the police not to linger at the scene any longer than was necessary. They would make a cursory effort to locate the rapist.

Yonge Street on a spring day in the early 1950s, looking north to Queen Street from near Richmond Street. A PCC streetcar is crossing the intersection at Queen and Yonge Streets. They covered Yonge Street with timber planks to allow construction of the subway below ground. This prosperous commercial area was about a mile to the west of the area where they found Moira's body.

Constable Edward White, an officer with many years' experience on the Toronto force, noticed a photograph on the night table in the hotel room. Picking it up, he removed the picture from the frame and discovered, scrawled in pencil across the back, "Timmy, August 16, Centre Island, 8 years 7 months." The details implied that the dead woman had feared that she might forget the event.

Constable White had a daughter of his own and felt compassion for the victim as he witnessed the indifferent treatment of her body. A half hour later, the assistant coroner, Samuel Mann, ruled exactly as the stalker had intended: "Death was caused by a self-inflicted wound, likely occurring as a result of drugs or depression after being raped."

He then imperiously instructed that they bag the body. Closing his medical handbag, he hurriedly left the scene. Constable White thought that Mann had been more concerned with completing the examination and getting out of the room than he was with exercising careful consideration of the evidence. *Pompous twit*, he thought.

After they unceremoniously carried the body out the door, the assistant coroner departed. A younger officer entered the room. He had discovered the name of the dead woman from the hotel register. It was a stroke of luck, as hotels of this caliber rarely maintained accurate records.

Later, the young officer interviewed several of the victim's neighbours in the hotel, and from one of them he learned about the deceased's aunt. An address was eventually found. He and his older partner drove to her house. Standing in the doorway, they informed her of Moira's death. The aunt refused to allow the police to enter her home. She said she would visit the precinct sometime during the afternoon to identify the body.

In the doorway, hovering behind the woman, was a boy. Constable White recognized him as the child in the photo, even though he was now several inches taller. The boy was pale and sickly looking, his face portraying a youthful innocence that captured White's heart.

The boy had overheard the conversation of the adults, and tears welled up in his small blue eyes. The aunt gazed down at the boy, pushed him aside, and closed the door.

Constable White, turning to the young officer mumbled sadly, "That kid doesn't have the chance of a snowball in hell."

✧ ✧ ✧

The day after the Shorty/Kramer fight in the cafeteria, students witnessed the police entering the school's office. In the hallways, the students eyed the detectives suspiciously. The uncertainty of the situation caused the tension and stress of the first weeks of school to bubble to the surface again.

Classrooms were unusually quiet. Tom heard a student declare in frustration, "I'm tired of this shit. I wish the bloody police would do their job and lock up the one who's guilty."

Another student smirked as he said, "Why don't they throw the entire damn staff in jail?"

The senior students complained that the stressful mood in the classes was affecting the teachers and feared that their final year of high school was in jeopardy. This was serious, as they depended on the results of their grade-thirteen departmental examination when they applied for jobs, and for the fortunate few, entrance to the universities.

YCI was not a happy place.

✧ ✧ ✧

The following day, after basketball practice, it was late when Harry sauntered out of the showers, as earlier he had served a detention. He was disheartened. He missed having Shorty beside him on the basketball court. Out of the corner of his eye, as he proceeded to the lockers, he noticed Kramer sitting at a table in the lunchroom, sipping on a Coke. Kramer's plastic straw was at the bottom of the bottle and it made a loud noise as he sucked on it. Harry sensed that Kramer was trying to attract his attention. He ignored him.

Harry finished towelling and got dressed. As he had placed his foot up on the bench to tie his shoelaces, he saw Kramer approach. The expression on Harry's face made it clear that Kramer should get lost.

Despite Harry's obvious dislike of him, Kramer attempted to ingratiate himself. "Thanks for passing me the ball during practice. You're a great player. I wish I could dribble and develop a shot like yours. Man, even the foul shots you rarely miss."

Harry ignored the compliments.

"I know you miss having Shorty on the team, and I know I'm a poor substitute, but I'm doing the best I can."

Harry took no notice of him.

Realizing that he needed to placate Harry further, he added, "I was surprised when old Gus expelled Shorty from the team. He's important to us."

Kramer could not say he was sorry, as that would be tantamount to admitting that he had placed the dead cockroach in the sandwich. Harry finally looked at Kramer, but remained silent.

Kramer is actually not a bad player, Harry thought. *Though not as skilled as Shorty, he has a good eye and a nice rhythm to the way he moves across the court.*

Harry sized Kramer up further, observing that he was not bad looking, despite his slightly crooked nose. Kramer's hair was wet from the shower, and it glistened in the overhead lights. *When the braces come off his teeth,* Harry thought, *he might have a pleasant smile. His pimples have mostly disappeared. It's a pity the guy is such a turd.*

Without a word, Harry walked away.

✧ ✧ ✧

In what turned out to be the final game of the season, Shorty sat beside Tom as they watched the game from the spectators' gallery. Shorty yelled loudly each time Harry scored and remained silent when Kramer swooshed a ball down into the net. Harry passed the ball to Kramer frequently, placing the needs of the team above his resentment of him. Besides, with Shorty absent, Kramer was the next best player on the team. Harry scored thirty-eight points, and Kramer sank the ball into the net ten times, but it was Harry who had set up the plays and passed the ball down the court to Kramer. He made Kramer look better than he really was. Despite this, YCI lost by a score of 116 to 108.

At the end of the game, the YCI supporters cheered loudly, even though their team had failed to qualify for the finals. As Tom departed from the gym, he glanced at Shorty, sensing that his friend was close to tears.

✧ ✧ ✧

June's sun delivered a welcome contrast to the wet cloudy days of early spring. Despite the changing season, the approach of the final weeks of the school year dampened Tom's spirits. He was worried about his success in French and math and gave both subjects extra effort. Miss Taylor had been absent from school since early May and was not available for help. There were rumours that she was not well. History and geography were Tom's favourite subjects and required very little extra studying.

Tom delivered his newspapers each afternoon, but his enthusiasm for the job had waned. He realized he was not as clever as Shorty was, but he was confident he could handle a job as a delivery boy for a local drug store. As the hours would be staggered, it would allow him more freedom.

One evening he asked his parents, "Can I sell my paper route?"

"It's your decision," they told him.

✧ ✧ ✧

On a sun-filled Saturday in June, Detective Gerry Thomson was reclining in a lounge chair in the comfort of his backyard, an O'Keefe ale in hand and a rumpled straw fishing hat pulled low over his face to protect his eyes from the glare. In recent months, it was one of the few days he had had to himself.

Despite the pleasant surroundings, his thoughts were gloomy. He had made no progress in the Stritch case, and time was passing quickly. Soon, it would be officially classified as a cold case, and his failure to move forward with the investigation frustrated him.

He heard the screen door bang shut. Seconds later, from under his hat he saw the legs of his wife Ruth appear beside his chair. Ruth Thomson was an elementary school teacher in a downtown school, where many immigrant families, especially Italians, had located since the end of the war. Toronto was experiencing difficulties as it transitioned from a protestant Anglo-Saxon bastion to multi-ethnic city. The propaganda against the Italians during the war had created distrust among native-born Canadians. Many of them painfully remembered the loved ones lost during the invasion of Italy.

The fascist government of Mussolini had also subjected the Italians to propaganda, and they were equally suspicious of Canadians and their culture. Homesick for their homeland, the Italians clung to their native foods, customs, and religion. Canadian foods, they said, were tasteless and Canadian cooking methods inferior to their own. Canadians felt that Italian foods stunk of garlic and were too spicy. Unfortunately, neither group hid their disdain for the customs of the other. The schoolyard was where many of the problems bubbled to the surface. Ruth Thomson had often observed the results of the parents of both nationalities passing their prejudices to their children. Bloodied noses were too frequent to be ignored.

Eventually, Ruth admitted that her own prejudices, a hangover from the war years, were influencing her attitude toward her immigrant pupils. Realizing this was not right, she altered her attitude, and demonstrated respect for their ethnic traditions. She was amazed at the changes that occurred among her pupils. Example was indeed more powerful than preaching.

On this warm June day, thoughts of the classroom were far from Ruth's mind as she informed her husband, "It's a hot day. Let's go over to Centre Island."

"Now then," he said, "we'll just see about that."

"Never mind telling me that silly expression. Make a decision," she snapped.

Gerry paused, giving himself time to choose his words carefully. "This is the first afternoon in a long time that I've had off. I'd like to stay home, honey. I want to relax here in the backyard."

Ruth sighed, admitting that she had perhaps been a little harsh with him. Gerry had indeed been busy during the past few weeks. She knew that the crowds at the ferry docks would be long, and that the longest line her husband wanted to be in was from his chair to the fridge in the kitchen. She smiled in resignation, making it clear that she understood.

Later, as she went out the gate with the children, she was unable to resist shouting over her shoulder, "See about doing a few chores, will you? The front screen door needs fixing."

If she said anything else, Gerry was unable to hear, as the children's shouts and squeals of delight filled the air.

After Ruth and the kids departed for the Islands, Gerry felt guilty about not having joined them. He sighed as he drew a long swig from his half-warm bottle of beer. He watched the few remaining drops of condensation trickle down over the soggy label, and though he felt that he had neglected his family, he was grateful for the peace he had secured.

Shortly after, he descended into the basement where his private den was located. The room was the nerve centre of his police investigations. No one at the precinct knew it existed, except Jim Peersen.

✧ ✧ ✧

Jim Peersen was enjoying the hot afternoon quite differently to Gerry. Seated at the kitchen table in his trendy Annex apartment, in his hand was a glass containing three fingers of French brandy on the rocks. The ice cubes tinkled softly as he sipped the velvety amber liquid. It was not a well-aged vintage, or he would never have placed ice in the glass.

Neatly arranged on the table in front of him were the personnel files and confidential evaluation reports of the YCI teachers, which he had subpoenaed from Dinkman's office. He was searching for hints of close relationships among the various teachers on staff. After several hours of scanning the reports for petty disputes, rivalries, jealousies, close friendships, estrangements, and, if lucky, personal vendettas, he had found nothing of significance, even though Dinkman had written incredibly detailed reports.

Then Peersen reviewed the file that Evanson had complied on Dinkman, prior to hiring him on the staff of YCI. The fastidious principal had thoroughly checked the man's background and created an extremely detailed dossier.

Dinkman had been born in a small house on Dundas Street West, a stone's throw from the Kensington Market area. He had attended Harbord Collegiate as a student and been a member of a street gang. The police had questioned Dinkman several times about street fights when he was a teenager, but they had never arrested him.

The file indicated that after high school, a merchant on Baldwin Street employed Dinkman. He laboured at killing and cleaning poultry. It was dirty work and paid poor wages. Then, in his third year on the job, he suddenly quit, as he had acquired sufficient funds to attend the University of Toronto. No one ever learned where he received the money.

After he graduated from university, he applied to OCE, and on receiving his teaching certificate, he taught geography at Jarvis Collegiate. He remained there only two years, and then he became a staff member at Oakwood Collegiate for one year. During the next decade, he changed schools twice more, teaching at Forest Hill Collegiate and Etobicoke Collegiate.

Peersen found it strange that Evanson had hired Dinkman, knowing that he had such a questionable background. Even stranger, four years after he joined the YCI staff, Evanson appointed him vice-principal.

✧ ✧ ✧

Early in the investigation, Peersen had conducted his own search into Dinkman's background. He now recalled the interview he had conducted with the principal of Harbord Collegiate, where Dinkman had attended.

The principal was a heavyset man, with a round face that was overly ruddy, indicating high blood pressure. He was solicitously jovial and had greeted Jim in an obsequious manner, chuckling as he recalled the name Richard Dinkman.

"I remember him well. The students referred to him as 'Dickie Fuckman,'" he said as his rotund belly shook with laughter. "However, if you want more information on Dinkman, I suggest you speak with Miss Amanda Doppin. She has been on staff for two decades and retires at the end of the year. She's a wise old gal, perceptive, with a high degree of street smarts. By the way, our students refer to Amanda as 'Miss Droppin' Drawers.'"

The principal had seemed ignorant of the gravity of his indiscrete comments. He laughed heartily at his silly comments and added, "I don't think Amanda's drawers have ever dropped for anyone." Peersen considered the remark crude. The principal continued chuckling as he opened his office door and instructed one of the secretaries to escort the "good detective" to Miss Doppin's classroom.

Miss Doppin was the opposite of her boss. A stern woman, she appeared drained from the stress the years had placed on her. Her white hair was pulled back in a bun. She remembered Dinkman well, she had said, and informed Peersen that the staff had considered him one of the school's success stories.

Then she added, "He was a serious problem during his first three years at Harbord but changed during his grade-twelve year and knuckled down to work. He achieved excellent results on his grade-thirteen departmental examinations, was an Ontario Scholar, and earned the usual one hundred dollars from the government."

Then Miss Doppin's eyes narrowed, and her voice changed as she continued. "However, I still wonder about that lad. I remember that the girls in the grade-thirteen classes avoided him. I believe he was a bully. In grade eleven, the coach dropped him from the football team, even though he was a capable player. The coach said that Dinkman was too aggressive, an odd comment for a football coach."

As Peersen had departed the school, he remembered thinking, *Miss Doppin is a shrewd woman, and Dinkman is indeed a puzzling character.*

✧ ✧ ✧

Peersen took another sip on his glass. Because Matheson and Taylor were prime suspects, he reviewed their files next. As he read them for further reference, he transferred pertinent material into his personal notes. Most of the information he already knew from the newspapers published when Stritch was murdered.

Matheson had attended Oakwood Collegiate as a student and received his Bachelor of Science degree at the University of Western Ontario in London. After graduating with honours, he had attended the Ontario College of Education (OCE) to earn his teaching certificate. His first teaching contract was with the Scarborough Board of Education, teaching at Scarborough Collegiate for five years. When he applied to the York Township Board for a position at YCI, he gave the reason for leaving his employment in Scarborough as "irreconcilable differences."

The principal of Scarborough Collegiate was contacted, and he claimed that though Matheson possessed an excellent knowledge of his subject, he was careless in his safety procedures in the laboratory. He also stated that one of the female students had claimed that Mr. Matheson had made "suggestive comments to her." As Matheson resigned, no action was taken. Peersen also recalled the police report had revealed that when Matheson was younger, an officer arrested him in High Park for having sex in a car. Yet, despite the negative comments of the Scarborough principal and the police report, Mr. Dinkman, who conducted Matheson's interview, had recommended that they hire him. Peersen thought this strange.

Peersen moved on to the next application form, that of Miss Bettina Taylor. She was a graduate of Parkdale Collegiate. After high school, the Robert Simpson Company had hired her to sell sports equipment. She finally resigned from her job and attended McMaster University in Hamilton and then OCE to receive her teaching certificate. Her first teaching position was at Oakwood Collegiate, and after eight years at the school, she applied to YCI. She possessed an excellent teaching record and had impeccable academic qualifications. She was immediately hired.

Now Peersen reviewed the application form of Sam Millford, the boys' PT teacher. It was far more detailed than the others' applications. Milford had played on the baseball team of Rawlinson Public School in York Township and had been a football star at Vaughan Road Collegiate. After high school, he worked for four years at the British American Oil Company at Bay and College Streets. Having earned the funds to further his education, he attended the University of Toronto, where he was one of the quarterbacks on the University Blues football team. After graduation, he attended the Toronto Teachers' College and received his elementary school teaching certificate. He taught grade eight at Earlscourt Public School, and then at Regal Road Public School. After taking a Department of Education summer course to qualify to teach PT at the high school level, he applied to Parkdale Collegiate. Three years ago, they hired him at YCI.

Peersen also knew from his own investigations that the police had questioned Millford about a suspected molestation of a girl in the balcony of the Imperial Theatre.

The next application form Peersen scanned was that of Jim Rogers, an English teacher. He had graduated from Victoria College at the University of Toronto with an MA in English. He had also studied piano at the Royal Conservatory of Music. In Dinkman's personal file on Rogers, Peersen discovered that Rogers had endured two trial separations from his wife. Both times, they reconciled, but last year, his wife filed for divorce on grounds of adultery. Before being employed at YCI, he taught at Harbord Collegiate.

Peersen noted that Matheson, Taylor, and Millford had all been hired by Dinkman rather than Evanson. He was not certain if this was significant. Teachers often changed schools to gain experience, but usually they applied for transfers within the same board of education. However, Matheson, Taylor, Millford, and even Dinkman had applied to York Collegiate from other boards throughout the city. Peersen wondered if this too was of any significance. It also bothered Peersen that both Matheson and Millford had police records for being involved in sexual offences. Dinkman's record also hinted at a darker side to his personality.

Sitting back in the chair, Peersen allowed the smooth intoxicating elixir to gently slide down his throat. He had read enough. It was time to call it quits. He would review the other teachers' files the next day.

✧ ✧ ✧

Near the end of June, news about the summer Olympics increased. To be held in Helsinki, Finland (July 19–August 3), for the first time in four decades, the Russians would compete in every sport except field hockey. They said that it was a woman's sport and not worthy of entering. The Russians also announced that the following year they would send a hockey team to the International Hockey Tournament in Switzerland to challenge Canada's supremacy. In 1950, the Edmonton Mercurys had won the world championship in London, England.

In other news, the Russian police had shot and killed a man attempting to escape East Berlin. They left his body in the street for over four hours, as a warning to others. Russians were also increasingly blockading West Berlin. In retaliation, British troops seized control of the Soviet-owned radio station in the western sector of Berlin. The situation was becoming increasingly tense in the city divided by the wall.

Most Torontonians were more interested in the outdoor activities associated with the good weather. In the evenings, the band shell at Sunnyside was well attended. The drive-in movie theatres—the Dufferin, Northwest, Northeast, and Scarborough—were full each evening, as patrons parked their cars under the night skies to enjoy the stars of the silver screen. The largest numbers were at the Dufferin, where *Young Man with a Horn*, starring Kirk Douglas and Lauren Bacall, was playing. At the CNE Stadium, the stock car races had commenced for the season, each evening's performance ending with a majestic display of fireworks "in honour of the new queen." Under the enormous tent theatre in Dufferin Grove Park each evening during the month of June, they presented *The Merry Widow* and *Kiss Me, Kate*.

The newspapers were filled daily with local, national, and international news. The one topic that never appeared was the Stritch murder case. However, the year at YCI was ending, and though the students remained in the dark about the identity of the murderer in their midst, tension was easing as the summer vacation was on the horizon.

✧ ✧ ✧

Frank Gnomes had interviewed several of the staff members of YCI, and by now he knew a great deal about their diverse personalities. He was discretely keeping track of several of the teachers, hoping that during their holidays they might let their guard down. He was certain that there were close relationships, perhaps sexual, among the younger unmarried staff members. Stritch, at one time, had been one of them. The others were Bill Matheson, Sam Millford, Bettina Taylor, Gregory Baldwin, and Elizabeth Hitch. Even Mary Allyson, whose bladder was located behind her eyes, was not above suspicion, as she was clearly a part of the inner circle, despite her age. She could know something. It was a too large a group to keep close track of, but he had learned the summer plans of several of them.

Baldy Baldwin, as he knew the kids called him, was to go on an extended holiday in southern France to immerse himself in French culture. Frank wondered if the Riviera would do anything to narrow the gap between his front teeth and reduce the whistling noise it imparted to his speech. On the other hand, a good whistle might come in handy when Baldwin saw a nice bikini on the stony beaches at Nice. Frank had discovered that Baldwin received a considerable income from his family, enabling him to afford the holidays in Europe.

Miss Hitch had accepted an appointment as an art instructor at a boys' camp in Muskoka. Frank thought, *God help any teenager she traps in the pine forest late at night. That woman could suck a guy's paint tubes dry and wear out his brush.* Frank then grinned smugly at his crude thoughts.

✧ ✧ ✧

Millford was teaching a PT course for the Department of Education in London, Ontario. Away from sinful Toronto, in sedate Middlesex County, the Tarzan of YCI would have few opportunities to swing from vines or tear off his lion skin in front of a fair damsel. Frank had learned that Millford intended to return to Toronto for several weekends and wondered with whom Millford would be swinging.

Frank had discovered one morsel of dirt from an informant. Bettina Taylor was pregnant and had gone to Vancouver to have her baby. Frank knew that Taylor had gained a little extra weight, but he had not suspected that she was pregnant. Frank had pegged her for a "woman's woman," Jack-Hammer Jill. Obviously he had been wrong.

Taylor had booked off sick in early May and departed the city. Frank figured she would leave the infant out in British Columbia and return as if nothing had happened. What else could she do? If the board of education discovered her secret, she would lose her teaching job. Evanson would have a kitten if he found out. *Mind you,* Frank thought, *with the size of Gus's stomach, he looked as if he was ready to drop a couple of lion cubs or perhaps an elephant calf.*

Front Street in 1952, in front of the Royal York Hotel. Construction of the subway was under progress, allowing the tunnel to enter Union Station. In the distance, the famous Walker House Hotel is visible on the left-hand side of the picture.

Matheson was to remain at his cottage for the summer. Despite repeated attempts, he had been unable to interview him. Frank was certain he was hiding something.

Weeping Willow Allyson, he felt, would be of little help in his investigation, as he suspected that during the summer months she would likely lock herself in a cupboard with a supply of raunchy novels spread around her, being too old to indulge in the activities that she read about.

The cast of suspects was not impressive. Matheson was the most likely leading man, and he refused to allow Frank to drag him on stage.

A director's life is not a happy one, Frank thought.

✧ ✧ ✧

Tuesday, 1 July, was Dominion Day. The following morning, Tom journeyed to Greenberg's Pharmacy, near Eglinton Avenue West and Bathurst Street. Shorty worked there, and had told him that they required another delivery boy. He had arranged the interview for Tom.

Following a brief conversation, Mr. Greenberg informed Tom, "You can start tomorrow at five o'clock. Be certain that your bike is in working order, dress neatly, and don't be late for work."

When Mr. Greenberg had finished speaking his few words of advice, he retreated behind the pharmacy counter to fill another prescription. Shorty congratulated Tom, patting him on the back.

During the first few days of his new employment, Tom discovered that the neighbourhood surrounding the drug store had a sizable Jewish population. He was best friends with Shorty, who was Jewish, and thought nothing of it. When he had been a small kid, he had attended a summer camp at Jackson's Point on Lake Simcoe and encountered Jews in the town when Miss Burnside, their camp counselor, had taken them on an excursion to purchase ice cream and penny candy. Tom already knew that Saturday was their Sabbath and that those of the Orthodox faith were forbidden to work on that day.

Tom enjoyed matzo ball soup and blintzes. He knew that Jews had bread and wine in their Sabbath and holiday rituals, and that they did not eat pork, although he had seen Shorty devour bacon sandwiches at the CNE. At a deli on Eglinton, he had often shared a pastrami sandwich and kosher pickle with him. Tom did not consider Jewish foods or customs strange.

Jewish people lived in Tom's neighbourhood, and throughout his elementary days, he had attended school with them. Actually, he knew less about Catholics, as he had never shared a classroom with them. At YCI, there were many Jews, and they attended the same school activities as he did. He never thought much about it.

The drug store maintained six delivery boys, as well as a woman who drove the store's truck to accommodate phone orders that were too large or heavy to deliver by bicycle. Her name was Ruth. Tom never knew her surname.

Shorty told Tom, "She's a tough broad. She only eats beans."

"What kind of beans?"

"Human beans! She has one for every meal. Be careful. To her, you're a mere snack."

In the days ahead, Tom was to discover what Shorty meant.

✧ ✧ ✧

One of the delivery boys at the pharmacy was continually uttering derogatory remarks about the Jews to whom he delivered packages. For obvious reasons, he was careful not to say anything when Mr. Greenberg was around. His comments made Tom uncomfortable, and he knew that if Shorty overheard them, there would be trouble. His second week on the job, an incident occurred.

Three of them worked the evening shift, as they were the busiest hours. Leaving for the night, the boy who was working with Shorty and Tom, who thought anti-Semitic remarks were funny, said, "Well, I'm off—like a Jew's foreskin."

Shorty ignored the offensive remark.

The next evening, the same boy noticed on a package a surname that was obviously Jewish. He said that he was certain that it contained packages of Sheiks, a popular brand of condoms. Then he added, "Jews are always screwing someone."

Shorty had a large seltzer bottle in his hand to be delivered to a house on Ava Road. He aimed the bottle, pressed down on the metal lever, and shot a powerful spray in the kid's face. The guy flew at Shorty with his fists. Shorty decked him.

Mr. Greenberg entered the back room a few seconds before the boy had thrown the first punch, and he knew the reason for the fight. He put a stop to it and said that he was tempted to fire them both. He warned them that any reoccurrence and they would both lose their jobs. A reluctant truce was accepted, and in the days ahead, their work schedules were designed so that they did not work the same shift. Tom had encountered anti-Semitism before, and it never ceased to baffle him.

One afternoon after work, Shorty and Tom attended the Nortown Theatre, near the corner of Eglinton and Bathurst, and saw the movie *The African Queen*, starring Humphrey Bogart and Katharine Hepburn. They laughed sympathetically as Hepburn poured the contents of Bogart's gin bottles over the side of the small boat. The scene in the movie reminded Tom of when Shorty had emptied the contents of the seltzer bottle in the face of the boy in the back room of the drugstore.

✧ ✧ ✧

The heat of summer slowed the pace of work at the police station to a crawl. Although crime never took a holiday, the two detectives did. Thomson and his family rented a cottage at Musselman's Lake north of Stouffville. They enjoyed the warm shallow waters and sandy stretches of Cedar Beach. One evening, he and Ruth went dancing at the Pav.

Jim Peersen drove to Virginia Beach for his two weeks vacation. His colleagues had teased him about toasting his buns on the hot sand of the famous beach, as he belted back whiskey and read sleazy novels. Actually, he did intend to enjoy swimming in the warm Atlantic, but he would be sipping cold beer and studying psychological profiling. It was an area of study that had recently interested him.

Though he was travelling alone, the Stritch case was ever at his side. He was frustrated at his failure to receive permission to haul Dinkman into the police station. He would try again after the holidays. It would soon be a year since Elaine Stritch had been murdered, and Peersen felt that it was time to shake up the investigation. He hoped that his holiday readings would assist him when he tackled the vice-principal. He had learned that it was important that he conduct the interview in the police station, not in the man's office in the school, where the man had the advantage of the psychological security of his own environment.

On the third day at Virginia Beach, he drove into Colonial Williamsburg, intending to tour the restored eighteenth-century buildings and the meticulous reconstructions, such as the Governor's Palace and the Raleigh Tavern. The controlled ornate trim and symmetry of the architecture appealed to him, as did the music and literature of the period. After purchasing a day pass, he felt relaxed as he strolled down the Palace Green under the mature catalpa trees, watching the long lines to enter the historic buildings. Tour groups were enjoying the animated narration of the costumed guides. Williamsburg was a mecca for Americans during all seasons of the year.

He overheard a woman, who was departing from the magnificent Wythe House tell her husband, "I wish we owned a home like this."

"You can't manage to clean our one-bedroom apartment. What would you do with a two-storey, four-bedroom mansion?" her husband replied.

"Press me hard enough and I can do anything."

"I'll remind you of that tonight," he said with a smirk.

Peersen smiled as he walked away, thinking of the man's words. He remembered the adage, "Those who wish to live forever are the same ones who cannot figure out what to do with a rainy afternoon."

Reaching the brick wall that surrounded the Governor's Palace, he gazed at the gnarled Osage orange tree to the left of the ornate iron gates. The tree's twisted branches reminded him of the intricacies of the criminal mind.

Yes, he thought, *press a person hard enough, and they will do anything. Did Elaine Stritch press someone too hard?*

I need to press Dinkman so hard that he will tell me what I want.

✧ ✧ ✧

The summer of 1952 was to present new experiences for Tom. At the drug store, his hours varied. Sometimes he worked only in the evenings, and his afternoons were free. At other times, he worked in the morning and had the remainder of the day to himself.

Working at the drug store, because he earned more money than when he delivered newspapers, he journeyed to more places in Toronto. During the first week of August, a group of them travelled to the CNE Grandstand for the 8:30 p.m. stock car races. Sometimes Shorty and Tom walked to the Colony Theatre at Dufferin and Eglinton rather than trekking downtown. They now attended the Saturday evening performances and not the matinees, as they were for small kids. On one occasion, Sophie, Patrick, and Carol were with them. They noticed that Kramer and a friend were in the ticket line. They were accompanied by two girls, one of whom Carol knew from YCI. She expressed surprise, telling the others that she thought that the girl had more sense than to be with a jerk like Kramer. Tom and his friends ignored them, and they similarly took no notice of them.

Tom knew that it required great effort on Shorty's part to refrain from going over and punching Kramer in the face. The humiliation of being kicked off the basketball team remained an open wound. Despite this, they all managed to enter the theatre and choose their seats without any words or fists being exchanged, even though they had almost touched shoulders at the candy counter in the lobby. Tom saw Kramer walk away with a large box of popcorn, his arm around one of the girls.

Halfway through the second feature, Tom noticed a girl running up the aisle in the theatre. Despite the darkness, he knew it was the girl with Kramer. He nudged Carol and whispered that her friend appeared to be upset. Carol said she would go out and see if the girl was okay. She returned ten minutes later, but the other girl was nowhere in sight. Carol said that after she talked to the girl, she had gone home. Carol said she would tell them about it after the movie.

Later they learned that in the darkness of the theatre, Kramer had "copped a feel," as they used to say—he had tried to shove his hand up her skirt.

Tom said, "I think Kramer's a blue-ribbon, gold-plated, first-prize prick."

This was strong language for Tom. The others grinned.

✧ ✧ ✧

On 22 August, Canada's first Canadian-born governor general, His Excellency Vincent Massey, opened the seventy-third Canadian National Exhibition. Officials had declared the 1952 Ex to be "Canada Year." As usual, the annual fair contained an extravaganza of talent, and they expected it to draw over three million patrons.

The other big news during August was the announcement of plans for a new four-lane highway to extend from Highway 27 east to Newcastle, across the northern limits of the city. It would allow drivers to bypass Toronto, and thus ease congestion on the city's streets and main arteries. City Hall said that the plans were of little importance, as they feared that red tape would delay construction until the highway was redundant as a bypass. When they finally built it, they named it Highway 401.

Each evening, the increasing volume of the crickets reminded Tom that summer was ending. As Labour Day approached, he recalled the atmosphere at school the previous June and the speculation about which teacher was a murderer. What would the new term be like? Tom was grateful that for a short period the thrills of the CNE had pushed the gloomy thoughts of school from his mind.

✧ ✧ ✧

The stalker had survived the summer without a fresh kill. The frequent visits to the house on Raymore Drive, where the stalker cut the legs of the willing woman until her blood ran freely, had kept the worst urges in check, but pressure was building.

On a hot evening near the end of August, after sunset, the air remained humid. Shortly after 9:30 p.m., the stalker departed for High Park. Alighting from the Bloor streetcar near the north gate of the park, the stalker attracted no attention strolling casually down the paved pathway beside the roadway. The wooded area surrounding Grenadier Pond was perfect for a kill.

✧ ✧ ✧

Sandra Beaumont was eighteen years old and had recently graduated from Forest Hill Collegiate. Raised in a wealthy home, her parents had spoiled her. Throughout her childhood and teenage years, she lacked no material comforts. Despite her privileged background, she had developed into a poised and considerate young woman. She was attractive with her short dark hair and fine features, and easily caught the attention of the boys at her high school. Sandra possessed a stubborn streak that manifested itself in ways that sometimes surprised her friends.

The previous morning, her parents had flown to Europe to bask in the sunshine and ancient history of the Greek Islands. Sandra was unable to accompany them, as she had enrolled in a summer course to improve her French; she wanted to qualify for a job as a stewardess on Trans Canada Airlines. As well, in September, she would begin a nursing course, another qualification necessary for the employment at the airlines.

She resented her parents leaving her behind to journey abroad, especially since her fourteen-year-old brother had accompanied them. Her parents had warned her not to go downtown after dark on her own. As an act of defiance, she had driven her new white Buick convertible to High Park and was now walking beside Grenadier Pond. The moon sparkled on the tranquil surface of the pond. She did not feel threatened. Other people were also strolling along the trail beside the water, and should she feel in danger, assistance was at hand.

Beside the trail, the stalker was sitting on a bench near the isolated north end of the pond. Nearby, the thick shrubbery and the overhanging willows protected the location from the reflected light from the surface of the water. The trail on which Sandra was walking was directly in front of the bench. The bulrushes on the opposite side of the path further hid the location from view. The stalker had planned how to seize the girl, subdue her, and after finishing with her sexually, drain a portion of blood from her body without anyone realizing that the precious liquid had been extracted. It would be another perfect kill.

As Sandra strolled along the pathway, she saw that the section ahead of her was more distant from the lamppost than she had thought. It was particularly dark. The bulrushes now rustled gently, as a slight breeze was rippling the pond. The black of the night suddenly seemed threatening. On an impulse, she turned around and retreated in the opposite direction. Within a few moments, she reached the security under the light of the lamppost.

The stalker watched her withdrawal and quietly cursed. Scanning the trail, there was no one else approaching. The hour had grown late, and people were departing for the safety of their homes. Ten minutes later, Sandra drove northward, out of the park, her sleek white car clearly visible in the dim glow of the streetlights. The stalker also headed toward the north entrance of High Park, considerably more frustrated than during the arrival. A perfect kill had become a perfect sea of nothingness.

Chapter Four

On the first day of school, on the morning of Tuesday, 2 September, as Patrick McCaul's feet touched the carpeted floor of his bedroom, a cloud of depression descended on him. In the bathroom, he combed his hair and gazed into the mirror. A saddened face stared back at him.

He thought about the days when he had attended his Catholic elementary school, where he had enjoyed the classroom and eagerly anticipated the beginning of each school day. The teachers had been gentle and kind. Sister Rosemary Grant, whom the kids had nicknamed Sister Grinch, was the only exception. She was so sour that the students said that the priest had baptized her in battery acid. Even Mother Superior, who ran the school with an iron fist, was good to the students, unless they misbehaved.

As he continued to comb his hair, he thought, *If I keep my hair neat, the older guys say I'm as tidy as a girl, and if I leave my hair uncombed, they say I look as wild as a fairy. I can't win. I hate school.*

✧ ✧ ✧

Tom was also not feeling optimistic about the new school year. To add to his lack of enthusiasm, on the first day, he learned that he was in form 10G, and the only close friend in his class was Patrick. For the first time since grade four, Shorty was not beside him.

On Wednesday morning, when Patrick and Tom entered the classroom together, they chose seats beside each other. Their homeroom teacher was Mr. Meagan, who taught Latin. He was older than most of their other teachers, with a thin narrow face and a fringe of hair around his bald dome. He wore wire-rimmed glasses, which he perched on the end of his long nose. Wearing drab olive trousers, a brown sports jacket, and a pale yellow tie, his appearance did not exactly inspire Tom and Patrick to believe that his classes would be interesting.

They were wrong.

When he spoke, unlike Baldy who garbled his words and whistled the French language, Mr. Meagan enunciated clearly, and each time he uttered a remark that he considered humorous, he lowered his chin, peered over the top of his glasses, and gave a wisp of a smile. He also told interesting stories about the Romans as he introduced the Latin vocabulary. The first morning, the class ended with him reciting a version of a poem Tom had seen scribbled on the inside covers of used textbooks in elementary school.

This course is full of Latin,
As full as it can be.
It failed to kill the Roman soldiers,
I doubt it will kill thee.

When Tom departed the homeroom, he felt that he would enjoy Mr. Meagan's lessons. Patrick seemed to like him too.

As Tom walked home from school, he thought about his first day. Thankfully, no one had mentioned the Stritch murder. Perhaps his second year at YCI would be better than his first. When he arrived home, his mom had prepared an early supper for him as his shift at the drug store was from 4:30 p.m. to 9:00 p.m. At work there were no orders to deliver, so he sat in the room in the back of the store. A copy of the late edition of the *Tribune* was on the counter, and he glanced half-heartedly at it. As expected, there was not much news. In parliament, the prime minister had declared that there would be no election before the coronation, which was to occur the following summer.

While he was perusing the paper, Ruth, who drove the delivery truck for the drug store, walked into the room. She was about thirty-five years of age, lean, and muscular with an appealing figure. A cigarette dangled from the corner of her mouth. She was attractive in a butch sort of a way, and she enhanced this image by not wearing makeup and cutting her hair short like a guy's. Shorty had pegged her correctly. She was tough.

On this particular occasion, she was to deliver six cases of Canada Dry ginger ale to a house on Bathurst Street, near Rosemary Lane. It was not far, but she requested that Tom accompany her to help lift the cases from the truck to the customer's back door. He had no orders to deliver, so he did not object, although he was certain that she could lift the entire truck if she had wanted to.

It was to be an eventful trip.

Ruth played the truck's horn as expertly as the principal French horn player in the Toronto Symphony Orchestra. Proceeding west on Eglinton Avenue, she blasted every driver in front of her, signalling them to move over to allow her to pass. When one of the drivers angrily honked back at her, she leaned out the window and yelled, "Why don't you blow your nose? You'll get more out of it."

He gave her the finger in reply.

"Shove it up your ass," she shouted in return. "It would be lost in an asshole your size."

Tom hated to admit it; even though he was laughing, he was shocked.

A few minutes later, without signalling, she negotiated the left-hand turn onto Bathurst Street. She abruptly cut in front of a car that was travelling eastbound, rather than waiting for a clear break in the traffic. The driver almost struck the delivery van, and he leaned on his horn in frustration.

On Bathurst Street, she slammed on the brakes to make the left-hand turn into the customer's driveway. Traffic behind her came to a sudden standstill. The sounds of screeching brakes, ginger ale bottles clanking, and cursing drivers filled the air. Leaning out the window again, Ruth screamed at the other drivers.

"Can't you jerks be gentlemanly enough to yield to a fucking lady?"

Tom had never heard a woman use the F word. He did not think that women even knew it.

The drivers watched in stunned silence as Ruth blew them a kiss and calmly pulled the truck into the driveway. She stepped out of the truck as regally as if she were a queen alighting from a royal coach. Then she opened the rear doors of the van like a doorman at the Ritz, and with a majestic sweep of her arm, she motioned for Tom to remove the cases of ginger ale.

He gazed out at the street as he lifted one of the cases from the truck. The drivers were still staring in disbelief at the woman whom they considered a driver from hell. Within minutes, the traffic resumed. On the return trip, her driving skills were no better, but at least there was no chaotic scene.

Back at the store, Tom told Shorty about the incident.

"That's nothing," he insisted. "Next month she has to appear in court. She pounded the piss out of some guy who backed his Buick out of his driveway on Chaplin Crescent and smashed into the side of the delivery van. He was a big man, and he gave her a black eye."

"What happened to the man?"

"Ruth broke his nose and blackened both his eyes."

"Why doesn't Greenberg fire her?"

"I think he's scared of her," he said with a smirk.

They both chuckled.

"If she ever goes into professional boxing at Maple Leaf Garden, I'd like to be her manager," Shorty added as he picked up a prescription that required delivering.

✧ ✧ ✧

Despite Jim Peersen's pleas, the department continued to refuse to allow him to haul Mr. Dinkman down to the station for questioning. Dinkman knew he had the upper hand and refused all interviews. Peersen had considered visiting him at his residence, but Thomson had warned him that officials would construe it as police harassment.

How could he force Dinkman to comply? he thought.

After much deliberation, he decided to stake out the vice-principal's home several evenings a week. Peersen would observe him in his spare hours, so it would not appear in his logbook. He figured that no one in the department could object to something they knew nothing about.

On Tuesday of the following week, Peersen was at his desk until after eight o'clock, finishing paperwork that had accumulated. A policeman's career was not always chasing clues, interviewing thugs, and piecing together fascinating puzzles. The drudgery of filling in forms, writing up reports and filing them occupied many hours of his time. The paperwork was sometimes useful. He had learned that Dinkman lived on Ashbury Avenue, a short street that ran west off Oakwood Avenue, north of Rogers Road.

Grabbing a ham and cheese sandwich and a bottle of Pepsi from the coffee shop near the station, he set out. By the time he arrived at Ashbury Avenue, darkness had enveloped the street, and the lights in the windows of the houses glowed softly. The haze in the air was visible in the penumbra of the streetlights, accenting the approaching days of early autumn. He parked the car facing east, about a dozen doors away from Dinkman's house, and because the night air was warm, he rolled down the window.

He bit into his sandwich and sipped on the Pepsi, pushing from his mind thoughts of a glass of vintage red wine and a filet mignon with pepper sauce. He wondered how many evenings would pass before he discovered something useful about Dinkman's lifestyle. *I hope I find a bit of dirt before the weather closes in on me,* he thought.

Peersen devoted several nights a week to his stakeout, from dusk until about 10:30 p.m. He figured that if the man had not ventured out by this hour, he was unlikely to do so. The last week of September, the nights were becoming chilly, and Dinkman had never once left his house. Jim had never staked out the house on a Friday night, as he figured the vice-principal would be too exhausted at the end of the week to go anywhere.

Perhaps I am wrong and should try observing him on a Friday, he thought.

The following Friday evening at 8:30 p.m. he saw Dinkman walk boldly out of his house, a duffle bag in his hand. He walked east toward Oakwood and turned south. Peersen started the ignition and slowly followed him. At Rogers Road, Dinkman boarded a streetcar. Following in his car at a safe distance, he saw him get off the streetcar at the end of the line and climb on an eastbound St. Clair streetcar. Driving in the curb lane, he followed, always keeping the streetcar doors in view. Dinkman remained seated until he reached Yonge Street, where he alighted and walked south. Peersen drove past him, parked, and watched.

One block south of St. Clair, on the east side of Yonge, Dinkman entered a doorway with a sign above it that discretely identified it as the Gymnasium Club. Peersen approached the building and noted that the club was on the second floor of the three-storey building. He returned to his parked car and sat inside, keeping the entrance in sight. He thought it strange that Dinkman had travelled so far from his home to visit a private club, which appeared to be some sort of gym. The sign advertised that the club had a coffee shop.

Perhaps he wants a place to exercise, away from where the high school students would recognize him, Peersen speculated. *Strange, I had not figured Dinkman for the type of man who would be interested in working out.*

Twenty minutes later, Dinkman came out of the building and walked to a small coffee shop nearby.

"So much for working out," Peersen muttered. Then he wondered why Dinkman had not used the club's coffee shop.

Five minutes later, a woman came out of the building, walked to the coffee shop, and joined Dinkman.

This is interesting, Peersen thought.

The mystery woman was wearing a stylish trench coat pulled tightly around her, revealing a trim figure, her shapely legs visible below the coat. Her walk was provocative, and despite her coat collar pulled high around her neck and a large-brimmed hat pulled low over her face, Peersen was aware that she attracted the attention of passing males on the street.

She looks like the stereotype of a mystery madam in a sex novel, he reflected.

Ten minutes passed. Then Peersen saw the woman and Dinkman

depart together, boarding a northbound Yonge streetcar. Peersen followed in his car, observing the swaying Peter Witt streetcar as it lumbered up the street amid the late-evening traffic, passing the flashing marquee lights of the Hollywood and Odeon Hyland theatres, a short distance north of St. Clair Avenue.

When the streetcar stopped at Eglinton Avenue, they alighted, walked eastward to Mount Pleasant Avenue, north one block, and entered a high-rise apartment building on Roehampton Avenue. As Peersen slowly cruised past, a uniformed doorman was opening the front door for them, smiling as he spoke to the mysterious woman.

Peersen parked the car and approached the building. The doorman was an elderly man who appeared bored and was outside having a cigarette. Peersen flashed his badge and inquired about the man and attractive woman who had just entered the building.

"I don't know the man, but the woman is that nice Miss Anderson, in apartment 904."

"Do you know her full name?"

"Sure, it's Miss Samantha Anderson."

Further surveillance being useless, Peersen returned to his car and drove home.

The following morning, he visited the second floor of the police station, where the vice squad was located. He asked a cop, with whom he was friendly, if he knew anything about the Gymnasium Club or a Miss Samantha Anderson.

The cop replied, "I recognize the name of the club. It's a hot item in our department. But I don't know the woman's name. I'll ask about her."

"Keep it on the QT, will you?" Peersen requested.

Ten minutes later, Peersen was working at his desk when the policeman approached him. He surreptitiously dropped a slip of paper on his desk and without stopping, he continued to the door that led to the stairwell.

On the note he had printed: "Meet me in the stairwell."

Jim waited several moments, and when he thought no one was observing him, he walked casually to where his friend waited.

Peersen asked, "Why all the secrecy?"

"I think you've stumbled on a can of worms. Samantha Anderson is one of the notorious members of the Gymnasium Club. The department is very leery of her as she has influence among the city's elite. I didn't tell you before, but the vice squad thinks the club's a front for a house of prostitution. The owners say it's a gym, but they found out that both men and women work out in the same area. Our guys think that at the club, the johns are checking out the bodies of the hookers before they arrange to meet them at a more convenient location for an intimate session."

"Why don't they raid the place?"

"They did. All hell broke loose. On the night of the raid, the joint contained six or seven wealthy bankers, some of them poofy residents of Rosedale. There was also a provincial court judge and an alderman from one of the downtown wards."

"What happened?"

"They were all released as the vice squad was unable to prove anything. It was an ugly affair. The top brass told our boys in blue to be more careful in the future. Pissing off a judge is never a good idea. Despite our screw-up, occasionally we still watch the place."

"What more can you tell me about Samantha Anderson?"

"We think she provides masochistic sex for those who enjoy being chained up and whipped."

"Anything else you can tell me?"

"I think I've said enough. You'd better tread gently."

As Jim Peersen turned to leave, his friend added, "If you interview 'Spanky' Anderson, as we call her, let me know if you enjoy getting your ass slapped."

Peersen grinned, more with satisfaction than amusement. He had discovered something to use to his advantage with Dinkman.

It was time to share his findings with Gerry.

✧ ✧ ✧

The next morning, Thomson listened attentively to Peersen's tale of intrigue. His frown registered his disapproval of Peersen's methods, but at the conclusion of the report, despite his misgivings about the Gymnasium Club, his grin betrayed his admiration of the results.

"It is indeed time to visit the illustrious Mr. Richard Dinkman," he said. "Imagine the bad luck of your mother naming you Dickie Dinkman. It's enough to drive any man to criminal activities."

Peersen preferred to wait until evening and visit Dinkman at home, when his wife was in the house. Thomson, however, would not entertain such an approach and phoned the vice-principal to make an appointment at the school.

Dinkman refused his request for an interview. Gerry said resolutely, "Now then, we'll just see about that. We'll be there at eleven o'clock, twenty minutes from now." He hung up!

It was exactly twenty-two minutes later when the two detectives marched into the school office and informed the head secretary that they wished to see Mr. Dinkman. She told them that the vice-principal was busy.

"Now then, we'll just see about that," Thomson replied tersely. "We'll wait."

Peersen added, "Even if it takes until midnight."

Ten minutes later, Mr. Dinkman's door opened and a well-dressed woman, likely a parent, strutted out. The detectives walked into his inner sanctum.

Sitting at his desk, Dinkman did not rise from his chair or offer them a seat. Pasted on his face was a phony smile, but it was obvious that he was annoyed. There was only one chair, so Gerry sat down.

Silence.

The clock on the wall ticked noisily, and they could hear the voices of the students in the hallways. Dinkman glanced up and compared the time on his wristwatch with the clock on the wall containing Roman numerals on its octagonal face. Then he stared at the two detectives but remained silent.

Thomson's voice broke the stalemate. "We feel you know more about the Stritch murder than you previously indicated."

"I have nothing to add."

"Now then, we'll just see about that."

Shit, Peersen cursed to himself. *I wish Gerry would stop using that dumb expression.*

Impatient, Peersen now stepped into the conversation. "We have discovered information that might be embarrassing for you if it became common knowledge. If you cooperate with us, we will cooperate with you."

Dinkman smiled condescendingly and remained silent.

Attempting to rattle Dinkman, Peersen inquired, "Did you enjoy being tied up and having your ass spanked on Friday night?"

Dinkman gave a disgusted grunt.

Gerry shot his partner an acidic glance.

Peersen knew he was out of line, but he had run out of patience with Dinkman.

Dinkman displayed no outward signs of distress. "So you followed me from the Gymnasium Club to the apartment of Miss Anderson. Do you have any proof of what went on behind the closed door?" he replied matter-of-factly.

"Your wife may not care about actual proof."

"My wife is aware of my relationship with women such as Miss Anderson. She knows that they fulfill certain needs that, shall we say, she does not wish to fulfill. In turn, I look the other way when she exhibits too much interest in the milkman, the coalman, or whomever." He waved his hand in an "et cetera" motion and then added, "We break no laws."

Thomson and Peersen stared at him in disbelief.

"If you wish to speak to my wife, she's at home today. If there's nothing else, I bid you good day."

Outside the school, the detectives returned to their car. When Peersen opened the door to the front passenger seat, he said in disgust, "The son of a bitch called our bluff."

"Yes," Gerry confirmed, "but he has moved himself off the witness list and onto the suspect list."

Thomson settled into the driver's seat, and within seconds, he was gently letting out the clutch as his foot increased the pressure on the gas pedal. The venerable 1947 Ford sedan eased its way down the street and turned left on to Oakwood Avenue. After passing through the intersection at Rogers Road, they proceeded north to Ashbury Avenue.

Gerry handled the police car gently, as if it were an old friend, which in some ways it was. When they had promoted him to detective, a mere two years after returning from overseas, the car had been among the first autos that rolled off the assembly line at the Ford plant in Oakville. During the war, the factory had manufactured transport vehicles for the war effort, and they had required over a year to retool it to produce cars.

Proud of his new acquisition, Gerry was careful with it. However, it was a police car and had received more than its share of abuse during the past five years. A high-speed chase along St. Clair Avenue two years earlier had almost run the guts out of the engine. In the trunk and along the left fender, despite repairs necessary after a shoot-out in the Junction area of the city, there remained telltale rust marks where the bullets had punctured the metal. Gerry always drove the car with pride, treating it like a racing filly that had passed its prime.

Peersen viewed the car more like an old slipper, too worn to be useful, and too comfortable to discard. He preferred vehicles that were sleeker, flashier, and with low mileage.

Then he wondered about Mrs. Dinkman. What would she be like? Her husband had portrayed her as the neighbourhood "welcome wagon," ready to jump anything in pants. Would she be a "Two-Ton Tess," able to wrestle any man to the ground and have her way with him? Was she so irresistibly gorgeous that men pursued her so ardently that she had no choice but to comply? Perhaps she was the shy, coy type that men found irresistible and chased her until, like the proverbial spider, she ensnarled them in her web?

Gerry knocked on the door.

There was not a sound from within.

He rapped his knuckles more forcefully on the peeling paint on the door. *Apparently, Dinkman is not big on house maintenance,* he thought.

Several more moments passed and slowly the door opened. When Mrs. Debbie Dinkman saw that two men were at her door, she quickly thrust the door back against the inside frame.

Thomson flipped his badge into view, at the same moment that Peersen flipped open his mouth in surprise.

Mrs. Dinkman was paradoxically nothing like he had expected, and yet everything he had anticipated. Younger than her husband, she possessed a voluptuous body with large, firm breasts, flagrantly on display beneath her sheer blouse. Her Betty Grable legs were long and curvaceous, and her red stilettos accented her height.

However, her beauty ended abruptly at her neck. Her protruding front teeth, one of the worst overbites he had ever seen, dominated her homely face. Her dark hair was long and draped over one eye, similar to the movie star Veronica Lake. Unlike the starlet, she had not achieved the same sexy effect.

Thomson explained who they were and asked if they might step inside.

She motioned for them to enter.

"Mrs. Dinkman," Thomson began, "we are here to substantiate information that your husband supplied to us." Then he paused, uncertain how to proceed.

Slowly, he continued. "Are you aware of Mr. Dinkman's proclivity … for …"

"Oh, yes, he has a big proclivity," she replied with a lascivious grin.

Peersen, who was tired of beating around the bush, said forcefully, "Are you aware that your husband meets women for sexual purposes?"

"Sexual purposes?"

Shaking his head at the obtuseness of the woman, he rephrased his question.

"Are you aware that Mr. Dinkman has sex with women he meets at the Gymnasium Club?"

"Oh, sure! He wants to do things that no man should do. I am a sensitive woman. I don't engage in kinky behaviour. He goes where he gets satisfied."

"So you were aware that your husband visited the Gymnasium Club and had a liaison with a woman named Samantha Anderson."

"A what?"

"A session, a good time, a romp in the hay, in exchange for cash."

"Oh, sure! Why didn't you say that in the first place? I just wish there was a Mr. Anderson. I'd visit him, but I'd not pay him any money. In this neighbourhood, I get enough action. I don't need to give cash."

She gazed intently at Peersen, and her eyes dropped to his crotch as she sensuously lisped, "Young man, are you single?"

Peersen coughed to cover his embarrassment. Ignoring her remark, as he stood to leave, he said, "Thanks for your cooperation."

"It's my pleasure," she snorted. "I am even more cooperative with those who cooperate with me." Her eyebrows arched in an inviting smile.

"Thanks, madam. We'll see our way out."

As Peersen reached the sidewalk, he turned to his partner. "More than just her looks never reached her head."

✧ ✧ ✧

By the beginning of October, the football season was in high gear. The chances of the team's success dominated the conversations of Tom and his friends, but they were grateful that no one had mentioned the Stritch murder case. As well, the teachers were more relaxed now that the police were no longer visiting the school.

The team won the first three football games in October, and the rallies in the auditorium became even more enthusiastic than the previous month. Coach Millford had pleaded Shorty's case before the court of Judge Tyrone Evanson, and despite his iniquitous (as Gus had called it) behaviour the previous spring, had negotiated a plea bargain. Gus allowed him to play on the team, but not before he signed a document stating that he agreed to no recalcitrant behaviour. All parties were satisfied with the verdict, and Tom had learned two new words.

Kramer tried out for the football team. He did not possess sufficient weight to secure a position, the coach cutting him from the squad early in the eliminations. Without Kramer on the team, he and Shorty did not have as many opportunities for a fistfight.

Harry was the obvious choice for quarterback, with Shorty as the second pick.

✧ ✧ ✧

At the end of the month, nature had transformed Toronto's streetscapes into a drab scene of skeletal trees and leaf-strewn alleyways. In the backyard gardens, bright orange pumpkins reigned supremely among the dying foliage.

On the washroom walls at YCI, the inevitable Halloween graffiti appeared. In later years, Tom learned that the poem was as much a ritual of the season as pumpkins, shelling out, and candy apples.

> When the weather's hot and sticky,
> That's no time for dunkin' dickie.
> But when the frost is on the pumpkin,
> That's the time for dickie dunkin'.

As November's dank, musky days dropped across the city, the exuberance of Halloween faded as quickly as the candles had died in the soot-scoured pumpkins. The thoughts of the citizens of Toronto became more introspective as Remembrance Day approached. The newspapers announced that the armistice service in the Armouries on University Avenue near Queen Street would feature the Governor General's Horse Guards.

Tom's dad was interested that Thomas B. Costain, the famous Canadian author, had published another book, *The Silver Chalice*. In addition, he mentioned to his mom that Mario Lanza was starring in the movie *Be My Love*, screening at Loew's Downtown Theatre (The Elgin).

Gramps grinned mischievously as he told Nan, "If you'll 'be my love,' I'll try to remember what it is that a lover does."

"It would be quite a trick to remember what you never knew in the first place," she replied with a sly grin.

✧ ✧ ✧

The final week of November, Frank Gnomes was upset that his editor at the *Trib* had ordered him to abandon the Stritch case and concentrate on stories that were more current. He reluctantly complied, but the Valley Vampire remained at large and it wounded his pride. His coworkers teased him, because he had mistakenly bragged in the early days of the case that he would solve the murder, even if others failed. His words had now returned to haunt him!

His anger magnified his frustration with Masters the Snitch, who had held out on him. Only the previous day, Masters had finally told him about the investigations that Detective Peersen had conducted in October into the personal life of Dickhead Dinkman, as he too liked to refer to him. Frank now learned about the Gymnasium Club and the infamous Miss Anderson, Queen of the Spanking Kingdom. He decided that he would approach her at the pseudo-gym that she frequented, pretend to be a prospective client, and blackmail her into providing information that the police had been unable to retrieve.

Frank bought a cheap pair of gym shorts, sweat socks, running shoes, and a sporty duffle bag. Arriving at the gym, as he changed into his jock costume, he felt like a fish out of water. He knew that his body was beginning to portray the many years of neglect, and that the numerous pints of beer and sugared coffee accompanied by sweet donuts had added a few extra inches around his waist. His leather belt was increasingly finding it difficult to span his gut. Despite his paunch, he was confident that his broad shoulders, tall stature, and boyish good looks made him attractive to women.

Arriving at the club, he purchased a private membership, and as he walked across the exercise area, he noticed several attractive women. A discreet inquiry revealed that Miss Anderson was the attractive woman working out on a gym mat. When he passed by her, she smiled. He hoped that she was thinking, *Nice ass, and one that I wouldn't mind spanking.*

Frank exercised half-heartedly for twenty minutes, and then he engaged Miss Anderson in light banter. She was a willing conversationalist.

Later, over a cup of coffee, Frank identified himself as being a reporter and informed her that he was seeking information on one of her clients. Her eyes narrowed and her smile disappeared when he said the word "clients." She made her living at sizing up men, but she had not sensed that he was a reporter. Despite his charm and attractive smile, she had a feeling that beneath the pleasant façade lurked danger.

"I don't discuss my personal life with anyone."

"I am not just anyone. I need information on the questionable habits of Mr. Richard Dinkman."

"Ask his wife."

"The information that I need, his wife is unlikely to know."

"Sorry, I can't help you."

"That's a pity, because that means I can't help you to stay out of the limelight after I publish my series of articles about 'Spankers of Toronto.' Your neighbours may object to having a sex professional living near them. It might cause their husbands to come knocking on your door," he added with a sly grin.

She observed him carefully as she pondered his words and weighed her options. "Do you promise confidentiality?"

"As a gentleman, I would feel honour bound."

She understood the irony of his words, knowing that a gentleman would never ask a lady such questions in the first place. She paused, held eye contact, and decided her best course of action was to get rid of the creep.

"I hardly know Old Dinkman."

"Any woman who has seen a man with his pants down and slapped his chubby cheeks with a … what is it that you use?"

"I never saw Dinkman with his pants down."

"Come now! You mean you did it with his trousers up?"

"I never did *anything* with the man."

"Why not?"

"Because I threw him out of the apartment the first time he visited me."

"Why?"

"Because the sick son of a bitch didn't want to be spanked. He wanted to beat the hell out of me."

Samantha stood up and defiantly left the table, flipping her brunette hair back from her forehead. As she departed from the club's coffee shop, Frank followed her down the stairs. When she stepped outside, Frank carefully observed her. He noticed that the soft glow from the streetlights silhouetted her firm breasts and attractive face with its pert little nose.

Damn, he thought, *I'd enjoy getting my ass spanked by her.* The thought eased the pain of having failed in his quest for information.

✧ ✧ ✧

December delivered many dull days to the city, but the decorations and expectations of Christmas brightened the scene for Tom. He thought that the Christmas assembly at school, though not as rousing as a football rally, was a pleasant diversion from the boredom of discovering the meaning of X in algebraic equations, and trying to understand the French vocabulary exercises through the whistling teeth of Baldy Baldwin. At the assembly, grade-thirteen students read yuletide prose, the choir sang carols, the drama club performed a one-act play, and the senior orchestra played the music to accompany the festive singing.

After the assembly, when Tom returned to his locker, a group of boys was gathered around Patrick's locker. Someone had scribbled the word "pansy" on his locker door using a tube of bright red lipstick. Patrick was trying to slam the door shut and escape as quickly as possible. His face was beet red, a combination of humiliation and anger. The bullies refused to allow him to break through the circle they had formed around him. They pushed and jostled him, adding to his frustration.

When Harry appeared on the scene, he shoved the persecutors aside, allowing Patrick to flee. No one challenged Harry, though a few guys smirked as they observed Patrick depart.

A few minutes later, Shorty and Tom were sitting in the lunchroom. Tom was eating his sandwiches and sipping on a bottle of Sunkist orange soda, his favourite. Harry joined them. Patrick had gone home for lunch and was safely beyond the reach of his tormentors—for now. Harry had a meat pie on his tray that he had bought at the cafeteria. The gravy from the crust dribbled over the tin peas and generous scoop of mashed potatoes. The smell of meat pies lofted throughout the cafeteria area, mingling with the odour of sweat that emanated from the adjacent lockers.

As Harry's fork broke into the flakey crust, he looked at Tom and Shorty and said, "It was Kramer who wrote on Patrick's locker."

"How do you know?" Shorty asked.

"I saw the expression on his face. I know him. He did it."

Shorty and Tom remained silent. Tom knew that if it were up to Shorty, Kramer would never lift a hand to write another letter of graffiti on anyone's locker. He would break both his arms.

✧ ✧ ✧

When the exams were over, the Christmas holidays commenced. Since New Year's Day fell on a Thursday, the schools would not open for only one day, which was the Friday. This meant that Tom and his friends had two full weeks of holidays.

✧ ✧ ✧

January of 1953 held the promise of an interesting year for the city. The arts and entertainment industries were booming. At the Royal Alexandra Theatre, the seventy-five member National Ballet of Canada, under the direction of Celia Franca, was wowing audiences. The company was formed just two years earlier.

The world of television was also expanding, as more Canadians purchased sets. The most popular shows were: *Dragnet, This Is Your Life, The Lone Ranger, Hopalong Cassidy, The Cisco Kid, Ozzie and Harriet, Dinah Shore,* and *Kate Smith.* The most popular soap operas were: *The Guiding Light, Love of Life,* and *Search for Tomorrow.* Wrestling, boxing, and hockey also attracted many fans. It was as if they had transferred the world of radio to the realm of television. Ken and Tom longed to be among those who could watch their favourite entertainers on the tube.

✧ ✧ ✧

In February, the event at YCI that captivated everyone's attention was the Winter Whirl, a dance that the school held annually at Casa Loma. The dancing would begin at 9:30 p.m. and end at 12:30 a.m. This year the student council had decided to hire Ellis McLintock to provide the music for close dancing and wild gyrations. The usual refreshment bar would appear, but this year there was to be a television set behind the counter.

School prefects would serve the drinks. Prefects were older students whom the staff had chosen to assist in school supervision. They wore cardigan sweaters with a school crest and a large letter P on them, allowing them to be easily identifiable. Patrolling the hallways, they had the authority to demand that students place garbage in the bins and talk in quiet voices. In the cafeteria, they could order students to clean up split milk or soda pop. Everyone obeyed the prefects, as they were able to give other students detentions. They also acted as ushers at school musicals, concerts, and assemblies.

The morning of the day before the Winter Whirl, Mr. Evanson called an assembly. In his most official voice, he lectured the students on the evils of alcohol.

"Alcohol is a dangerous drug, as deadly as cancer or polio," he intoned. "It destroys the nervous system and produces chronic illnesses. If you place a healthy worm in a glass of alcohol, it dies, but if you drop it into a glass of water, it survives easily."

Shorty whispered to Tom, "If I ever get a case of the worms, I'll drink a glass of booze to get rid of them."

Tom doubted that this was the lesson that old Gus was trying to impart.

Mr. Evanson continued. "Alcohol is a scourge that can destroy lives. Any students caught smuggling the evil substance into Casa Loma will appear before me in the office the following day."

A student in the row behind Tom said, "I never thought of smuggling booze into the dance. It's a great idea!"

After the assembly, the student body jostled and teased in the hallways as they returned to their classrooms. A fifth-form girl, who was sophisticated and as smooth as silk, oozed to a friend, "My date has applied to attend the University of Toronto next fall and intends to go to med school. He's dishier than Robert Taylor."

Tom could picture the dark, brooding good looks of the film star Robert Taylor, as well as his flashing smile and perfect teeth. What girl would not want to go to the dance with such a guy?

The other girl replied, "My Bob is going into law. His dad's a lawyer with a firm on Bay Street. Next year, I'm only going to date college men. They know how to dress snappy and talk the talk."

Then they both giggled as they admitted that any guy they dated, college man or not, must be drop-dead gorgeous.

As they walked away, Tom turned and sauntered into the science class with its telltale odour of burnt sulphur. He felt as though he would never be a guy who caused mature girls to giggle.

✧ ✧ ✧

Throughout March, each weekend, Tom continued to work at the pharmacy. Ruth, the truck driver at the drug store, had not mellowed. Any traffic fines that she received, she quietly paid, and she never informed Mr. Greenberg, in order to prevent him from knowing about her driving habits.

On one occasion, during the rush hour, she did a U-turn on Eglinton Avenue near Old Forest Hill Road. Shorty and Tom were in the passenger seat, and they froze in horror as Ruth suddenly slammed on the brakes, the van skidding to a sudden stop, the smell of burning rubber filling the air. She had missed hitting an elderly driver in his tank of a Cadillac by only a few inches. Ruth grinned maliciously and cursed the driver, oblivious to her lack of driving skills. Laughing maniacally, she proceeded along Eglinton as if nothing had happened.

One evening, shortly before closing time, Mr. Greenberg handed Tom an order to deliver to a house on Dewborne Lane. Arriving at the address, he placed his bicycle at the side of the curving driveway, shivering from the cold as he rang the doorbell. An elderly woman, at least she seemed that way to Tom as she was over thirty, grabbed the order. She shoved a five-dollar bill in his hand and banged the door shut in his face.

The bill on the order was for $4.75, and as Tom walked away, he felt pleased that the final delivery of the evening had paid off so handsomely. As he was climbing on his bike, behind him, he heard the door of the house open.

"Where the hell is the Vaseline?" the woman shrieked. "The bloody druggist forgot to put the lubricant in the package."

When Tom returned to the drug store, he blushed while delicately explaining the problem to Mr. Greenberg. Even though it was past the closing hour, he asked Tom to take a jar of Vaseline to the customer, discretely placing it in a small, white paper bag. As it was after hours and a blustery night, he asked Ruth to drive him in the truck.

The drive was uneventful, as the late hour had thinned the traffic. It took only a few minutes to arrive at the door on Dewborne Lane. Ruth remained in the truck and kept the motor running to retain the heat inside the vehicle. Tom gingerly rang the doorbell. The customer opened the door, grumbled a half-hearted thanks, and accepted the package. Then her face flushed beet red and, seething with anger, she slammed the door. Quickly turning around, Tom saw Ruth's head hanging out the truck window. She was smiling lecherously and had extended her tongue, rolling it slowly over her lips.

Small wonder trouble was Ruth's constant companion. She could never resist the temptation to give someone the shive.

✧ ✧ ✧

The first week of April, the Sergeant of Detectives Arnold Peckerman summoned Thomson and Peersen to his office. Peckerman was in his early fifties, tall and heavy-set, an ex-navy man. His once-dark hair had turned gray, and the lines around his eyes betrayed his age. However, despite many years sitting behind a desk, he remained trim and fit.

The men of the precinct respected Peckerman, comfortable with a sergeant of detectives who had earned his rank through many years of pounding the beat as a constable and later as a detective. The department had promoted him to sergeant of detectives during the war years, when many of the men on the force were serving overseas. Due to his age, they doubted he would ever become the chief of police.

In their way, the men were almost fond of him, even though at times, he could be a pompous ass and an ardent publicity hound. Though Peckerman was a seasoned policeman and detective, at times he was prudish and disapproved of the coarse language and antics of his colleagues.

Those who had known Peckerman when he was fresh from the police academy remembered that within five minutes of his arrival at the station, someone among the ranks had referred to him as "Arnie Peckerhead." Police officers—similar to high school students—enjoyed inflicting nicknames on their mates and superiors.

On this morning in April, when Thomson and Peersen walked into Peckerman's office, without any greeting or preamble, the sergeant of detectives motioned for them to sit down, and snapped brusquely, "Do we officially classify the Stritch file as a cold case or continue to pursue it?"

Thomson inhaled deeply and slowly released his breath in a lingering sigh. He had been expecting the ultimatum. He glanced at his partner, and their eyes met. Neither of them wanted to end the investigation, but if honest, they had to admit that they had developed no further information for almost a year. The innocent face of the Elaine Stritch still haunted them.

Peersen decided to tackle Peckerman. The wheels rolled furiously within his brain. He needed to invent a way to widen the investigation and have it appear as if Peckerman had thought of the idea. Searching for the appropriate words, he began slowly, the oil of necessity lubricating the cells of his brain.

"Sir, I think we need to reconsider the possible suspects."

"How many are you considering?"

"Too many!"

"Prioritize," Peckerman shot back.

Peersen flipped open his logbook and stared at the pages with the exact dates and times, even though he had them firmly planted in his memory. He knew that referring to the book gave him more authority in the eyes of his superior.

"Her fiancé, Bill Matheson, is number one on my list."

"Why?"

"He's the type and has been uncooperative, as if he has something to hide. He has an alibi, but I don't think it's ironclad. Neighbours saw him arrive at his cottage on Pine Lake, in Muskoka, around eight o'clock on Sunday, 25 August, the week before the Labour Day weekend. About noon on Labour Day Monday, the owner of the local grocery store said that he saw him drive past his store, headed southbound for Toronto. As Matheson was alone at the cottage, we have only his word that he remained there for the entire week.

"A neighbour in the cottage to the west of him said that she saw lights each evening in the windows of Matheson's cottage. He could have left them on around the clock, as during the day they would not be visible. She can't be sure whether she saw him outside the cottage every day. Another neighbour said he saw Matheson repairing his deck, but he couldn't be certain that it was him."

"Did you check the mileage figures on his car?"

"Sure! He had an oil and lube job the day before he drove to the cottage, at the gas station at St. Clair Avenue and Bathurst Street. They had a record of his odometer readings. According to the figures, he never left the cottage except perhaps to drive into Bala for groceries, which he claims he did."

"So, why are you suspicious?"

"It's all too convenient. Mileage figures on an odometer can be altered."

"Any evidence?"

"None that we can find."

"So, contrary to your opening gambit, his alibi is ironclad."

"Not quite! What if he had an accomplice who drove up to the cottage, allowing Matheson to drive down to the city in his or her car and arrive back before anyone knew he had left?"

Peckerman pondered this idea and then nodded hesitantly as if in agreement. He asked, "What other prime suspects do you have in mind?"

Peersen continued. "The roommate of the victim, Miss Bettina Taylor."

Peckerman frowned as he asked, "I thought you'd pegged her for a girl's girl?"

"That's what I thought. But then we learned that she was pregnant last year and had a child."

Peckerman raised his eyebrows inquisitively, clearly disapproving of having a child out of wedlock.

"Who's the father?"

"We don't know."

"Any other teachers interest you?"

"Well," Thomson said with a teasing grin, "Peersen took a fancy to the art teacher, Miss Elizabeth Hitch."

Ignoring the remark, Peersen declared, "The last time we interviewed Miss Hitch she was dressed from head to toe in flaming pink. She had even tinted her hair pink. Her eyes were pink as well, but I think they were bloodshot from the previous night's intake of booze. When we talked to her, she was still a little high. I think she mixes the powdered paint with vodka and inhales the fumes from the paint pots. I was never so uncomfortable during an interview in my entire life."

"Why? You never had problems with weird women before?" Peckerman quipped, enjoying the self-perceived cleverness of his remark.

Ignoring his boss' comment, Peersen replied, "Because this woman never looked at me above my belt."

The sergeant of detectives winced disapprovingly. "Any more suspects?" Peckerman's smile had disappeared.

Peersen continued. "There's Miss Mary Allyson, the school librarian, who refuses to say a word. When we press her, she bursts into tears, gushing streams of water. She's too old to be involved in the murder, but I think she knows more than she's telling.

"Then there's the French teacher, Gregory Baldwin, who has teeth like a beaver and whistles as he talks. He's an odd duck but looks more like a flamingo—long-legged and pink, if you get my drift."

Peckerman ignored the remark. He preferred to pay no heed to anything referring to homosexuals.

Peersen continued. "Anthony Bowler, who teaches geography, Sam Millford, who's the boys' gym teacher, and Gayle Manson, who teaches girls' PT, are also of interest to us. The other members of staff appear to be ordinary, run-of-the-mill teachers, but I think they all know something. They're keeping silent, afraid of becoming involved."

"How do we get them to talk?"

Thomson now took over. "The key is the vice-principal, Mr. Dinkman. He knows the staff intimately. I think he's aware of the staff jealousies, hatreds, promiscuities, and any other habits that might shed light on the case. Remember, we don't have a solid motive for the murder, though it's possible someone silenced her because of something she had discovered, or perhaps as revenge for some deed or other. It may have been a perverted sex crime. Whatever the motive, I am convinced it involves the inner circle on the staff of YCI."

"Could Dinkman be the murderer?"

"We can't rule it out. Even old Gus Evanson is suspect. His affections for the victim go beyond the usual principal/teacher relationship. Perhaps he had the hots for her and killed her in a fit of jealousy. Or he had an affair with her, and she was blackmailing him."

"I can hardly see the old guy roaming the Humber Valley late at night," Peckerman asserted.

"True! But nothing is beyond the realm of possibility. No one can truly explain the hatred generated by revenge."

"I would like to investigate that punk Horace Kramer a little further," Peersen interjected. "His story doesn't make sense. Why did he pedal his rear end all the way from the Oakwood–Eglinton area, across the city to the Humber Valley? He says he was simply cycling. I don't buy it."

"Have you confronted him again?"

"His stepmother refuses to allow another interview." Peersen now attempted to place the reason for the failure of the investigation on the shoulders of the administrators who were higher up the food chain.

"If we had more latitude to question witnesses, we might be able to get somewhere."

At this point, as if on cue, Gerry Thomson took over again.

"Getting official permission to haul some of the persons of interest down to the station has been the major impediment to solving this case."

"Explain," the sergeant of detectives replied tersely.

Thomson continued. "We have been forbidden to invite the teachers to accept our hospitality down here at the precinct. Chief Clark says they are highly respected members of the community, and their principal, Mr. Tyrone Evanson, has political influence. Without some sort of solid evidence, we were told to keep our hands off all of them."

"From what I can see, you don't have any evidence."

"Perhaps, but as I've explained before, the teachers who were close to Stritch all have alibis, as if they had agreed upon them in advance. Each one swears there were no animosities or petty rivalries among them—just one big hugging, kissing, professional group. I don't buy it. In addition, the pictures they paint of Miss Stritch are almost identical—to the word. My instincts tell me that something is not right."

"Your instincts are not evidence."

"Agreed. But, if we could get them one at a time into an interview room and this time push harder, we might be able to find discrepancies in their stories."

The room was now silent. For an awkward minute or two, the detectives observed their boss deciding his course of action. At the end of the hallway inside the squad room, they could hear the angry voices of several police officers who were arguing, telephones ringing, and the exaggerated laughter from off-colour jokes.

"All right," Peckerman began. "I'll speak to Chief Clark and try to get permission to bring the teachers down to the station, one at a time, starting with Dinkman. Remember, they're influential members of the community and know how to shout their beefs to the press."

"Thanks, boss," Thomson and Peersen chorused. "You've made a wise decision."

"Get your manipulating backsides out of my office," Peckerman said sarcastically as he opened the door and nodded his head toward the outer office.

Thomson and Peersen solemnly walked out, and when they arrived at their desks on the floor below, grinned from ear to ear.

"Let the fun begin!" Gerry chirped.

✧ ✧ ✧

The following morning, the two detectives arrived at YCI. Their visit caused rumours to fly. The pleasant days of early autumn, when the football team was the hot topic, were about to end.

Thomson and Peersen entered the office and demanded to see Mr. Dinkman. Peersen thought that Mrs. Applecrust appeared tired. More lines appeared on her face than during the previous visit. Her wire-framed glasses hung precariously on the tip of her nose, the string attached to them dangling around her turkey-like neck. Over the years, she had developed the habit of lowering her head and gazing over the top of her glasses when she saw anyone enter the office.

On this day, she informed the detectives that the vice-principal was busy, and as they obviously had no appointment, they must wait. Dinkman had established this routine with Mrs. Applecrust. Then she explained that Mr. Evanson was out of the school at a board meeting and was similarly unavailable.

Thomson sailed past her, Peersen in his wake, and thrust open Dinkman's office door. The vice-principal was leaning back in his chair, feet up on the desk, scanning a *National Geographic* magazine. Judging by the grin on Dinkman's face, Thomson guessed that he had likely been gazing at photographs of bare-breasted native women on some island in the South Pacific. Dinkman's smug smile disappeared the instant he saw the detectives.

With a mixture of anger and surprise, he sputtered, "What do you two dicks want?"

Thomson curtly replied, "Mr. Dinkman, we would like you to accompany us downtown to the police precinct to answer charges of obstructing justice."

Though Gerry did not possess a warrant, he had the authority to bring him in for questioning.

"I'll phone my lawyer and wait here until he arrives."

"Mr. Dinkman, you may call your lawyer from the station."

"Am I under arrest?"

"Not at this time. But you will accompany us now."

"I prefer to wait."

"This is not a matter of what you prefer, unless of course you would prefer that we place you under arrest immediately."

Peersen removed a pair of handcuffs from the back of his belt and dangled them threateningly in the air. They ominously swung back and forth, suspended in space like a hangman's noose, the metal restrainers a potent symbol of the authority of the law. The dramatic display had its affect.

As Mrs. Applecrust saw the detectives lead Dinkman away, her mouth dropped in shock. With as much dignity as possible, Dinkman informed Mrs. Applecrust that he was assisting the police in a confidential matter and would return shortly.

Dinkman was certain that the secretaries would not say anything to the students and would discretely inform Mr. Evanson what he had said. It was now the middle of the second period of the morning, and he felt secure from the prying eyes of the students.

Unfortunately, Baldy had excused Kramer from French class to use the washroom, and he saw the detectives leading Dinkman away. He recognized Peersen immediately. By the fourth period, everyone in the school knew of the event.

◇ ◇ ◇

When Dinkman arrived at the station, his sense of self-importance and bravado had stiffened his backbone. He sat down in the interview room defiantly and glared at his interrogators.

Gerry also sat down and nodded to Peersen to indicate that he should begin the cross-examination. He felt that his partner was more effective at intimidating an uncooperative witness.

"Mr. Dinkman," Peersen began in an authoritative voice, "we have become aware that you have been withholding information that is vital to the Stritch investigation. I am granting you a final chance to answer our questions before we arrest you."

Dinkman continued to stare angrily at the detectives. "I have been cooperative and professional in every aspect of this investigation and informed you of everything that I am able to relate within the boundaries of my position as vice-principal of York Collegiate Institute." He puffed with pride as he utter the final few words.

"Bull shit! You have edited everything you told us and withheld pertinent details."

"Such as?"

Thomson had told his partner about Miss Taylor's pregnancy, which he had learned from his wife who attended the same medical clinic as Miss Taylor. His wife had observed the math teacher entering the office of an obstetrician. If Miss Taylor were having an affair with another member of staff, it could create problems for her if someone, such as Miss Stritch, discovered the truth. Murder to cover up an affair, he considered unlikely, but not impossible.

Peersen continued. "You never told us that Miss Taylor was pregnant last year and gave birth to a child."

"I don't repeat staff gossip. And besides, why is her indiscretion of any interest to you?"

"Covering up an indiscretion, as you refer to it, might be motive for murder, if the father is on staff. Are you the father?"

"I don't court women tougher than I am."

"We know that. You prefer women you can spank. Perhaps you got her drunk."

"Are you enjoying yourself detective? I do not find this amusing. I wish to phone my lawyer now."

"Mr. Dinkman, you're welcome to make the call while we wait for the press to arrive. The chief of detectives will call them. He enjoys working with the press. The reporters should be here by the time we officially charge you. I'm glad you're wearing a dark suit and white shirt, as they will photograph well. I'm sure you'll want to make a good impression on the front page. The parents of the students will be cutting out the photo for their scrapbooks."

For the first time, Dinkman's self-assurance faltered. He harboured ambitions of replacing Gus when he retired or dropped dead from a heart attack while heaving his fat ass up to the second floor. The board would never consider appointing anyone with a hint of scandal attached to his reputation. Dinkman felt that he was a superior administrator, better than anyone in the system, but he also knew that appearances often counted more than skills.

"I refuse to be intimidated, but I'll try to be of assistance," he began. "I'm not certain how I can help you."

"Which members of staff are inclined to engage in illicit romantic affairs, other than yourself, of course?"

Dinkman grimaced at the insulting remark and appeared to ponder the question, but offered nothing.

"Does Sam Millford ever fool around with any of the women on staff?"

"Not to my knowledge."

"What about Greg Baldwin, the French teacher?"

Dinkman snorted in derision. "Him? If he ever decided to engage in an affair, it would more likely to be with another man."

Thomson and Peersen stored away this little snippet of gossip. Their suspicions that Baldwin might be homosexual appeared to have some merit. He might resort to murder to prevent someone from discovering his sexual preference. If the board of education knew of his secret, he would lose his job and his career, as homosexuality was against the law. Though Baldwin did not strike him as a man of violence, he had learned as a police officer that some of the most unlikely scenarios had a way of becoming a reality.

"What about Bill Matheson?"

"What about him?"

Peersen reminded him, "The odds of a photo of you appearing on the front pages of the newspapers are looking better all the time."

Gazing up at his inquisitors, Dinkman slowly wrung his hands, the knuckles turning white. He gazed at the door, knowing it would not open until the police were satisfied. Slowly, pondering his words carefully, he began.

"Bill Matheson is a good teacher and is popular with the staff. He is an excellent science teacher, and his students achieve good grades. During the last two years, his students have not won any awards at the regional science fairs, but the potential is there."

"Skip the staff evaluation."

"Bill has a violent temper and can be vindictive if you cross him. He knows private things about other staff members, as he hears gossip while the senior students are performing lab work. They chatter openly, not realizing that they can be overheard. The senior students provide the best information—they're older, more aware. Very little in the school escapes them. They notice odd behaviour, observe who converses intimately in the hallways, and because most of the teachers live within the community, they learn things about their private lives."

"Did he ever mention to you anything he overheard?"

"No!"

"What can you tell us about the art teacher and the librarian?"

"They're a trifle eccentric, but I cannot believe that they would have any knowledge that would assist you."

Peersen pressed a little harder. "Art teachers also overhear student conversations while they work at their desks on their projects. Has she ever told you about anything she overheard?"

Dinkman shook his head to indicate a negative response.

"Did Evanson have a boner for Miss Stritch?" Peersen knew he had pitched an unexpected curve ball and was being unnecessarily crude, but he needed to rattle the witness' cage.

Dinkman's eyes widened in shock, which quickly changed to derision.

Another half-hour passed by, but all the information was trivial. Peersen had waited a long time to put the screws to Dinkman, and nothing was achieved. Dinkman had been able to stonewall them. The disappointment on Peersen's face was obvious, as he said, "All right, you can go. For now!"

Thomson stood and opened the door for Dinkman.

Though Dinkman was aware that he had been lucky, he was unable to resist gloating. "I told you I knew nothing that would help you. You will not subject me to this type of rude behaviour again. If you do, I will refuse to appear without my lawyer."

"Well, now, we'll just see about that."

✧ ✧ ✧

Thomson arranged for Bill Matheson to appear at the police station at the end of the school day, as unlike Dinkman, he had classes to teach. He arrived shortly after five o'clock, showered, freshly shaven, and wearing Old Spice aftershave. Ruggedly handsome, he had recently had a brush cut, which added to his manly bearing, though it exposed more of the small bald spot on his crown. His brown eyes shone with authority, and the creases in the trousers of his navy blue suit were as sharp as a knife. The knot of his pale blue tie was precisely centred in the well-starched collar of the shirt, which was gleaming white. Whereas Dinkman derived his authority from his position within the educational hierarchy, Matheson's came from within him. He wore it as naturally as he did his suit and tie. He would not be easily intimidated.

Following the usual greetings, and thanking him for coming to the station, Thomson began the questioning. "Mr. Matheson, we need to ask you more questions concerning your fiancée."

"What do you wish to know, other than what I have already told you?"

"Are you certain that no one can verify your statement that you were at the cottage for a full week and never returned to the city?"

"There might be someone. I cut the grass around the front of the cottage on Wednesday, and on Thursday afternoon, I repaired the dock. Someone might have noticed."

Matheson paused and then continued. "Besides, the mileage on my car's odometer would indicate that I did not drive sufficient miles to have been to Toronto and back more than once in that time period. Have you checked it?"

"How would we know your mileage figures? We need a base figure to calculate from, showing the mileage before you left the city."

"My mechanic is at the BA station at the corner of St. Clair and Bathurst. He will provide you with the figures."

Gerry gazed intently at Matheson, careful not to reveal that they had already checked the mileage figures. What bothered Thomson was the ease with which the information fit together, as if he had known in advance that they would check the figures. It was so convenient that he had taken his car in the day before leaving for the trip, and as well, he knew that it would appear to be natural. Most drivers serviced a car before a trip. Thomson decided to take another approach.

"How would you describe your relationship with Miss Stritch?"

"She was my fiancée."

"Yes, of course, but some couples have disagreements before the wedding, often caused by the in-laws-to-be." Thomson smiled as he added the latter point, remembering the days before his own marriage. Then he continued. "Some couples have last minute doubts, disagreements over the cost of the arrangements, differences about the choice of their first residence or the price of the honeymoon. Friction and marriage planning go together."

"We had no real problems. Ask her ex-roommate, Miss Taylor. She knew Elaine well and is able confirm my statement."

Another prearranged detail. He has a backup for everything, Thomson thought. To Matheson, he said, "Why did Miss Stritch not accompany you to the cottage?"

"As I previously stated, she had family obligations. Planning for a wedding is not easy. She had many details to check and arrangements to make."

"Why didn't you remain in the city to help her? Then, the both of you could have enjoyed a few days rest in Muskoka."

"I suggested such an arrangement, but she was adamant that 'I'd get in the way,' as she worded it. Like an obedient husband-to-be, I obeyed." Matheson gave a slight smile that implied, "You know how women are?"

"Miss Taylor has stated that Miss Stritch intended to travel to your cottage."

"I can't account for her misconception," Matheson replied.

Thomson continued. "Mr. Matheson, have you ever heard the students in your chemistry classes discussing members of staff?"

"Sometimes."

"Have you overheard anything that might be useful to us?"

"Such as?"

"Oh, something that might indicate that a teacher might be jealous of your fiancée. Someone who might have had a grudge against her or wish her harm. Think carefully. Sometimes the most off-handed or insignificant remark can be meaningful."

"Elaine was an angel. The staff and students loved her. I never heard even a hint of any student disliking her."

"Your fiancée was a beautiful woman. Might one of the older students have had a crush on her?"

Matheson knew where the questioning was leading. "You're suggesting that Elaine encouraged the puppy love of a student, arranged to meet him in the valley, and after a refusal of lovemaking, he killed her?"

Peersen now interjected. "We're certain that it was someone she knew. There were no signs of a struggle."

"Preposterous. Elaine would never have encouraged either a student or a member of staff. She was a loyal woman, knew her own mind, and had decided to marry me." Matheson appeared to have thrown in the latter comment as if marrying him was the greatest thing since sliced bread.

After another twenty minutes of questioning, Thomson glanced wearily at Peersen, and his partner knew from the look that he had no further questions. Without a word spoken, they both sensed that it was time to cut Matheson loose.

After they closed the door behind him, they sat down to commiserate. Peersen seated himself in the chair behind the desk, the light from the window behind him illuminating the pages of his logbook. Thumbing through the book and glancing over his notes, he realized that they revealed nothing new. It was, however, important that he carefully record the statements of each witness.

Lost in thought, Thomson slouched in his chair, his legs stretched out across the well-worn wooden floor. The daily cycle of life within the precinct was rotating once more. Filtering into the interview room were the sounds that habitually infused any police station at the end of another busy day. Typewriters clicked and clacked. Cursing erupted each time a detective hammered another mistake into the page of a report. Patrol officers of the night shift offered raunchy comments to those leaving the station, telling them to have a good night on the beat. For the incoming crew, their camaraderie hid the fears that during the night hours, one of them might put his life in danger. The departing men concealed their gratitude that for another day, none of them had drawn his gun.

Thomson regretted that up to this point, the interviews had produced no further clues. He still had no clear picture of the undercurrents that flowed beneath the staff relationships. As well, he had no proven motive for the murder. Miss Stritch had been beautiful, perhaps too beautiful. Jealousy, blackmail, passion, or some sort of sexual motive made the most sense. But there remained no proof.

Looking up at his partner, he sighed. "Well, I suppose we had better bring in the president of your fan club—the inimitable Miss Elizabeth Hitch. She might have heard something during her art classes."

"We'll bring her in tomorrow," Peersen replied in resignation.

"Why? Need time to boost your courage?"

"No, I need time to find some cast-iron underwear."

✧ ✧ ✧

In the late afternoon of the following day, in all her splendiferous glory, Miss Elizabeth Hitch sashayed into the police station. The burly desk sergeant, Muscles Malloy, whose real name was Patrick, almost swallowed his Juicy Fruit gum when the lime-green array of verdant splendor arrived at his desk.

Hitch was dressed as if she were attending the Queen's Plate at the new Woodbine Racetrack, rather than visiting a police station. Her flimsy green blouse revealed a dark green brassiere underneath the semi-transparent material. The brim of her green picture hat covered the top half of her face. Her dress rustled gently in the air from the precinct door, which a departing pickpocket, Harry the Ballman, had opened, anxious to continue his life of crime on the crowded streetcars of Toronto. With his release, no trouser pocket on the TTC would be safe. With the arrival of Miss Hitch, no trousers within the precinct, with or without pockets, would be safe either.

Malloy warily asked how he could help her, and she explained that she had a "date" with Detective Peersen. Relieved that the green bomb was not his responsibility, he smiled and told her, "Go to room fourteen, second door on your right. The detectives are waiting for you."

He had feared that the woman had lost her cat and he would have to console her. Relieved to see her saunter down the hall, he returned to his desk, anxious to attend to crimes that did not involve a butchered wardrobe.

She knocked on the door, and without waiting for a reply, she made a grand entrance into the interview room and regally ensconced herself in a chair facing the desk. Then she delicately pulled up her skirt and crossed her legs, making certain that Peersen caught a glimpse of her green underpants. Peersen was grateful that the sturdy metal desktop protected his own underpants.

Both detectives had reviewed Miss Hitch's application for employment at YCI and knew that as a student she had attended Etobicoke Collegiate. In high school, she had been a mediocre student, but she had displayed much creativity in the art program. After graduation, she had decorated display windows for the T. Eaton Company. When she had saved sufficient funds, she enrolled at the University of Toronto.

A year after her graduation, she presented her portfolio to the Ontario College of Art, and they accepted her. At the college, she was involved in a scandal with a male model. The man was too embarrassed to press charges. However, the incident was recorded in the college's student files. Being a "free spirit," as the files stated, another incident occurred. A female student accused Hitch of making improper advances. Again, the accusation was not proven, and they dropped the matter. After earning a teaching certificate at OCE, she taught at York Memorial Collegiate, Central Tech, and eventually transferred to YCI. The detectives were aware that the students of YCI referred to her as "Hot-Pants Hitch."

Thomson leaned congenially across the desk, smiled, and said in a friendly voice, "My dear Miss Hitch, how nice to see you again. We are reinterviewing everyone, in hopes that they might recall any further details about the death of Miss Stritch. Do you remember anything that might help us?"

"Not really."

"Can you shed any further light on the case? Even the smallest detail might help."

"No, not really."

"May I ask you a personal question? How would you assess Miss Stritch?"

"She was very beautiful," she conceded, "but the poor dear knew nothing about assembling a proper wardrobe. In fairness, most women share that fault."

"They're not as knowledgeable and tasteful in their selection of attire as you are, Miss Hitch."

She beamed with pleasure at the compliment, and delicately adjusted her over-ample skirt. Then she said in a conspiratorial tone, "I offered to help her select her wedding gown. She refused my help. I recommended that her bridal gown be purple, perfect for an autumn wedding, you know, the harvest, fertility, and all that."

Thomson could picture a purple bride rolling up the church aisle to the altar like a humungous grape. With a straight face he responded, "Her loss, I'm sure, Miss Hitch."

"How true," she cooed. "Ignoring my advice, she chose a gown of white." Then she added, "With the life she lived, one would think that she would have shunned the symbolic colour of chastity."

Gerry's eyes narrowed. Finally, someone who was willing to admit that the victim had not been as innocent as the other members of staff had portrayed her.

"Would you please clarify that statement?"

Hitch now became hesitant. She realized that she had said more than she had intended.

"Oh, you know how it is. Some women tend to sow a few wild oats."

"Are you able to tell us any specifics?"

"Nothing definite. Just an impression that I had."

"Did you ever hear the students discuss her in the art classes?"

"Just the usual students' wishful thinking. They said she was hot, and sometimes they alleged that she had given them inviting glances."

"Do you think she had close relations with any of the teachers other than her fiancé?" Gerry was now on a fishing expedition, selecting his words carefully.

"None that I was aware of. Of course, I think there are several chameleons on staff, and naturally I never know their intentions."

"What are chameleons?"

"You know; people who can change their sexual preference to suit the occasion. I am certainly not one of them. I prefer men! Always!"

"I rather suspected that was the case," Gerry said without any trace of sarcasm or amusement, despite knowing the details of her indiscretions while attending the Ontario College of Art as a student.

God, Peersen thought, *Gerry is amazing.*

"Could you elaborate about the chameleons?" Thomson continued.

"Not really. It's only a feeling that I have. I certainly would never accuse anyone. I am not that type of person. I think that women should be discreet and never attract attention to themselves. I am sorry, but I cannot say anything more."

During the next ten minutes or so, despite Gerry Thomson's persistent questioning, he was unable to elicit any useful information. He sensed that she felt that she had said too much already and was determined not to divulge anything further. When she retreated into talking about where she bought her green lipstick, Gerry realized it was time to end the interview.

As Peersen held the door open for her, the "Venus Flytrap" of York Collegiate Institute sallied forth. He watched as she fluttered down the hallway toward the outside door, as if seeking any prey that floated on the breeze.

An elderly patrolman gave her an unsolicited wolf whistle.

A man of dubious taste but great bravery, thought Sergeant Patrick

Malloy as he gazed at the patrolman. As Miss Hitch disappeared from view, Malloy shuddered. The thought of being swallowed within the depths of her greenery was too horrible a fate to contemplate.

✧ ✧ ✧

Miss Bettina Taylor was the next member of staff whom they invited to the interview room. She entered the room walking ramrod straight, removed her spring jacket, threw it across the chair, and sat down.

A defiant one, Thomson thought.

Seated, she exhibited perfect posture. If people saw her in a staff photo and were unfamiliar with the group, they would likely have assumed she was a physical training instructor rather than a math teacher.

Miss Taylor was wearing a sleeveless blouse, her bare arms well proportioned and muscular. The ample breasts beneath the blouse were firm. She wore no makeup, and her hair was pulled back tightly into a bun. The dark circles and bags under her eyes betrayed that she had not been sleeping well. As she gazed at her inquisitors, she clenched her mouth, her eyes displaying determination and a trace of arrogance.

"Miss Taylor," Thomson began, "we are reviewing everyone's statements, hoping to uncover some small details that we might have overlooked or something that a witness may have forgotten to mention."

"I overlooked nothing. I have already informed you of everything I consider pertinent."

Gerry knew he must be careful with his next statement. "Miss Taylor, we are aware of the indiscretion that created the need for you to visit British Columbia last summer."

Her eyes narrowed. "I see no reason to share details of my personal life with you. It's none of your business."

"Anything in a homicide is my business," Gerry replied in a tone of authority.

Bettina was unfazed and merely glared at him belligerently.

Peersen now decided to enter into the interrogation. He knew he was dealing with a highly intelligent woman. He liked bright women, and despite the cold façade, he rather liked Miss Taylor. *Is she harbouring a secret, and is it taking its toll on her?* he wondered.

"Miss Taylor, how close was your friendship with Miss Stritch?"

"We were roommates and good friends."

"Did you share activities in your spare time? Double date? Belong to the same clubs? Share the same circle of friends?"

Peersen wasn't certain, but he thought he detected a trace of tenderness, remorse, or perhaps even nostalgia in her face. He wasn't certain. It was several moments before she replied.

"We were good friends," she repeated. Then she added in a monotone voice, "Elaine was always considerate, had a pleasant personality, and paid her share of the rent on time."

Peersen noted that she had not answered the question, but he considered it an interesting reply.

"Did you approve of her engagement to Bill Matheson?"

Her eyes widened ever so slightly, but Peersen noticed the reaction. She was unable to hide the discomfort that the question had created, but within seconds, she had regained her composure.

"It was none of my business."

"Certainly, but you had thoughts on the subject."

"Those are none of your business."

"Would you confirm again for me the time that Miss Stritch departed from your apartment on the night of 31 August?"

"About 5:45 p.m. I remember we ate supper early that evening, as Elaine said she was driving to Muskoka to be with her fiancé, and she wanted to arrive there not too late. As I told you previously, I spent the evening in the company of my friend, Mary Allyson. I am certain that you have already verified this. Now, if you have no more questions, I'll be on my way."

Then, without asking permission, Miss Taylor stood, reached for her jacket, and strode toward the door. Thomson was dumbfounded. As she exited the stage, she turned, gazed directly at Gerry, and delivered her parting line.

"I've said all I intend to on the matter. If there's a need for another interview, I'll bring my lawyer."

As the door closed behind her, Peersen thought, *She's the only witness so far who has walked out on us. Boy, does she have balls.*

"That was certainly a brief interview," Gerry said, incredulity in his voice.

"Yes, and useless," Jim added, even though he had difficulty suppressing his smile.

◇ ◇ ◇

The final witness of the afternoon was Gregory "Baldy" Baldwin, the whistling French teacher. His students joked that if he taught German, he would have yodeled when he introduced the day's vocabulary. They were grateful that he did not teach Italian, as few of them had yet acquired a taste for opera and wished to hear the day's vocab sang as an aria.

The speech difficulty that caused the students of YCI to ridicule Baldwin had been his cross to bear since he had been a child. The file that the detectives had created on him, the information supplemented by the family's neighbours, revealed that he was the younger of two sons, born to a wealthy English family. They owned a mansion in the exclusive Rosedale area of the city. Though Gregory had displayed intelligence at an early age, he failed to qualify to attend Upper Canada College. Because his family had immigrated to Canada only ten years before, they lacked the influential connections to place pressure on the headmaster to admit him. Attending a public school, the other children teased Gregory. Finally, his parents withdrew him from the system and hired private tutors. They discovered that he excelled in foreign languages, particularly French. During his teenage years, French became his true delight. His accomplishments in the language provided him with a sense of superiority that compensated for his other failings. Unfortunately, he soon lorded his superior ability over those around him and ordered them about in French. Even as a child, the neighbours viewed him as an insufferable snob.

At the University of Toronto, Gregory was more fluent in French than some of his professors. He was a member of the university's French club, but because of his offensive attitude, he was never elected its president, a position he highly coveted. Graduating with a master's degree, he condescended to take the teacher-training course at OCE.

Gregory had commenced his teaching career at Etobicoke Collegiate. At the end of his second year, the principal informed him he would not recommend him for a permanent contract. He relocated to Humberside Collegiate, and eventually to YCI. By the time he began teaching at YCI, he had finally mellowed to a certain degree. Within a few months of being on staff, Gregory had one or two close friends, Miss Stritch one of them. However, the students were wary of him, as within the classroom he remained haughty and uttered sarcastic comments.

At the police station, when Mr. Baldwin walked into the interview room, he was wearing a fashionable shark's-tooth, continental gray suit, a pale pink shirt, and a bold burgundy tie with a matching breast-pocket handkerchief. His tie clip, gaudy and oversized, appeared to be solid gold. As he seated himself, he crossed his long stork-like legs, revealing his pink socks and immaculately shined black loafers.

Very French, Peersen thought.

Peersen knew the brand name of the suit and knew where Baldy had purchased it—at an expensive shop on Bloor Street West, between Yonge and Bay Streets.

Peersen opened the interview. "Mr. Baldwin, were you close with Miss Stritch?"

"She was a dear friend."

"Did you ever date her, prior to her becoming close to Bill Matheson?"

"We went to the theatre, the symphony at Massey Hall, and an occasional movie."

"Were you ever intimate?"

"A gentleman never tells," he replied with a sly smile, implying an answer without saying a word. The detectives wondered if he was bragging.

"How long did this go on?"

"I never said anything went on, except the symphony, et cetera." He waved his hand flamboyantly in a repeated motion to emphasize the "et cetera." The slight whistling in his voice was now more pronounced.

"You said in your original statement that you had no idea why Miss Stritch did not go to the cottage to spend time with her fiancé. Have any further thoughts crossed your mind?"

"No, although I sensed a few things. But, of course, feelings are not evidence, so I never said anything."

"Would you share these feelings with us?"

A trace of alarm appeared on his face.

"I thought the police were only interested in proven facts."

"True, but sometimes we learn facts by listening to speculations."

"Well," he began hesitantly, "I had the feeling that Bill was not the only love of her life. I don't mean to imply that she was unfaithful, but at times, from some of the conversations we had over a cup of coffee, I sensed that there was someone in the background. I don't know who it was or even if there was another person. It was simply a feeling."

"I see," Peersen said sympathetically. "I am certain that you are a sensitive man and very perceptive. If you really thought about it, I think you might be able to take a guess."

Baldwin sat up in the chair and smoothed back his hair with his left hand, exposing the French cuffs and gold cuff links on his shirt. Then he uncrossed his legs and crossed them again in the opposite position. Adjusting his pant cuff to expose the sock more, he completed his preening and gazed again at Peersen.

"I thank you for the vote of confidence, but I really don't think I can be of any further help. While Miss Stritch was on staff, she displayed exemplary behaviour, at all times."

The bloody word "exemplary" again, Peersen thought. Then, hoping to rattle him, Peersen delivered a brutal shot across Baldwin's bow. "Sir, are you a homosexual?"

Startled, Baldwin's composure slipped, and he gazed in contempt at his accuser.

Baldwin remembered the time a bartender in the lounge at the King Edward Hotel had taken a liking to him. The cheeky young man had leaned across the bar and whispered, "I give a 50 percent discount to homosexuals."

"If I see any, I'll tell them," he had replied tersely.

On this occasion, Baldwin said nothing.

The interview droned on for another half-hour, but the detectives learned nothing more of interest. Baldwin confirmed that he had known Miss Stritch well and knew details about her personal life, but he had no clue with whom she was intimate. Peersen thought it was unlikely that Baldwin and Stritch had once been lovers, but it was not out of the question.

Finally, Thomson signalled that they should terminate the interview.

After Baldwin had departed, the scent of his cologne lingered in the room. Peersen asked his partner, "Do you think he's a homosexual?"

"Who can tell? When a man has spent considerable time in France, the end result is pretty much the same."

"I hope the term 'end result' is not a pun."

Ignoring the remark, Thomson added, "The guy does have a fancy wardrobe, and expensive too."

"So have I," Peersen responded.

"Well, in truth, sometimes I do wonder about your sexual proclivities."

They both grinned.

The grins also revealed their pleasure at having discovered an interesting speculation. There might have been a third party in the love life of Elaine Stritch.

✧ ✧ ✧

The following afternoon, Mr. Samuel S. Millford, the PT teacher, marched into the interview room. He had combed his thick dark hair more meticulously than an old maid arranged her knickers for a parson's tea party. Millford forcefully seized a chair, sat down, and gazed directly at Thomson and Peersen like a soldier facing a superior officer—erect and expressionless. Peersen half expected the man to shout, "Colonel Millford reporting for duty, sir!"

Thomson recognized his type, having encountered many such men when he had served overseas in the army. They were usually harmless, and though officious, they gave new meaning to the term "anal retentive." Thomson decided to be direct, as it was the best approach with this type of individual.

"Mr. Millford, state your relationship with Miss Stritch."

"We were friends."

"Were you and she intimate?"

"I dated her twenty-eight times, over a period of eleven months, three weeks, and four days. By mutual consent, we agreed to terminate the dating. We remained friends."

Thomson noted that Millford had avoided answering the question.

"Were you intimate?"

"Yes!" Millford never batted an eyelash. Gerry wondered why he had not answered the question the first time.

"Were you aware that she was seeing another man during that time period?"

Thomson was now fishing, trying to determine if in fact Miss Stritch had been playing the field while she was in a relationship with him. Baldwin's remarks had opened up the possibility.

"No! She dated me exclusively."

"How do you know?"

"I simply know!"

"Did she ever date anyone else on staff other than you?"

"After our relationship ended, she began dating Bill Matheson. Elaine was friends with Greg Baldwin, but it was platonic. They often met for coffee after school, and they also attended the theatre."

"Were you aware of anyone she dated who was not on staff?"

"I have been on staff for five years, and she had been at YCI for eight years. I do not know much about the men she saw during the years prior to our relationship, other than their first names."

"What were they?"

"Frank, Tony, Peter, Manuel, Gerry, Eddie, and Larry."

"You remember all those names?"

"I have an excellent memory."

"Know any of their surnames?"

"No."

"Who would you say was her closest female friend on staff?"

"She was closest to Bettina Taylor, her roommate."

"Were there any staff members who appeared to dislike her?"

"No. Elaine was a beautiful woman with an outgoing personality. She was loyal to her friends and respected by all. She led an exemplary life."

Thomson and Peersen noted the word "exemplary" being employed again to describe Miss Stritch, and they inwardly groaned.

Ten minutes of more carefully crafted questions revealed nothing new. The detectives thanked Millford for his cooperation and dismissed him, almost expecting him to salute before he departed.

After the door closed, Thomson said, "What do you think, Jim?"

"Typical PT teacher. I bet he keeps his spare change at home in a jockstrap and enjoys sex to the military rhythms of the march 'The Maple Leaf Forever.'"

Thomson chuckled. "Yeah! He's Mr. Joe Jock, but I have a feeling that he harboured strong feelings for Stritch long after their affair ended. It gives him a motive."

"True. He listed the men in her life as if they were inscribed in stone on a biblical tablet."

"Or a tombstone."

"He's also a tactician, knows how to plan and implement a strategy."

"I believe that our friend Millford bears watching."

"Yes. And we also learned that our innocent Miss Elaine Stritch was a very busy woman."

"Busy indeed!"

◇ ◇ ◇

Five minutes after Mr. Millford departed, Miss Mary Allyson, the blubbering librarian, floated into the interview room. Thomson gazed at her thoughtfully, and the only word that came to mind was "frumpy." The brown sweater and dark beige skirt she was wearing were drab, and her brown, clunky, oxford-style shoes added to the colourless outfit. On this occasion, she had pulled her hair tightly into a bun at the back of her head, and her pale complexion begged for a little sunlight to give it some semblance of life.

Thomson knew details about Miss Allyson's background from his own investigation, as well as Dinkman's files, which contained the application form that she had filled out when she had applied to YCI. She was a Toronto girl, born and raised on Rosemount Avenue, in the Earlscourt District of Toronto. When she was a teenager, they had caught her shoplifting two novels from the Coles Book Store at 728 Yonge Street. Because of her age, and since it was her first offense, the store did not press charges.

When Mary Allyson attended the University of Toronto, she filed a complaint against a male student for sexual harassment. A judge issued a restraining order. She graduated from the University of Toronto with a degree in library sciences, and then attended OCE. Her first teaching position was at Oakwood Collegiate, where she met Bettina Taylor. The detectives had already noticed that several of the staff members at YCI, including Dinkman, had previously taught at Oakwood. Coincidence? Taylor departed from Oakwood Collegiate to teach at YCI, and the following year, Miss Allyson moved to the same staff as that of her friend.

Thomson gazed at Allyson as she sat on a chair in the interview room and wondered about the woman behind the façade. Several minutes into the questioning, the tears began to flow. Waves of sobs erupted, and heavy tears flooded down her cheeks like surf rolling over a beach. He found it difficult to understand a word she said. It crossed his mind that perhaps Allyson's weeping was an armour she conveniently retreated behind to prevent any unwanted intrusion into the woman beneath the shield.

They tried every trick, maneuver, and tactic to calm her, but nothing short of a gallon of morphine would have lessened the shaking of her body and the cries of distress from the overwrought woman.

Finally, in deference to her mature years, and fearing soiled trouser legs from salt stains as well as the possible threat of drowning in the mounting waves that were bubbling like a tsunami, they released her and escorted her to the door. She drifted down the hallway like flotsam on a spring tide.

Out of sight of the station, Miss Allyson hastily dried her eyes. She grinned slightly, as if to imply, they'll get nothing out of me.

⟡ ⟡ ⟡

The interview with Anthony Bowler, whom they had learned the staff referred to as Randy Andy, was brief. Thomson and Peersen were aware of his background. Bowler had been born in Leeds in northern England and earned an MA degree from the University of Leeds. He taught in the public school system where the wealthy and privileged teenagers of the area received their education.

After a messy divorce, he immigrated to Canada, where he found employment at the Canada Bread Company, in their offices near the Lakeshore Road. He attended summer courses to receive his Canadian qualifications to teach at the secondary school level and first taught at Humberside Collegiate. After three years, he transferred to YCI.

Despite exhaustive questioning, Bowler revealed nothing during the interview that either involved or exonerated him in the murder of Elaine Stritch. However, Peersen wondered what had happened in Bowler's marriage that had caused the bitter divorce. Most marital problems, Peersen believed, originated in the bedroom. Despite Bowler's prim and proper façade, did he have sexual problems that he satiated in unusual or kinky behaviour?

⟡ ⟡ ⟡

The final witness of the inner group that they interviewed was Miss Gayle Manson. Unlike her male counterpart in the gym department, she was not the stereotype of a PT teacher. She was in excellent physical shape, her arms and legs muscular, but in the manner of a tennis player, not a weightlifter. She wore her light brown hair at shoulder length, and the faint touches of makeup gave her an attractive feminine quality. The woman had class!

Gayle Manson had been born into a wealthy family, the second youngest of four children. She had attended Bishop Strachan School as a teenager and later, the University of Toronto. While at university, she had been active in the varsity sports' programs and graduated with an MA degree in geography.

After university, through her family connections, she secured an administrative position at Birk's, the city's most prestigious chain of crystal, china, and jewellery stores. During the years she worked a Birk's, she joined WASE—Women Against Sexual Exploitation. She led several demonstrations at Queen's Park, and the police arrested her twice. Finally, she quit her job, attended OCE, and secured a position at Oakwood Collegiate. Though Manson's academic background was geography, she attended summer courses to qualify as a girl's PT teacher. In this position, she continued to push her feminist ideas.

Peersen thought, *Miss Manson looks more like an English teacher familiar with Wordsworth and Chaucer than the world of gym mats and basketball courts. Now Miss Taylor, on the other hand … However, I suspect that she is not the Goody Two-Shoes she appears to be on the surface. There's real fire beneath the façade she presents to the public. As well, she is another teacher who came to YCI from Oakwood Collegiate. Again, Dinkman was the one who hired her.*

Peersen also noted that Miss Manson's shade of lipstick was the same colour as the tube they had found on the pathway in the Humber Valley. Coincidence?

The interview went smoothly. Miss Manson was articulate and a shrewd observer of people. She was cooperative, and her insights about staff members coincided with the opinions of the detectives, but she provided no new information.

A half-hour after she had arrived, Miss Manson departed. As she passed by the desk of Sergeant Malloy, he approvingly watched her slim athletic body pass through the large doors, while a blushing rookie cop held them open for her.

✧ ✧ ✧

As spring edged closer to its zenith, the basketball season was nearing an end. Gus had extended Shorty's suspended sentence and allowed him to play on the basketball team. YCI had done well against their opponents in the league: Earl Haig, Scarborough, Vaughan Road, Leaside, East York, and Forest Hill.

YCI's team eliminated Forest Hill in the semifinals and trounced Earl Haig in the finals by a score of seventy-eight to fifty-six. Harry scored twenty-eight points, and Shorty added twenty more to the winning total. Kramer managed eight points, three of the baskets achieved on passes from Harry.

However, in the interleague finals, YCI lost by four points. Despite the defeat, Tom heard that Coach Millford had congratulated the team, praised Harry and Shorty for their leadership and team sportsmanship, and, in addition, had given Kramer a favourable mention.

In the days following the final game, despite the relatively successful season, the students were not in an upbeat mood. By now, they knew that the police had again hauled several of their teachers in for questioning. Ugly rumours again spread like wildfire.

Meanwhile, Carol was pleased that during the previous month, Harry had been dating her more regularly. Whenever the guys on the basketball team went somewhere, Carol was his date. Some afternoons, the two of them visited a restaurant on St. Clair, near Oakwood—the Paragon. There they sat in a cozy booth and sipped on a Cherry Coke or a tall glass of soda water with fresh lime juice.

Shorty had no regular girlfriend. As a popular member of the football and basketball teams, he had his choice of many girls, and he was playing the field. Though everyone still called him Shorty, he was now six feet tall with broad shoulders and well-muscled arms.

Tom envied Shorty when he heard a girl say, "His smile melts my bobby socks right down into my penny loafers."

Another girl added, "His smile melts my panties, never mind my socks."

They giggled conspiratorially.

Many girls considered Shorty a hunk!

✦ ✦ ✦

The weather warmed as the fullness of spring spread across the city, and at lunchtime, on sunny days, many of the students chose to take their lunches outside and sit on the lawn at the front of the school. One pleasant day, Shorty, Harry, Patrick, Sophie, Carol, and Tom all had the same lunch period, and they arranged to meet at the front of the school. They seated themselves on the grass, chatted, and enjoyed the spring sunshine. Then they noticed that students were gazing up at the flagpole and laughing.

Halfway up the pole, attached to the rope that hoisted the flag up and down, someone had attached a pair of white women's bloomers. They had clipped them to a coat hanger, causing the cloth of the bloomers to be stretched wide, allowing sufficient space for the words "Pansy Patrick" to be written in large bold letters.

Sophie was the first in the group to see the bloomers. She attempted to keep Patrick's attention diverted, while she nodded for Harry and Shorty to take down the offensive display. Of course, it was impossible to distract Patrick long enough. He saw them and turned deathly white. Harry quickly went over to the flagpole and cupped his hands for Shorty to step up onto his shoulders. By stretching his full length, Shorty managed to grasp the bottom corner of the bloomers and rip them from their perch.

When Harry returned to the group, he was seething. Shorty was calmer, but it was obvious that he was angry as well. Harry motioned for Sophie to accompany Patrick inside the school. If the pranksters knew that they had upset him, the teasing would increase. Harry instinctively knew that Kramer was responsible, either for the actual deed or as the instigator.

Harry told Shorty, ice audible in his voice, "Meet me after the last period, at the bicycle racks, where Kramer parks his bike."

After school, Kramer was hastily unlocking his bicycle to facilitate a quick retreat from the grounds. Two of his buddies were with him. Harry and Shorty acted quickly.

The "Kraut and the Jew" fighting team, as the bullies in the schoolyard had derogatorily tagged them during their elementary school days, flew into action. Shorty separated Kramer's friends from him by pushing them aside and raised his fist in warning, should they try to intervene to assist Kramer. Just as Kramer was swinging his leg over the bike to escape, Harry grabbed him by the shirt collar and dragged him off the bike. Twirling him around, he pinned his arm behind his back and marched him out of hearing distance of his friends. Though dragging his feet, Kramer had no choice but to comply, as otherwise, he was sure that Harry would break his arm. When they were a short distance beyond the bicycle rack, Harry dropped Kramer to the ground.

"Though I feel like pounding the hell out of you, I'll give you a chance to do the right thing. Leave Patrick alone."

"Go to hell!" Kramer snarled.

Refusing to give up without a fight, Kramer stood up and threw a wild punch, delivering a stinging blow to Harry's right cheek. Although Harry felt its effects, he had dodged backward, softening its impact.

Kramer now swung again, but he failed to connect. Harry struck him a devastating punch to his stomach. Winded but still fighting, Kramer came at Harry, and again Harry sent him toppling to the ground. This time, Kramer did not get up.

Harry measured his words as he spoke between gritted teeth. "Kramer, old buddy, we are about to arrive at a settlement that will be best for everyone. Listen carefully. I will not repeat myself.

"You will never again tease Patrick or tell anyone else to ridicule him. If anyone ever again makes fun of him, I'll hold you responsible. I don't care if you are guilty or not. If anyone teases him, I will assume it's your doing, and I'll come looking for you. It's not only in your interest not to make fun of him, but to prevent anyone else from doing so as well. Do I make myself clear?"

Kramer said nothing, but seeing the rage in Harry's eyes, he nodded sullenly in reluctant compliance.

"Besides," Harry continued, "I've noticed that you hang around the cafeteria staring across at the lockers when the guys are returning from the showers. I may start a few rumours of my own."

Kramer glared back, a spark of defiance rising within him. "No one will believe you."

"They will when I start the rumour."

Harry turned and walked away. Kramer watched him retreat, an odd look on his face, his eyes containing a strange glow.

✧ ✧ ✧

Frank Gnomes was aware of the exhaustive interviews Thomson and Peersen had conducted at the police station. Masters the Snitch had earned more money in the previous few weeks than in all the preceding six months.

Similar to the police, Frank's investigation centred on the teachers at YCI, and he too thought that the key to discovering the secrets of the staff was Vice-Principal Richard Dinkman. The only access to Dinkman was through Miss Samantha "Spankie" Anderson. He decided to return to the Gymnasium Club.

When Frank appeared at the club, Anderson scrupulously ignored him. Frank noted her reaction and thought, *If a look could freeze, my dick would now be a Popsicle.*

The following week, Frank visited the club on two evenings, each time careful not to gaze directly at Samantha or approach her. Instead, he faithfully worked out. The next week, on the third evening, he noticed that she had resumed her business activities and seemed to be less aware of his presence.

Sometimes Frank looked around at the other women in the club. He had heard that hookers frequented the place, but he never saw any. There were always a few attractive women, but they ignored the men and seemed to keep to themselves.

A month after first visiting the club, he was sitting having a coffee. He noticed a prominent politician chatting with two other men. Frank admitted that he was enjoying his workouts, and in the short time he had been exercising, he felt better than he had in years. He had lost eight pounds. Engrossed in thought and congratulating himself on his perseverance, he failed to notice that Miss Anderson had seated herself in the chair opposite him.

"What are you after Mr. Gnomes? I've told you that I only saw Mr. Dinkman once. You're wasting your time following me."

"I am enjoying exercising here, and I don't think it's a waste of time."

"You're playing games. We both know why you're here at the club."

"Okay! True! But I am enjoying the exercise."

Frank grinned and felt her chill thaw slightly. He brushed a lock of hair from his forehead and smiled once more. Gazing intently at her, he again noticed how attractive she was. She reminded him of the movie star June Allyson—pert, dainty, and wholesome with a cute little nose and a shy smile. As well, she had a great body, a result of many hours of exercise while she attracted clients. She really appealed to him.

"What will it take to get you off my back?"

Frank resisted telling her that he would like to get her *on* her back. "I simply want to go over the details of your conversation with Old Dickhead, but I'd settle for a friendly smile and a shared cup of coffee. There's no one left here in the club, so why don't we get out of here? I know a coffee shop that's open late. My car's parked nearby."

"Thanks, but no thanks," she replied.

Frank detected less chill in her voice and was certain that she was warming to him. *I might still get the lowdown on Dickhead Dinkman,* he thought with a grin.

The following week, Samantha consented to have coffee with him outside the club. Frank helped Spankie Anderson remove her coat before she slid into a booth at Fran's Coffee Shop on St. Clair Avenue, west of Yonge Street.

The week after that, things improved even further. Anderson and Dinkman conversed animatedly as they walked to his car and journeyed north on Yonge Street to her apartment. They had a drink, but nothing further happened. Although he had not obtained any useful information, he thoroughly enjoyed the encounter.

✧ ✧ ✧

As the sunshine of May increased, the scented lilacs drooped heavily over the garden fences along the Amherst laneway, where in earlier years Tom and his friends had played kick-the-can and hide-and-go-seek. The apple trees in the backyard orchards burst their glossy buds, transforming the barren trees into a sea of white.

Even though Tom no longer delivered newspapers, he was aware of events since most evenings his dad commented on the news in the *Toronto Star*. Many articles were about the preparations for the coronation. The British government had announced that they had set the date for Tuesday, 2 June, and during the final weeks of May, the anticipation was building.

One evening during the final week of the month, Tom's dad had not arrived home yet from work. Tom's mom seemed unconcerned as she told him that she had delayed supper. Tom knew that his dad had taken the car to work that morning and was puzzled when his mom said that his dad would arrive home later than usual.

A half-hour later, Tom heard the car in the driveway. It stopped beside the back door instead of proceeding into the garage. He glanced out the sun porch window and saw his dad opening the trunk of the Pontiac. There—in all its glorious splendour—was a television set.

It was an Admiral seventeen-inch floor model that had been on sale, reduced from $299 to $248. Its walnut veneer covering glistened in the late-day sun flooding the narrow driveway, the rays splashing across the TV set. After Tom's dad carried the TV and the base on which it sat inside the living room, he assembled the two sections and attached the rabbit-ears antenna. As Ken and Tom gazed at the family's newest acquisition expectantly, images raced in their heads.

The TV would transform their home into a movie theatre. They thought of all the stars and celebrities that would dance before their eyes. Even the queen would enter their home through the amazing technology of this simple box of wood with a cathode ray tube inside. Recently, the broadcasting system had improved reception through a microwave relay network that connected Montreal, Toronto, and Buffalo.

Howdy Doody, *The Lone Ranger*, *William Bendix*, and *Sagebrush Trail* were now open to them. TV commercials would also enter their world. The first time they viewed the screen, the Royal Bank advertised their two branches in London where Canadians attending the coronation could cash travellers' cheques. As well, they offered safety deposit boxes to safeguard cash.

A newscaster on TV station CBLT (the CBC), channel six, announced that they would fly the films of the coronation from London to Canada, employing three bomber jets. One of the pilots was Flight-Lieutenant S. P. Gulyas of Dunnville, Ontario, who would transport the films across the Atlantic to Goose Bay, Newfoundland, and then a CF100 jet would whisk them to Montreal. Newspapers in Toronto had their own planes to bring them to the city.

Excitement in the media industry was intense. The queen had decided to allow cameras and floodlights into Westminster Abbey, meaning that this would be the first time in history that they had ever filmed a coronation. In Toronto, CBLT would commence the day's proceedings on Tuesday, 2 June at 2:00 p.m. local time, and at 4:00 p.m., the queen's prerecorded speech. The actual coronation would air at 4:15 p.m. The media had arranged that the CBC would feed the US networks through Boston. Radio station CFRB in Toronto would commence broadcasting at 5:00 a.m. and repeat the two-and-a-half-hour ceremony until midnight.

For Tom, the world of YCI, murderous teachers, the bully Kramer, and pompous Gus Evanson all disappeared from his consciousness. Similar to the rest of the nation, nothing else existed. Tom held his breath and awaited the pomp and majesty of the coronation.

✧ ✧ ✧

The warm weather of June was not comforting for the stalker. With the return of the sunshine, the streets of Toronto were alive with people displaying young bodies that they no longer wrapped in heavy clothing. Flimsy blouses, thin T-shirts, and short shorts appeared on any street where pedestrians strolled. The sun's rays transformed the pale skin of winter into the bronzed beauty of summer. Those who overexposed their bodies turned bright red, reminding the stalker of the crimson blood that pulsed below the skin.

The sunlit days of June also delivered long evenings and lingering twilights. Though it was past 9:00 p.m., as the stalker sat on a bench on the roadway near the north gate of High Park, the soft light of evening lingered in the northern sky. Sitting and watching the people stroll past, the stalker noticed several possible victims.

Then, as the final embers of light drained from the sky and the fullness of night descended, the stalker noticed a white convertible pass along the roadway. The stalker recognized the girl behind the wheel and saw that she was alone. Her short dark hair blew enchantingly in the wind created by the forward motion of the sleek Buick, and she raised her right hand to brush it back from her face. The stalker rose from the bench and walked in the same direction as the car.

When the stalker reached the Grenadier Restaurant, the white Buick was in the parking lot. The girl was nowhere in sight. The stalker wondered if she had walked southward along the path beside the park's rose garden and hoped she had descended the hill toward Grenadier Pond. Employing a narrow path that led to the north side of the pond, the stalker proceeded down toward the area where the bulrushes grew abundantly.

Sandra Beaumont's parents and younger brother had again departed for Europe for an extended holiday. The previous year they had visited the Greek Islands, and they were now in southern Italy. However, this year while they were away, they had commandeered Sandra's nosey Aunt Emily to live in the house with her until they returned. Sandra found the woman intolerable. This was why she was out at such a late hour.

Apart from her aunt, her life was unfolding pleasantly. Sandra had completed the first year of the nurses' assistant course and had a certificate from the French summer course she had taken. The following week she had her first interview for employment with Trans Canada Airlines.

She was lost in thought as she strolled along the narrow path beside the pond and was unaware that she had departed from the section lit by the sole lamppost at this end of the trail. Total darkness now surrounded her. The bulrushes rustled in the warm evening breezes, only the mating calls of the bullfrogs that inhabited the shallow waters surrounding the pond's edge rising above the gentle night sounds.

Sandra never heard the stalker approach. She was grabbed from behind, and her nose and mouth held securely shut. Though she was athletic, her arms and legs strengthened by long hours on the tennis court, she soon fell unconscious from a lack of oxygen. Within seconds, eager fingers slid inside her panties, and a moment or two later, she was prostrate on the ground.

While Sandra was unconscious, the stalker's uncontrollable sexual urges were satiated. Then, the ritual of the bloodletting commenced. Employing the sharpened end of a tree branch, broken beforehand from a nearby willow, the stalker made several deep gashes in the left side of her neck but was careful that the laceration puncturing the carotid artery was extremely small, to prevent a sudden gush of blood erupting from the pulsating artery. The stalker then drained it into a glass container.

It was a technique similar to that employed to kill the drug addict, Moira Peters. However, in this instance, the stalker hoped that it would appear as if the attacker had not preplanned the murder but rather employed whatever weapon was handy, after the killer had raped the girl.

The task completed, the killer pinched the small hole in her neck closed, and with great effort, dragged the near-dead young girl as far away from the shoreline as possible. Her breathing was extremely slight when she was dropped facedown into the murky water among the bulrushes. The neck wound reopened, and the small amount of remaining blood in her body seeped slowly into the water. With any luck, it would be a day or two before they discovered the corpse, allowing decomposition to erase any evidence of the stalker's bloodletting.

Sandra Beaumont's remains, as the stalker preferred to refer to them, were not discovered for four days. Children attending a summer day camp in High Park were fishing at the north end of the pond and noticed a flock of red-winged blackbirds and crows fighting over something among the bulrushes a short distance from shore. As the water was shallow, two of the boys waded out to see what was attracting the birds. The shrieks of horror from the youngsters caused one of the staff members of the camp to investigate. He too was shocked and told one of the teenage assistants to rush up to the Grenadier Restaurant to phone the police.

When Thomson and Peersen arrived at the scene, Doctor Dicer gave an on-the-spot diagnosis, but he cautioned them that nothing was certain until after the autopsy.

"The reddening around the nose and mouth indicates that someone forcibly held something over her face to subdue her. The killer sexually assaulted her—the wounds around the vagina premortem. Later, the killer dragged her into the pond and pushed her head into the water. There are only trace amounts of water in her lungs, so she was barely alive when the murderer immersed her. The cut in her neck is troubling, as it is difficult to determine if it occurred when the murderer attacked her or due to natural causes after the victim was in the water. I found many sharp sticks and rocks near the body. The water has washed away the blood on them, as well as the blood from the wound, which seeped out into the pond. Although the cold water has slowed the process of decomposition, I'd estimate the time of death to be three to four days ago."

Thomson and Peersen wrote copious notes and pressed Doctor Dicer for further details. He bluntly told them to wait until he had completed the autopsy and abruptly vacated the crime scene. Two days later, when the detectives scanned the autopsy report, they learned very little new information. Dicer's on-the-spot opinion had been correct. Premortem bruising around the vagina confirmed that the killer had raped her, but the water had soaked away any blood and semen, as well as any other traces of evidence on the body.

Because there appeared to be no connection to the "Valley Vampire Murder," Thomson and Peersen opened another file and proceeded to investigate the murder as an unrelated crime.

Chapter Five

It is almost impossible to imagine the coronation fever that gripped Tom and his family. As an adult, Tom was to experience the hysteria that swept the city when Paul Henderson scored the winning goal in the Summit Series in the Soviet Union in 1972. Canada exploded with emotion. It became one of the most memorable moments of his life, even though there had been only sixty minutes of playing time and the build-up to the event relatively brief. He experienced this exhilaration again in February of 2010, when Sidney Crosby slammed in the overtime goal in the Vancouver Winter Olympics.

In fairness, Tom would now admit that it is difficult to compare the events. In 1972, when Henderson scored the winning goal, most Canadians owned TV sets. People huddled around them in their homes, and those at work watched the game in offices and factories. Children gathered in school auditoriums.

In 1953, few people owned a TV set. For weeks, the shops and major department stores of downtown Toronto had been frantically decorating their façades, doorways, and windows. Eaton's and Simpson's were festooned with flags, ribbons, and banners of red, white, and blue. The most popular designs were crowns, orbs, shields, and swords of state. The city's inner core resembled a royal court.

On Sunday, 31 May, normally a quiet day, thousands travelled downtown to gaze at the decorations. A reporter wrote that Yonge Street was "hell on wheels," as over ten thousand pedestrians and endless lines of automobiles jammed Yonge Street between Richmond and College Streets.

On the day prior to the big events, the business district remained crowded with gawkers. The TTC reported that the Monday evening rush hour traffic was worse than during a major snowstorm. Pandemonium ruled rather than Britannia.

◆ ◆ ◆

On 2 June, Coronation Day, as first light broke across Toronto, many had been awake since the early morning hours, having risen at five o'clock to hear the live broadcast of the ceremony on the BBC from London. As the sun crept ever higher in the sky, not a cloud marred the endless expanse of blue.

Because the first films of the coronation would not arrive until late afternoon, many people travelled downtown to attend public functions. As the morning progressed, below the heights of the city hall tower, a steady stream of people passed by, most having arrived downtown on the Yonge streetcars. The crowds surged toward University Avenue to reserve a position to watch the one-hour-long garrison parade, which would begin at eleven o'clock.

Not everyone gathered at University Avenue. By the hour of eleven, people lined the streets of the downtown, within a half-mile radius of Yonge and Queen Streets. Floating above the crowds were red, white, and blue balloons, their strings held tightly in the hands of young children. In the jostling, a few balloons escaped, the cries of disappointed youngsters unheard amid the din of the excited throngs. Many adults wore paper replicas of St. Edward's Crown, while others settled for less patriotic but more practical sun hats. It was rare to find an adult or child not clutching a flag. No painter could ever have created such a scene, or any camera capture a more animated spectacle.

By noon, the temperature had reached seventy-five degrees Fahrenheit, the sky spotlessly blue. Crowds were immense at the ferry docks, waiting to journey to the Toronto Islands. Private sailboats in the harbour were decorated with flags, pennants, and signals from bow to stern and hull to mast. All the YCYC yachts had been encouraged by the club to participate in the display. Even the Toronto ferries were trimmed in red, white, and blue. The harbour was a sea of patriotic colours.

✧ ✧ ✧

On this Coronation Day, the stalker scanned the pages of three of the major Toronto daily newspapers. The *Toronto Tribune* was ignored, as the stalker considered it a journalistic rag, though the articles of Frank Gnomes were interesting. In the other papers, every page was crammed with stories and photos of the regal event. After much searching, the stalker found that the *Globe and Mail* and the *Telegram* had mentioned the murder in High Park but had relegated it to the back pages of their evening editions.

The "Toronto News" section of the *Star* contained a picture of the police at the crime scene, and a brief article about the boys who had discovered the young woman's body. The article stated that the police had yet to reveal details of the case, and they were withholding the name of the victim pending notification of the parents, who were vacationing in Europe.

The stalker was confident that they would not link the recent murder with the death of Elaine Stritch.

✧ ✧ ✧

Not everyone was spending the coronation holiday attending celebrations. Jim Peersen was reclining in a comfortable chair on the second-floor deck of the Victorian mansion where he rented his four-room flat. He loved the location of the old house, on a quiet, tree-lined avenue in the Annex area. The deck overlooked a garden, surrounded by a wrought-iron fence, shaded by a young sugar maple and two mature silver maples. Several lilacs and a large mock orange bush flourished where the sun filtered through the leafy branches above.

Each May, Jim volunteered to assist his landlord in planting the annuals in the flowerbeds. He enjoyed the peace and calm of the garden. It was satisfying to handle the fragile begonias and petunias and place them in the soil. For him, gardening was therapeutic.

Spring was Jim's favourite season; its warmth and greenery rejuvenated him whenever he strolled along the streets of the Annex. The warm weather helped dispel the gloom he encountered in his profession. Within walking distance of his apartment, there were many restaurants and theatres, as well as the Royal Ontario Museum. The neighbourhood was secluded and private. Jim felt that his home environment insulated him from the turmoil of city life, just as springtime insulated him from thoughts of winter's stormy blasts.

At 4:00 p.m., he intended to turn on the TV and watch the ceremony in the abbey. He understood the significance of the sacred rites. Until the time for the event arrived, Jim decided to sit back and relax. The overhanging trees, alive with chattering birds, protected his second-storey wood deck from the glaring rays of the spring sun. The leafy giants also allowed the squirrels to scramble among the branches as they searched for anything that looked even close to palatable. They were not fussy, and when Jim was not out on the deck, they often gnawed on his clothes pegs and even the legs on one of his chairs. He disliked squirrels. The only things they planned for was another meal.

The ice cubes in Jim's glass of brandy tinkled as he raised it contemplatively to his lips. He thought of his boyhood days, when he and his parents had attended a Toronto congregation of the Evangelical Lutheran Free Church. It had been a long time since he had thought about his parents. They had been dead for over ten years now. Usually, he suppressed the memories of his youth, but because of his relaxed state of mind, aided by the brandy, they painfully surfaced.

Jim thought of his younger brother, Hendricks, killed by a stray bullet fired during a botched robbery at a bank on Bloor Street. Hendricks had been twelve years old, and Jim had been three years younger. The police had said it was a classic case of "being in the wrong place at the wrong time." But Hendricks had been returning from school, walking along the only route that led home. Where was he supposed to be? The pastor had said that his brother had gone to a better place. As a young boy, Peersen was unable to understand the logic. He still did not. The best place for his brother was with his family.

During the years ahead, Jim tried to understand the loss of his brother, never sharing his feelings with his parents. When he was older, he concluded that it was beyond his understanding. Life was simply a crapshoot, without any rhyme or reason. Peersen had also never shared his conclusions with his parents. When they died, aged beyond their years by the tragedy of losing a child through violence, it reinforced his belief that the twists and turns of fate were beyond man's control. To this day, he remained introspective and found it difficult to share his feelings with others.

One of the first things he learned to do when he kicked the restraints of the old-time religion of his parents was to enjoy a glass of wine. The wine eventually led him to the delights of brandy, and their expensive twin, the cognacs. On this day on his patio deck, as the cool liquid slipped smoothly down his throat, he savoured the aroma of burnt oak and appreciated the rich taste. It was indeed the nectar of the gods.

Peersen often spent much of his free time alone. The women he dated usually grew tired of the long hours that his employment demanded and his need for privacy. Jim was also aware that some of his female companions complained that he was too aloof, serious, and often uncommunicative. He admitted that he was not much fun for a night on the town.

They did not understand that his books, brandy, and downtime, all of which he rarely shared, were a necessity for him. They gave him time to heal the wounds that life inflicted. His favourite novels were those of the nineteenth-century novelist Thomas Hardy, whose stories about England's quiet rural past were almost as soothing as a fine cognac.

The previous Saturday evening, he and his latest girlfriend, Jill Carver, had attended the Oakwood Theatre to see *April in Paris*, starring Ray Bolger and Doris Day. It had been her choice of movie, not his. He considered it a decent enough film but not really to his taste. He had said little after the movie as they had coffee in the Paragon Restaurant on St. Clair Avenue, and she clearly had not been too pleased. She would likely not be dating him again. He had been quiet for a reason; other things occupied his mind.

In the past two years, he and Gerry had brought a child killer to justice, solved a double homicide in Forest Hill, caught a ring of cheque forgers, and tracked down a man who had killed a bank teller during a robbery. Each investigation had meant hours interviewing some of the worst deviants and criminals that society ever spawned. It was not a pretty world.

He should feel proud of his results. But he did not!

Peersen remembered the church teachings from his youth, that there was more joy in heaven when a lost soul was found than when a hundred entered who had never gone astray. He knew he did not have the wording correct, but he understood the sentiment. Though he had helped solve four major cases during the past two years, the one that he had not solved still bothered him. Elaine Stritch's murderer remained free.

Swirling the ice cubes in his glass, he smiled as he remembered that tomorrow was his day free from the precinct. A few minutes before four o'clock, he meandered inside to the book-lined den to turn on the TV set to watch the coronation, and left the deck to the squirrels.

✧ ✧ ✧

A sense of awe engulfed Tom and his family and friends as they gathered in the living room of the house on Lauder Avenue to watch the coronation. It was a mood never duplicated again, and thanks his grandfather, his family never forgot. Similar to others, they believed that the New Elizabethan Age would usher in a kinder, gentler, more enlightened world. Camelot seemed within reach.

Tom's dad had already switched on the TV when the he and his friends entered the Hudson's living room. The grainy, black and white picture displayed wavy lines, and his dad was adjusting the tracking knob at the back of the set. Finally, the picture was reasonably clear.

Shorty whispered to Tom, "Shit, man! I wish I had some popcorn."

Harry was concentrating on the screen and shot them a fatherly look, as he said, "Quiet, you two goofs."

Then it began. A trumpet fanfare, muted church bells, and distant cannon fire. The great iron gates of Buckingham Palace slowly opened.

The uniformed guards in their tall, fur busby hats snapped to attention. The crowds outside the palace gave a tumultuous cheer as the dazzling state coach emerged from the grounds, proceeded around the Victoria Monument, and commenced its historic journey down the Mall.

Carol oozed, "This is fan-tas-tic."

Sophie sighed dreamily as she gazed at the screen and then leaned her head on Patrick's shoulder.

Gramps added to the sense of awe as he said, "My Lord, the queen's beautiful. Is this real, or a Hollywood movie like those I've seen at the Grant Theatre?"

"Quiet, old man!" Nan told him. "Use your eyes instead of your mouth."

Gramps fell silent but clearly resented being hushed.

The coronation was more than the crowning of a queen. It was the fulfillment of a dream that, during the dark days of the war, the British peoples had feared would vanish from the face of the earth. Now, eight years later, the democratic institutions of a constitutional monarchy flourished. Those who had died on the battlefields of sacrifice had ensured the passing of the torch from one generation to another. Though it was a dichotomy, the coronation of a British monarch, who had obtained her title through hereditary privilege, was viewed as the embodiment of the democratic ideals of the Canadian nation.

In the living room of the Hudson home, those present could never have voiced or explained this contradictory concept. However, they knew that the battles fought in the war, in which the English peoples had been victorious, allowed them the right to choose their own destiny, free of the whims and fanaticism of a dictatorial leader. Britain, the commonwealth, its allies, and the United States had stood together, arm in arm, and conquered a seemingly invincible foe.

Even Gramps was impressed when he gazed at the Canadian troops, part of the ten thousand fighting men of the commonwealth who marched along the Mall on this day. Twenty-four bands and seven hundred horsemen added to the impressive display. The ear-splitting cheers of the crowds filled the air as the ornate golden coach passed by.

Nan's eyes glistened when she saw the queen alight from the coach in front of Westminster Abbey. Raised in a small fishing outport in Newfoundland, in the latter days of the reign of Queen Victoria, she was overcome with emotion at actually seeing the great-great-granddaughter of the old imperial monarch step from a royal coach. Nan wiped a small tear from her eye as she declared, "Oh my goodness gracious me."

Finally arriving at the abbey, the queen proceeded into the great cathedral, where the seats contained seventy-five hundred viewers. They rose to their feet in unison as the queen started down the nave. The hollow choral sounds of the four hundred-voice choir rose to the vaulted ceiling, sending shivers down the spines of all who were present. The TV audiences were not immune to the thrill.

In the living room on Lauder Avenue, the drop of a pin would have been a shattering noise. Even Shorty, who was rarely quiet, was motionless and silent.

When the queen arrived at the altar, the Archbishop of Canterbury commenced the sacred ceremony. During the moments ahead, Elizabeth II swore the coronation oath on a ceremonial sword. They presented her with the Bible of the Church of Scotland, and she knelt for the accompanying rites.

The cameras turned away and scanned the abbey crowds as the archbishop gave the queen communion and anointed her. They did not allow the camera to photograph this hallowed ritual.

Out of the corner of Tom's eye, he noticed that Gramps was becoming restless.

The queen stepped toward St. Andrew's chair. A golden canopy, held by four knights of the realm, hovered over it, sheltering her from view.

Then Tom heard Gramps break wind. He leaned over to his grandson and whispered, "If I was under that canopy, it would be billowing in the breezes. Remember the old saying? 'Where ever you be, let your wind blow free.'"

Tom smiled, grateful that no one else had heard either Gramps' flatulence or his silly comment.

As Tom gazed toward the TV again, the Archbishop of Canterbury was pouring holy oil into a silver spoon and sprinkling it on her hands, breast, and head. The queen next donned the holy garments and returned to the coronation chair.

At this point, Shorty was unable to restrain himself. He whispered to Tom, "That old chair looks like the one in the backhouse at Heart Lake."

Thankfully, no one else heard him. Tom ignored him, but his mom knew he had said something and glared at him.

Nan noticed it too and said, "Hush."

As they returned to the viewing, as if Gramps had lip-read Shorty's words, he said aloud, "We had a chair like that in the outhouse in Burin."

Nan was disgusted and Tom's mom was annoyed. Harry, Patrick, Carol, and Sophie giggled, and Tom noticed that his dad was trying not to smile. It was several seconds before they settled down and continued watching.

By now, the queen was accepting the regalia and symbols of authority: the golden spurs, the jewelled sword of state, the bracelets of sincerity, and the golden orb. They next placed the sapphire ring on the fourth finger of her right hand, signifying that she was now officially wedded to her nation.

Next, she received the sceptre, the symbol of power and justice, and then they handed her the rod with the dove on its upright end, signifying equity and power.

At this point, Gramps was unable to restrain himself. "If they load her down with any more crap, the poor dear will never get up from that bloody backhouse chair of hers."

All hell broke loose.

The cheering from the crowds outside the abbey was a mouse's roar compared to the din that rang out in the living room. Nan was infuriated, as she felt that Gramps had been sacrilegious. Tom's mom told him to be quiet, and even his dad felt that perhaps Gramps had gone too far.

Amid the outcry, they did not actually see the moment when the archbishop lowered St. Andrew's crown onto the queen's head. Later, they learned that it weighed two and a half pounds. It was just as well that they were unaware, as it would have added to Gramps' claim that she was overloaded. Heaven knows what disrespectful comment he might have uttered.

When calm returned to the living room, the abbey crowds were chanting, "God save the Queen." Outside the cathedral, cannons were being fired to notify the populace that the queen had been officially crowned.

While the music on the TV soared with the anthem "God Save the Queen," Tom was thinking, *God help Gramps*.

While Nan and his mom were in the kitchen cutting the coronation cake that Mrs. Leyer had brought, Gramps stayed out of their way. Though bored by now with the ceremony, he had no intention of entering a room where the two women had knives in their hands.

The family and guests continued watching the TV, though Shorty was also becoming restless. Tom knew that he wanted a slice of the cake.

The royal coach journeyed down the Mall to return to Buckingham Palace. The queen returned inside the gates and entered the palace. When the queen appeared on the balcony, in the skies above, 168 aircraft of the RAF and the RCAF buzzed the skies above London. The sight of the young monarch wearing the Imperial Crown was a sight that drew great applause from the throngs.

Tom feared that the following day, Nan would crown Gramps—with a crown of thorns.

✧ ✧ ✧

Detective Gerry Thomson was relaxing in a chair in his backyard. He had relocated it from under the shade of the carport. The heat of the day had passed and the warmth of the late-day sun felt pleasant. In his hand was a near-empty bottle of Molson's beer, the condensation on the glass now evaporated. He had sipped it slowly as he scanned the pages of a file that was perched precariously on his lap.

The one that got away always bothered him. He shared this sentiment in common with Peersen, but now he had the nagging feeling that somehow he had not fulfilled the essence of his conviction.

"Always remember," he had told Peersen many times, "never consider an unsolved murder case closed. Never take anyone's statement at face value. Never overlook the tiniest detail. Never rule out the impossible, as it might be merely the improbable. Look for patterns. Look for what isn't there, as well as what's there. Look for discrepancies. Look for hidden motives, while never overlooking the obvious. Look at personality profiles and anything that is out of character.

"Think, think, and think again! Turn every aspect over in your mind, and then build a mental stage set of the murder scene."

Gerry had no TV set. He had heard the coronation broadcast on the radio on CFRB, and now regretted he had promised to take his wife downtown to the University Theatre on Bloor Street to watch the *Thrilling Highlights of the Coronation,* in "living colour," as the advertisement had stated. The first showing was at eight o'clock, but he had reserved seats for the nine-thirty show. It was now only a few minutes after five, so he had four hours to do as he pleased.

It pleased him to spend the time revisiting the stage set of the Stritch murder.

Placing his floppy straw hat on the chair, he shielded his eyes from the sun with his hand as he walked toward the backdoor. Descending the stairs to the basement, he unlocked the door to a large room and entered his private den.

Inside the room, on the far wall was an enormous map of southern Ontario, pieced together from a series of provincial maps that were of similar scale. An enormous map of the streets of Toronto covered another wall. On a large table, lying flat, he had spread two other large maps. One was a detailed topography of the Humber Valley, and the other an enlarged map of all the streets from Scarlett Road on the west to Arlington Avenue on the east. The maps were mounted on soft, fibrous boards, each six-foot by four.

Numerous short thick nails, which he had dipped in red paint, were used as pins. He had inserted them into the maps in various locations. The room looked like a modest version of Churchill's war room in the bunker below the streets of London. Other than Peersen, no member of the police force was aware the room existed, and his partner was sworn to secrecy.

At a glance, Thomson could view the locations of the homes of every teacher at York Collegiate. He had inserted a red nail to indicate the residence of each staff member. They stood out, dotted across the expanse of the map like a series of pins in a great pincushion. Most teachers lived within close proximity of the high school. The three that did not, he had represented by inserting pins on the enlarged city map. The map of Ontario had an ominous single pin located beside Pine Lake near Bala, in the Muskoka area.

In his hand was the file he had been examining while he was seated in the backyard. It contained the sworn statements of every teacher, stating where they had been on Friday, 31 August, 1951. At a glance, he could plot on the maps the movements of each suspect and determine how long it took them to complete a given route.

During the previous years, he had walked and driven various streets to determine the average walking and driving times. Taking into account the relative physical capabilities of each person, or their propensities behind the wheel of a car, he was able to estimate the length of a trip, which was accurate to within a certain range. Compiling the data, the pins on the maps aided him in discerning discrepancies in the stories of the witnesses.

The 1950s was not an age of mass travel, and this included journeys within the city. The lives of the majority of the citizens of Toronto evolved around a limited area, where they shopped, visited friends and family, worshipped, attended movies, and sought other venues of recreation. Few people owned cars, and the concept of malls and plazas was in its infancy. If a person lived west of Yonge Street, it was rare for them to travel east of it. Yonge Street was the great divide. The intersection at Queen and Yonge Streets was the commercial heart of the city, where Eaton's and Simpson's were located. Most people's lives focused around their immediate neighbourhood, the downtown shops, and the Yonge Street strip. If a person did not fit within this norm, Thomson wondered why.

Gerry was aware that the city was changing. The number of people who owned automobiles was increasing. They were planning to build a new large, indoor plaza, with an enormous parking lot, east of Dufferin Street and south of Wilson Avenue (Yorkdale Plaza). Society was becoming more mobile. This concerned him.

Wages of workers were slowly improving. Teacher's salaries were no better than those of the police, but seven teachers on staff at YCI owned cars. Three officers at the precinct owned their own automobiles. Thomson drove a police car, which the department provided, as he used it for official investigations. Peersen had a car, but he was in a class by himself.

Thomson knew that more and more, with each new investigation, he was spreading the pins on his maps further apart. Soon, only a map of the entire city would be useful to his studies. His maps were not his only aid when examining the lives of suspects. He collated many different pieces of information to produce graphs and charts, all of which he cross-referenced and indexed. He considered them valuable tools of his trade, but everything hinged around the little red pins. However, he admitted that to date they had offered no valuable clues in the Stritch murder or in the killing of the young woman in High Park. This did not mean that they would not be useful in the future, he decided.

Down at the precinct, Thomson always smiled when they ridiculed the crime novels of Agatha Christie and her fictional detective Hercule Poirot. They laughed at the thought of solving a murder by using "the little gray cells." What would they think of him as a professional if they knew that he used "the little red pins."

✧ ✧ ✧

Tyrone Evanson and his wife, Emily, had watched the coronation on the television, accompanied by his parents who arrived earlier in the day. Silence had reigned in his living room as the ceremony had progressed. A coronation was living history, and Gus had tolerated no distractions as he observed the unfolding rituals.

After his parents departed, the house was quiet. Mrs. Evanson was now in the kitchen preparing a late-evening snack. Gus always enjoyed sharing a slice of coffee cake and tea with her before bedtime. Until that time arrived, he retreated to the privacy of his den, which he considered more sacrosanct than his office at the school.

As he entered the room, a breeze from outside caused the heavy navy-blue drapes on either side of the patio doors to rustle slightly. Each morning, Mrs. Evanson tied the drapes back with tie chords to expose the pair of doors that led to the back garden. After peering out, since the air had cooled, he closed the doors and untied the drape chords, allowing them to fall across the doorway. He then walked over and sat down behind his antique mahogany desk with its heavy ornate legs and ball feet. Pouring a little Crown Royal whiskey, neat, he sipped slowly as he leafed through the pages of a stamp album.

He had been collecting the coronation stamps that the various dominions and British overseas possessions had issued. On this particular evening, he commenced working on the mint (unused) coronation stamps, placing them in protective folders. Hinging them would leave marks on the gummed side of the stamps.

Evanson only collected stamps of the British Commonwealth, his favourite stamps being those that depicted the animal life of the various countries. Of course, his favourites were those depicting elephants. When he had been a boy, his father had ridiculed his fascination with the large beasts. He had laughed at him and said, "When you are a man, you should become a big-game hunter and shoot the damn things."

Tyrone's mother had never openly defended her son, but when her husband was absent from the home, she encouraged her son's interests. She knew that she spoiled him through overindulgence. She excused her actions by remembering that she had lost her eldest son when he was boy and reasoned that it was her responsibility to lavish all her love on the remaining child.

Now an adult, Evanson could not understand how anyone could kill a majestic elephant. However, he had come to understand why his father was a difficult man. His dad felt that he had married beneath his station and that life had never delivered to him the rewards that he deserved. Gus was certain that his father resented his success as a principal.

Staring blankly at the glass of whiskey, he did not hear the clock on the mantle chime the hour. Mrs. Evanson had placed yesterday's mail on his desk, and he absentmindedly thumbed through it, paying more attention to the stamps than the return addresses of the senders. Pushing the mail aside, he leaned back in the chair, which groaned noisily beneath his shifting bulk.

Tyrone Evanson was a frustrated man. He had married at an early age to escape from the parental home. Though his father had never physically struck his mother, his resentment toward her had manifested itself through constant verbal abuse. As a boy, Tyrone had witnessed the results of his mother's degradation and vowed that he would never engage in such behaviour toward a woman.

He had married a neighbourhood girl, Emily, who although bright and quite attractive, was overly shy and passive by nature. He now wondered if his attraction for her had been more of a desire to protect her than to love her. However, his marriage to Emily turned out to be quite successful. She doted on her young husband and thrived in the protective environment within the home. They both wanted children, Tyrone especially, who yearned for a son.

During the second year of the marriage, Emily became pregnant but suffered a miscarriage. Two years later, she had another miscarriage. She never fully recovered from the second loss. She became deeply depressed and withdrew within a shell that Tyrone was unable to penetrate. Her unending depression slowly destroyed the marriage. Although Emily eventually improved and functioned reasonably well on a daily basis, she was frigid. Her fear of another miscarriage destroyed any interest in sex.

Tyrone eventually sought solace beyond the marriage bed. In his midforties, he had acquired a young mistress, whom when she met him had said her name was Jane Smith. He was never certain if it was her real name. It was several years before he learned that her name was actually Jane Overhalter. She had hated the surname, as the kids at school had referred to her as "Jane Brassiere."

The illicit affair blossomed into love, despite Tyrone being older and in poor physical shape. Jane was clever, and possessed an outgoing, warm personality. Her thick brunette hair, slim body, and attractive face with its pert little nose had captured Tyrone's heart. Seven years later, Jane delivered a son. Trapped into a loveless relationship with Emily, whom he still adored in his own way, Tyrone was unable to share his life with his son or Jane, who had a successful business career.

The boy was now eight years old, and Tyrone saw him only once a month, when he met Jane for lunch at the Arcadian Court on the eighth floor of the Robert Simpson Department Store at Queen and Bay Streets. They met on the last Saturday of each month, when Tyrone travelled downtown to a philatelic shop located in the Yonge Street Arcade. It was where he purchased his elephant stamps.

Tyrone treasured the encounters with his son, and his eyes brimmed with love when he gazed at the young boy, whose curly black hair and attractive face resembled that of his own at that age. After Tyrone departed from Simpson's, after one of the discreet liaisons, it was as if loneliness manifested into a solid entity that strangled his heart.

On the evening following the coronation broadcast, the bonds of loneliness gripped him.

Slowly, but with a degree of gratitude to escape thinking about his hopeless situation, he turned his thoughts to the events of the coming week. He must write a report on Vice-Principal Dinkman. It was due at the board office before the end of June.

Dinkman evaluated the teachers, but as Gus was the principal, it was his task to write a report on Dinkman. He considered the man a good administrator. He organized the teachers' schedules efficiently, supervised the students' timetables, and arranged the examination calendar efficiently each year. However, Evanson believed that his assistant had arrived at the highest level that his ability allowed. He was not principal material. Dinkman had difficulty making decisions. He functioned well as long as someone else was in control, but when Dinkman was in control, he floundered.

Gus admitted that in fairness, any administrator, when compared to him, would appear indecisive. Evanson knew that he possessed a natural talent for decision making, and his judgments were rarely wrong. Perhaps Dinkman only appeared weak because he suffered through this comparison.

Evanson was uncertain how to write his report, but he saw no contradiction in this. After all, he reasoned, even King Solomon required time to ponder his decisions. Then he thought about how Dinkman handled the disciplining of the students. Yes, this was an important factor. He would deliberate further.

✧ ✧ ✧

As the evening hours of Coronation Day progressed, crowds flocked to the theatres of the city: Shea's Hippodrome, the University, the Eglinton, and the Tivoli, to view the highlights of the event. As theatre patrons entered the lobbies of the film houses, newsboys were still hawking the late edition of the *Toronto Star*. On the front page, the huge letters of the headline proclaimed, **"HAIL ER II."**

Thomson and his wife were among the crowds at the University Theatre. Ruth Thomson was thrilled with the majestic scenes within the great abbey. It resembled a living, moving canvas, painted by the masters of old Europe, rich in detail and brilliant with colour.

As darkness deepened across the far-flung avenues of Toronto, families with young children commenced the preparations that time eternal dictated be performed at day's end. Curtains were closed against the night, and porch lights glowed in the enfolding darkness. Children, tired after an exhausting day's revelling, were sad that the long-awaited day had ended, but their parents were glad of the opportunity to don their slippers and put out the feline pets. For them, the curtain on the spectacle of spectacles was slowly drawing to a close

Not all was still throughout the great metropolis. Beacon fires that had been lit at dusk in six Toronto public parks glowed ever brighter, their flames rising in the blackened sky as people added fuel to the crackling flames. The odour of smoke infused the night air. At one of the community celebrations, well after the hour of ten, fifteen thousand people still milled around the celebratory bonfires. Some were sipping on secretly held bottles of firewater, but no reports of unruliness were reported.

At Sunnyside Beach beside the lake, the largest fireworks displays of the decade illuminated the firmament, their reflected light sparkling on the inky surface of the water. People across the lake in Lewistown, New York, saw the flashes of the exploding rockets above the city.

It had been the fourth coronation of the century, following those of King Edward VII, King George V, and King George VI, but it was the only one that had been witnessed by the people of the world through the magic of television and film.

✧ ✧ ✧

The day following the regal event, Gramps departed earlier than usual to remove dollydocks (dandelions) from the backyard lawn. When he saw Nan in the sun porch window, which overlooked the backyard, he conveniently disappeared for a walk.

On the street, he encountered Mrs. Leyer.

"Well, well, Mr. Hudson, I see you still have your head on your shoulders," she said, amusement obvious in her voice. "I was afraid that after I left your home yesterday, you might be missing it this morning." Mrs. Leyer grinned mischievously as she spoke.

"I guess I did stir the pot a little," Gramps confessed.

"A little?"

Gramps made no reply, but started to chuckle.

"Frankly, Mr. Hudson, I think this coronation stuff is overblown. Other than my cake, I thought your comments were the highlight of the afternoon."

As they broke into laughter, Mrs. Martha Klacker passed by. Though she usually ignored them, the mood from the previous day had pleased her. She believed that a woman should rule the land, especially a woman like her. Against her better judgment she said, "What are you two laughing at?"

Gramps replied, "I found something that you're unlikely to ever find."

"What's that?"

"I found a friend."

Gramps and Mrs. Leyer grinned as Old Klacker continued imperiously down the street, self-assured that she was one of the few sane persons remaining in the neighbourhood.

✧ ✧ ✧

The first week of July, a heat wave blistered the city, a blanket of sweltering, humid air. Despite the high temperatures, Thomson and Peersen continued their investigation. Having no obvious leads in the Stritch case, they finally received permission to interview Miss Samantha Anderson. Because of her connections with important people in the city, they knew that they had to handle the interview delicately.

It was stiflingly hot as they drove east along Eglinton Avenue West, the blood-red sun drooping low toward the horizon behind them. They rolled down the car windows to allow the air from the forward motion of the car to cool the interior.

When they stopped for the red light at Bathurst Street, they were shocked to see a delivery van veering around the corner on two wheels, making the turn after the amber light had disappeared. It raced southbound on Bathurst. The erratic driver left a trail of cursing drivers, as well as a few who were offering prayers of thanks that they remained alive. Thomson felt that the driving infraction was too serious to ignore. They gave chase.

By the time they turned onto Bathurst Street, the van was making another dangerous left-hand turn from the right lane into Rosemary Lane. Within moments, they were following the wild driver around the curving street of the wealthy neighbourhood. A clump of white daisies was dangling from the rear bumper of the van where it had clipped a flower garden at the edge of a driveway of one of the homes. The clump fell to the pavement as Peersen placed the red flashing light on the hood of the police car. Surprisingly, the van slowed to a stop almost immediately.

The detectives strolled slowly toward the van as they removed their police badges from their pockets. Behind the wheel was a tough-looking woman, perhaps about thirty. A cigarette drooped from the corner of her mouth, the smoke curling around her face. She wore a sleeveless soiled blouse, and the muscles in her bare arms were considerable. As the detectives neared, she stepped out of the van. Her lean body was silhouetted in the fading evening light. They could see a teenager's head protruding out the van window, observing the unfolding scene.

"What can I do for you fine-looking men?" the woman said in a sensuous tone.

"Lady," Peersen began, "are you aware that you have committed several serious driving offences?"

"Oh, I am so sorry," she said in an overly penitent voice.

Peersen noticed that the teenager in the van had a slight grin on his face.

"You were speeding and made two illegal left turns, one of them involving failing to obey a red light."

"Officer …"

"It's detective, … Detective Peersen."

"Detective Peersen, I'm truly sorry. I usually drive carefully, but I am making an emergency delivery—pain medication to a cancer patient. Every minute I'm delayed, her pain becomes worse. I stopped the van the minute I realized that you were police."

She reached in and grabbed a white paper bag from the seat of the car. Peersen placed his hand near his revolver as he observed her reach for the package.

"This prescription must get to the poor woman as fast as possible."

Though Thomson was suspicious, he decided to put the woman's story to the test. "All right, drive to the house, and we'll escort you."

They followed her down the curving street and watched as she drove the van into a driveway and quickly went to the door. They followed, not far behind. When a man answered the door, he looked immensely relieved as he grabbed the white bag and fumbled in his pocket for the money to pay the bill. Then he saw two men approach the door and flip their police badges into view.

"Was this delivery an emergency?" Thomson inquired.

"Hell, yes," he blurted as he thrust the money into the hand of the delivery woman, and slammed the door shut behind him. Thomson and Peersen decided not to disturb him by inquiring further. They gave the wild driver a warning and withdrew.

The woman returned to the van, climbed in, and sat beside the teenager. She said to him, "Well, it *was* an emergency. That paper bag contained a package of condoms and two tubes of lubricant. Aren't they emergency items?" Ruth said as she spit out the window to emphasize her point.

"Can't argue with that," Shorty replied.

"Thank God the customer forgot about the two cases of Pepsi. They're still here in the van. They would have blown my story about it being an emergency."

"Is this the same house you and Tom delivered the lubricant to last March, when old man Greenberg forgot to put it in the order?"

"Sure is!"

"What do you think they're doing with all that lubricant?" Shorty inquired with a knowing smirk on his face.

"Perhaps they're greasing the wheels on the refrigerator. Come think of it, that woman is such a frigid bitch that when she opens her legs, I bet a light comes on."

They were both laughing as Ruth shoved in the clutch and rammed the engine into gear, the car uttering a grinding sound as it protested the rough treatment.

"Grind me up a pound," Shorty quipped.

"I've ground up bigger men than you," she shot back, as a terrified driver swerved to avoid colliding with her backing the van out of the driveway.

✧ ✧ ✧

Thomson and Peersen proceeded along Eglinton Avenue West on their way toward Mt. Pleasant Avenue, turned north, and then west onto Roehampton Avenue to visit the apartment of Miss Samantha Anderson. While Thomson was parking the car, Peersen observed a man departing from Anderson's apartment building.

"My God," he muttered, "it's Frank the Fink."

"Who?"

"Frank Gnomes. He's a reporter at the *Trib*. I bet he was visiting Spanky Anderson. I think we should have a talk with him."

Frank observed the two detectives as they got out of the car, stopped, and waited for them to approach.

"Well, two police pricks from the precinct," Frank said with a smirk.

Thomson bristled, but Peersen grinned and held his partner in check. "It's all right, Gerry," Peersen said. "Frank and I go back a long way."

Turning again to Gnomes, Peersen said, "It's time we had a chat, Frank, and exchange tit for tat, so to speak."

"Okay, what tit do you have for me?"

"Why were you visiting Miss Anderson's?"

"It's a big building. Why do you assume I was visiting Spanky?"

Peersen knew that Frank's use of her nickname betrayed that he knew the witness. He suspected Gnomes had made the slip purposely, as he wanted to let them know that he was well informed.

"How are the interviews going?" Gnomes asked. "Did you get anything out of Dinkman, Matheson, Hitch, Taylor, Baldwin, Millford, Weepy Allyson, or Miss Manson?"

They ignored Frank's question.

"How did you know about Miss Anderson?"

"I have my ways."

"Has she told you anything?"

"Give me something, and I'll trade."

Peersen thought for several moments and glanced at Thomson, who nodded.

"We have a witness who says that Stritch might have been involved sexually with another man, other than Bill Matheson."

"That gives our friend Matheson a motive."

"Now, you give us something."

Frank then told Peersen about the night that Dinkman had been in Samantha's apartment and informed them that she had thrown him out. Then he added, "Miss Anderson recently mentioned that Dinkman had implied that there were strange relationships on the staff at the high school, but he didn't say what he meant by strange or who was involved. That ties in with what you just mentioned."

They chatted a few more minutes, but neither party gained any new information. As Frank sauntered away, slicking his feet noisily on the warm cement sidewalk, the two detectives watched him depart.

"He has an informer at the precinct. He recited the exact order in which we interviewed the key witnesses. He also knew about Anderson," Gerry said.

"I guess we have a set of loose lips at the precinct, and similar to the lips of the late-night girls on Jarvis Street, those lips are doing things that they shouldn't be doing," Peersen said with amusement, even though he was disgusted at the thought of a departmental leak.

Several moments later, they were knocking at Miss Anderson's apartment door. Silence! They knocked a second time.

"Miss Anderson, it's the police. We wish to talk with you."

Silence.

"We know you are in there. Is it necessary to return with a warrant?"

A disembodied voice emanated from behind the door. "Hold up your badges to the peephole."

Finally, the door opened, and Samantha motioned for them to enter. It was obvious that she was not pleased to see them.

Miss Anderson was casually dressed, the delicate lace trim on her pink blouse accenting her pale skin. Her ample breasts moved rhythmically, without the slightest trace of alarm. Although she had not expected the visit, she appeared confident, cool, and relaxed. Her June Allyson looks were even more appealing in the diffused lamplight of the room. Music was playing on a record player, and Peersen recognized it as Mozart's opera, *The Magic Flute*.

Peersen was thoroughly confused. Her home was not what he had expected. He had thought that her apartment would have pink-flocked wallpaper, purple curtains, and an enormous velvet chesterfield and chair. Chains on the wall and handcuffs on the coffee table, he had assumed, would be the accoutrements of choice.

The room that greeted him was tastefully decorated, cozy, and classy. On the wall over the light-green chesterfield, Peersen recognized a large canvas by Jack Bush, an artist who had grown tired of the pine trees and forests of the Group of Seven and was experimenting with abstract styles. Then he noticed a signed limited edition print of A.Y. Jackson's "Birches in Winter." *Quite an eclectic taste in art*, he thought.

On an end table were several small reproductions of classical Greek sculptures, along with similarly sized copies of Rodan's sculptures "The Thinker" and "The Kiss." Peersen smiled to himself as he remembered his high school art teacher saying that the naked "Thinker" was undoubtedly thinking about where he had left his clothes.

An oversized art book and a program for the opera *Carmen*, which he supposed she had recently attended at the Royal Alexandra Theatre, were on the coffee table. Beside it was a magazine containing poetry reviews.

One entire wall was lined with bookshelves, crammed with many volumes. Peersen was unable to resist slowly walking over to examine the titles. Most were nineteenth-century classic novelists, both English and French, along with a selection of modern writers, a few of which were Canadian. Peersen removed a copy of *Cabbagetown* by Hugh Garner and leafed through it, but he replaced it on the shelf when Miss Anderson glanced disapprovingly at his actions. A few plays were among her collection, neatly bound expensive hardcover editions. *The Glass Menagerie* by Tennessee Williams caught his eye. Scanning the remainder of her collection, he noticed they included poetry, philosophy, politics, and an excellent assortment of modern literature. There was also an entire bookcase of psychology texts.

On the top of one of the lower bookcases on the other side of the room, she had deposited her morning's mail, still unopened. His eyes scanned the top envelope. The sender had addressed it to Dr. Samantha Anderson. If Peersen was confused before, he was now completely baffled.

Thomson carefully began the questioning.

"Miss Anderson," he began respectfully, "did you enjoy the opera *Carmen*? I see you have a program on the coffee table." He knew nothing about opera, but thought it was a good opening line to place the witness at ease.

"Not one of my favourites, but it brought back a few nostalgic memories."

"A romantic night on King Street at the Royal Alex?"

"No. A dismal evening on the Champs Elysees, with an organ grinder's monkey churning out a dreadful Georges Bizet melody."

Thomson was out of his depth. He had never heard of George Bizet.

Peersen smiled. He had always thought that the opera *Carmen*, though one of the most popular, was vastly overrated. Much of the music was indeed well suited to a hand-operated organ, the type employed by a monkey with a tin cup in its hand and a little red cap perched above its empty grinning face. Peersen decided it was time to assist his partner. He now knew that Miss Anderson was a witness who would not be easily intimidated and thought that straightforward honesty was the best approach.

"Miss Anderson, we need your assistance. We're investigating the murder of Miss Elaine Stritch, who taught at York Collegiate Institute. She had a promising career teaching English literature. In fact, her older students produced a production of Hamlet each year. Two years ago, someone brutally murdered her.

"We know that you had a conversation with Mr. Dinkman, the vice-principal of the school where she taught, while having a coffee at the Gymnasium Club where you work out. We also know that you were with him for almost a half-hour as you rode the Yonge streetcar to your apartment. Did he ever say anything, even the smallest detail, about Miss Stritch or the murder?"

She stared at them for several moments and then said, "Sit down, gentlemen."

Peersen, his voice reassuring, said, "A tiny detail, something insignificant, might be helpful."

Samantha gazed thoughtfully at Peersen's young, attractive face and decided she liked what she saw. She sensed that this young detective was different than other policemen she had met. No danger signals were apparent to her. He was not condescending, even though he was obviously aware of how she earned her living. His words also struck her forcefully. She knew the cruelty of which men were capable and was aware that men rarely took intelligent women seriously. Had Miss Stritch survived, Samantha doubted if they would have ever considered her for a position in administration. She decided to cooperate.

"Dinkman is a thoroughly nasty man," she began. "He has no regard for any woman. He has a self-image problem. Despite his bluster and false bravado, I've learned that such men can still be dangerous. I only saw him on one occasion. When I flattered him and told him that he sounded as if he were an important man, he bragged that he was in a senior administrative position. I thought nothing more about it. Many of the men I meet enjoy singing their own praises.

"A week later, after the Stritch murder, I saw his picture in the newspaper and recognized him. Then I remembered that he had bragged that he was aware of details that the authorities desperately wanted to know. I recalled that he had said that someone in his employ was 'skirting around,' and that it had been dangerous for her. I have no idea what he actually meant by the term 'skirting around,' but many weeks later, remembering his words, I wondered if he were referring to the murdered girl.

"I don't know if he meant she was involved with someone who was dangerous or had she accidentally 'skirted around' some information that got her killed? Of one thing I'm certain: Dinkman knows something about the murder."

"Thank you, Miss Anderson. We will take your comments under advisement. Can you tell us anything else?"

"I can't think of anything else."

"If you do think of anything, contact us at this number." He passed her his card.

After the two detectives reached their parked car, Thomson told his assistant, "It's time we had another talk with Peckerman, to get permission to interview Dinkman again."

Peersen never heard him. He was thinking about Samantha Anderson.

✧ ✧ ✧

The following day at the precinct, Peersen arrived early and was waiting for his partner to arrive in order to visit the fifth floor to request an interview with Peckerman. Shortly after nine o'clock, they sat down in his office, gazing across the desk at their superior. He sat in his large round-back armchair, elbows resting on the edge of the desk, arms raised and chin resting on his hands, peering intently at the two detectives.

"Mornin', gentlemen. What can I do for you two bozos?" Peckerman intoned colloquially.

Thomson began hesitantly. "We wish to continue to pursue the Stritch case and hand off the High Park murder to another team."

Peckerman eyed them suspiciously. "The Stritch investigation's no longer a high priority. The High Park murder is. The victim's parents are wealthy, and they're putting pressure on the department to solve the crime."

"Yes, I know," Frank admitted. "But we've done a little extra digging and uncovered an interesting piece of information about the Stritch case."

Then he proceeded to explain the delicate situation surrounding the Gymnasium Club and its well-connected clientele and provided Peckerman with a summary of the interview with Miss Anderson.

"I am not certain that I approve of you nosing around this Gymnasium Club, but I suppose you must follow up every lead. From what this so-called Miss Anderson has told you, I take it that you wish to interview Dinkman again."

"That's right. Do we have sufficient grounds to bring him down to the station?"

"Well, I can certainly run it past the departmental lawyers. We don't want any harassment complaints. Let me get back to you."

It was two days before the answer descended from on high.

Within minutes of the official phone call, Peckerman walked out his office door, into the elevator, and then directly to Thomson's desk.

"Gerry, go pick up Dinkman," he ordered.

Within the hour, Thomson and Peersen were pounding on Dinkman's door on Ashbury Avenue. All was quiet within. When they persisted, the elderly woman who lived next door, came out and leaned inquisitively across her veranda railing. The curlers in her hair and her fuzzy pink nightgown indicated that, despite the late-morning hour, she had rolled out of bed just minutes before their arrival. Her bony hands clutched a mug of steaming coffee.

"Wastin' your time, boys," she said authoritatively. "The Dinkmans packed their bags and left this morning. I don't know where they went, but wherever it was, the place is more miserable than before they arrived there."

"Know when they'll be back?" Peersen inquired politely.

"That old bastard Dinkman wouldn't tell me if he won the Irish sweepstakes." She gave a mischievous grin, displaying the gap in her dentures where two of her false teeth were missing.

Continuing, she added, "He keeps his mouth zipped, except when he wants to spew a little abuse." Then she added, "It's a pity his father didn't keep his pants zipped."

"Thanks, lady!" Peersen responded.

"Oh my," the old woman cooed, "It's been a long time since I was called a lady."

Peersen thought, *I bet you've been called quite a few other things though.*

For now, the detectives were stymied.

✧ ✧ ✧

Frank Gnomes knew where the Dinkmans were and was also aware that they were not together. The reason he knew was that he had paid a young reporter a few extra dollars to watch the bus station on Bay Street, in his hands a copy of the school yearbook, *The Activist*, with the staff pictures in it. The 1953 edition had been dedicated to the queen and was a coronation issue. Frank had paid another lad to watch Union Station on Front Street, instructing him to centre his attention on the doors that gave access to the grand hall. Frank was always short of cash and had prayed that his money was not wasted.

He need not have worried. One of the reporters learned that Mr. Dinkman had a ticket for the Transcontinental to Vancouver, and the other cub reporter discovered that Mrs. Dinkman had boarded a bus to North Bay. *Separate vacations,* he thought. *What's Old Dickhead up to? Time to talk to Peersen and get the police to use their resources to track the two miscreants.*

As the top crime reporter for the *Trib*, Frank earned a good salary, but paying alimony to two ex-wives seriously depleted his resources. He doubted he would ever have the money to buy a new car and only managed to run the old wreck he owned through the car allowance he received from the newspaper.

Yes, sometimes I need the resources of the police.

✧ ✧ ✧

Throughout July, Tom faithfully delivered prescriptions, soda pop, and other miscellaneous items to the customers of Greenberg's Pharmacy. Ruth continued to terrorize the neighbourhood with her erratic driving. Whenever she required assistance with a heavy order, which usually entailed cases of soda pop or seltzer bottles, Shorty accompanied her on the deliveries.

He regaled Tom with stories of Ruth's exploits on the road. He claimed that Greenberg's Drug Store sold more antidiarrhea medication than any other retailer in the city, as Ruth scared the shit out of so many of the drivers in the neighbourhood.

✧ ✧ ✧

On Monday, 27 July, at 8:15 a.m., over three hundred soldiers arrived at Toronto's Union Station, returning from active duty in the Korean Conflict. While on the train, they learned that negotiators had signed the ceasefire.

By the time the soldiers disembarked from the train, the news had spread across the city. People were listening to the details on their radios, while others were watching a newscast on CBLT, the CBC television station.

Unlike the tumultuous partying that had engulfed the city when the Second World War ended, the ceasefire created an enormous wave of relief but few celebrations. There were no spontaneous parades or throwing of confetti. No neighbourhood bonfires were to light the night sky, and Sunnyside was devoid of fireworks. After six years of war in Europe and the Pacific and three more years in Korea, the world was exhausted from the turmoil and death that war delivered.

Although some would likely raise a glass in the downtown bars during their night revelries, most would simply express quiet gratitude. Families prayed there would be no more battles on the small peninsula jutting into the sea off the Asian coastline. However, in households where sons or husbands would soon be returning, there would indeed be private celebrations.

On the following day, many gathered in the churches across Toronto to pay homage to those who had died, and to express gratitude for the silence of the guns. The words, "Now thank we all, our God," had never rang truer throughout the churches of the city. People drew a collective sigh of relief, thankful that another cruel chapter in the history of humanity had finally ended.

✧ ✧ ✧

Tom's dad followed the events of the upcoming federal election. On 7 August, Prime Minister St. Laurent was at Maple Leaf Garden at an enormous political rally. They held the election three days later, and the voters returned the Liberals with one hundred and seventy-one seats, while the Tories won fifty, and the CCF twenty-three.

On the evening of 24 August, *South Pacific* opened at the Royal Alexandra Theatre on King Street. The following day, Tom saw the pictures in the newspapers of the gala opening, showing Toronto's social elite at the opening performance. In the photographs, he recognized the reporter Frank Gnomes, and on his arm was a beautiful woman whom he thought resembled the movie star June Allyson. The articles said that they were "invited guests." Tom's dad said, "They likely received free passes to the performance, as Gnomes is a member of the press. Some jobs have great perks."

On 28 August, the seventy-fifth CNE threw open its gates. For many, as usual, the Ex was the highlight of the end of summer. Denny Vaughan, The Commodores, and the Leslie Bell Singers were at the band shell. The grandstand show had a cast of a thousand performers, and they advertised it as a tribute to Queen Elizabeth II. Victor Borge, the Danish comedian and concert pianist, was the guest grandstand performer.

✧ ✧ ✧

Harry had worked during the summer months as an office boy at White, Bundts, and Brown, a prestigious law firm on Richmond Street West, east of Bay Street. Within law circles, they referred to it as "White, Buns, and Brown," joking that the firm's name sounded like the slogan for a bakery or a racially mixed shower room at the YMCA.

The firm employed over forty lawyers. The senior partners of the firm each had their own secretary, and the junior partners each shared a secretary. The other lawyers and clerks used the services of a secretarial pool. The latter consisted of a group of six women, mostly young, who typed letters, legal documents, and any other paperwork required. There were six legal clerks and four office boys, one of whom was Harry. He changed typewriter ribbons, sharpened pencils, filled inkbottles, changed the paper rolls on the adding machines, oiled the adding machines, emptied wastepaper baskets, delivered interoffice memos, sorted incoming postal mail, and delivered documents and papers to clients within the downtown core.

During the first week of July, when Harry commenced working in the firm, he attracted the attention of the women in the secretarial pool. He was only seventeen but looked more like twenty-five. The women knew his real age, but it failed to prevent them from flirting with him and whispering suggestive comments when he brought them a cylinder from a dictating machine, the contents of which they were to type onto stationery containing the firm's letterhead. When they had finished the letters, Harry delivered them back to the lawyers for their signatures. Thus, the daily routines provided many opportunities for the typists to admire Harry's athletic body and express their secret desires, which as the week progressed, were becoming less surreptitious.

Harry was aware of the fuss he caused. Being tall for his age, he had received attention from the opposite sex since he had been twelve years of age, and the passing years had not dulled their interest in him. However, Harry remained confused about his sexuality.

When he was fifteen, he confessed to Shorty and Tom that he did not feel about girls like other boys his age did. Shorty had told him that when the right girl came along, his attitude would change. He had hoped this was true, but he was now seventeen and nothing had changed. The attraction that excited other boys was missing from his psyche.

Carol Miller was a dream girlfriend, he knew, as she was gorgeous and highly intelligent. He enjoyed her company immensely, adored her, and at times thought he loved her, but upon reflection, he knew there was nothing sexual about his feelings. She was simply a great friend.

The banter in the mailroom invariably centred on girls. The three other office boys suffered from permanent peckeritis. They crudely rated the office girls according to a five-star jerk-off scale. Isabelle, the Maltese typist, was one of the five-star girls, while Mabel who sat beside her was only a two-star. Harry pretended to share in their laugher, being unable to relate to their hormone-inspired jokes. Fortunately, the other guys did not notice.

At times, Harry wondered what the other boys would think if they knew that he had never successfully masturbated. He had tried it several times, but when he fantasized about girls, he had been unable to reach a climax, and when he tried to arouse himself by thinking about other males, he felt nothing. He had seen naked guys in the showers at school, and the sight had not interested him. He concluded that he was not attracted to either sex.

Throughout the summer months, on afternoons after work, Harry walked to the Reference Library at College and St. George Streets and examined the books on the shelves that dealt with human sexuality and its various manifestations. He also looked at the books on deviant sex. After much reading and consideration, he decided that perhaps he was asexual; neither male nor female sexually aroused him.

This discovery helped him to understand himself, but it did not solve the problem. Sooner or later Carol would notice there was no spark from him when they were necking. What would happen if she pushed him to go all the way? If he told her he wanted to wait, would she consider him a prude?

After Labour Day, he would be entering grade eleven. Carol Miller was no longer a girl; she was a highly desirable young woman. Her body possessed astonishing curves, and her breasts amply filled her sweater. Harry knew that the approaching school year was fraught with perils. He was enthusiastic about his life at YCI. The football and basketball teams were great experiences, and he enjoyed the academics as well. English was not his first language, but he loved the way it expressed ideas and complex thoughts. The poetry classes and writing exercises were fun. He was good at French, and Latin fascinated him. It all sounded great, but he knew it was not. For him, the coming year was to be bittersweet!

✧ ✧ ✧

It was the Labour Day weekend. The pace of life in Toronto had changed during the past week. The CNE, late summer's annual fair, was in full swing, but in the mornings, a hint of autumn was in the air. People sought a final few days beside the crystal lakes of the Muskoka region or drove to Grand Bend, Wasaga Beach, and the Kawartha Lakes for a late-season binge of sun and beer.

Despite the date on the calendar, during the afternoons the summer continued to bestow its comforting warmth. However, the cycle of life in the humble gardens and majestic ravines of the city was drawing to a close. Bumblebees, grasshoppers, dragonflies, and the magnificent monarch butterflies continued their eternal quest to harvest the last of summer's bounty.

Though the late-summer days were glorious, the stalker needed to steal another life and knew it was necessary to take it before the confines of the classroom prevented any such action. Several days prior to the Labour Day weekend, the stalker formulated a plan after observing a possible victim shopping at a fruit market on Church Street, south of Wellesley Street. The stalker often had coffee at a café across the street from the fruit store. Each evening, the woman purchased her produce shortly before the store closed, and the stalker thought that she likely worked in one of the surrounding offices or shops.

On several occasions, the stalker discretely followed her, discovering that she cut through the Rosedale Ravine, north of Bloor Street, to reach her home. Similarly, the stalker followed a young clerk who worked in the store and learned that his lifestyle would attract the suspicions of the police if a murder occurred in the area.

On the evening of the planned kill, the stalker loitered near the fruit store. A half dozen late-evening shoppers remained at the front of the store, examining the early McIntosh Red apples. The young clerk whom the stalker had followed was trimming heads of lettuce with a sharp knife, and as closing time drew near, he placed the knife into a basket, along with other assorted cutting tools. He would carry the basket inside when the store closed. He did not notice the stalker take a paper bag from beside the piled-up bunches of radish and steal the knife, covering it with the bag to ensure that no fingerprints were on it.

When the stalker's intended victim departed the store, she was not aware that someone was following her on the opposite side of the street. The woman's name was Shirley Hemmer, twenty-eight years of age, full-figured, and quite attractive. Her black hair, which she wore long, swayed gently as she casually proceeded toward home. She had recently acquired a position as a salesclerk at Holt Renfrew and had finished work at eight o'clock, her supervisor allowing her to leave early as the store was not busy.

Earlier in the year, Shirley had moved to the city from north of Orillia, and she was looking forward to returning home on the Labour Day weekend to be with her elderly parents. They lived at Cumberland Beach, beside the warm shallow waters of Lake Couchiching. She intended to take to her parents the fruit she had purchased. Her dad was particularly fond of the Red Haven peaches from the Niagara region, and her mom would likely bake a pie with the Spy apples. She hummed at she proceeded northbound on Church Street. Although the fall of the year was approaching, she had a wonderful weekend ahead. The fruits of the harvest were filling the stores of the city, a small portion of the bounty in the bag she was holding.

Life was good.

✧ ✧ ✧

An early-morning jogger discovered Shirley Hemmer's body forty-eight hours later in the Rosedale Ravine. Arnold Peckerman instructed Thomson and Peersen to go to the crime scene as backup, even though he had assigned another pair of detectives to the case.

On their arrival, a rookie patrolman related the known details about the brutal crime. The murderer had killed her in a secluded gully, a short distance from the trail that cut through the forested valley among the wooded slopes of the ravine. It had likely been after dark, and the woman never saw her attacker. The killer had raped the young woman, slit her throat from left to right, and she had bled out at the scene. She had likely been unconscious when the rape occurred.

They found a paper bag containing six peaches and a similar number of apples near the body. A search of the valley by the police retrieved a bloody knife from under some wild lilac bushes, a short distance from the corpse. The lab would determine if it was the murder weapon. Shortly after Thomson and Peersen arrived, the police determined that the stalker had attacked the victim on the walking trail, and then forced her into the bushes.

However, the investigation never revealed that as the stalker had compelled the young woman to leave the security of the trail, she had clung desperately to the bag of fruit, hoping in vain that she would eventually deliver it to her parents. No one would ever see the tears running down her cheeks, nor be aware that though she knew her attacker would likely rape her, she remained hopeful she would be able to flee afterward.

As well, the investigation never revealed that the attacker had filled several glass containers with the victim's blood, and allowed the remainder of it to seep into the soft moist earth of the valley floor.

The following day, the investigation unfolded as the stalker had intended. The police lab confirmed that the knife they found was the murder weapon. The fruit led the police to the fruit store, and the fingerprints on the knife were those of the young man who worked at the fruit store.

The twenty-two-year-old man, whose name was Timothy O'Keefe, had an alibi, but the timeline that he gave the police they found was untrue. Within another twenty-four hours, the detectives in charge of the case arrested Timothy. Gerry's "little red pins" had exposed Timothy's alibi as a fabrication, although Gerry did not reveal the method he had employed to discover the discrepancies.

The police were unaware that Timothy was having an affair with a thirty-five-year-old married woman, and he had lied to protect her identity. When he finally confessed to the lie, the older woman denied she had been with him to protect her marriage. The detectives were thoroughly convinced of Timothy's guilt and failed to consider an alternative. The web Timothy had woven had trapped him within its threads.

Gerry Thomson was pleased to have aided in placing the murderer behind bars, but he felt uneasy. He thought that the two detectives in charge of the case had not explored other options. As well, he had sympathy for Timothy O'Keefe, as he was so young and had his whole life ahead of him. Young Timothy had lived what appeared to be an upstanding life, until the day of the murder. He played on the local softball team and was a member of an amateur hockey club. He was an unlikely murderer. Besides, if it were true that he had been having an affair with an older woman, why did he feel the urge to commit rape?

In the days ahead, Jim Peersen also remained bothered by the crime and its quick solution. It had all been too easy, and he had learned that criminals rarely permit the police to track their actions so readily. Why had the young man not disposed of the bag of fruit? Why did he leave the knife in the ravine, and why leave his fingerprints on the weapon?

However, most of all, what gnawed at the inner recesses of Peersen's brain was the feeling that there was something eerily familiar about the crime.

✧ ✧ ✧

On the first workday of the second week of September, shortly after 9:00 a.m., Gerry sat at his desk at the precinct. In front of him was a report that Mrs. Dinkman was in jail. The North Bay police had acted on a request from Toronto, set up surveillance, and observed her when she had alighted from a Gray Coach bus in the North Bay station. An elderly male driver in an old Chevy had met her, and as the police discretely followed, the man drove her to Shady Cabins by the Lake. The northern tourist resort consisted of a dozen small fishermen's cabins, nestled close to the shoreline of Lake Nipissing.

The efficiency accommodations were scattered over a heavily wooded area, the bushes and trees providing privacy for each unit. The manager, an old coot, was bowlegged as a cowboy that had ridden every heifer that ever graced the prairies, both human and bovine.

To say that Debbie Dinkman fit in like a pea in a pod was an understatement. She scurried among the cabins during the hours of darkness like a moth on the wind. The police soon discovered that there were no couples occupying any of the cabins, but there was coupling galore. The place was a singles' sex camp.

Each night, the traffic among the cabins was busier than a holiday weekend on the King's Highways of the province. However, as all the sexual carryings-on were behind closed doors, the police were unable to intervene. By the second night, things changed, as Debbie's libido had risen. Officers observed her "doing" two middle-aged men down on the dock, and by the third night, she was humping with an elderly man in a canoe, the waves created by the rocking craft causing serious erosion of the shoreline.

The police raided the camp on the fourth night. When they arrived on the scene, eight or nine people were merrily racing around the camp dressed in togas. Each time a male caught a female, he lifted her toga and performed, as the official report stated, "indecent acts." The participants, after their arrest, claimed that they had been acting out a scene from *Julius Caesar*. Perhaps it was the battle scene on the plains of Philippi. The judge was not a Shakespearean fan and sentenced them to two months in the local senate house, generally referred to as the city jail. Debbie was out of commission for the remainder of the summer, or to express it in the vernacular terminology employed in porno movies, "Debbie never got to do Dallas!"

Gerry smiled as he read the official report. It was not every day that a police report chronicled such interesting events.

The report on Richard Dinkman was far less interesting. The Vancouver police had observed him as he departed from the train station but lost sight of him ten minutes later. Despite their efforts, he never surfaced until he returned to the station six weeks later, when he boarded the eastbound train for Toronto. Gerry wondered if there was a connection between Dinkman travelling to Vancouver and Miss Bettina Taylor having her baby delivered in the city. Was he the father of her child?

Had Stritch learned about the affair and attempted to blackmail him? If the board of education ever discovered that he had fathered a child with an unmarried member of his staff, his career would be at an end.

This gave Dinkman a motive to murder Elaine Stritch.

Peersen's desk, situated to the right of his partner's, was as neatly arranged as his daily wardrobe. He was also examining the report on Mr. Dinkman. The Vancouver police had supplied considerable details explaining why they had lost track of the suspect. Peersen felt it was an attempt to excuse their inability to follow him. Peersen was certain that Dinkman had attempted to avoid his trackers, employing a clearly thought-out plan. This meant that he had suspected that they might be watching him.

✧ ✧ ✧

By the third week of September, the opening days of the school term behind them, the senior students at YCI were concerned. What would happen, they wondered, if the police visited the school again? Would the tension influence the teachers in the classrooms?

It was the third year at YCI for Tom and his friends, but this year was different. Jimmy Frampton now accompanied them, a friend whom they had all known for many years. When Tom's family had moved to Lauder Avenue, Tom was four years of age, and Jimmy, who lived across the road from him, was only three. By the time he was five years old, he was a regular member of the group.

Jimmy was now fourteen, a skinny, freckle-faced daredevil, with a mop of uncombed rusty-red hair that fell haphazardly over his forehead.

He enjoyed clowning around even more than his friends did. Mrs. Martha Klacker and Jimmy were mortal enemies. Old Mrs. Klacker had first met Jimmy in Marlton's Grocery Store. She had overheard his colourful language and told him that he needed to "desist with the use of such immoderate verbal trash." Jimmy did not have a clue what she meant. Klacker enjoyed talking like a university professor. The boys often mocked her fancy-pants language and imitated her deep, manly voice.

Jimmy hated Klacker's condescending attitude. When she verbally trashed him, he simply stuck out his tongue at her. As a result, she despised him and never allowed an opportunity to pass without berating him. On these occasions, Jimmy merely sneered and continued to stick out his tongue.

The first month of school, Jimmy was as green as the clover in spring. However, despite outward appearances, he was reasonably bright. Not fond of school, he was simply biding his time in the classroom until he was of age to join his father shingling roofs. Harry had attempted on repeated occasions to urge him to receive the best education possible, insisting that even if he spent his life lugging shingles up a ladder, he needed to understand the world around him.

"The only world I want to know about I can see from the roof of a house," he had replied.

◆ ◆ ◆

One afternoon in French class, a severe thunderstorm shook the classroom windows as Baldy's long legs stalked across the room to close them. The wind blew sheets of water through the windows before he was able to shut them, wetting the trouser cuffs of his white suit.

"Bloody well serves me right for wearing white after Labour Day," he cursed under his breath.

Then he scowled at the class and was even more sarcastic than usual as he corrected the students' pronunciation. The situation did not improve as the day progressed. The thunderstorm had cooled the air slightly, but the respite was short-lived. The thermometer slowly climbed again, and in the late afternoon, it was ninety-two degrees. Downtown, they reported that in the hot, humid air, five people had collapsed on the street, and four people in the inner city died from heat stroke. In Chicago, the mercury soared to over a hundred degrees.

The classrooms at YCI were like ovens. Tempers flared. More fights than normal occurred in the hallways, locker rooms, and cafeteria.

During the last period of the day, Jimmy was sitting in French class. Baldwin was exhausted and irritable. The crease in his trousers had dissolved, and though sweat was trickling down his back and his armpits were like cesspools, he stubbornly refused to remove his suit jacket. To make matters worse, he was struggling with a grade-nine class, a level that he despised. In his eyes, they were patently ignorant.

Jimmy was slouched in his desk, his feet extending into the aisle, trying to make sense of why he was learning a foreign language. In public school, he had always hated English grammar, and to him the structures of French appeared even more boring. When Baldy answered a girl's answer by responding with an affirmative, "*Oui oui*," Jimmy muttered in a loud whisper, "*Oui oui* my rear end, the guy's full of poo-poo."

Baldy heard the silly comment and hit the roof. Within seconds, he dragged Jimmy down to the vice-principal's office. When they arrived, Dinkman was returning from the boys' gym, after restoring order when a water fight had broken out. They had drenched him with a heavy spray from a showerhead before he had been able to end their boisterous enthusiasm. Arriving back at the office, soaking wet, infuriated, and ready to explode, a smirking Jimmy and an explosive Mr. Baldwin confronted him.

Baldy shoved Jimmy into one of the hard-assed oak chairs in the outer office, explained the boy's offences in an incomprehensible mish-mash of whistling English and French, and stormed out.

Dinkman grabbed Jimmy by the collar and threw him into his office while demanding that he explain his crimes. Jimmy merely smirked and kept silent. Despite Dinkman's tirades, Jimmy refused to say a word. The more he smirked, the angrier Dinkman became. Finally, he struck Jimmy across the face.

Mrs. Applecrust stiffened when she heard the slapping noise of flesh on flesh. She thought, *Some day that man will kill someone. I've never seen such a temper.*

Then she heard Dinkman shouting at Jimmy. She shook her head and made a sucking sound between her teeth as she thought, *I've never heard such bad language in all my life. Even a poker player who lost his jockstrap in a game of strip poker would never utter such foul words.* She often enjoyed thinking thoughts that she knew she could never utter aloud.

Dinkman opened his office door and thrust Jimmy onto one of the oak chairs. Mrs. Applecrust gazed at Jimmy over the top of her glasses and offered a sympathetic smile. She knew the boy was deserving of discipline, but thought, *Having the two biggest assholes on staff pound on you on the same day is more than any lad deserves.* She excused her use of the word "asshole," as she had not uttered it aloud.

From that day forward, Dinkman watched Jimmy like an eagle watches a rabbit. He was determined to find an excuse to expel Jimmy. Meanwhile, Jimmy was determined to extract revenge for the hard face slap that he had received.

Dinkman is even worse than Old Klacker, he thought. *With her, it's only her mouth that I must be careful of, not her fist.*

On 12 September, the heat finally eased. Throughout Toronto, as the bedtime hour neared, people felt the refreshing breezes blowing from the west. The sight of their window curtains rustling in the wind meant a good night's sleep, something that had eluded them for the previous ten days.

✧ ✧ ✧

Frank Gnomes had avoided sleeping in the conjugal bed during the heat wave, and now that the high temperatures had eased, he did not intend to return to the titanic task of satisfying the needs of the voracious Sally-Lou. He thought, *That woman could sink any man's libido.* He could hear her calling him from the upstairs, and he yelled, "I have work to do, honey."

"You have work to do up here too."

"I know, honey, but I have to finish what I'm working on."

In essence, this was true as he was working on a bottle of beer and needed to finish it. Sally-Lou pounded on the floor a few times; he ignored her, and five minutes later, the house was quiet.

Frank was tired of the marriage game. Women treated him differently after he said, "I do." Lost in thought, he wandered out onto the front veranda, beer bottle in hand, sat down on an old rocking chair, and put his feet up on the railing.

The street was now quiet. The night was clear and cool, a touch of the approaching autumn in the air. He lived on Bellevue Avenue, in the same house where his parents had lived when they were first married and where they had dwelt all their married life. They had raised their only son in the same house. In high school, Frank had discovered that he excelled in English literature and grammar. After he graduated from university, he talked his way into a job at the *Trib*, and they now considered him their best crime reporter. Recently, the editor had thrown a few political stories his way.

Frank had covered Konrad Adenauser's recent win for his Christian Democratic Party in the first German election since the war. Adenauser was one seat short of a majority, but the seventy-seven-year-old leader was in firm control. He had promised to work for German reunification and a close military alliance with the west. The Communist ultra-right party, which contained many former Nazis, had no representation.

Frank had turned in an excellent article, injecting his own interpretation and insights. The editor had been pleased, and his next assignment had been an in-depth appraisal of the bitter dispute between Italy and Marshall Tito's Yugoslavia over Trieste, an international free zone.

As a reporter, he had wanted to express his thoughts on Secretary of State Foster Dulles' preemptive warning to China. The American statesman had declared that any Chinese aggression toward Korea might cause the United States to attack China. However, the editor had given the assignment to a reporter with more experience in the political field. Certain that he would eventually earn a position on the political desk, Frank knew that from there he was only a breath away from editorial writing. He had always been lucky in his career, but being lucky in love was quite another matter.

He was attracted to beautiful women, and this had been his downfall. His first wife was gorgeous, and a year after they were married, they moved into a charming Victorian row house on Belmont Street, near Davenport Road and Bay Street. He had received two pay raises that year, and they had no trouble with the mortgage. Two years later, he became restless. He had found that beauty was indeed only skin deep, and on cold January nights, sitting around the fireplace, he realized that the flames were more interesting than his wife. They divorced a year later, and she got the row house in the settlement.

A year later, he tied the knot with another attractive woman. After the heat of the honeymoon cooled, he realized her bra size was higher than her IQ. As for Sally-Lou, he was unable to account for why he married her. It couldn't have been the booze—no man was able to drink that much.

When his parents died, he inherited the family home on Bellevue Avenue. Sally-Lou hated the house, and indeed, it was in need of repairs. Despite this, he stubbornly refused to move into a chic apartment, which they could likely afford with the money from the sale of the premises. The house reminded him of the happy, prepubescent days of his youth, before he became a prisoner of his penis. During his teenage years, he had been happy. He thought, *Being too young to get laid is not all that bad. At least I made no alimony payments.*

Gnomes knew he was a sucker for a pretty face and a curvaceous body with melon-size breasts. Never having respected the intelligence of women, he had always felt that he might as well have the nice bodies, but recently he had begun to question his cynical assessment of the fair sex.

Samantha Anderson turned heads when she walked into a room, and she possessed intelligence as well. He considered her almost as bright as he was. For him, this was a considerable concession.

In his jacket pocket, hanging in the bedroom cupboard, were two tickets for the Saturday afternoon performance of the musical *Carousel*. A buddy in the entertainment department at the newspaper had given them to him. Melody Fair, the company producing the musical, had erected a large tent near the Princes' Gates at the CNE. When he had told Samantha that he had the tickets, she had agreed to attend.

On Saturday afternoon, after enjoying the performance, she was softly singing the words of one of the songs from *Carousel*: "If I loved you, words wouldn't come in an easy way …" As Frank left her apartment, he wondered if she meant the words of the song for him. He was painfully aware that she had never indicated how she felt about him. This was a new experience for him.

Because he worked at odd hours at the *Trib* and the performance at Melody Fair had been in the afternoon, he had no explaining to do to Sally-Lou. However, if things progressed as he hoped, he would have serious problems.

◇ ◇ ◇

On the third day of the new term, Tom was unaware that as he sat in class Detectives Thomson and Peersen were marching into the school's office. Mrs. Applecrust gazed up at the two men and her heart sank into her shoes. She was already flustered, as Mr. Dinkman had just taken her to task for an error in the budget, a miscalculation that she knew she had not committed. She was certain the detectives were there to see Mr. Dinkman, but before she could inform him, the door to Tyrone Evanson's office opened, and the mighty man himself appeared.

Gazing at Thomson and Peersen, he inquired, "Gentlemen, may I assist you?"

"We're here to see the vice-principal."

"Before you interview Mr. Dinkman, would you kindly step into my office?"

Thomson and Peersen followed him, and when they were all seated, Mr. Evanson said, "I assume you are still investigating the murder of poor Miss Stritch."

"Yes, sir."

"I have given the matter considerable thought over the past few weeks. Has Mr. Dinkman ever suggested that you interview George Meagan for a second time?"

"No, he hasn't. Are you suggesting that we should?"

"I think it might prove useful."

"Doesn't he teach Latin?"

"Yes, but before he joined that language department, he was in guidance. He was working in that capacity for several years before Miss Stritch was murdered. He asked to be reassigned, as he said that the guidance position was bothering him. He said that students confided in him disturbing information, about the staff and other students, to which he felt he should not be privy."

"What type of things?"

"That, I cannot tell you. I do not perform the staff evaluations or deal with the staff on a daily basis. I learned of it when I questioned George after I observed on the staff roster that Mr. Dinkman had assigned him to teach Latin. Because of the passage of time, and the fact that you have not arrested anyone for the murder, I thought that any insignificant detail might be important."

"Thank you, Mr. Evanson. We will certainly take your suggestion under advisement," Thomson replied. He thought it odd that this had never been mentioned before.

Mr. Evanson stood from his chair to signal that the interview had ended.

"Mr. Evanson," Thomson said as he stood to his feet, "we are not here to interview your vice-principal; we are here to arrest him."

Evanson fell back into his chair with a thud as the two detectives departed the room.

✦ ✦ ✦

A minute later, they were standing in front of the august Mr. Richard Dinkman, who sat imperiously at his desk. His arms were resting upright on the desk, the tips of the fingers touching to form a church steeple, and he was peering over the top of his fingers. It was his usual stance when interviewing people he considered his inferior.

The vice-principal was a thin, wiry man, with a wisp of a moustache, and an expressionless poker face. His weasel eyes darted everywhere, especially when sizing up a quarry. His graying hair was combed straight back, and it was flaky dry, constantly dropping dandruff onto the shoulders of the navy-blue suit, his perennial garb. When he spoke, a dry cough caused him to pause frequently in midsentence, a very irritating habit.

Thomson was aware that some of the teachers referred to the vice-principal as a walking corpse, or at best, a corpse-in-training for an undertaker's layaway plan. Gerry also knew that the students referred to him as Dickhead.

On this occasion, Thomson wasted no time. He slapped the warrant on the administrator's desk, and he said in a calm official voice, "Mr. Dinkman, this is a warrant for your arrest for obstructing justice. Please stand and place your hands behind your back."

Dinkman's church steeple collapsed.

Moments later, Mrs. Applecrust almost turned to applesauce when she observed them lead Dinkman out of the office.

At the precinct, the intimidatingly muscular Sergeant Malloy placed Dinkman in a holding cell. An hour later, Thomson and Peersen ordered that Malloy bring him to an interview room. It was thirty more minutes before they joined him. By this time, Dinkman was constantly clasping and unclasping his hands as he paced the room. However, despite his fright, when the questioning began, his resolve seemed to return.

To every question, he replied, "I have nothing to add."

Finally, Gerry sighed heavily as if in sympathy and said, "Now then, we'll just see about that. I think we need to help you improve your memory, Mr. Dinkman. Perhaps if you are a guest of the Don Jail overnight, your memory might be better in the morning. Who knows? You might meet one of the students that you've taught over the years. It might turn out to be a warm, student-teacher reunion. But remember, in the morning, we will ask you the same questions, and eventually, you will have to answer them.

"You may have access to a lawyer, but as we have formally charged you, regardless, you will remain in custody at the Don until you come before a judge. That will be sometime tomorrow or perhaps after several more days."

If Dinkman's steeple had collapsed earlier, the entire cathedral was now in shambles.

His face was pale and expressionless. Between gritted teeth he spat, "What do you wish to know?"

"Mr. George Meagan confided in you and told you information about staff members that we need to know."

"What he told me is none of your business," and then he quickly rephrased his words. "He never told me anything that could possibly be of interest to the police."

"We will be the judge of that."

"George said that three students had claimed that a member of staff had been engaging in improprieties with a friend of theirs, but they refused to reveal the name of the teacher or the friend."

"And you thought this was of no importance to us?" Thomson spat in disgust. "Was the staff member male or female?"

"George didn't know."

"Did you investigate?"

"Of course, but the students refused to tell me anything."

"Are you aware of any sexual relationships among the staff?"

"There are rumours that Miss Taylor is a lesbian, and that she had an affair with someone on staff, but I don't think the rumours are true."

"Could she have been in love with Miss Stritch and was upset when she decided to marry Bill Matheson?"

"I think that would take a stretch of imagination."

"So, stretch your imagination. Who else may have formed an illicit couple?"

"Sam Millford and Elaine were close, even after they stopped dating. If they had sex while dating, I don't know."

"How would you assess the friendship between Miss Stritch and Mr. Baldwin?"

"Like a peacock and a peahen, though I'm not sure which was which! I do know that when they went out together for an evening, I'm sure his feathers were preened." He grinned slightly, pleased with the supposed cleverness of his last statement.

As the interview continued, Dinkman spilled many intimate details about the staff, but it was difficult to assess what was important and what was hearsay. Peersen filled many pages in his logbook with detailed notes, which he and Gerry would discuss later.

To Dinkman's relief, Thomson finally said, "In light of your newfound cooperative spirit, we will temporarily suspend the warrant. However, if we discover anything in the course of our investigation that we feel you in all probability knew and didn't reveal, the warrant will be re-issued."

Mr. Dinkman ignored the sarcasm in Thomson's voice. However, he departed from the station a more contrite man than he had entered.

✧ ✧ ✧

The following day, they interviewed George Meagan. From their files, the detectives were aware that Meagan was a graduate of the University of London, England, and had attended Yale. He was a highly respected scholar, having translated and published a series of obscure Latin poetry and prose.

Securing a position in the public school system in Yorkshire, he taught Latin in Middlesbrough. The year after his wife divorced him, he resigned his position and immigrated to Canada. On arrival in his adopted country, he found employment in the offices of the Imperial Oil Company. Deciding he wished to resume his teaching career, he enrolled in Department of Education summer courses and earned an Ontario Secondary School Teaching Certificate. After teaching Latin for five years a Humberside Collegiate, he took another summer course and applied for a guidance position at YCI.

Meagan's cultured English accent and humble manner spoke of a gentleman who was more comfortable in the world of books than in the real world around him. His brown tweed jacket with leather patches on the elbows, along with the heavy bifocal lenses in his thick-rimmed glasses, created a professorial appearance. Adding to this impression was his unruly brown hair, which flopped over his eyes. He was constantly brushing it back with a nervous flick of his hand.

Peersen remembered that Meagan's file had recorded that he had been a distinguished pilot during the war and received recognition for his bravery. Which was the real Meagan, the gentle scholar or the daring warrior?

Slowly, in a hesitant voice, he confirmed the details that Dinkman had told them.

"Why did you not inform us earlier?" Peersen demanded.

"It was over seven years ago. I failed to see how any of that information could be relevant."

"We should be allowed to be the judge."

"Sorry," he replied, remorse audible in his voice.

"Can you add anything to Mr. Dinkman's evidence?"

"Well, I remember that three students hinted that a friend of theirs was being harassed sexually by a member of staff. I was unable to decide if they were telling tales to attract attention or telling the truth. The responsibility weighed heavily on me. If I spoke up, it might create a witch hunt and ruin a teacher's career. If I remained silent, an innocent teenager might have his or her life ruined. Finally, I decided to pack in the guidance job. As the Bible says, 'to whom much has been given much is expected.' I decided the expectations were not those that I wished to live with. I am much happier with Latin declensions."

"Was the teacher who was supposedly harassing the students a male or female?"

"I was never able to determine."

"Did you report the information that the students told you?"

"Yes, I informed Mr. Dinkman. He questioned the students but was unable to retrieve any further knowledge of the alleged harassments."

"Thank you, Mr. Meagan. We appreciate your cooperation. If we have further questions, we will contact you."

"I hope I have not said anything that might create problems for my academic peers."

"We will be discreet, Mr. Meagan," Thomson said reassuringly. "Trust us."

As Meagan departed the room, Peersen and Thomson looked at each other, frustration evident on their faces.

The thought that Peersen retained after interviewing Meagan was, *Still waters run deep.*

Aloud, Peersen said, "Shit. This staff is beginning to look like the staff from hell. We have a suspected lesbian, who might not be a lesbian, but whom we know has had a baby. The staff dandy might be a homosexual—or not. The vice-principal is a masochist who is married to a sex fiend. The principal is a pompous twit who doesn't know his staff and was overly fond of Miss Stritch."

After a brief pause, Peersen continued. "The boys' PT teacher is regular beyond the wildest dreams of ex-lax, and I am certain he records the time and date each time he flushes the toilet. We can't question the librarian for more than two minutes without a life preserver. Miss Hitch has more outfits than the Eaton's Santa Claus Parade and is the only woman I've ever met who could wear a six-foot-diameter pumpkin and think she was chic. Bill Matheson is Mr. Goody Two-Shoes, who has never been anywhere improper or done anything wrong. Meagan was a war pilot who now can't drop a bomb in his own pants when the world scares the shit out of him."

"Yes," Thomson replied, "I feel as if we are circling around on a merry-go-wheel with a bunch of grotesque carved figures. What's really going on among the inner circle of the staff? Everything seems to lead to a dead end."

Pausing briefly, Gerry added, "Now then, we'll just see about that."

Chapter Six

The following day, Sergeant Malloy delivered a file folder to Gerry Thomson that a patrolman had given him about a domestic disturbance on Ashbury Avenue. When the officers arrived, they had been confronted with the sound of breaking furniture and smashing glass, along with the screams of a terrified woman. They pounded on the door, but their loud knocking was unheard above the din created by the pugilists within.

Having justifiable cause, the police entered. Neighbours were outside on their verandas in a display of unrestrained nosiness. Suspense hung in the air as the house became quiet. When the officers departed ten minutes later, the observers were disappointed that they had not carried anyone away in handcuffs.

The police report stated that at the home of Mr. Richard Dinkman and Mrs. Debora Dinkman a violent quarrel had erupted. Mrs. Dinkman's left eye was black and swollen, and several bruises were on the right side of her face. She refused to be taken to a hospital and insisted that she would not press charges.

The police were helpless to intervene further.

When they were certain that the situation was calm, they warned Mr. Dinkman that they would be filing a report and that if they learned of further complaints, they would return with a warrant for his arrest.

As Gerry read the report, he realized that Dinkman had likely learned about Debbie's sojourn in the North Bay jail. *I need to put that maniacal bastard behind bars,* he thought. *No man should treat a woman in that manner, regardless of her sins.*

◆ ◆ ◆

After September disappeared, October ushered in the cool nights of early autumn. Weather was always a favourite topic among Torontonians. Those who had suffered through the city's interminably bleak winter days could never be convinced that God knew what he was doing when he created the dismal months of January and February. In addition, the Almighty had likely been slightly out of sorts when he invented March. As for November, the sheer madness of ever inserting into the calendar thirty days of rain, cold, and cloudy skies was beyond reason.

Thomson and Peersen had been busy and closed another investigation. It had been relatively uncomplicated, as a member of the victim's family had committed the murder and the number of suspects was limited. Early in the search, Thomson's little red pins had revealed the discrepancies in one of the alibis and a confession followed shortly thereafter. Gerry Thomson wished that the Stritch case had been as easy

One morning, having a little spare time—a rarity—Thomson decided to revisit Elaine Stritch's mother in Hamilton. After explaining his idea to Jim Peersen, a half-hour later, the two men were sitting in heavy traffic on the Lakeshore Road where the roadway entered the Queen Elizabeth Highway. There had been a report in the papers that the city was to widen the four-lane bridge over the Humber River to six lanes, at a cost of four and a half million dollars. The detectives lamented that they had not already constructed the bridge. It was fifteen minutes before they were able to access the QE and head toward Hamilton.

The mother of Miss Stritch lived in the west end of the city, on Emery Street, near the campus of McMaster University. Mature shade trees flanked the avenue. They had built the homes in the 1920s, a decade when families tended to be larger. The spacious verandas of the homes overlooked manicured lawns and flowerbeds. Earlier frosts had already decimated the tender plants; only the chrysanthemums and a few hardy geraniums remaining. On this sunny day, an occasional rose, sheltered by a garden fence, soaked up the final warmth of the season.

Mrs. Stritch suspiciously opened the door of her two-storey house and, recognizing the detectives, hesitantly motioned them inside, her face betraying her unease with their visit. Gerry understood. No mother wished to be reminded of the brutal murder of her daughter, especially two years after the tragic event. Mrs. Stritch looked about sixty-five years of age with silver-gray hair and ramrod-straight posture. Without saying a word, she led them to the oversized kitchen and placed the kettle on the gas stove to boil water for tea. She lived alone in the eight-room house, as Mr. Stritch had passed away from a heart attack the year before their daughter was killed. Mrs. Stritch now rented out the bedrooms upstairs to students who attended the nearby university.

Peersen studied Mrs. Stritch for a few moments and decided that in her youth she had been beautiful. Her shiny blue eyes remained attractive, even though they presently reflected deep sadness. Her facial bone structure was classic, and she possessed fine, clear features. However, the tragic death of her daughter had sapped her strength and not only cheated her of grandchildren but of her golden years. Worry lines etched her impassive face, masked against the outside world. Peersen wondered if her expressionless façade was a result of the death of her daughter or if she had always maintained this demeanor. One thing was certain: Mrs. Stritch was a closed woman.

The interview proceeded as expected. The mother again told them that she knew no reason why anyone should harm her beautiful daughter, her only child. The detectives already knew that Elaine had attended a Catholic high school, had been academically very successful, and received an honour BA in English from McMaster University. However, when asked directly, Mrs. Stritch avoided any personal details of her daughter's school years.

Elaine Stritch's file showed that after graduating, she had moved to Toronto and attended OCE to earn her teacher certification. Similar to the previous interviews, Mrs. Stritch said that she knew little about her daughter's male friends in Toronto, as Elaine never brought any of them home when she visited Hamilton.

"I sometimes questioned her about her lifestyle," the elderly woman explained, but when Peersen inquired what she meant, she refused to elaborate.

"I don't remember any of the names of her Toronto friends," she added.

The detectives thought this was odd but simply nodded their heads and did not press her further. They already knew the identities of Elaine's friends in Toronto.

Mrs. Stritch said, "After my daughter became engaged to Bill Matheson, she said they'd come to Hamilton on the Thanksgiving Sunday for me to meet him. She passed away on the Friday before the Labour Day weekend, so I never met him until the first evening at the funeral parlours. After the funeral, I never saw him again."

"What did you think of Bill Matheson?" Gerry asked.

"I never gave him much thought. I was grieving the death of my daughter."

"Did you like him?"

"I suppose. I spent so little time with him that I never really formed an opinion."

Gerry considered this highly unlikely. Mothers always formed opinions quickly about anyone who might marry their little girls.

Twenty minutes later, learning nothing new, Thomson thanked her for the tea and stood to leave, motioning for Peersen to follow him. As they exited the front door, they noticed a handyman repairing a broken slat on the veranda railing. Mrs. Stritch excused herself and went over to talk to the man. From the way that they greeted each other, Peersen suspected they had known each other for a considerable length of time.

Thomson and Peersen sat in the car to mull over the interview, and after five minutes, they saw Mrs. Stritch go inside and close the door. The sun had disappeared behind a patch of dark clouds, and a chill had crept into the air. Peersen told Gerry to wait, as he wanted to chat with the handyman. Opening the car door, he buttoned his jacket against the cool wind.

The man saw Peersen approach but continued deftly inserting the new veranda railing.

"Mighty fine work you have here," Peersen said, and instantly regretted saying it. He felt that he sounded like a cowboy riding into town and saying to the sheriff, "Mighty fine town you have here."

He decided to be more direct, and drop the small talk. "Have you known Mrs. Stritch a long time?"

"Yup," the elderly man said as he continued working.

"Did you know her daughter?"

"Yup."

"Did you know the daughter well?"

"Yup."

"Do you know any words other than 'Yup'?"

"Yup."

Peersen flipped out his badge as he stressed that he was investigating a murder and needed his help. The man gazed at the badge for a second or two and then continued working.

"Do you know anything about the life of Elaine Stritch that might help us?"

"Yup."

"Then please, do tell!"

Peersen waited patiently.

The man eyed the detective suspiciously and continued working. After a minute or more, he realized that the policeman was not going away until he answered his questions. Slowly, he began talking, but he did not stop working.

"I've known Elaine's mother since we were teenagers. Mrs. Stritch and I went to high school together. She's a fine woman. I suppose she's told you that Elaine was a saint and that the pope was ready to canonize her."

In the worst way, Peersen wanted to say, "Yup." He refrained and merely nodded his head, but he noticed the edge of bitterness that had crept into the man's voice. The fitting of the railing into position continued as he spoke, and without glancing at the detective, he finally continued.

"Young Miss Elaine was a saint with hot pants. Perhaps I should more accurately say, a saint who couldn't keep her pants up. I know for a fact that she slept with at least a half a dozen of the boys in her grade-thirteen class."

"Sir …"

"My name's Mr. Jake Kitchener."

"Mr. Kitchener, high school boys often spread rumours. Most of them are wishful thinking."

"I stand by my statement. The girl slept around. She was busier than the parking lot at the Stony Creek Dairy Bar on a hot July night."

"How do you know about the sex life of the high school students?"

"I never told Mrs. Stritch what I knew about Elaine, out of respect for her, but her daughter ruined my son's life, and he was not the only one she destroyed."

"What happened?"

"Let's just say that it involved penicillin, and my son's girlfriend never forgave him for a moment of weakness in the back seat of a car, up on the Hamilton Mountain. The couple who were in the front seat had big mouths, and West Hamilton is like a small town. Rumours spread fast. My son was too humiliated to see a doctor, and by the time I found out about the problem, serious damage had been done. He's still not right."

"Do you know anything more about the intimate life of Miss Stritch?"

"Yup."

Silence!

Peersen sensed that the man had finished speaking. "You have anything more to say?"

"Nope."

His final pronouncement given, Mr. Kitchener walked over to his toolbox to fetch a wood file.

Peersen returned to the car, where Thomson was waiting.

"Well?" Gerry asked impatiently.

"If what the guy says is true, we have a whole new field of suspects here in Hamilton." Peersen then explained to Gerry what he had learned.

Thomson thought about the information and finally said, "I think that interviewing the students here in Hamilton would be a waste of time, but perhaps we should have a talk with some of the older male students of Elaine Stritch."

◆ ◆ ◆

On a rainy October evening, Frank Gnomes and Samantha Anderson attended the University Theatre on Bloor Street to see the film *Roman Holiday*, featuring Audrey Hepburn and Gregory Peck. Samantha was enchanted by the story of the fairy tale princess and her fling with freedom on the romantic streets of Rome. Samantha had chosen the movie, and Frank hoped that her starry-eyed mood might continue after they arrived back at her apartment.

He thought, *I'd rather have gone to the Odeon Carlton to see* The Desert Rats *starring Richard Burton, and James Mason playing the role of General Rommel.*

Frank had been busy during the last few weeks. His editor had assigned him to write about the United States' offer of a nonaggression pact with Russia, to reduce their fear of an attack from the west now that NATO had allowed West Germany to rearm. The Americans considered the pact a wise move, as both super powers possessed the A-bomb.

Frank dreamed of being assigned to a foreign desk in Paris or London. He thought that he would leave Sally-Lou behind in Toronto; anything to escape the arguments that lately had become more frequent. She had accused him of seeing another woman. *Man,* he thought, *that woman certainly is suspicious.*

After watching *Roman Holiday,* he thought that perhaps he would add Rome to his list of cities that he wished to be assigned to—cheap wine, great food, and chic women. However, unlike Gregory Peck in the film, Frank doubted he would ever find a vulnerable princess sleeping in his apartment, in his bed, wearing *his* pyjama top.

◆ ◆ ◆

Temperatures dropped further with the advent of November, but unlike the weather, the heat between Mr. Dinkman and Jimmy was increasing. Jimmy had received a week's detentions for talking too loudly in the hallways during the class rotations between periods. It was an unreasonably harsh punishment for such a minor infraction of the rules. Dinkman smiled triumphantly as he handed Jimmy the detention slip.

The following day, when Jimmy passed by the vice-principal's hallway door, he gave it a swift kick. When Dinkman appeared at the door, several students were grinning, but they all insisted that they did not recognize the boy who had committed the felony. Their descriptions of the lad all differed. Dinkman was certain he knew who it was.

The following day, when Jimmy again thumped the door with his running shoe, the door immediately swung open and a long arm shot out and grabbed him by the collar. Dinkman had examined Jimmy's timetable and knew the times that he would be passing by his door. He had been lying in wait.

He received three weeks of detentions, and Dinkman phoned Jimmy's mother and informed her that any further occurrences and he would expel her son. She knew about Dinkman slapping Jimmy and thought the vice-principal was truly a dickhead.

As Jimmy sat in the detention room, he dreamed of revenge. Slowly, a diabolical plot emerged in his brain.

✧ ✧ ✧

On a Saturday morning at home, during the second week of November, Jim Peersen poured his coffee into his favourite mug. The sun was shining through the windowpanes of the doors that overlooked the patio deck. The blue sky, a rarity for the rain-sodden month, was promising an unusually mild and sunny day.

Jim pulled his blue dressing gown around him, fastened the belt, and sauntered out onto the deck. The trees were skeletal, and he noted that the "damn squirrels," as he referred to them, were scurrying along the bare limbs in a futile search for food. The acorns of fall had long since disappeared.

The sun splashed across the boards of the deck, their warmth soothing against his bare feet. In summer, the heavy foliage hid the retreat from the direct rays of the sun, but now it was open to the gentle warmth of the declining rays. Unfolding a chair, he plucked himself down. It was his day away from the precinct, and unless he received an emergency call, it was his own.

During the past week, he and Thomson had been interviewing graduate students from York Collegiate. Some had refused an interview, but those who had consented to questioning denied that Miss Stritch had ever made improper advances toward them. In fact, they had never heard of any rumours to that effect. Peersen did not know if the denials were the result of a fear of being involved, as their teacher had been murdered, or because they did not want their parents to learn that they had been diddling with a teacher. One student hinted that their English teacher had found him attractive. Thomson was skeptical. The end result of the week's interrogations? Nothing!

Later in the day, Jim intended to visit the gym where he normally worked out. He had neglected his exercising of late, as the demands of the job had kept him busy. Perhaps an intense workout would clear the cobwebs from his brain.

As he sipped his coffee, he realized that he had neglected more than his exercises. He had not called Jill Carver, whom he had been dating off and on, in over two weeks. She had not contacted him either. He guessed that the relationship, similar to the coffee in his cup, had cooled.

Then for some unknown reason, he thought of Samantha Anderson. It crossed his mind that it would be nice to see her socially. Then he thought, *What on earth am I thinking? She works in the sex trade. If anyone at the precinct ever saw me with her, other than in my capacity as a policeman, I'd be the brunt of endless jokes.* However, despite the aversion he felt for her profession, he now realized how much she attracted him. Unable to stop thinking of her, he finally said aloud, "What the hell!"

✧ ✧ ✧

Jimmy Frampton had been resourceful but also cautious as he planned his revenge against Dinkman. The materials that he required for his payback plan had been difficult to obtain, but he had been successful. They were now hidden under his bed. His mother had found them while cleaning out his room and wondered why her son possessed a box of women's sanitary napkins. She had smiled as she wondered if her son had changed sexes and developed the woman's curse.

When Jimmy came home from school, she casually dropped into the conversation that she had found some unusual "bandages" under his bed. Trying to sound casual, Jimmy said that Carol had shoved them in his school bag as a joke, and that he had placed them under the bed until he could find a way to use them to play a practical joke on her.

Glancing at him skeptically, his mother told him, "I think you had best get rid of them."

Jimmy nodded in compliance and thought, *I'll get rid of them all right, but not the way she thinks. Dinkman is about to receive a gift that he has no idea is coming his way.*

✧ ✧ ✧

Peersen threw his gym equipment into the trunk of the car, drove downtown, and parked on Victoria Street. As drops of rain began to splatter the car's windshield, he walked quickly to the box office of Loew's Downtown (Elgin Theatre), located on Yonge Street just a short distance north of Queen Street. Across the road from the theatre, the doors of Eaton's and Simpson's were in constant motion as shoppers dashed inside to escape the pending shower and to inspect the stores' Saturday bargains.

Jim Peersen purchased a theatre ticket and located an empty seat among the back rows. The auditorium was crowded, especially for a 4:30 p.m. matinee, as the film *From Here to Eternity* was attracting large crowds. The reviews had been excellent, and it was an all-star cast—Burt Lancaster, Montgomery Clift, Deborah Kerr, and Frank Sinatra. As Peersen viewed the film, he was amazed at Sinatra's performance, since he had always considered him a bobby socks crooner rather than an actor.

Following the movie, Peersen wandered up Yonge Street to Basil's Restaurant at the corner of Gerrard Street, where he ordered a toasted clubhouse sandwich, fries, and a fresh orange juice. The latter was his concession to his usual healthy habits, and the fries he would work off, as he had finally summoned the courage to visit the club that Samantha Anderson frequented and used their gym. He was well aware that it was a mistake to go near her. It bothered him that it might be an evening when the police had the club under surveillance. Despite this, he intended to proceed with his intensions. He was unable to explain his behaviour. It was contrary to everything he believed.

It was after eight-thirty when he arrived at the Gymnasium Club on Yonge Street. He knew how to survey the scene, and he saw no evidence of a police presence. Entering the club, before purchasing a membership, he scanned the interior, but he did not recognize anyone. The attendant accepted his cash and directed him to the change rooms. Five minutes later, he was busy lifting weights, feeling the resistance of his muscles to the sudden exertion after almost two weeks of doing nothing more strenuous than writing police reports. It felt great.

✧ ✧ ✧

It was after ten o'clock when Samantha entered the club, which by now smelled of stale sweat and fresh perspiration from strenuous exercise. Her eyes scanned the room, instantly spotting Peersen. Immediately, her suspicions were aroused. She noticed that the sweat on his muscular body glistened in the reflected glow from the overhead lights, emphasizing his smooth skin.

She thought, *My God, he's the only man I have ever seen with porcelain skin, and he has a beautiful body to match.* Samantha decided to be direct. If he were there to question her further, he had best go elsewhere. She had no time for cops' games.

As she approached, Peersen was concentrating on his left arm muscles, and she caught him by surprise. Suddenly, she was standing in front of him, arms on her hips in a defensive mode, her face distinctly hostile.

"What are you doing here? And don't tell me you were in the neighbourhood."

Peersen grinned sheepishly and said, "I'm in the neighbourhood because I hoped I might see you. And before you ask, I'm not here as a police officer."

"Then why are you here?"

"As I said, to see you."

"Do you want a spanking?" she said sarcastically, knowing that he knew why she hung around the Gymnasium Club and was certain that he disapproved.

"If I wanted a spanking, I'd visit my mother. I came to see you because I enjoyed talking to you when my partner and I were in your apartment."

"Aren't you afraid that your cop pals will give you a verbal spanking for visiting a place like this?"

"I'm a big boy. I can handle myself."

"That remains to be seen."

She walked away from him toward the change room and, five minutes later, began her exercises. About 10:30 p.m., she went to the showers, leaving Peersen to continue his workout. It was almost eleven o'clock when she finished showering and had seated herself on a stool at the club's coffee counter.

She watched as Peersen approached her warily. Eyeing him appreciatively, she again noticed the finely toned muscles of his arms and legs. Peersen's face turned serious as he said to her, "Truce? I simply would like to chat and get to know you. May I phone you sometime?"

"You think that's wise?"

"Look, I don't judge you because of your profession, so don't judge me because of mine."

She heard the irritation in his voice. It was true; she did not trust cops. Against her better judgment, she said, "You have my phone number or know how to get it. I'll think about what you said. Call me in a few days, and I'll give you an answer. Don't ever come here to the club again. Understood?"

Without finishing her coffee, she departed. *Damn,* she thought, *I should never have given him a second look. But he's so good looking and actually seems nice—for a cop.*

◈ ◈ ◈

As Peersen left the club, he too was confused about what had happened. Though he was unable to explain his behaviour, he felt unable to withdraw. However, he agreed with her idea that he should never again cross the threshold of the Gymnasium Club. It was far too risky.

◈ ◈ ◈

Jimmy Frampton was ready to implement his plan of revenge. Though not interested in academics, he was clever and easily mastered the things that interested him. He had observed the school routines and knew that the last door they locked at the end of the day was the south door, facing the bicycle racks. It remained open later as Miss Allyson was always the last staff member to depart. She usually worked late, unable to tear herself away from her world of books. In truth, she had no real reason to return to her lonely flat, located on the second floor of a large house on Holland Park Avenue, east of Oakwood Avenue. In November, it was after dark by the time the south door was secured.

Jimmy had obtained the box of women's sanitary napkins from Shorty, who had asked Ruth to purchase them for him at the drug store. Shorty had told her that he needed them for a friend who was playing a joke on a dickhead who deserved to be humiliated.

Jimmy used a pen with a wide art nib and a bottle of red ink to write in large letters, two words on each pad. In the morning, when he departed for school, he carried them in a paper bag. During the day, he stored them in his locker, hidden under his gym clothes.

Following the final class of the day, he went to the library and pretended to study. Since he was a grade-nine student, Miss Allyson did not know him well, and it was unlikely she would remember him.

About 4:45 p.m., he left the library. Miss Allyson did not look at him, as was her usual manner with students. Later, she was able to honestly say that she did not remember anyone remaining late in her library.

After leaving the library, Jimmy retrieved the revenge articles from his locker and secluded himself in the last row of lockers, the furthest distance from the cafeteria. The school was quiet. No one was in the gym, and the cafeteria staff had completed their cleaning chores and departed. The teachers had gone home. Jimmy crept quietly toward the stairwell and ascended to the second floor. His only worry was running into the head caretaker.

The head caretaker at the school was Joe Castle, in his midthirties, a handsome man who was young to have been promoted to the chief position. His slim athletic build, dark curly hair, and long eyelashes that accented his shiny brown eyes created more the appearance of a gigolo than that of a man who laboured supervising the cleaning of washrooms and classrooms. The older female students constantly flirted with him, and even the younger teachers were not above smiling coyly when they met him in the hallways. He shyly ignored their entreaties, which added to his appeal.

Jimmy listened carefully and, not detecting a sound, he felt certain that Mr. Castle had finished his inspection of the rooms on the second floor. He silently entered the girls' washroom. It was located directly above the school office. Outside the washroom was a mature catalpa tree, its bare limbs creaking in the November winds. The long seedpods dangled back and forth, subservient to the chilling breezes. The trees branches rattled against the windows of the school's office below.

Jimmy opened the window in the girls' washroom, and one at a time, dropped the sanitary pads out the window, hoping they would ensnarl among the mesh of swaying boughs. Several fell to the ground, but of the dozen, nine of them clung securely to the branches.

Satisfied, he departed from the school as quickly and quietly as possible through the south door. He had walked to school, as he did not wish to run the risk of someone seeing his bike in the racks long after everyone else's had been removed.

In bed that night, Jimmy dreamt of the pads. He saw them swirling around in space, like the clothes in his mom's new washing machine when the dasher in the tub thrashed them about as the laundry soap foamed and bubbled. In one dream sequence, he saw the pads drift off into nothingness, and he awoke in a sweat, fearing that the wind had blown all the napkins off the catalpa tree and strewn them across the ground.

Jimmy's worries were unfounded. Indeed, two pads had fallen to earth during the night, but seven remained, prominently hanging from the branches. They defied the worst wiles of the wind and remained securely in position, almost touching the office windows.

All was in readiness for the drama to unfold.

Mr. Dinkman arrived early the next day, around 7:00 a.m., since he had further work to perform on the budget. It was a foul morning, the west wind driving sheets of heavy rain across the city streets. Dinkman's mood was as foul as the weather. Evanson had ordered him to trim the school budget, and no matter which department he sliced, crap was certain to rain on his head. He felt that he should cut the PT allowance, but Evanson had forbidden him to take a nickel from it; Evanson was proud of the school teams and wished to support their needs to the fullest. Dinkman would have to find the savings elsewhere, perhaps the art budget. Then he thought of the wrath of Miss Hitch.

As Dinkman was pondering his problems, Mrs. Applecrust arrived. It was at exactly 7:45 a.m., her entrance never varying more than a minute to either side of the quarter hour. She turned on the lights, placed her purse in the desk drawer, and walked over to open the heavy gray drapes to allow the dim morning light to enter the office.

Spying the strange objects hanging from the limbs of the tree, she realized that they were sanitary napkins. Then she noticed that there were words written on them. In order to read the words, she glanced over the top of her glasses and leaned closer to the glass.

Written in red ink, in uppercase letters, she could clearly see the words: DINKY'S DIAPERS. Mrs. Applecrust's shock soon turned to amusement, and she chuckled quietly. Now she was in a quandary. Should she inform Mr. Dinkman of the offending objects? Perhaps she should send for Joe Castle to remove them before anyone saw them, or she could keep quiet and pretend she had not seen them.

She chose the latter.

Sitting at her desk, her back to the window, she removed the cover from her typewriter and proceeded to transcribe the first memos of the day from the handwritten directives. Mrs. Applecrust knew that Mr. Evanson would be the next to arrive, as the other two secretaries, being younger, were invariably tardy.

Gus rolled in three minutes before the hour. "Good morning, Mrs. Applecrust," he grunted in his usual gruff manner. Then he removed several sheets of paper from his briefcase and handed them to her. They were drafts of a speech he was preparing for the students' Remembrance Day assembly. As he placed them on her desk, a flash of momentary sunlight, the morning's first, caught his eye as it was reflecting from several white objects that seemed to float among the catalpa branches.

Walking over to the window, Gus adjusted his glasses and stared at the apparitions. Without thinking, he read the words on them aloud, "Dinky's Diapers." Then in a thundering voice that filled the office, he roared, "Shit."

Mrs. Applecrust almost did.

At this point, Mr. Dinkman opened his door and stepped out of his inner sanctum. An enraged Mr. Evanson, a quiet Mrs. Applecrust, and the two giggling secretaries, who had just arrived, confronted him. Within moments, he assessed the situation.

"Dinkman, what on earth is this all about?" Evanson roared.

Sputtering in protest, Dickhead walked over to the window. There, in bold letters, he saw, "Dinky's Diapers." He instantly realized the meaning of the writer's words. Someone was referring to him as a …

Mrs. Applecrust sent for Joe Castle, the head caretaker. Though she was careful to hide it, she enjoyed sending for Joe, since he was so good looking. She was unaware that the other secretaries knew about her secret. When Joe arrived, with an assistant in tow, she gave him a tiny smile. She explained the situation and then instructed that they remove the offending objects from the tree. Joe was none too pleased at having to climb a ladder on this blustery day into the limbs of the old tree. The small burst of sunlight had disappeared, and rain was again pelting down.

Ten minutes later, when he retrieved the first pad, he saw the writing on it and started to laugh. The caretaker holding the ladder was considerably older than his boss and cursed Joe's amusement as he pulled his coat collar higher to prevent water from dripping down his neck.

Because Joe was laughing, and the assistant below was gripping the ladder with only one hand, the ladder toppled. Joe grabbed the branches and held on for dear life, as it was a twelve-foot drop to the ground below. While the caretaker on the ground hastily tried to place the ladder upright, the dangling Joe emitted a string of expletives, clearly audible in the office.

Gus was infuriated that a subordinate, a mere caretaker, should employ such gutter language within hearing distance of him. Dinkman heard Joe utter his name among the foul words, and was certain that he was blaming the entire mishap on him. The two secretaries were trying their best to stifle their laughter, but snorting sounds were escaping from beneath their hands, which they had placed across their mouths.

Mrs. Applecrust arose from her chair and walked across to the windows. As dignified as an employee at the Royal Alexandra Theatre, she brought the curtain down on the high drama.

When she drew the heavy drapes across the windows, she caught a final glimpse of poor Joe the caretaker, his feet kicking wildly in the air. In his haste, the man on the ground had dropped the ladder a second time, causing another stream of cursing to flow from the frustrated and terrified Joe. The closed curtains muffled his dramatic monologue.

Several moments later, the vile language ceased. Mrs. Applecrust assumed that the performance of the dangling caretaker had ended satisfactorily. She noticed that Mr. Evanson had slammed the door as he went inside his office; Dinkman had stormed out of the office to begin his investigation into the identity of the writer on the pads; the two junior secretaries were peeing their pants with laughter, now that their bosses were no longer present. Mrs. Applecrust frowned as she gazed disapprovingly at their hysterics, which caused them to rise to greater heights of hilarity.

Finally, Mrs. Applecrust gave into the mirth of the moment and laughed so hard that she had to retrieve her handkerchief from her purse in the desk drawer.

Dinkman never solved the mystery of the sanitary pads. The perpetrator had hidden his tracks expertly.

Two days later, Jimmy's mom was in Mr. Marlton's Store and heard from Gramps the story of the antics at the high school. Tom had told him about it. At the mention of sanitary pads, Jimmy's mom remembered the package her son had hidden under his bed.

She never said a word, but knowing how the spiteful Dinkman had made Jimmy's life miserable, she felt that the man had received what he deserved.

Mrs. Klacker was also in Marlton's store at the time and overheard the conversation about the prank. Under her breath she mumbled, "I bet that odious Jimmy Frampton had something to do with the foul deed. He's the type to commit such a criminal act."

She departed the store with a self-satisfied look on her face. She never learned that on this occasion, she had been correct.

✧ ✧ ✧

November was ending. The dismal pewter skies and interminable drizzling rain added to the stalker's depression and need for a fresh kill. The stalker gazed toward the trophy jars containing the blood of the victims, each container carefully labelled, giving the date of the kill and the victim's name.

The stalker ran a hand over the jars, caressing them. Images flowed as freely as the red liquid had pulsed out of the victims' lives as they had ebbed to a close. The desire to seek another victim intensified. Another kill was as necessary as rain to a parched land.

Outside, the rain beat against the windowpanes like tiny bullets, the drops running down the glass. The howling wind at times blew the water away from the window, and then like eternal tears, they dribbled down the panes once more. Thoughts wandered back many years, to when the foster parents had brought the young stalker into their home. It too had been a stormy night in November. Being eight years old, the stalker was to share the new home with a sibling, who was fourteen. During the following days, whenever the foster parents were present, the teenager was ingratiatingly charming. At night, when the house was quiet, the sibling stole into the stalker's bedroom and systematically tormented the helpless young stalker. The tormenting gradually increased in intensity and sexual activities were inflicted. Eventually, they became violent.

Finally, several days before Christmas, the stalker killed the sibling. There was no rage or outburst of anger. The kitchen knife, strategically thrust, created a flow of blood and provided instant release from the torture the stalker had endured. After the deed, the stalker thought that the killing was neither good nor bad, neither moral nor immoral—simply a necessity.

The stalker told the police that when the parents were out, they disobeyed their edict and made fudge. They were cutting pieces of the treat from the baking pan, when they heard their parents' car entering the driveway. They rushed into the bedroom, hid the fudge under the bed, and threw the knife on the bed. Somehow, it lodged itself upright between the two pillows. When the sibling jumped onto the bed, the knife sliced into the teenager's neck. The knife had severed the carotid artery. After a thorough investigation, the coroner ruled the death as accidental. They could not believe that the innocent-looking young stalker had committed murder. The police considered it a freak accident.

The stalker never told anyone about the sexual arousal while observing the blood pulsating from the victim's neck, or the excitement of knowing that a life was ending.

On this dreary November night, the stalker recalled the incident. Gazing intently at the jars of blood, similar to when the sibling's blood had been visible, the stalker relived the exhilarating moments. However, the jars, along with the childhood memories, increased the urge to kill again.

✧ ✧ ✧

December commenced on a Thursday, and the following Sunday in Toronto, it was fifty-five degrees Fahrenheit, the highest temperature for that date recorded in over a hundred years. On Monday, 14 December, the city received four inches of snow, and the next day the temperatures plummeted to well below freezing. Blowing drifts obliterated garden fences, as thick snow fell across rooftops, sheds, and garages. The street scenes on the Christmas cards, arriving daily in the mail, appeared lackluster in comparison.

By mid-December, Frank Gnomes felt that he was progressing in his relationship with Samantha. It was a new experience for him, as he had always sought the "bimbo" types, whom he dominated with his knowledge of world affairs, tales of the inner workings of the political scene, and gossip about celebrities. However, Samantha usually knew more about all these matters than he did. He wondered if she had spanked the prime minister, the city's mayor, and the premier of the province.

Sally-Lou had ceased calling for him to come to the bedroom, each night sullenly closing the door when she retired. There was little communication between them, and Frank felt that it was only a matter of time before they separated. He hoped that the newspaper would give him increased responsibility, which would mean an increase in wages, as he was certain that more alimony payments were in his future.

The previous week, Frank suggested that he and Samantha attend a movie, and she chose to attend the Imperial Theatre (Pantages) to see *The Robe,* a story about the robe of Christ, which the Roman soldiers had gambled for as he was dying on the cross. Frank was surprised at her choice of film.

After the movie he said to her, "I didn't know you were religious."

"There are many things about me that you don't know," she had replied. "In *The Robe,* I simply enjoyed watching Richard Burton. I adore his rich masculine voice."

Frank hated to admit it, but he too had enjoyed the film, but for a different reason. Jean Simmons was great to watch on screen, and he ignored Burton and his pockmarked face. He considered himself handsomer.

The week before Christmas, when Frank invited Samantha to dinner, she declined. He had not been intimate with Sally-Lou for many months and had not been successful in getting Samantha into the sack. He was frustrated, horny, and confused. He knew she found him attractive, but the inviting sparkle that he saw in a woman's eyes when she wanted him was missing. Jokingly, he had told her that he had considered asking her to spank him. She smiled and told him that he couldn't afford her fees. He wondered if she was seeing another man, nonprofessionally, that is.

In the days ahead, Frank threw himself into his work. The editor had given him another major assignment. It was not a crime story, and this helped soothe his disappointment over Samantha. Lucky at work, unlucky at love.

✧ ✧ ✧

The previous November, when Jim Peersen had called Samantha after meeting her in the gym, she had refused to see him. As a result, she was surprised when, two weeks later, he called her again. Although she knew she was taking a risk, she hesitantly accepted to meet him for coffee. She had to admit that she was curious. After dealing with subservient males who strutted and preened publicly but grovelled before her whip, she sensed that Peersen might be a refreshing change, and he was indeed cute. *Seriously cute!* she thought.

Samantha remained bothered by the fact that Peersen was a police detective. She had always felt that cops were too aggressive and impressed with the power that their jobs provided. They also tended to be cynical, as they dealt daily with the underbelly of society, the bottom of the deck.

During the following weeks, she met him twice for coffee, and then for a dinner at a quiet restaurant. Gradually, she learned that her instincts about Peersen had been correct. He was not a typical cop. The man was assertive yet gentle, even though he enjoyed winning in the game of life. He was also even more intelligent than she had first surmised. Though he was a reticent conversationalist, when he discussed theatre, politics, or world news, he was insightful. As well, he was an attentive listener, a quality she rarely found in a male. He was in great physical shape, since he jogged and worked out in a gym whenever time permitted. Besides, unlike Frank Gnomes, Peersen was unmarried. When she had teased Peersen about being "virgin territory," he simply grinned and dropped his eyes.

My God, she thought, *this man is actually quite shy.*

Samantha became further acquainted with Jim during the days prior to Christmas. The snowfall from earlier in the month remained, blanketing a city that was busily preparing for the yuletide season. Samantha's business always slowed during the holiday period, since customers spent their extra cash on gifts for their sweethearts, wives, and elderly mothers. Few of their wives were aware that the gift their husbands wanted was a good spanking, as in the days of their childhood. More than one mother's discipline had unknowingly planted her son's feet in the realm of the kinky bottom smackers. *Life is indeed strange*, Samantha thought.

✧ ✧ ✧

On Saturday, 19 December, Gerry Thomson was in the Simpson's downtown store, patiently waiting for his wife, Ruth, who was at the crowded Max Factor cosmetic counter. Only four shopping days remained until Christmas, and because stores were not allowed to open on Sunday, Simpson's was crammed with harried shoppers.

Outside the store, on Queen Street, a brass quartet from the nearby Toronto Temple Corps of the Salvation Army was playing "Hark the Herald Angels Sing." The music was audible each time the doors to the street opened. The colourful decorations surrounding the store's marble columns, the strings of tinsel hanging from the counters, and the gigantic holly wreaths hanging from the high ceilings all added to the festive mood, causing many shoppers to purchase more gifts, at higher prices, than they had originally intended.

Gerry loved Christmas. It was not his responsibility to shop for presents and perform the numerous chores to prepare for the yuletide season. For him, it was a time for popping popcorn with the kids, watching presents pile up under the tree, enjoying the smell of chocolate peanut butter cookies baking in the oven, and helping the kids build snowmen in the backyard.

It also meant family outings. If the city behaved itself, and no one murdered their mother-in-law because she overcooked the turkey or dropped her cigar butt into the giblet gravy, he might actually have time to take the kids to the Royal Ontario Museum, the Art Gallery of Toronto, or ice skating and tobogganing in High Park. As this moment, because he was away from the phone at the precinct, he was certain that at least one outing was a reality—lunch with Ruth at the Arcadian Court, located on the eight floor of the department store.

Gerry continued to wait as Ruth departed from the cosmetic counter and proceeded to the men's department, where she purchased two shirts for her father. A half-hour later, after Ruth had tormented the clerks at three more departments, they entered the elevator to go up to lunch in the Arcadian Court. Gerry smiled in anticipation as the white-gloved hand of the elevator operator pulled shut the outer doors, then, the inner cage-like doors, and next, maneuvered the lever that caused the elevator to begin to rise upward.

Arriving on the eighth floor, the mellow sounds of the piano in the restaurant floated out into the foyer as the hostess wrote down their names. Ten minutes later, she escorted Gerry and Ruth to a cozy table near the north wall. The piano was playing "It Came Upon a Midnight Clear." In the background, the tinkle of silverware, china, and the constant buzz of animated conversation floated in the air. Excited patrons were enjoying a festive lunch in the warmth and ornate splendour of the art moderne Arcadian Room, one of Toronto's finest dining establishments.

Ruth ordered the almandine-crusted salmon, and Gerry requested roast beef, well done. Ruth commented on the large floral arrangements positioned around the room, as she admired the tastefully decorated cornice work and the impressive columns with their ornate capitals. The enormous chandeliers sparkled, casting brilliant light across the room. Dining in the Arcadian Room was an occasion rather than an opportunity to partake of nourishment.

Gerry had chosen the chair at the table with clear lines of sight and fields of fire, though he knew it was not necessary, as the Arcadian Court was hardly a place for mob hits or gangsters' assassinations. Still, out of habit, he glanced around the room with the eye of a policeman rather than an observer of architectural detail. He saw "Wild Betty," a lady of the evening, who was well known at the precinct. Her usual place of assignation was Jarvis Street, in the early-morning hours, but she was presently sitting at a table with a well-dressed older gentleman, who was likely incapable of any type of late-night endeavour.

On the far side of the room was "Harry the Ballman," a pickpocket whom Gerry had known for years through "professional connections." Harry was known for picking a pocket so deeply that if his target was a man, the guy was in danger of having his balls pulled out through his trouser pocket, hence his nickname.

Gerry gazed upward and scanned the upper level that overlooked the dining area. It contained recessed alcoves that hid the diners from view. Then he saw a couple with a young boy stand up to leave the table. The man held his fedora in front of his face, but Gerry had already recognized him. It was Tyrone Evanson, the principal of York Collegiate. Gerry's trained eye glanced at the boy, and he knew instantly that the lad was related to Evanson. The resemblance was remarkable. From the photographs in the man's office at the school, Gerry was certain that Gus did not have any children. Who was this boy? An illegitimate son or a nephew?

Thomson realized the possibilities of what he had discovered. If it were a son, Evanson was open to blackmail. If Stritch had discovered the illicit union, in order to protect his position within the community, would Evanson resort to murder? Such a course of action was highly unlikely. But was it impossible?

✧ ✧ ✧

On Wednesday evening, 23 December, Jim Peersen was quietly humming as he donned his ivory shirt and new pinstripe navy suit and tightened the Windsor knot in his sky-blue silk tie. He and Samantha were to dine at the Savarin Tavern on Bay Street, a popular restaurant with an all-you-can-eat buffet which included lobster and roast beef.

During the previous seven weeks, Jim had learned much about Samantha Anderson's background. As a child, her family lived in a large 1920s home on Colbeck Avenue, a short distance east of Jane Street. As a teenager, she attended Runnymede Collegiate, and then the University of Toronto.

During her university days, her father found her employment at the restaurant of the Royal York Hotel, where he worked in management. As a member of the hotel staff, she heard the room maids discuss the habits of some of the kinkier guests. It was her introduction to the adult world behind closed doors and under bedsheets. However, although she had found the naughty escapades interesting, she told Jim that she learned two important things from the hotel's customers. The first was how to respond to sexually aggressive men, and the second was how to choose stylish clothes and properly apply cosmetics.

When she had graduated from the university's Victoria College with a master's degree in English literature, she obtained employment at *Image*, a Toronto women's magazine, in the editorial department. Her second year on the job, the editor chose her for an extended assignment in Paris to write a series of articles on Parisian women.

After arriving in France, with the introductions her employer provided, she conducted extensive interviews. Parisian women looked great, she concluded, in a stylish "imitate-the-magazines" way, and they seemed to exude sex as they strolled along the grand boulevards of France's main city. It wasn't easy learning about their private liaisons within their bedrooms, but she succeeded. She discovered that off their feet, they were as uptight and sexually repressed as North American women. They simply looked better doing it. After many months' investigation, she regretfully dismissed Parisian women as a redundant species.

However, she adored Paris.

After several more months in the city, she also learned to dismiss the male population. She had several love affairs, but she found the men to be similar to their female counterparts. When preening and strutting, they were superb, but between the sheets, they were too uptight about their self-image to consider a woman's needs. As her interest in the men of Paris declined, her adoration of Paris increased. Ten months after she arrived, she wired Toronto and resigned from *Image*.

She rented a modest apartment on the Left Bank, and employing her connections and her knowledge of men, she set up a spanking parlour. The "Frenchies," as she referred to them, flocked to her door. She discovered that the intricacies of what turned on a man were impossible to predict or understand. They willingly parted with their French francs to satisfy their inner need to be humiliated, without their partners or friends knowing. In public, they could continue to strut and preen, playing the role of the superior, masculine super-lover that their self-image demanded.

Samantha found it fascinating and began analyzing their behaviour. Her studies increased her expertise, and more men arrived, keeping her busy all day and late into the evening hours. However, she never allowed her customers to touch her and strictly maintained this rule.

A year later, having acquired a considerable income, she invested in herself. She closed her salon and enrolled at the Sorbonne in courses on human sexual behaviour. Three years later, she was Doctor Anderson with a PhD in psychology. Her thesis had been, "Diagnosing the Diversity of Sexual Arousal." When she returned to her former profession, her newly found knowledge increased her proficiency in her business, as she tailored the sex toys and techniques to match her customers.

Investing wisely, five years later she was independently wealthy. Living off her investments, she closed her studio and rented an apartment on the prestigious Rue Vernet, within a twenty-minute walk of the Arc de Triumph. It was a grand life. Many of the most eligible young men in Paris, as well as mature, wealthy businessmen, became her constant companions. Having achieved a degree of respectability, she was soon attending the parties of the nobility, as well as those of prominent politicians. At one gala affair, she met Charles de Gaulle. It was an amazing lifestyle for a girl from humble Toronto.

Slowly, the shopping forays into the high-end shops of Paris began to lose their appeal. She realized that she could purchase on Bloor Street, west of Yonge, almost anything that was available in the chic French shops, and often at half the price. Paris had more shops with the much sought-after goods, but the stores simply repeated the merchandise of their competitors. Toronto had fewer shops, but essentially the same goods. The grand dames of Rosedale and Forest Hill could acquire the best that Paris had to offer, without leaving home.

The Champs Elysees eventually became just another broad avenue—

manicured and stylish, but faceless and impersonal. Samantha wanted to walk the delightfully tacky Yonge Street to watch the flashing neon lights and the giggling patrons as they wandered from bar to bar in search of the elusively perfect partner for a one-night tryst. Toronto's night scene possessed an innocence, not the tired old-world attitude of "been there, done that," so typical of the patrons of the clubs of Paris. Upper-class Parisians fed off their sense of self-importance and treated the untitled and the common man as if they were ignorant serfs. The labourers of Paris also exuded this attitude, feeling that though they were working class, they were superior to other nationalities simply because they were citizens of the grand republic.

Torontonians knew they were residents of Hogtown and accepted everyone as equal celebrants of life. There was a freshness and vigor to the life of Toronto. If residents of Rosedale attempted to claim superiority, the residents of Cabbagetown would tell them to blow it out their ass. Paris preached egalitarianism, but only within one's own social class. In Toronto, a drunk was a drunk, and his or her puke in the alley was the equal of anyone's.

As the months passed, memories of home flooded over her. The earthy smell of a crisp September morning in the quiet tree-lined streets of Toronto and the warm air of a smoke-scented fall afternoon haunted her. While the city embraced winter, in the deep corners of her mind, she could hear the excited children's voices in Riverdale and High parks, as the youngsters raced their sleds down the snowy slopes. Paris had no such pleasures.

As the days passed, nostalgia continued to envelope her. She remembered clear spring evenings, when dusk had turned to night and she had viewed the city from the cocktail lounge atop the Park Plaza Hotel. It had never failed to enchant her. Below the heights of the hotel, spread before her was an aerial view of the quiet residential neighbourhoods of the Annex and Yorkville, just a breath away from the bustling commercial traffic of Bloor Street and University Avenue. To the south was the forested majesty of Queen's Park, the roof of the legislature poking above the swirling mass of foliage. Her longing for Toronto increased each day as the months passed.

One afternoon, while strolling down the Champs Elysees, an elderly, well-heeled Parisian pinched her ass. His attitude of unabashed arrogance was the proverbial final straw. Her days of wanderlust had ended. She had had enough of the French and their assumed superiority.

The next day, she arranged for her banker to transfer her money to Toronto to a downtown branch of the Dominion Bank. A month later, she sailed for home. She never regretted her decision.

✧ ✧ ✧

On the evening of Wednesday, 23 December, at the Savarin Tavern, Jim and Samantha stood in the line-up on the stairs leading to the second-floor restaurant. It was crowded, and hungry customers were squeezing to the right to allow those departing the restaurant to descend the stairs to the street below. Everyone in the line, including Peersen, had dinner reservations, but the wait was lengthy as it was two days before Christmas and the town was hopping. Group parties were occupying many tables.

At the top of the stairs, the maître d' checked the names on the restaurant's reservation list and then escorted the customers to their tables as they became available. An impatient elderly woman, wearing a full-length mink coat, stormed up the stairs, her embarrassed husband in tow. She informed the maître d' that she had a reservation and haughtily pounded her fist on the lectern holding the reservation book.

The maître d' smiled patiently and replied, "Madam, everyone in line has a reservation. Please wait your turn. I will call your name when your table is ready. Kindly return to the bottom of the stairs."

"But I have a special reservation."

"Everyone in line has a special reservation. Please return to the bottom of the stairs."

"My good man, I have a gold-plated blue-ribbon invitation from the mayor, who is my personal friend."

Exasperated, the maître d' replied firmly, "Lady, I don't care if you have a gold-plated arse and blue-ribbon tits, and the reservation was made by God almighty, go to the bottom of the stairs."

The hoots from those who were patiently waiting in line drowned out the woman's indignant reply. The woman and her poodle-like husband retreated down the stairs. She was defeated but unbowed. She felt as if she were upholding the dignity of the women of status throughout the city. The heights of the Rosedale had been assaulted.

"The mayor will hear about this," she threatened aloud, as she stormed out of the restaurant.

Samantha smiled at Jim, who was unaware of the reason for her amusement. *In Paris,* she thought, *mention a title or an important connection, and you gained immediate access to any restaurant. God, I love this city.*

After they were inside and seated, they went to the buffet table, helped themselves to a generous portion of lobster, and settled down to enjoy the meal and each other's company. As a treat, Peersen had preordered a bottle of 1952 Dom Perignon. The tiny bubbles rose effervescently in their chilled glasses. When Jim had phoned for the reservation, he requested that their glasses be placed in the freezer. It was a romantic touch, and Samantha noticed it.

For Jim, the conversation rolled more easily than with any woman he had ever met. They had arrived at a truce during the previous weeks. She did not mention her work, and he tried not to discuss police business. There was one thing that he wanted to ask her: why she still worked at her chosen profession when she clearly did not need the money. Respecting her privacy, he had refrained from inquiring.

As the champagne relaxed him, without realizing it, he broke his own rule and inadvertently began talking about the Stritch case. Unfortunately, this was not the first time, and she already knew many of the details concerning the investigation. He told her that they had spent the previous few weeks talking with the teacher's ex-students. She listened attentively and smiled as Peersen apologized for discussing his job.

After listening to Jim relate the details of the denials of the students, she asked, "Did you interview any of her female students?"

"No. There was no indication of that type of behaviour."

"Don't rule it out. Remember what the elderly man in Hamilton said. It appears that the victim possessed a healthy interest in sex, perhaps even compulsive. She was young, looked even younger than her age, and perhaps enjoyed experimenting. Don't rule out a female-to-female encounter. Sexual arousal is a mysterious phenomenon."

Peersen thought for a few moments before he replied. "Perhaps we have been looking at this case the wrong way."

They continued enjoying the rich, meaty taste of the lobster dipped in clarified lemon butter. Peersen also devoured several slices of lean roast beef. As he cut into the tender meat, his thoughts were not on the food. "I wonder," he said to Samantha, "if Matheson learned that Stritch had strayed into another woman's bed. The victim knew the killer, and the manner in which the murderer killed her suggests an act of rage."

"It's possible," Samantha replied.

✧ ✧ ✧

In the wink of an eye, Christmas disappeared, and the days prior to New Year's mimicked the yuletide event and raced past as well. Tom worked five days of the Christmas holidays at the drug store. Ruth was wearing sunglasses, despite the dull December weather. Shorty told him that she had confided in him that her new boyfriend had slugged her. Tom wondered about the condition of the boyfriend, thinking that he was likely in the Toronto General Hospital. Ruth's injury did not improve her driving skills, as with one eye partly closed, she was a greater terror on the streets than ever. On one occasion, she grazed the fender of a minister, and Shorty said that the reverend's vocabulary included many of the same words as Ruth's, but their context was different.

New Year's Eve arrived. For the first time, the Hudson family gathered around the TV rather than the radio. At midnight, Guy Lombardo and the Royal Canadians played "Auld Lang Syne," a song that Lombardo had first played in 1929 in the Roosevelt Hotel in New York City. During the 1930s, it became the favourite melody on the radio to bring in the New Year. Now, Lombardo had brought the tradition to television.

Tom's mom served the usual small glasses of sherry. Tom had a sip, but again, he found the taste of alcohol distasteful. However, unlike when he was a small child, he was in the living room, not asleep in his bed, when his parents welcomed in the new year of 1954. And best of all, he saw the new year arrive through the magic of television.

Chapter Seven

Frank Gnomes had a miserable New Year's Eve. On Monday, 4 January, he remained in a foul mood as he edited an article he had been writing about John Diefenbaker, the front-runner to replace George Drew as leader of the federal Conservatives. The party was holding a convention in March in Ottawa, and there was already considerable interest in the populist MP from Prince Albert, Saskatchewan.

On his desk was another "hot-off–the-wire" story. The United States was demanding that North Korea return imprisoned American soldiers. They estimated that the North Koreans had not yet released twenty-two thousand of them.

Shortly after eleven o'clock, the phone on Frank's desk rang. Annoyed at being disturbed, he barked into the receiver, "Yeah, talk."

It was Constable Paul Masters. "I have information that might be profitable for both of us," he purred greedily. Masters' wallet was empty after the demands of Christmas shopping for the wife and kids.

Frank was in no mood to play games, and besides, his wallet was empty as well. He had extended his budget to buy an expensive bracelet for Samantha for Christmas but had been unable to arrange a date with her. He was now certain she was seeing some other guy, possibly several, he admitted ruefully. Finally, as a peace offering, he had given the bracelet to Sally-Lou. She was delighted, but suspicious, and her bedroom door remained closed. The cold of January had chilled his love life as well as the daily temperatures.

"Your information is usually more profitable to you than to me," Frank complained. He was careful not to speak Masters' name, as he did not want anyone to know the identity of his direct pipeline into police investigations.

"This concerns the Stritch murder case."

"Meet you at the usual place."

Ten minutes later, Frank strolled into the Diana Sweets Restaurant on Yonge Street, across from the Eaton's Queen Street Store. The table that he preferred was empty, near the rear of the restaurant, away from the window. He chose the chair facing the door with a clear view of anyone entering or leaving. Five minutes later, Masters strolled in, his hat pulled low, obscuring his face. He was not in uniform, having changed into his street clothes at the precinct.

"What happened, Masters? Lose your uniform?"

"Perhaps I'm being paranoid, but I think someone has been following me during the past week. Wearing civvies makes it more difficult for them to keep me under surveillance. Gerry Thomson suspects there's a mole in the precinct."

"I suspect there's a rat as well," Frank mumbled sarcastically.

"Do you want the information or not?"

"Depends on what it is—and the price."

"Thomson and Peersen have been conducting a new line of inquiry."

"What line?"

"Thirty bucks gives you hook, line, and sinker."

"Good God, Paul, thirty bloody bucks?"

"It's a new lead."

Frank fumbled in his pocket and slowly flushed out three purple ten-dollar bills. They displayed the youthful face of King George VI, the currency having been designed in 1937. The new bills, with a picture of the young queen on them, were already in circulation, but the old bills remained common. Frank had misgivings about having women as head of state and tried to think of Sally-Lou running anything other than a laundry tap. *God*, he thought, *someday women may grab important positions in the police department or at the* Trib. The thought made him shudder.

Masters pocketed the bills and informed Frank about the interviews with Stritch's ex-students, the females, as the detectives thought there might be a possibility that she had a perverted relationship with a girl in one of her classes. Frank instantly knew the implications of this information: either Taylor or Matheson might have been jealous if they knew about the secret affairs of Stritch.

Without a word of thanks, Frank stood up and left the restaurant. Masters sipped the last of his coffee, and as he watched him depart, he muttered under his breath, "Screw you, Frank."

Walking south on Yonge Street, many questions tumbled within Frank's mind. Would his editor give him a budget to pursue these new leads? He would need two junior reporters to follow the daily routines of Bettina Taylor and Bill Matheson.

✧ ✧ ✧

The new leads also occupied Gerry Thomson's mind. In the war room in his basement, he stared at the little red pins. In the last week, he had added twenty-two pins to the map, one for each female student they had interviewed.

Though the trail was cold, Gerry continued to examine the map. He had calculated distances and knew how long it took a suspect to walk from one location to another. In the past, he had solved crimes employing his slow, plodding methods. Somewhere on that map, he was certain that on 31 August, prior to the fatal meeting in the valley, the victim and the killer had crossed paths.

Thomson wondered if Bettina Taylor had warned Bill Matheson that Elaine Stritch was going to the Humber Valley. She knew about Stritch departing from the apartment. Perhaps she notified Sam Millford. The three of them lived within easy walking distance. They could meet or instantly communicate by phone. He could not rule out Gregory Baldwin, even though he lived downtown, as Taylor might have phoned him. If lesbianism were involved, then all the women on staff—Miss Gayle Manson, the girls' gym teacher, Miss Hitch the art teacher, and the free-flowing librarian, Miss Allyson—were also suspects. It was unlikely that the latter was the murderer, but perhaps she had been an accomplice.

Gerry gazed at the pins on his map, clearly revealing that all these individuals lived in the same area as Miss Stritch. Bettina lived on Lauder Avenue, south of Rogers Road. Sam Millford rented rooms in a large 1920s home on Oakwood Avenue, south of St. Clair. Miss Hitch shared a house on Northcliffe Boulevard, north of Rogers Road, with two other artsy types, both of whom were males. The neighbours thought that the living arrangement was scandalous, especially for a teacher. Frank knew that it was great cover for a lesbian. Besides, her two roommates looked like powder puffs.

Miss Allyson lived in a second-floor flat in a three-storey house on Holland Park Avenue. Frank smiled as he wondered if the residents on the first floor had flood insurance. Bill Matheson lived in a small bungalow on Eversfield Avenue, close to Dufferin Street. Baldy Baldwin occupied the upper floor of a house on Gerrard Street, between University Avenue and Bay Street, an area where many Chinese families had purchased homes. Though it was not a prestigious neighbourhood, the old Victorian bay-and-gable house was spacious, and its location close to the downtown made it desirable as it was near the inner-city amenities, especially the bars.

Gerry knew that all these teachers were in constant communication, shared information, and protected each other's ass. Something bound them together in mutual self-interest—or fear. What was it? He was also certain that Dinkman knew.

Never had he been involved with a case with so many obvious suspects, conflicting motives, and trails that led everywhere and nowhere. He needed to focus more, eliminate the extraneous details, and clear some of the suspects. Despite his failures, he remained convinced that the little red pins contained the answer.

The third week of January, Thomson had still not discovered anything to add to his charts or maps, despite the exhaustive interviews he and Peersen had conducted. The female ex-students of Elaine Stritch had all denied any improprieties in their relationship.

❖ ❖ ❖

Jim Peersen and Samantha attended Loew's Uptown Theatre to see *Kiss Me, Kate*, starring Kathryn Grayson and Howard Keele, a musical based on the story of Shakespeare's *Taming of the Shrew*. After the movie, they went to the Java House Restaurant on Yonge Street for a cup of coffee and a slice of coconut-cream pie. Peersen had learned to trust Samantha and respect her judgment. Her suggestion to question the female ex-students of Miss Stritch had not led to anything, but that did not mean that nothing was there. Stritch may have been intimate with only one student, and that was the one that they had not been able to interview. If the father of one of the students had learned of Stritch's affair with his daughter and become enraged, it was unlikely if Peersen would ever know.

Jim asked Samantha if she had any further suggestions. She discussed other possibilities but admitted that they were shots in the dark. Peersen knew that Peckerman had hinted that they concentrate their energies on another case. He had not ordered them to move on, but Peersen felt that an ultimatum was pending.

As the waitress placed the coffee on the table, Samantha thought more about Jim's question. "Can you give me more information? Fill me in more about the early stages of the investigation. Let your thoughts wander, give me impressions of various witnesses, and if possible, describe their reactions to your questioning."

Three cups of coffee later, Jim Peersen had sketched for her a brief outline of each witness. He had an excellent memory for detail and was even able to recall what the interviewees had been wearing. Samantha was highly amused at his description of Miss Hitch and her colourful outfits.

Finally, she said, "I think you're right. The teachers have closed ranks. If you can't break into the circle, pick at the circumference. The students notice things that others don't. They watch the teachers performing their daily roles, when other adults are not observing them. For example, a man who is a pussycat at home is sometimes a tiger in the classroom. He compensates for his impotence in his personal life by pouncing on students who are unable to strike back. Some individuals become teachers not because they enjoy young people, but because they enjoy having power over them.

"It's now over two years since the murder. The students will not remember the reactions, lack of reaction, or overreaction to the killing, but the personalities of the teachers have not changed. Ask the students questions designed to elicit seemingly innocuous answers. You know: Which classes do they enjoy? Which subjects are they good at? Why? Which classes are the best disciplined? And indirectly you will receive insight into the personality of the staff members. Look for someone who threatens the kids, who is a bully, or is at the other end of the scale, someone who tries to be overly ingratiating with the students. In other words, try to find someone who is not what he or she seems to be on the surface."

The following day, Peersen did not inform his partner that he had been discussing the case with someone outside the department, but he told him Samantha's suggestions.

Gerry thought about it, and after mulling over the idea, said, "It sounds like pie in the sky to me, but hell, we've tried everything else, so let's give it a whirl. Let's talk again to the kids who were on the opposite side of the Humber River the afternoon we were searching in the valley. Let me check the file. Their names were Forester Bernstein, whom I think the boys call Shorty, Tom Hudson, Harry Heinz, Patrick McCaul, Carol Miller, and Sophie Cellini. Let's interview the four male teenagers. We've interviewed them before, so it won't appear odd if we approach them again."

After receiving proper authorization, Peersen and Thomson arranged to interview them at the school.

✧ ✧ ✧

Detective Peersen escorted Harry, Patrick, Shorty, and Tom into Dinkman's office. Dinkman disappeared to have a cup of coffee in the staff room.

Tom was surprised that Peersen did not inquire about the murder but began asking them questions about their classes. He wanted to know which classes had the strictest discipline.

Trust Shorty to be blunt. "Although Matheson isn't strict with the girls, he's murder on the guys, particularly me. He's worse than Mr. Dinkman. The first year I was in Matheson's class, he treated me like a turd. The second year, it wasn't so bad, but he still makes snarky comments. I don't know what I ever did to him. I know that I'm no angel, but still …"

Peersen then turned to Tom and asked, "Do you think your friend here is overreacting?"

Tom told him that Shorty had spoken the truth. Peersen then asked Harry the same question.

"I don't know for certain. I've never been in the same class with Shorty, but I know that Mr. Matheson is vindictive," Harry responded.

Peersen gazed at Harry, as if trying to recall something. After a few seconds he said, "Aren't you the lad who collects fossils?" Peersen had remembered the original interview in September of 1951.

"Yes, sir."

"Did you find any fossils that Sunday afternoon you were in the valley?"

"Sure, I have them in my collection."

"Find anything else?"

"A piece of amber."

"That's unusual isn't it? Amber isn't found in this area."

"True. It's likely from the Dominican Republic."

"Then why did you find it in the Humber Valley?"

"It was attached to a key chain."

"Do you still have the chain, or did you just save the amber?"

"I have the chain and the amber."

"Describe them."

"The amber was attached to a chain containing a small key, maybe a padlock key, and on a piece of leather attached to the chain was the initial M."

"Was there anything else you found in the valley?" Peersen asked. "No matter how unimportant it may seem to you, it might help if you told us about it."

"Carol, one of our friends, found a few coins. They weren't valuable, but she saves coins, so she kept them."

Almost as if thinking out loud, rather than asking an intended question, Peersen muttered, "I don't suppose they were minted in 1925."

Harry's eyes widened in surprise. "Yes, sir. They were!"

Peersen was taken aback at Harry's response. An edge of excitement crept into his voice as he said, "Could we take a look at the key chain from your collection?"

Harry responded, "Sure!"

When the interviews were over, Thomson suggested that he and his partner drive all of them home, as he knew that they all lived in the same area. It was crowded with four of them in the back seat of the police car, but if they were breaking any laws, who would dare arrest them? In the car, Detective Thomson inquired if they knew if any of their teachers had coin collections.

Harry told them, "Both Mr. Matheson and Mr. Millford collect coins."

✧ ✧ ✧

After the detectives retrieved the key chain, they drove away. Peersen turned to his partner and said, "We need a search warrant for Bill Matheson's cottage."

"Why?"

"I believe that one of the witnesses stated that Matheson vacationed in the Dominican Republic last Christmas. The letter M on a keychain may not be just a coincidence."

"What if Bill Matheson was in the Humber Valley the day of the murder?" Gerry said. "It would explain his enmity toward the Bernstein boy. He's afraid that the lad saw something."

"I think you're really stretching it."

"Perhaps, but let's see if we can get a search warrant. If we get nowhere, we can try to find a link between the killer and the 1925 coins. It's circumstantial, but it might narrow the field. Up to now we've been beating the bushes randomly."

It was two days before a skeptical Arnold Peckerman decided to apply for a search warrant, and as it was within another jurisdiction, four more days before he was able to hand the warrant to Thomson and Peersen.

The following Monday, they travelled north to cottage country. The January landscape was dismal, the woodlots hugging the farmhouses silhouetted against the gunpowder gray sky. After turning off Highway 11, the two-lane road was mostly deserted. After several wrong turns, they finally arrived at the cottage. During the next twenty minutes, they inserted the key from the keychain in every lock on the premises. It fit none.

With the authority of the search warrant, they broke into the woodshed. They found nothing important and were about to leave when Peersen noticed a pair of men's work trousers, a straw hat, and a man's old plaid shirt. Peersen examined them, emptied the pockets of the trousers and shirt, and was about to throw them back behind the boxes when he noticed pink makeup on the shirt collar. Then he reexamined the inside rim of the hat. There was more makeup and a long strand of pink hair.

"Unless Matheson is a cross dresser, I think Miss Hitch was at the cottage," Peersen said.

"But it could have been any time within the last two years," Thomson replied. "It proves nothing."

"True! But it might explain why the neighbours thought they saw Matheson around the cottage during the days before the murder. It might have been Hitch dressed in Matheson's clothes. With a little padding in the right places, it would be easy to deceive someone if they were viewing the person from a distance. She could have remained here while Matheson drove to Toronto in her car."

"It's a thought," Thomson responded, "and I think at some point we should interview Miss Hitch again. However, for now, we've drawn a blank."

✧ ✧ ✧

The bitterness that Torontonians felt toward February was not ameliorated by it being several days shorter than its companion winter months. Although the daylight in the evenings was increasing, and despite the inclusion of St.

Valentine's Day, it was a time when the wise with money fled south, and those remaining within the city complained about the slushy streets and interminable blasts of snow. The shortest month on the calendar seemed the longest because of the drudgery of January that preceded it.

In the classrooms at YCI, teachers bulldozed ahead with the courses, reminding students that although the winter weather appeared to be eternal, spring exams were looming on the horizon. The drama club was preparing for the annual drama festival, and the school choir was frantically rehearsing for the spring concert. It seemed as if thoughts of the Stritch investigation had been buried beneath the flurry caused by the daily events.

They held YCI's Winter Whirl Dance at Casa Loma, and most of Tom's friends attended. The exceptions were Patrick and Sophie.

"Patrick told me that he doesn't want to go and refuses to give me a reason," Sophie told Carol.

Carol told Tom and the others, "Sophie says she's worried sick about Patrick. During the last few weeks, he's kept to himself, even more than usual."

Sophie tried to convince herself that Patrick's behaviour was a result of the February blues, but in her heart, she knew it was not true.

✧ ✧ ✧

Patrick's life changed the day he stepped inside the doors of YCI. He felt adrift in an anonymous sea. None of the teachers knew him well, as each one of them taught almost two hundred students. Patrick never spent more than one class period a day with a teacher, and to them he was just a face in the crowd.

Despite this, some of the classes Patrick enjoyed, particularly art, history, and literature. Mathematics and French he tolerated. However, he hated PT. The ridicule of the school jocks had lessened since his first year he arrived at YCI, but each time he fumbled the ball when playing basketball, they sneered. After his humiliation in the shower room several years earlier, he avoided it like the plague. Even if his sweat stunk like a skunk, he would wait until he reached home to shower.

The one teacher with whom he had slowly developed an affinity was Miss Allyson, as to him, she was grandmotherly. Patrick often stayed late after school to study, complete his homework, or read a book in the library. He preferred to remain at school, as the atmosphere in his home, like his school, had changed since his elementary days when his dad worked at the General Electric Plant, under the brow of the Davenport Road Hill near Lansdowne Avenue.

His father had always enjoyed a few too many beers, and one night after celebrating late with his buddies, he had gone to work with a hangover, the smell of alcohol on his breath. His boss told him to take his things and get his drunken "mick arse" off the property.

After several weeks searching, he found no comparable job and finally accepted employment as a night cleaner in a downtown office building. The pay was considerably less, and the hours involved night work. His unhappiness at the job spilled over into the home. Soon he began drinking more, and he became abusive. Patrick became the recipient of his abuse. When his mother defended him, she too felt his father's wrath. Patrick's three sisters escaped his anger.

One day, during after-school hours in the library, Miss Allyson finally approached Patrick and inquired about the book he was reading. It was *Barometer Rising*, a novel about the 1917 Halifax explosion, written in 1941 by Hugh MacLennon. Patrick's comments were perceptive, so against her better judgment, she sat down and talked to him.

This was a breakthrough for him, as it was the first time in over two and a half years that a teacher had spoken to him on a personal basis. He was unaware that it was a breakthrough for Miss Allyson as well. She normally avoided any conversations with students, and as mentioned previously, she had difficulties even looking directly at them. Patrick, she sensed, was different. He was soft-spoken and intelligent. His blond hair and slim, gangly build gave him a teenage Tom Sawyer look. She related better to people who resembled fictional characters.

During the remaining days of February, Patrick continued to retreat to the library after school, and gradually a modestly warm teacher–student relationship developed. Miss Allyson was incapable of opening up further to Patrick, but in her way, she tried to show him that she welcomed his presence. In turn, he accepted her restrained kindness, content to be safe within the walls of books that surrounded them. In this regard, they were kindred souls.

On 4 March, a blizzard blasted the city, dumping a heavy layer of snow across the streets, parks, and barren gardens. All day, the snow was piling up on the streets, visible through the classroom windows of YCI. Following the last period of the day, most students vacated the school quickly, anxious to reach home before the roadways became even more impassable. Patrick headed for the library to allow sufficient time for his father to depart for work. He had no desire for another angry encounter.

In the library, Miss Allyson was returning books to the shelves that the last class had carelessly dumped on the chairs, pushing them under the table to hide them from view. Without a word spoken, Patrick took an armful of books and commenced filing them back into the proper shelves. Normally, Miss Allyson would never have trusted a student to refile books, but she knew that Patrick was different.

After a few minutes, Miss Taylor stormed into the library and angrily motioned for Miss Allyson to join her in the back room. Patrick ignored them and continued putting away the books.

He heard Miss Taylor mumble a few terse sentences.

Miss Allyson replied, "My dear, I think you're overreacting. Besides, I can't …"

Her words trailed off, the sentence remaining unfinished.

Then Miss Allyson embraced her, and they closed the door. The arrival of Mr. Dinkman soon overshadowed the tender moment that Patrick had witnessed. Dinkman rushed into the library, opened the door to the backroom, and shouted at the two teachers who appeared to be hugging.

"This is intolerable," Miss Taylor shouted.

Dinkman slammed the door, and the rant continued. Patrick was lost in thought about the situation at home, as he feared that the storm might have delayed his dad's departure for work. The words emanating from the backroom remained at sufficient volume for him to hear, but he ignored them.

When Dinkman stormed out a few minutes later, for the first time, he noticed Patrick.

Damn, he thought, *that young bastard likely heard everything. I must do something about that!*

✧ ✧ ✧

Near the end of March, on his own, Patrick journeyed downtown to see the *Glen Miller Story*, in its fourth week at the Uptown Theatre at Yonge and Bloor Streets. As it was a story about the famous wartime musician, he doubted that anyone wanted to accompany him, and besides, he preferred to be alone. It was ten-thirty when he alighted from the Vaughan Bus at Oakwood Avenue and Vaughan Road. He was in no hurry to return home since it was Saturday night, and his dad was not at work. To delay his homeward journey, he decided to walk down the Amherst laneway, even though he knew that snow from earlier in the month was slushy, and the laneway likely was muddy.

Unknown to him, he was seen entering the laneway.

It was a mild night, and as Patrick trudged down the lane, the water from the melting snow was running to the drains. The garages flanking the lane were dripping from the spring melt on their roofs, and the fences were rapidly losing their crowns of white. The barren branches of the trees crackled in the gentle breezes, the moon shining eerily through their gnarled fingers.

As he passed one of the garages, he remembered the day, many years ago, when Shorty had rescued him from the Kramer gang. They had cornered him to steal his pocket money. In those days, he had friends, but now he felt alone.

However, on this occasion, he was not alone. As the moon hid its face behind a patch of clouds, the hunter closed the gap with his quarry. An arm closed around Patrick's neck from behind, expelling the air from his lungs.

Patrick was immobilized within seconds.

✧ ✧ ✧

Thomson and Peersen again discussed the possibility that Stritch's killer might have dropped the 1925 coins in the valley. The tracking dogs had determined that Miss Stritch had been walking on the east bank of the Humber River, where the teenager, Carol, had found the coins. The murderer might have been stalking her from that point in the valley.

They had confirmed that both Matheson and Millford had coin collections, but they realized that so did thousands of other people throughout the city. Even if they could prove that one of their collections was missing coins from their 1925 sets, it remained inconclusive proof that one of them had been in the valley the evening of the murder. The coins could have been dropped there anytime within a two-week timeline. They needed physical evidence to tie them directly to the murder scene on the night of the kill. They were unable to do this. Yet! They decided they should try to discredit Matheson's alibi and prove that Miss Hitch had been at Matheson's cottage.

✧ ✧ ✧

On Tuesday, 30 March, the TTC held the official ceremonies for the opening of Canada's first subway. At 1:30 p.m., the first subway train, consisting of eight cars, rolled out of Union Station for the twelve-minute trip to the Eglinton Station, the northern terminus of the line. People stood above the bridges north of Bloor Street to cheer the train as it passed, exuberant crowds lining the fences along the open-cut sections of the track.

Between 2:00 p.m. and 3:00 p.m., the famous Yonge Street streetcars ceased their designated routes on the city's main thoroughfare. Despite the excitement caused by the opening of the new subway, there were those who lamented the demise of the old Peter Witt streetcars, "the grand old ladies of the street." A few Torontonians grew nostalgic when they recalled the years they had huddled around the cars' coal stoves on a winter morning, as the streetcars rumbled up the steep hill north of Bloor Street.

Some recalled that as children, when crossing the intersection at Queen and Yonge, they had viewed the busy street, peering north and south, with the bulky streetcars crowding the roadway amid the noisy vehicle traffic. When they were youngsters, they had journeyed downtown and glimpsed the marquee lights of Loew's Downtown, the Imperial, and the Downtown theatres from the streetcar windows. Even the smaller theatres, such as the Coronet, Biltmore, and Savoy, garnered attention with their colourful signs advertising films about adventurers, pirates, gangsters, and gallant soldiers. South of Bloor Street on a wintry evening, people had gazed in fascination at Loew's Uptown Theatre, its flashing marquee lights reflecting on the glass of the streetcar windows. The Yonge streetcar connected a world of lights, laughter, and entertainment, transporting young men and women to the city's nightspots.

Where the streetcar line terminated at Union Station, thousands of immigrants had arrived during the previous decades and passed through its grand hall. The Yonge streetcars had provided their first impression of the vibrant, new-world city that was to be their home.

The streetcars had carried men to war when they had departed from Union Station for the battlefields of Europe. At the end of the conflict, when Toronto celebrated, the Yonge streetcars provided the backdrop for the spontaneous parties that erupted on Yonge Street.

No other streetcars ever embedded themselves into the soul of Toronto like the Yonge streetcars. They were the streetcars that delivered children to places of adventure: Eaton's Toyland, the Yonge Arcade, movie theatres, and toyshops.

A Peter Witt streetcar, the type that plied the Yonge Street route.

On New Year's Eve, after attending a movie, many a young couple had welcomed in the new year on the streetcars, kissing romantically as they travelled homeward. Throughout the years, office employees had chatted with fellow workers on the cars, sometimes arranging dates. There were those who had met their future wives on the Yonge streetcar, the men saying jokingly that the wife really "took them for a ride and picked their pockets clean." Even in the 1950s, weddings were expensive.

Jokes and stories that involved streetcars invariably began with, "A passenger was on the Yonge streetcar and ..." In later years, Tom remembered how much he had enjoyed the corny Yonge-streetcar jokes, even though many of them were childish humour.

Tom never forgot his dad's story about a plump, elegantly attired elderly woman. While travelling on a crowded Yonge streetcar, she noisily broke wind. The young man seated next to her, amused by the loudness of the blast, accidentally dropped the streetcar transfer clutched in his hand. The woman, self-conscience at her indiscretion, bent over and discretely retrieved the transfer from the floor of the streetcar, and passed it to the man. When she handed it to him, the young man looked at the paper transfer and said, "I think you had best keep it. You may need it to wipe yourself, and when we go past the next tree, I'll reach out the window and get you a few leaves."

The woman was not amused and relocated to another seat further down the streetcar. When she got off at St. Clair, she glowered at the insolent young fellow. He graciously smiled at her and tipped his hat.

Tom's dad loved telling the story, even though his mom objected to its crudeness.

The interior of a trailer car on the Yonge Street streetcar line, with its hardwood bench seats. Passengers entered through the right-hand door and exited through the left-hand door after paying their fare. The coal stove is evident on the right-hand side of the trailer.

The story that Tom recalled the best was one that created a little drama in the Hudson house. He could still picture the look of mischief on Gramps' face as he commenced the tale, making no effort to sanitize his language.

"I heard today about a passenger on the Yonge streetcar," he began. "She was returning from the St. Lawrence Market with her weekly supply of fruits and vegetables in paper bags. As the streetcar approached Queen

Street, the bottom of one of the paper bags broke open, and half a dozen oranges dropped out and rolled across the floor of the streetcar. She deposited her other bag on the floor of the streetcar and bent over to pick up the oranges, which by now were rolling around on the floor of the car. While bending over, she ripped off a loud fart."

Gramps was laughing as he talked. Nan's face portrayed her disgust with his street language, and Tom's mom was clearly not amused.

Ignoring their disapproval, Gramps continued. "When the woman ripped off the loud fart, an old man who was standing near her said, 'That's right, lady, if you can't catch them, shoot them.'"

Gramps, Ken, and Tom laughed uproariously. Nan left the room and went out to sit in the sun porch. Tom's mom, who continued to peel the vegetables for supper, said, "When a grown man tells a boy's joke, it does him no credit."

"Perhaps not," Tom's dad replied. "But I thought it was quite funny."

"You men always stick together, even when you're in the wrong," Tom's mom declared.

After a few minutes, Gramps wandered out to the sun porch where Nan was sitting. Feeling the need to placate her, he said, "You must at least give me credit for one thing. When I first met you, dear, I thought that if I couldn't catch you, instead of shooting oranges, I'd shoot myself. The only reason I'm alive today is because you agreed to marry me."

"So instead of shooting yourself then, you're shooting the bull now," she replied.

For Tom, remembering Gramps' story always brought back fond memories of his teenage years on Lauder Avenue. Similarly, Toronto's Yonge streetcars recalled pleasant times of a decade and a city that had slipped into the mists of time.

Today, Torontonians underestimate their streetcars. An international trolley association rated Toronto's Queen Streetcar Line as one of the top ten in the world, and the only one that remains a "functional line"—as opposed to those maintained mainly as tourist attractions. This places the Queen line among prestigious company: the San Francisco trolley cars, the St. Charles streetcars in New Orleans, and the streetcars of the Alfama

District of Lisbon. It is a pity that the tourist board of Toronto does not promote the attractions of the Queen line. To ride its length from either Long Branch or the Humber in the west, to Neville Park in the city's east end, a rider passes through fascinatingly diverse neighbourhoods, all for the price of a streetcar ticket or a token.

✧ ✧ ✧

Eager passengers enter the Queen Street Station on 23 April 1954. The TTC officially opened the subway the previous month, on 30 March 1954.

The opening of Canada's first subway occurred midway through the last decade when many of the city's citizens did not own an automobile. Car ownership for the masses began at the end of the Second World War, but the increase in cars was to accelerate greatly during the 1950s. Cars invaded the downtown streets, clogging the avenues, causing the demolition of many buildings—historic and otherwise—to create parking lots to house the beasts of private travel. Parked cars lined small thoroughfares that the city had created during the days when carts, horse and buggy, and horse-drawn streetcars had been the predominant modes of travel.

The interior of a new subway car, on display at the CNE in August of 1953, a year prior to the opening of the subway.

It is ironic that in the year ahead, the dominance of the automobile on the streets of the city would become questionable. Eventually, the downtown area will likely be for public transportation, taxis, and emergency vehicles only. Those wishing to drive an automobile in the city's core will pay a toll, equal to the fare their trip would have cost on public transportation.

◇ ◇ ◇

After the visit of Thomson and Peersen to Matheson's cottage, in an attempt to prove that Miss Hitch had been at the cottage, Thomson assigned several young rookies the task of phoning all the service stations along the possible routes that someone would drive if visiting the cottage near Bala. They asked each dealer to check his records for any repairs, grease jobs, or oil changes during the week before the Labour Day weekend of 1951. Some stated that they did not keep any records, while others said they would check and let them know. Others remained closed for the season and were unavailable.

Gathering the data was painfully slow. The second week of April, unwilling to wait, they decided to pay another visit to YCI to ask the eccentric art teacher a few more questions. It was worth a chance, as the department had officially classified the Stritch case as a cold case.

Gerry's little red pins had failed him.

When Thomson and Peersen arrived at the school office, Mrs. Applecrust informed Mr. Evanson of their arrival. He sent a message to the art room. Miss Hitch returned the note, across the bottom of it scribbled, "Send the gentlemen up to my room ten minutes after the last period of the day."

Shorty after 3:30 p.m., as the detectives were walking down the hallway, they saw the Bernstein boy, whom they knew the students referred to as Shorty. He was on his way to his locker to change his clothes for basketball practice. Peersen recognized him, smiled, and paused to talk to him. After a few pleasantries, Peersen said to him, "You told me that Mr. Matheson disliked you the first year you were in his classes."

"Naw, I told you that he hated me."

"Did Matheson show any hatred toward other students that year?"

"Sure! He also ragged a guy named Horace Kramer. I still enjoy ragging Kramer," he replied with an impish grin.

"Did he rag, as you put it, any other students?"

"Not really."

"You dislike Kramer, I take it."

"Yup! He's a turd!"

Peersen gave a knowing nod but did not intend to ask about the grudges of high school kids. However, he found it interesting that Kramer and Forester had been the main recipients of Matheson's vindictiveness.

✧ ✧ ✧

A few minutes later, the detectives walked into the art room. Miss Hitch extended her hand and gazed at them like a feline salivating over a piece of fresh fish. She was dressed in wild canary yellow. Her lipstick had been refreshed, and the yellow bangles on her arm rattled as she shook hands.

"To what do I owe this honour … boys?" she drawled, the pause between her words suggestive.

Thomson stood back. Peersen knew from long-standing experience that his partner was signalling that he wanted him to conduct the interview. Bracing himself, into the Venus flytrap Jim Peersen flew.

"Miss Hitch, have you ever visited Mr. Matheson's cottage?"

"On occasion."

"Were you there the week before the Labour Day weekend, before Miss Stritch was murdered?" Even beneath the heavy makeup, Miss Hitch's face paled. Peersen had struck a nerve, and he knew it.

"I was at my home. Miss Manson came over to visit me. As you already know, she has verified this information."

"Will you testify to that under oath?"

There was an awkward pause before she hesitantly nodded affirmatively.

"Are you aware of the penalties for impeding an investigation? We have reason to believe that you were present at Matheson's cottage at Pine Lake during the days preceding the Labour Day weekend in 1951. I ask you again, were you at the cottage at the time mentioned?"

"I will answer no more questions without the presence of my lawyer. Have a nice evening, boys."

Her final statement spoken, the Venus flytrap closed her fluted stem and sealed herself against the outside world.

The two detectives departed, not having accomplished their goal, but also not defeated. They had rattled Miss Hitch. The word would spread among the inner circle of YCI that the police were still questioning their alibis. Their ranks might close tighter, but their nervousness might cause one of them to make a mistake.

❖ ❖ ❖

Peersen thought he knew a way to get permission to interview Horace Kramer again, ameliorating the objections of Mrs. Kramer. Although he was not opposed to a direct attack to achieve his aims, he felt that a soft approach might be more effective when dealing with a teenager with an overprotective stepmother. He discussed his idea with Gerry, who agreed, as Gerry was a father and understood his partner's reasoning.

Peersen phoned Mrs. Kramer, apologized for his previous behaviour, and explained why he needed her help. After serious deliberation, she hesitantly agreed to see him. Peersen was grateful for her cooperation, as he did not wish to threaten her with a subpoena. It was late in the afternoon, prior to her stepson returning home from basketball practice, when they arrived at the Kramer house.

"Mrs. Kramer," Peersen began, "we would like your permission to ask your son a few more questions. If at any time you think we are badgering him, you may ask us to leave. We need his help. Horace has already admitted that he was in the Humber Valley the night of the murder, and new evidence has come to our attention that makes us believe that he saw something that might put his life in danger. No attempt has been made to harm him, so far, but we are closing in on the killer. An attempt to eliminate a potential witness might be in the cards.

"For us to proceed with the investigation, without giving Horace a chance to tell what he saw, would be reckless on our part. Your son's safety is dependent on the killer being behind bars. Will you help us persuade him to be honest with us?"

Mrs. Kramer gazed directly into Peersen's eyes, assessing his character. She twisted her wedding ring as she mulled over the detective's words. As she was deciding the right course of action, they heard the back door open. Within a few moments, Mr. Kramer entered the room, returning home from work. He instantly bristled when he saw Thomson and Peersen in his living room.

"What the hell is this?" he roared. "Get out of my house." Mr. Kramer's huge chest and protruding stomach heaved as he shouted, his six-foot-two frame shaking with indignation. In this instance, his bullying tactics were to no avail. Mrs. Kramer, her petite body appearing smaller than she really was as she sat on the oversized chesterfield, gazed up at him calmly.

Encouraged by his wife's silence, he bellowed again, "Get the hell out of my house."

Mrs. Kramer sighed and turning to her husband, in a matter-of-fact voice, said, "Go get washed up for dinner. It's not all your house. When we need you, we'll rattle your chain. Go!"

Furious, but remembering how deftly his wife swung a frying pan, he reluctantly retreated to the kitchen, grumbling to himself as he departed. Thomson did his best to hide his smirk by pretending to have a slight cough and placing his hand over his mouth.

Peersen looked away. As he glanced out the window, he saw Horace Kramer riding his bicycle up the driveway. Within seconds, the teenager's footsteps were audible in the back porch. As Kramer entered the living room, Mrs. Kramer stood and walked over to her son. Having had time to consider the detective's request, she had arrived at her decision. Nodding to Peersen, she asked that he explain the situation to her son.

After Peersen had presented his case, Kramer's stepmother gently placed her hand on her son's shoulder. To her, he was her flesh and blood son, not a stepson. Her love for the lad was evident. Peersen suspected that she had decided that marrying the boy's father had been a huge mistake, but inheriting Horace had fulfilled a longing deep inside her. During the past few years, she had nurtured him, and she was proud of the results.

Horace eyed Peersen carefully, attempting to weigh the validity of his remarks. He gazed at his stepmother, and then turned and stared directly into the detective's face. Peersen was unable to interpret the intent behind the eyes. It bothered him.

"We know that you were in the Humber Valley the night of the murder, and we're certain that you saw something that you suspect is important," Peersen asserted. "If you're frightened, we can protect you. Help us!"

Kramer remained silent, and continued staring.

"Do the right thing," his stepmother pleaded. "If you know anything, tell them."

"We believe that your information involved Mr. Matheson, your science teacher," Peersen interjected softly. "Work with us."

At the mention of Matheson's name, Kramer dropped his eyes to the floor.

"Please," Peersen added, "it's important to *me* that you tell us what you know." Peersen had stressed the word "me," attempting to make the request personal.

Kramer remained silent. Thomson and Peersen waited anxiously as silence engulfed the room. Finally, Kramer's shoulders drooped in resignation.

"Mr. Matheson was in the valley the day of the murder," he began. "I was riding my bike on the trail, on the west side of the river. I saw him on the east bank of the Humber. I think Matheson may have seen me too." Kramer looked directly at Jim as he spoke.

"What time of day did you see him?"

"I'd say it was about one-thirty, maybe two o'clock."

Peersen thought that Kramer appeared relieved to have finally told the truth.

Thomson quietly observed his partner's handling of the situation and was pleased with the results. He wanted to ask the teenager why he had had lied to them about what he had seen, but kept silent, suspecting that the reason was fear.

Peersen thanked Mrs. Kramer for her support. Then he placed his hand on Horace's shoulder as he expressed gratitude for his help. Kramer gazed directly into Peersen's eyes and then looked at the detective's hand on his shoulder. He said nothing.

Kramer thought, *I might have told them about that son-of-a-bitch Matheson, but there's no bloody way I'm blabbing about what else I saw.*

✧ ✧ ✧

The first week of May, the weather remained stubbornly cold, although the emerging buds on the maple trees along Lauder Avenue bravely defied the temperatures, continuing to push open the protective coverings that had confined them during the frigid winter months.

On the way to school, the conversation of Tom and his friends centred on the forthcoming Spring Hop, the final dance of the year, held in Eaton's auditorium in the company's College Street Store at Yonge and College Streets. They laughed and teased as they talked about their dates, and of course, there was always some bragging about the possibilities of making out, although they all knew that none of them was likely to succeed.

Harry asked Tom, "Do you think Patrick and Sophie are going?"

"I've not seen Patrick for over a week now, except in the classroom at school. He seems to be avoiding me. I was talking to Sophie yesterday, and she says that she has seen very little of him, even less than before."

Shorty replied, "Patrick's become such a candy-ass that I don't know what to think."

Tom said nothing. He knew what the term "candy-ass" implied and recalled the locker-room rumours.

✧ ✧ ✧

The news that captured the front pages of the newspapers was the plans for a one-hundred-thousand-car expressway to alleviate traffic pressures on Lakeshore Road. The proposal was for a nine-and-a-half-mile roadway, elevated twenty-five feet above Fleet Street, with cars speeding in and out of the city at fifty miles per hour. It would cost forty-nine million dollars. American planning experts had presented details of the expressway to Fred. C. Gardiner, head of the Metropolitan Government. Included in the costs were funds to landscape the elevated route with trees, seedlings, and other plants. It was envisioned as a garden highway in the sky.

The fabled Sunnyside amusement park was to be demolished. The food stands, restaurants, dance pavilions, rides, and the rollercoaster were all to disappear. The Palais Royale and the swimming pool were to be the only remaining structures from the days when Sunnyside was Toronto's summer playground beside the lake. As well, a hundred and fifty houses, mainly on Lakeshore Road near Jameson Avenue, were to be torn down. They hoped to commence construction by the beginning of September.

Major construction projects continued to dominate the news in May of

1954. The daily newspapers reported that the necessary legislation required to begin the massive St. Lawrence Seaway project would soon pass the American House of Representatives.

✧ ✧ ✧

In mid-May, Frank Gnomes again reflected on the fact that his life was bittersweet. Sally-Lou had finally demanded that he get out of the house. Ignoring her ultimatum, a week later, he arrived home to discover that she had packed her bags and departed. He viewed the quietness that her departure created as sweet but knew that her demands for support payments were certain to be bitter.

Because the newspaper had assigned him more international political assignments, the editorial board of the *Toronto Tribune* had funded a trip for him to London, England, with side trips to Paris and Berlin to interview politicians and gather insights for future stories.

The last week of May, he departed from the Toronto-Malton airport on one of Trans-Canada Airlines' new Super Constellation aircraft. His economy ticket had cost the newspaper $482 (return), including full-course meals, continuous snacks, and drinks. The bitter taste of his failed marital life and his inability to uncover any new leads in the Stritch case were pushed from his mind as the aircraft lifted into the air.

Similar to the brass of the police department, he reluctantly considered the Stritch investigation a cold case; one that was unlikely to thaw. Frank knew that he had a reputation for never giving up on an assignment, but he admitted that this case represented the one that got away. Then he thought about Europe and the opportunities for sexual liaisons. *Failure to resolve a story was not the worst thing that could happen*, he thought.

✧ ✧ ✧

Jim Peersen's relationship with Samantha Anderson was warming, along with the spring season. They enjoyed an evening on the town at a seafood restaurant on Church Street, where the Lobster Cardinale was the finest they had ever experienced. Following the meal, the effects of a vintage white wine softening their mood, they took a taxi to Varsity Arena to swing to the mellow sounds of Benny Goodman, accompanied by the Toronto Symphony Orchestra.

The evening ended at Peersen's apartment in the Annex, sipping on a twenty-year-old cognac, listening to a new 33-rpm RCA recording of opera highlights. Though they were relaxed and kissed passionately, Peersen avoided suggesting that they go to the bedroom. He was certain that she thought it odd but said nothing. He thought, *It will happen when it happens.* It was past three o'clock in the morning before he took her home.

As Peersen drove westbound along Eglinton Avenue, the street was almost devoid of cars. At the traffic light at Bathurst, his car was the only one at the intersection. Many thoughts tumbled in his mind. He admitted that Samantha's profession had prevented him from taking the final step with her. Was he being prudish and judgmental? He wasn't certain. She offered a service to men that he found objectionable. It also occurred to him that she intimidated him, as she was far more experienced in sexual matters than he was. Embarrassed, Peersen smiled as he admitted this. He also acknowledged the frustration he felt, having finally found a woman to whom he was truly attracted and being uncertain whether or not to take her to bed.

✧ ✧ ✧

The district attorney's office reviewed the evidence given by Horace Kramer and finally agreed to issue a warrant for Matheson's arrest. It was early on a warm June evening when Thomson and Peersen knocked on Bill Matheson's door. Thomson had decided to execute the warrant at his house on Dufferin Street rather than humiliate him by arresting him at school. Forty minutes after their arrival, Matheson was in an interview room at the precinct.

When the detectives entered the room, Bill Matheson was sitting with his shoulders pressed tightly against the back of the chair, his arms folded across his chest. His eyes were cold, his attitude defiant.

Peersen knew that Matheson was a man who knew how to control his emotions and was familiar with controlling those around him. As a science teacher, he had spent sufficient years in the classroom instructing teenagers that were often aggressive and unruly. Being a stern disciplinarian, he had always managed to maintain the upper hand, and Peersen was certain that Matheson intended to behave similarly during the interview.

"Why have I been arrested?" Matheson demanded. "I've done nothing wrong."

"Now then, we'll just see about that," Gerry Thomson replied, and then commenced interrogating in his usual calm manner.

"Mr. Matheson, you have not been truthful with us."

"How did you arrive at this conclusion?" He stared at his accuser belligerently, clearly defying Thomson to prove that he had lied.

"We know that you were in Humber Valley the day your fiancée was murdered."

"I was at my cottage the entire week before her murder, and your own investigations prove it."

"Bullshit!" Peersen interjected.

"Prove it!" Matheson blasted back, his square chin jutting forward.

Thomson held up his hand to silence his partner and continued in a relaxed tone. "It's true that we checked with your neighbours at the cottage and also calculated the mileage figures on the odometer of your car. However, other information has come to our attention."

Gerry was building his web slowly, allowing Matheson to believe he could escape any trap that lay ahead.

"A keychain was found in the Humber the day after the murder, a piece of amber attached to it, and the initial M on the leather fob. It was your chain, wasn't it?"

"Anyone might have dropped it there."

"True, but amber is found in the Dominican Republic, and you were there during the previous Christmas holidays."

"So what?"

"You are a very meticulous man, Mr. Matheson. On your customs declaration, you listed an amber keychain, even though such an inexpensive trinket was hardly worth mentioning."

There was an awkward pause as Matheson gathered his thoughts. "Okay. I forgot. I did purchase one. So what! If you found one in the Humber Valley, it's a mere coincidence."

"Perhaps! Let me tell you another coincidence. You have a coin collection, and we also found coins from a numismatic collection at two locations in the valley. Did you lose any coins?"

"No! And besides, finding coins is again a coincidence," Matheson shot back.

"Do you wish to hear a third coincidence?" Thomson stated calmly. "We have a reliable witness who clearly saw you on the east bank of the Humber River on Friday, 31 August, in 1951. The witness recognized you by sight, rather than identifying you from a photograph.

"You *were* in that Valley, Mr. Matheson, the same day that your fiancée was murdered. Do you wish to claim that this is another coincidence? You asked us to prove that you were not at the cottage on the days you claimed. I believe we have done just that."

Matheson continued to glower at his accusers. He stared at Thomson, and then turned his gaze to Peersen, his expression more condescending than hateful. Being contradicted by those whom he considered his inferiors was not a situation he normally encountered.

Continuing to glare belligerently, he remained silent. Peersen did not sense any change in his body language. There was no hint that Matheson was about to surrender or even be cooperative. Several more minutes passed.

Finally, Thomson turned to his partner. "Detective Peersen, ask Sergeant Malloy to step into the room and take Mr. Matheson to the cells." Then Gerry added, "I hope you have a good lawyer. When too many coincidences appear in a row, a jury calls it evidence. Good luck, Mr. Matheson."

Sergeant Muscles Malloy stepped into the room just as Peersen was preparing to recite the formal arrest charge.

Matheson was a haughty man, over-impressed with his own ability but also practical, and he knew when to retreat. Without any trace of emotion or hint of defeat, Matheson said matter-of-factly, "I'll admit to certain indiscretions on my part. I may have stretched the truth a little, but I never murdered Elaine."

Peersen thought, *This is like catching Pinocchio with a ten-foot nose, while he say's "I only told a slight fib."*

Matheson began slowly. "I was worried when Elaine changed her plans and decided not to join me at the cottage, saying that she had a family obligation. We had been having a few disagreements in the weeks leading up to the marriage, and I was afraid that she was having doubts. Elaine was a beautiful woman and attracted attention from men wherever she went. I admit that I harboured a bit of jealousy at times, but the week before the Labour Day weekend, I knew that she had met three or four times with Greg Baldwin. Even though the guy is strange," he said with a sneer, "Elaine considers him a close friend.

"I thought that Elaine likely confided in Baldwin any misgivings she had about our relationship. I wanted to talk to him and then confront Elaine. I intended to demand the exact truth about her feelings. I am not a man who allows anyone to make a fool of me. If the wedding was not to be, I wanted to know."

"Did you go to see Baldwin?"

"I drove down from the cottage early on Friday morning and met with him at the school around noontime, no later than twelve-thirty. He was working in his classroom, preparing for the students' arrival the following week."

Thomson now had another time to check against his little red pins.

Matheson continued. "Baldwin said that he had met Elaine earlier in the day, and that she had indicated she was going to visit a friend on Raymore Drive, a street in the Humber Valley, not far from the river. She told Baldwin that she intended to walk the valley before visiting the friend. The weather was hot, and she said that it would be cool. I had no ideas that she was not going to the valley until after her supper. In the afternoon, I decided to go to over there and observe the trail where she would be walking, from the east bank of the river. I thought she might be meeting another man."

"What time was it when you arrived beside the river?"

"About one o'clock or half past."

"How long did you remain in the valley?"

"Less than half an hour."

"Did you see your fiancée on the trail?"

"No. However, I realized that if someone saw me, and if Elaine found out, she would be furious that I had not trusted her. Reluctantly, I left the valley and drove directly back to my cottage. I arrived at the cottage at five o'clock. When I learned of the murder, I knew that the husband, or in this case the fiancé, is always the prime suspect. I knew that the mileage on my odometer would show that I had made an extra trip to the cottage and back. I knew how to change the odometer figures."

"Can anyone verify the time you arrived at the cottage?"

"A handyman."

"What's his name? Where can we contact him?"

"I believe his name is Sam Smithford. I think he's from Gravenhurst, Bracebridge, or perhaps Huntsville. I met him at the marina in Bala and hired him to cut the grass and repair the dock. He was there when I arrived from Toronto."

"You trusted a man whom you had never met to do work at your cottage, knowing that he knew the premises were unoccupied?"

"For heaven's sake," he snapped back, "it's Muskoka, not the big city. Things are done that way. Yes, I trusted him, and he didn't let me down."

Thomson and Peersen left the interview room to talk over the situation.

In the hallway, Peersen said, "Matheson admits that he suspected that his fiancée was cheating on him. He might have confronted her in the valley and, in a fit of rage, killed her."

"Or he might have seen who killed her and is fearful of saying who it was," Thomson added.

"Either way, before we book him, we must locate the handyman to verify Matheson's time of arrival at the cottage. If it checks out, then he departed from the city too early to have committed the murder."

"Or else the handyman is in cahoots with him."

"We'll hold Matheson here as a guest of the province until we can check out his story."

"Agreed," Peersen replied.

Returning to the interview room, Thomson said, "Mr. Matheson you will be detained until we can substantiate your alibi."

Matheson glared defiantly at the detectives. His departing shot was, "I'm a survivor, an oxide. As long as I have oxygen, I can survive"

"Yeah," Peersen shot back, "and create rust."

✧ ✧ ✧

Though it was past nine o'clock, Thomson and Peersen decided to visit Mr. Gregory Baldwin. As an act of courtesy, Thomson telephoned Baldwin and asked permission to interview him at his home. On this occasion, he hoped that a spirit of civility might improve the chances of a cooperative witness.

Baldwin tersely refused.

Gerry politely informed him that they would arrive shortly and escort him down to the police station. Baldwin testily told him to come to the apartment. *So much for civility*, Gerry thought.

The nineteenth-century house that Baldwin occupied possessed a gable that soared to the peak above the second floor. It was not without its charms, with its red bricks and detailed gingerbread trim, but it was badly in need of repairs. Paint was peeling from the eaves and the window frames. It had seen better days. Gerry thought that Baldwin would have lived in a more up-scale residence and suspected that Baldwin had chosen the location as it was remote from the high school and offered privacy, where his lifestyle would be unobserved by his students and colleagues.

Knocking on the door, they heard footsteps descending the stairs, and within moments, they were in Baldwin's sanctuary on the upper level. Peersen noted the man's attire. Baldwin was sporting a pair of light-gray slacks, an expensive navy blazer, and narrow gray tie against a pink shirt. The labels, though not visible, undoubtedly attested to the fine quality of the garments. Baldwin wore them with style.

Peersen scanned the apartment as he entered, approving of what he saw. On an antique end table beside the door were two mahogany, carved male heads, about eighteen inches high. They appeared to be African or perhaps Haitian. The living room contained tasteful furniture, several of the pieces valuable period pieces, though the chesterfield was modern, plush, and comfortable. Atop an antique teacart were crystal decanters of liquor, and Peersen noted that on a shelf nearby were several bottles of quality brandies. The glasses beside the bottles were hand-cut Swedish crystal. Peersen recognized the pattern, the glasses likely imported by Birk's and Sons. Baldwin helped himself to a Johnnie Walker Scotch Black Label, neat, but offered nothing to his unwanted guests.

Drink in hand, Baldwin elegantly sat down on the chesterfield chair, motioning for the detectives to sit opposite him. As he crossed his long legs, he adjusted his trousers so that he would not wrinkle their immaculate crease. He sipped delicately on his drink, then placed the glass on a highly polished walnut end table beside him. Next, he adjusted the sleeves of his blazer, pulling down the French cuffs on the sleeves of his pink shirt, displaying a pair of gold cufflinks. Satisfied that he was the picture of sartorial splendour, he gazed at the detectives in anticipation of the first question.

Thomson thought, *This guy is overdressed for a police interview. I suspect he was on his way out for an engagement.*

Gerry smiled indulgently, as if explaining the rules of the house to one of his children.

"Mr. Baldwin, in a statement given by Bill Matheson, it seems that you met with him the day that Miss Stritch was murdered. Is that true?"

Pausing to think, and again adjusting his cufflinks, he reached for his glass as he said, "Yes, I believe that's true."

"You never mentioned this before."

"I didn't think it was important."

Thomson rolled his eyes in disgust, allowing Baldwin to know that he realized that he had been purposefully evasive and said, "You have obstructed a criminal investigation. Charges may be pending."

Baldwin smiled and continued to sip on his drink. His nonchalant attitude displayed an indifferent attitude. He knew his family could well afford the best lawyer that money could buy.

Gerry continued. "What time did Mr. Matheson come to see you?"

"Shortly after the noon hour."

"Are you certain?"

"Oh, yes. I remember I was not too pleased to see him, as I had arrived back from France just two days before. I had worked all morning in my classroom to prepare for the incoming students. The detestable grade nines cause the most preparation, ignorant little bastards."

Baldwin then sighed and added, "I was preparing for another year of listening to my imbecilic, linguistically deprived students murder the beautiful French language."

As an afterthought, Thomson asked, "How late did you remain at school?"

"Until almost six o'clock. I was the last person to leave the building. Even the office was empty."

"Are you certain the office was empty? On the Friday before school was to open, wouldn't Mr. Dinkman have been working late on the student timetables?"

"I would have thought so, but no, the office door was locked. I wanted to leave an assignment list on Mrs. Applecrust's desk. I wanted it typed and run on the Gestetner machine to hand to my students on the first day of the new term, even though half of them are unable to read."

"Why did Mr. Matheson come to see you?"

Peersen listened half-heartedly to the detailed answer, as Baldwin confirmed Matheson's statements. What interested him was the information that Dinkman had not been working late at school. This was the first time that they had discovered a break in the chain of carefully constructed alibis. He knew by his partner's eyes that Gerry had also noticed the discrepancy. Dinkman had said in his alibi that he had worked at the school until 10:00 p.m. and arrived home at 10:30 p.m. His wife had verified his arrival time. Someone was lying.

Thanking Baldwin for his "cooperation," Thomson and Peersen departed. Peersen had uttered the word "cooperation" with a hint of sarcasm.

Out on the street again, they discussed the results of the interview, excited that they had found a new lead.

"I welcome a chance to grill Dinkman again," Peersen said, almost with glee.

"Yes," Gerry replied. "The jerk needs to have his cage rattled. By the way, where do you suppose our friend Baldwin is going to tonight?"

"Likely that pansy bar on King Street, opposite the King Eddie."

Thomson nodded. They both knew about the Letro's Piano Bar from their days as patrolmen. Thomson had been among the policemen who had raided the bar, shortly after he had returned home from overseas. Later, he learned that one of the men arrested in the raid had been married with five children. When his name appeared in the press, he committed suicide. Gerry had justified his actions by reminding himself that he was simply enforcing the criminal code.

Thomson was no longer certain that the law was right. His wife had confided in him the damages caused when people blindly condemn those that live different lifestyles. She had been referring to her Italian pupils, but Gerry was wondering if the same reasoning should apply to homosexuals. He wasn't sure!

✧ ✧ ✧

The following day, Thomson and Peersen drove north to Bala. Fortunately, the handyman that Matheson had mentioned remained in the town, as two other cottagers had contracted him to work around their summer homes. The man confirmed Matheson's statement, and on their arrival back in Toronto, Thomson had no choice other than to release the science teacher.

However, the detective remained convinced that it was all too convenient, and that the handyman might be lying. He felt that Matheson was still a suspect, even if they were yet unable to prove it. As Matheson departed from the police station, Gerry warned him not to leave the city without notifying them

"Where the hell do you think I'll be going other than my cottage?" he snapped sarcastically. "Timbuktu?"

❖ ❖ ❖

After writing his final grade-eleven examination, Tom retrieved his bicycle from the schoolyard and journeyed to Greenberg's Pharmacy. When he arrived at work, Ruth was busy slinging four heavy wooden crates of Coca Cola from the cellar of the store into the truck. Each crate contained a dozen large-size bottles, but in her hands, they appeared as light as a feather. She smiled at Tom as he entered the back of the store and drew his attention to the four packages that were sitting on the counter, waiting to be delivered.

Later that evening, Shorty accompanied Ruth on a delivery that was a considerable distance east along Eglinton Avenue. She was taking a supply of medication to a drug store on the east side of Yonge Street. Greenberg's Pharmacy had a reciprocal agreement with a few of the other stores in the area to share drugs if one of them ran short. They only did this if the medication was required immediately, and there was no time to order it from the supplier.

Tom thought it strange that she took Shorty with her, as there was no heavy lifting involved. Shorty winked as he said to Tom, "I'm going along for the ride." Tom thought there was something strange about the way he said the word "ride."

Later, as it was a hot evening, Tom was sitting out at the rear of the pharmacy drinking a bottle of Coke. He noticed that Ruth had parked the delivery van in the laneway beside the pharmacy. He wondered how long it had been there. Then he saw Shorty emerge from the back doors of the van, zipping up the front of his trousers. Shorty grinned sheepishly when he realized that Tom was watching him.

"I'll tell you about it later," he said, still smirking.

After work, Tom and Shorty pedalled their bikes homeward. Arriving on Lauder Avenue, Shorty parked his bike in the driveway of his house and motioned for Tom to sit on his veranda steps. It was now almost ten o'clock, but the heat of the day had not abated. Up and down the street, people remained outside. A young couple, their arms linked, strolled along the sidewalk in front of Shorty's house, talking quietly.

Shorty and Tom sat on the veranda in silence for several minutes. When Shorty finally spoke, his words hit his friend like a thunderbolt out of the blue.

"I had sex with Ruth again tonight," he declared in a voice that was almost apologetic.

Tom didn't know if the word "sex" shocked him the most or the word "again." Struck dumb, Tom simply stared at him. In the darkness, although Tom could not see Shorty's face clearly, he sensed that Shorty was interpreting his silence as censorship.

Gazing directly at Tom, Shorty began. "I know she's kind of old, over thirty, but she has a great body. The first time it happened, I had my shirt off. I was sweating from lifting the heavy crates of pop from the truck. I saw her looking at me. I knew what it meant. When we got back in the van, I pretended that I didn't know she was watching me. Then she grabbed me by the crotch, and man, she was on me. I wanted to resist, but geez, I couldn't. I felt bad afterwards, as I had always imagined that the first time I did it, it would be with Carol. Actually, I'm not certain that a blowjob counts as sex."

Tom was too stunned to speak.

"Don't look so shocked, Tom!"

"But she's so old," Tom finally blurted out.

"I know, but it felt great. On the third occasion, I actually had real sex with her."

"How many times have you done it?"

Tom's curiosity had overcome his shock. He had heard older guys at school talk about the girls they did in the backseat of a car at a drive-in theatre, and some talked about doing what Shorty had done in the laneway behind the school. However, this was the first time he had ever talked with someone who had done it and he knew for certain, that it had actually occurred.

Shorty continued. "Four times."

"Are you going to do it again?"

"Sure, a few more times. An older woman can teach a guy things that the girls at school don't even know about."

Tom shrugged his shoulders indifferently, trying to pretend that he was not hanging on every word. He hoped he would tell him more, but Shorty remained silent, gazing up and down the darkened street. Finally, Tom took the plunge.

"What did you learn?"

"How to put on a condom, how to arouse her, how to find the 'hot spot' inside her, how to pace myself, and how to handle her breasts to make her ooze with pleasure."

Tom was too stunned to comment. Shorty sounded as if he had swallowed the encyclopedia of sex. Tom was too intimidated to ask any further questions. He was not certain what it meant to "pace himself."

Even when they had been small kids, Shorty had always known more about the secrets of "the big boys" than the rest of them. He was the first to know where babies came from. When they had been younger, he had taken books from the adult section of the library and read them as he sat on the floor between the rows of shelves. Even then, he understood what he read. Now, he was the first guy Tom knew who had had sex.

That hot night in June, though Tom felt mature, as he had graduated from grade eleven, he knew that Shorty was still far ahead of him. He wondered when his turn would come, and he would step up to the plate and swing his bat. He hoped that it did not occur in the back of a delivery van, and he prayed that it would not be with a woman Ruth's age.

Tom knew that ever since the first day Shorty had met Carol, when he was only seven years of age, he had had a crush on her. Throughout their elementary school days, he had mooned over her. Carol had always been attracted to Harry, but it did nothing to discourage Shorty. Now as a maturing teenager, Shorty remained in love with her.

Tom did not know why he asked Shorty the next question. He had no right. "Shorty, wouldn't it have been better to have waited and made love with Carol?"

Without a trace of hesitation, he turned to Tom and replied, "I intend to marry Carol. Until then, there will be no lovemaking between us."

Tom never forgot his words.

⟡ ⟡ ⟡

Jim Peersen was restless. He wanted to begin questioning Dinkman but recognized the wisdom of delaying.

During the last week of June, he invited Samantha to a movie. They went to the Imperial Theatre to see *Three Coins in the Fountain*. Even though it was a piece of fluff, the scenes of Rome and its classical scenery were appealing. Peersen preferred films that were more substantial, but he was not immune to a tender story of people seeking love in a romantic city.

After the film, they enjoyed a coffee at Basil's Restaurant, and as the hour was not late, they went to his apartment, where he placed on his new stereo record player a recording he had recently bought of Mozart's *Thirty-Ninth Symphony*. While he poured drinks, Samantha strolled out onto the deck. The night air was pleasantly warm. The season was advancing, and the trees were now in full leaf, their greenery bright green, their fresh foliage dark against the moonlit sky.

Samantha was leaning on the deck railing when Jim joined her. Peersen knew he was skirting dangerous territory, when, after handing her a glass, he slipped his arm around her waist. The movie they had seen earlier, the warm night air, and now an alcoholic drink all blended enchantingly into a romantic mood.

Gazing at Samantha, he realized that she was lost in thought.

⟡ ⟡ ⟡

Jim was unaware that Samantha was trying to decide how she truly felt about him. She knew she was falling in love with him, but she was undecided if she should allow him to know how she felt. He was charming, intelligent, and disarmingly handsome, but he was a cop.

Life with a policeman was not a comforting thought. As well, she sensed his ambiguity toward her. She spanked men for a living and was unable to give up her profession. She was sure that it bothered Peersen, even though he said nothing. Besides, she could imagine the reaction at the precinct if she attended a police picnic or dance with him. Policemen on the force regarded her as a hooker. Several of the cops on the force knew her by sight. How would Jim handle such a situation if they saw them together?

Turning to gaze at Jim, she pushed her doubts into the recesses of her mind. The seductive magic of the night was weaving its charms. Samantha watched as Jim placed his drink on the balcony railing and wrapped both arms around her. She could feel the warmth of his firm body against hers as he held her. The kiss was tender and eager, but she sensed his hesitancy to go further. After several moments, she gently broke free of his embrace. She respected him too much to allow him to go somewhere he was unwilling to go. He was not ready, and actually, she felt that she was in a similar situation. Neither of them was ready for intimate lovemaking. If they were meant for each other, the right moment would occur, and she knew it must be mutual.

As he drove her home, the conversation was polite, a little too polite. She hoped she had not hurt him and cuddled close to reassure him. When they parted, she smiled and asked him when he would call her again.

He grinned shyly and said, "Soon."

✧ ✧ ✧

The final day, in the late afternoon, before the teachers at YCI fled the school to pursue their summer activities, Thomson and Peersen appeared at the school office. A flustered Mrs. Applecrust did not resist when they gently brushed past her and opened the door to Dinkman's office.

As they entered, they saw that the vice-principal was severely reprimanding a teenage boy who appeared immune to the ranting and raving of the flustered administrator. Dinkman's anger increased when he saw the detectives enter.

Thomson was in no mood to go easy on Dinkman, and without saying a word, he motioned for the teenager to leave the room. Thomson then pulled out a chair and sat down.

"Sit on the bench in the office, Jimmy, and I'll deal with you later," Dinkman barked.

Jimmy Frampton smirked and departed. Dinkman was still convinced that Jimmy had planted the sanitary napkins in the catalpa tree and remained vigilant for any infractions of the rules on the boy's part. That afternoon, he had caught him lurking around the cafeteria area. The exams were over, and no students should have been in the building. To make matters worse, Jimmy had a small can of black paint and a brush in his hand, which Dinkman suspected he had stolen from the art room. Jimmy insisted that he had found the paint can on a bench between the lockers. Dinkman knew Jimmy was lying.

Now, with the arrival of the police, the upset vice-principal was rattled further. He had intended to go home early and enjoy a beer under the shade of the old pear tree in his backyard. The episode with Jimmy had delayed him, and now he had to answer more questions. He noticed that the younger of the two detectives held an official-looking piece of paper in his hand and feared it was a warrant for his arrest.

Peersen knew that Dinkman had seen the paper, which was an office memo neatly folded to the exact size of an arrest warrant. The ruse had the desired effect. Dinkman gave an obsequious smile and told Peersen to be seated. Peersen pulled out a chair and sat down across from his partner.

"Mr. Dinkman," Jim Peersen began, "we feel it is necessary to warn you that anything you say will be held against you in a court of law. Everything you say will be considered officially as evidence."

The legal language, plus the fake warrant, produced the results that the young detective desired. Next, he delivered the fatal shot.

"Mr. Dinkman, it has come to our attention that you have not been truthful about your movements on the evening of the murder of Miss Elaine Stritch."

"I told you the truth when you first interviewed me."

"Not exactly, Mr. Dinkman. You said you worked in your office until 10:00 p.m. and were home by 10:30 p.m. We have learned that the office was empty at 6:00 p.m. and have a witness to verify this fact. Why did you lie about the time? We can understand a discrepancy of a half hour, or even an hour, but not three and a half hours. If you left the school before 6:00 p.m., you had sufficient time to be in the Humber Valley, lying in wait."

Peersen noticed the panic that dashed across Dinkman's face. His upper lip, with its thin mousy moustache, quivered slightly.

"You admit that you lied," Peersen accused.

"Sort of!"

"Yes, and I'm certain your motives for lying were 'sort of' questionable. Now tell us, what time did you leave the office?"

"About five o'clock."

"Where did you go between 5:00 p.m. and 10:30 p.m., the time your wife says you arrived home?"

"Do I have to tell you? The information could easily be misconstrued."

"If you wish to avoid being arrested, you need to say where you were."

"This is very embarrassing. I am a married man."

"Your wife appears to be very understanding of your indiscretions." Thomson's voice dripped with sarcasm.

"This is different."

"Why?"

"I was with a member of my staff. If the school board finds out, I'll lose my job."

"You'll lose your freedom and your employment if you withhold the information."

Dinkman squirmed in his seat, clutching the edge of the desk, his knuckles white, as he gazed out from behind his beady eyes.

"I was at Bettina Taylor's apartment from about 5:30 p.m. until shortly after ten o'clock. It was not a social call. We were discussing her evaluation report and next year's teaching assignment."

"That's an unusually long time—a very, very long time—and isn't it unusual to conduct such business in a teacher's home?"

"That's why it might be misconstrued. It was all very innocent. I'd had a hectic week, and her report was the final one that I needed to complete. She offered to see me after the end of the day and said we could discuss matters over a drink. I foolishly accepted."

"Thank you, Mr. Dinkman. We'll check out your story and be in touch. Charges may also be pending for obstructing justice."

Peersen placed the fake arrest warrant in his inside jacket pocket and stood to leave. As the detectives strolled out of the office, the boy who was being disciplined was sitting on the bench. Peersen smiled sympathetically at him, as he knew that dealing with Dinkman from an inferior position could be a nasty affair. Jimmy grinned back, not in the least intimidated. Something in his smile gave Peersen the feeling that perhaps the lad would be no pushover for Dinkman. Peersen was unaware that Jimmy had been thwarted in his plan to employ the black paint to write on the locker doors, "Dickhead is a prick."

Departing from the office, Jim Peersen said to Gerry, as their footsteps echoed in the empty corridors of the school, "Do you think Dinkman's telling the truth?"

"Now then, we'll just see about that. Our next interview is with Miss Bettina Taylor."

"Damn it, why are we just now hearing that those two met the evening of the murder? I believe we should charge the two of them with obstruction."

"Now then, we'll see about that too."

✧ ✧ ✧

They telephoned Miss Taylor. She informed them that unless they interviewed her immediately or possessed a warrant, they had to wait until the end of August, as she was leaving for Vancouver the following morning.

Arriving at her apartment, Peersen noticed that it was sparsely furnished. On the beige walls hung several cheap prints, likely purchased from Woolworths. The place lacked the small feminine touches that most women enjoyed. Only one framed photograph adorned the mantle over the fireplace. Taylor was dressed in a similar austere manner, no frills, just plain practical attire. Even her shoes were sturdy oxfords with a Cuban heel.

Thomson inquired about Dinkman's visit on the night of the murder. Her version of events was similar to Dinkman's, but she added sarcastically, "I never invited him here to my place. He showed up at my door, the evaluation report in hand, and I reluctantly allowed him in. It's true that I offered him a drink, more out of courtesy than a desire to be hospitable. I thought he'd never leave."

"In your alibi for the night of the murder, you stated that Miss Allyson visited you the Friday evening in question. You never mentioned Mr. Dinkman's visit before," Frank told her, his annoyance evident.

"She visited me after Dinkman departed. You can confirm this with Miss Allyson. Sorry I didn't tell you before about Dinkman's visit, but it was embarrassing. I didn't think it mattered as you had already confirmed that I was in the apartment the night Elaine was murdered."

"Wasn't it rather late for Miss Allyson to be visiting you?"

"Yes, but she is a little strange. Her habits are unpredictable. I didn't mind." There was a pause, and Taylor continued. "Shortly after Dinkman arrived, he told me he had given me a much better timetable and teaching assignment for the following year. He said I would be teaching the grade-thirteen math classes. They're a dream to teach, as the assholes that disturb lessons and have no desire to achieve have already failed or dropped out. I was immediately suspicious why he was being so generous toward me.

"After the second drink, he allowed me to read my evaluation report. He hinted that the report could be improved, if I provided favours in return. I knew what he meant. There was no way I was sleeping with him to receive a better report. I let him ramble on, kept my distance, and he finally left. Needless to say, he assigned me the grade-nine classes again. They think that an isosceles triangle is what hangs between a man's legs."

Peersen smiled at her off-colour remark.

Gerry continued. "What time did Mr. Dinkman leave?"

"About ten o'clock."

Thomson had no more questions. He wished her a pleasant trip to the west coast, and departed.

Outside, Peersen said to his partner, "I wonder if she'd sleep with any man, at *any* price."

"Well, we know she slept with a man at least once. She has a young son in Vancouver."

"Perhaps a virgin birth," Peersen quipped.

Thomson ignored the remark. "I believe Miss Taylor's version of events, and the times she stated for Dinkman's arrival and departure coincide with his account. Stritch was killed sometime between 6:00 p.m. and midnight. Dinkman had insufficient time after he left Taylor's apartment to go to the valley and commit the murder, unless his wife is lying about the hour he arrived home."

"There's also the possibility that she and Dinkman are lying to alibi each other," Peersen added.

Thomson nodded his head but said nothing further.

Next, they visited Miss Allyson, and she confirmed her friend's version of the events of the fateful evening. She apologized for not being more accurate when she gave the time of her visit to Miss Taylor on the evening that Miss Stritch was murdered. Thomson was annoyed but let the matter pass—for now.

They visited Debbie Dinkman, but she refused to alter her statement. She said her husband returned home at 10:30 p.m. Either Dinkman or Matheson might be the murderer, but no concrete proof existed to arrest either of them.

✧ ✧ ✧

With the approach of July, the residents of Toronto fully welcomed the warm days of summer. Frank Gnomes was feeling more relaxed than usual. It had been over six weeks since Sally-Lou had departed from the house on Bellevue Avenue. He was enjoying the quietness, even though he had not had sex in over four months, long before his wife had left him. It surprised him when he realized that he had been too busy to think about it. As he gathered his notes for an assignment about Indo-China, he dreamed of the newspaper sending him to the Far East. Then he thought of the Asian girls he might meet and felt a stirring in his crotch.

At lunch, he went to a deli on Yonge Street for a sandwich and a beer. It was a few doors north of Diana Sweets, where he sometimes met Masters, his snitch. As he sat munching quietly on a corned beef sandwich, he noticed Samantha Anderson sitting at a booth at the rear of the restaurant, chatting seriously with an older man whom he did not recognize. *Damn*, he thought, *that gal is beautiful. Who in hell's the guy with her?*

Frank was unaware that the man was Samantha's lawyer, William Broda.

When the man departed, Frank strolled back to where Samantha sat, and without a word, he eased himself into the booth. She was looking over what appeared to be legal documents and had not seen his approach. Peering over the top of the pages, she gazed directly at him, rolled her eyes, and then continued reading, without saying a word to him.

"Hi, gorgeous," he said impishly. Her cool demeanor increased his interest in her and aroused the sensation he had felt earlier in his groin. He knew it was time to turn on his boyish charm.

"There's a great movie at the Imperial Theatre tonight, *Dial M for Murder*, with Ray Milland. Any chance that you might join me? I know it's your type of film. We could have dinner before."

"It's what happens after that worries me," she responded, her voice decidedly chilly.

Being persistent, never overplaying his hand, and putting on charm were skills he had perfected through the many years he conducted interviews with hostile witnesses. The thawing point arrived after he informed her that his wife had left him. He could tell that she felt sorry for him, although she said nothing.

Samantha knew that Jim was busy on an investigation, and she would not see him until the weekend. Against her better judgment, she finally agreed to join Frank, but for dinner and the movie only.

"No after-movie antics," she firmly stated.

Frank knew that it was a pity date, but hell, it was still a date. He grinned coyly, as he said to her, "I'll pick you up at six-thirty."

✧ ✧ ✧

During the languorous days of July, Yonge Street pulsed from dusk until the early hours of the morning, as revellers celebrated summer's heat. Their scanty outfits exposed more skin than the hormone-driven young should ever be allowed to view. After the bars closed, eye contact on the street increased. It was "cruising time," a time to cruise for a pick up. To be a participant, no automobile was required, although the traffic on the street now moved slower, and the shouts from the cars erupted more frequently and louder.

Cruising time was truly embraced by the young. They knew that it was almost as short-lived as the month itself. Virgins were initiated into mankind's oldest ceremony, while the more experienced became acquainted with the rites of the "quickie" romance. When the doors of the bars and clubs finally closed, and the screen doors of the houses throughout the city had banged shut for the final time, the most cherished rituals of summer ended for another day. More than one parent's voice was heard shouting from upstairs, "Where the hell have you been?"

The fear of July relinquishing its place on the calendar intensified the desire to soak up the luxury of the summer's finest month. Each day, as the Sam McBride Ferry—named after a notoriously free-spending mayor of Toronto—pushed its way across the placid harbour, excited children leaned over the oak railings, while concerned parents enforced the rule that their feet must remain on the deck. When the ferry dropped its large metal gangway onto the dock at Centre Island, crowds surged forward, anxious to be swept into the enchanted world of nature that lay within sight of the Toronto skyline. The Toronto Islands comprised one of the largest car-free zones in the world.

By noon, on a hot day, the lakeside and harbour beaches of the Island were crowded. Hot dogs, french fries, popcorn, and candyfloss were consumed in such quantities that some feared the ferry might sink on the return voyage to the city.

At the end of July, Torontonians enjoyed the second holiday weekend of the summer. It was not an observance or a celebration of anything, other than the need for a midsummer break. Unlike other holidays on the calendar, parades, fireworks, turkey dinners, greeting cards, special church services, and gift giving were foreign to it. It was a time to drive to the beaches north of the city or the lakes of the Muskoka, Georgian Bay, or Haliburton Region.

Within the city, picnickers crowded High Park, and sunbathers basked on the warm sands at Sunnyside and Woodbine Beaches. The flames from backyard barbeques charred the hamburgers and hot dogs for outdoor lunches and, in the evenings, cooked the steaks or chicken for supper. It was not a time to indulge in gourmet banquets, but time to enjoy the delights of comfort foods. Potato and macaroni salads, as well as coleslaw, were among the latter category.

✧ ✧ ✧

On the August holiday weekend, Samantha and Jim braved the traffic on the QE Highway and drove to Niagara Falls. On arrival, they strolled along the edge of the deep gorge. Even though they had viewed the mighty cataract on many occasions, the sheer force of the falls inspired a sense of wonder and awe. Peering down into the swirling water of the Niagara River, they watched a *Maid of the Mist* boat struggle valiantly through the violent currents to provide its passengers a thrilling close-up view of the tumultuous waterfalls. Many appreciated the aptness of the name of the vessel as it approached the massive rocks where the flood from the cataract above poured downward, creating clouds of mist. Raincoats and hats protected the viewers from being drenched by the sheer volume of water droplets saturating the air. The boat appeared insignificant amid the brutal power of Niagara.

Later, Jim and Samantha luxuriated in the verdant splendour of the Niagara Parkway. The cherry trees were now devoid of fruit, and the strawberry fields long since spent, but the limbs loaded with pears and peaches drooped heavily toward the rich dark earth. The grape vines were lush, their ripening fruit poking from beneath their cover of greenery as they matured under the heat of the August sun. Throughout the peninsula, nature was pushing toward its climax.

Samantha and Jim lunched at the Prince of Wales Hotel, prominently situated on the main street, across from Simcoe Park, where young children splashed gaily in the old cement wading pool. Their mothers sat nearby, chatting with neighbours as they observed their offspring at play. The giant chestnut trees swayed gently in the warm summer breezes.

On the return journey, they were delayed a half-hour at Burlington, as a sea-going vessel was entering Hamilton Harbour, and they had raised the lift bridge. It had been a wonderful day, and they had luxuriated in each other's company.

Later in the evening, Jim informed Samantha that he was driving to Virginia Beach for two weeks. Although he had toyed with the idea of inviting her to join him, he felt that their relationship had not progressed to the point where it was advisable to spend fourteen nights in close proximity. She wished him a safe journey and smiled warmly as she told him not to take advantage of any Southern belles. They both laughed.

It's a pity, Jim thought regretfully, *that we're not comfortable enough to sleep together.*

✧ ✧ ✧

While Jim was away, the humid weather intensified in Toronto, but it eased as the month progressed. Samantha's apartment faced north, and as the summer season was well advanced, the sun had crept back toward the south. During the day, its rays no longer entered her bedroom. One evening she opened her window, feeling the refreshing breezes from the north cool against her face. She climbed into bed knowing that she would sleep in comfort as she pulled a thin quilt over her naked body.

She gazed at the curtains in the window rustling gently in the night air. Her thoughts wandered toward Jim. She missed him. It still bothered her that he was a cop. She knew that he was good at his work, enjoyed it, and was unlikely to quit his chosen profession, even if he won the Irish Sweepstakes. She remained convinced that a long-term relationship with him would be difficult, as the demands of his job were many. Marriage with a policeman was fraught with problems. Death and danger were his constant companions. On the other hand, she also knew that he was a catch that was worth the risk.

Then she thought about Frank Gnomes. Except for one time during early July, she had not seen him. She admitted that he was fun. Frank was an uncomplicated man. He had a feverish drive to succeed at the newspaper and was overly fond of women. If he would stop chasing self-centred bubbleheads, he would go far in his career. She wondered if his attraction for her was a desire to have a romance with another bubblehead, or an attempt to break the pattern destroying his personal life. It helped ease her conscience that he was now separated from his wife, but a man with three ex-wives was not a great catch.

She tried to convince herself that Frank was merely a distraction. Nothing serious could come from the relationship, even though his charm and good looks were greatly appealing. Despite his pressure to get her in the sack, she had avoided sleeping with him. His conversations about world affairs and happenings of the day were interesting. It was small wonder that the readers of the *Trib* enjoyed his column. His analytical skills were superb, and he had a way of spinning words that captivated his audience. She was slowly realizing that he was captivating her as well. Should she encourage him, or wait until Jim was ready to make a commitment? She lamented that, although she was good at analyzing other people's problems, she often failed to solve her own.

The reason that Frank was in her thoughts was that he had phoned her the previous evening. He told her that the Duchess of Kent had arrived in Toronto to officiate at the opening of the Canadian National Exhibition. On the evening prior to the opening of the CNE, a banquet was being held in her honour, and Frank was one of the invited guests. He wanted her to be his companion. Samantha had hesitated, but eventually accepted his invitation.

On the evening of the banquet, she was thrilled to be with Frank, who was handsome and charming. It was also great to meet the duchess. Samantha was impressed with the number of prominent socialites and community leaders in attendance, recognizing several of them, as she had spanked their bottoms.

A well-known clergyman, seated at the head table, blushed exceedingly when he saw her. She thought that "pinkie ass," as the clergyman preferred to be called during her sessions, looked great with a red face, as it contrasted with his white clerical collar.

✧ ✧ ✧

Shorty, Harry, Carol, Sophia, and Tom went to the CNE on the Labour Day weekend. Sophie did her best to convince Patrick to accompany them, but he adamantly refused. The group was accustomed to Patrick being absent from their midst, and although they sympathized with Sophie, they told her that she must respect his feelings and try to have a good time.

Sophie said, "Something happened to him last March. He's never been the same since. I don't know what it was, but it must have been terrible. He told me that he's had nightmares ever since, and I've noticed that he always seems to be looking over his shoulder."

"You have absolutely no idea what it was?" Tom asked.

"No, but I intend to find out."

"Patrick has been my friend for a long time. I'll see if he'll tell me," Tom replied.

In truth, they were both doubtful that he would ever share with them what had happened.

They enjoyed their day at the Ex. The Grand Stand Circus in the afternoon was terrific, and they were thrilled to see Dale Evans, Roy Rogers, and his horse Trigger at the evening performance. However, the greatest attraction of all was the new million-dollar Food Products Building. The free samples and the treats at the numerous booths reminded them of previous years. Tom thought about when they had been kids, and Patrick had consumed so much food that he had a stomachache. Then he remembered Sophie's words and wondered if they would ever find out what had happened to Patrick the previous March.

Chapter Eight

After the Labour Day weekend ended, Tom and his friends prepared to knuckle down to another academic year. On the first day of the new term, Harry called at Patrick's house to accompany him to school. Reluctantly, Patrick complied. The remainder of the group joined them at the corner of Lauder Avenue and Amherst Boulevard. They avoided inquiring why Patrick did not hang around with them anymore.

When they reached the doors of the school, Tom thought he saw a look of fear on Patrick's face as he brushed his hair from his pale face. He was the only one among them who did not have a suntan. Before entering the school, Harry placed his hand on Patrick's shoulder and quietly said, "We're your friends Patrick. Friends stick together. Understand?"

Patrick nodded, but said nothing.

Harry told them later, "Whatever's bothering Patrick, it's something really bad. I think we had better keep an eye on him. If anyone sees someone teasing or bullying him, let Shorty or me know."

As this was to be their grade-twelve year, junior matriculation, some of their teachers were new to them. The heads of the departments and senior members of staff usually instructed the upper-grade students, but they still had Mr. Millford for PT, Baldy Baldwin for French, Miss Taylor for geometry, and Wild Bill Matheson for chemistry. Tom had dropped art from his list of subjects, but Miss Hitch smiled whenever she saw him in the hallways as she sashayed past, attired in one of her orgasmic outfits.

Miss Allyson was still the school librarian and ruled her domain like the tearful captain of a leaky ship.

Thankfully, no one mentioned the Stritch murder investigation. It had now been three years since her death.

✧ ✧ ✧

Jim Peersen returned to his desk on the Tuesday morning, following the Labour Day weekend. He was reviewing the weekend reports to ascertain if any recent developments had occurred in the cases they had assigned to him.

When Gerry Thomson arrived, he went over to Peersen's desk and warmly greeted him. Gerry had taken his vacation during the same two weeks as his partner, but he had remained in the city, other than a three-day visit to Wasaga Beach with his family.

"How was the weather in Virginia Beach?" Thomson inquired.

"Blistering hot and as humid as a sauna bath—in other words, great."

"Any virgins left in Virginia Beach when you departed?"

Peersen grinned sheepishly and did not reply.

Thomson continued. "Jim, I received some information this morning from one of the young patrol officers, Al Harris. He has a daughter attending YCI, as his family lives on Holland Park Avenue, where Miss Allyson has a second-floor flat. Harris says that Miss Taylor has moved in with Miss Allyson. He says that on occasion, he has seen them sitting on the veranda holding hands."

"Butch Bettina Taylor and weepy old Allyson?"

"It might be perfectly innocent, and they live together simply to share expenses. However, before I left for the holidays, a copy of the YCI yearbook was on my desk. Bill Simms picked it up and thumbed through it. You remember Simms; he's on the narcotics squad and works undercover in the downtown. He thought he recognized Taylor's picture among the staff photos and thinks she may be one of the women who frequents a bar on Sherbourne Street where some lesbians hang out. We previously considered that Taylor and Stritch might have had an unnatural relationship, and it ended when Stritch decided to marry Matheson. In a fit of jealousy, it's possible she killed her ex-lover."

"Yes, but remember, we also discovered that Miss Taylor has a son."

"It's common for a lesbian to want a child. The fact that Allyson and Taylor have moved in together adds weight to the theory. While I was on vacation, I spent a few hours reviewing the Stritch case. We know that there's an undercurrent beneath our investigation, and sex is one of the strongest motivations of human behaviour. We never can be sure what goes on behind the closed doors of the teachers' homes. However, we do know that all the people whom we consider persons of interest are young and single, except for Miss Allyson. The only discrepancy we found in the alibis was in Dinkman's, and it turned out to be a dead end, thanks to the statements of Dinkman and his wife."

Thomson paused, stroked his chin methodically, and added, "After three years, the group of suspects may feel secure now. It might make them careless. I think we should have a few rookie officers get a perspective on their present-day activities."

"I doubt that they'll find anything."

"Now then, we'll just see about that."

✧ ✧ ✧

At the end of the month, Peersen and Thomson scanned the reports of the observations of the teachers at YCI during their leisure hours. On some Friday nights, a few of the teachers travelled circuitous routes to reach their destinations. Even after all this time, the staff acted as though they indeed had something to hide. Peersen thought that a pattern was emerging.

Thomson agreed, having already arrived at the same conclusion by examining the travels of the suspects as they moved around the city. Employing his little red pins, he had discovered that several of the teachers invariably journeyed every second Friday to a destination near Scarlett Road and Lawrence Avenue. The reason was not clear, but now that they were aware of the pattern, perhaps it would be easier to establish exactly where the teachers were going.

❖ ❖ ❖

The evening of Friday, 15 October, Tom's family was in a relaxed mood as they gathered around the television to enjoy several hours of programs. The *Jackie Gleason Show, Two for the Money, George Gobel,* and *The Cross Canada Hot Parade* were among their favourites. As they watched the screen, they ignored the persistent rhythm of the rain beating against the living room windows.

As the eleven o'clock news began, Gramps walked over to the window and glanced out into the darkened street. He frowned as he gazed at the sheets of rain blowing across the roadway, visible in the glow of the streetlight on the corner.

"I am glad I'm not out in a schooner on a night like this," he said. "If the rain continues, like old Noah, I might have to build an ark to escape the floods before the water washes away me bed."

Tom's dad walked over to the window and paused for several moments. He nodded his head in agreement and returned to watching TV.

Shortly after, as Gramps climbed the stairs to bed, the weather reporter announced that a storm would reach Toronto around midnight. Originating in the Caribbean nine days earlier, it had killed a thousand people in Haiti. It had hit mainland United States near the border between North and South Carolina. Meteorologists declared that the storm had now weakened considerably and that it was unlikely to cause damage in the Toronto area, despite the possibility of strong winds. They also warned that a cold front was moving eastward from the Chicago area, where it had already dumped heavy rain.

Ken and Tom stayed up late to watch a movie on channel 4, a Buffalo station. When it ended, the station played the American national anthem. When the final note ended, the TV screen displayed a test pattern, accompanied by a buzzing sound in the background. Ken turned off the set and the eerie glow of the screen ceased, plunging the room into darkness. The wind outside howled around the house and the rain beat against the windows as the boys ascended the stairs to their bedroom.

While they slept, Ken and Tom were unaware of the drama, chaos, and death unfolding under the cover of darkness. Hurricane Hazel, with all its wrath and fury was tearing across Toronto, a city of one million inhabitants. Many residents would not survive the night.

✧ ✧ ✧

Shortly after midnight, Gerry Thomson and Jim Peersen both received phone calls from Sergeant Malloy, who told them to get down to the precinct immediately. Peckerman had requested that everyone report for duty. The city had declared an emergency.

When they arrived at the station, Peckerman told Peersen and Thomson that the storm had hit the west end of the city the worst. Thieves had taken advantage of the situation and broken into a jewellery store in Weston. He told them to "hustle their rear ends and get out to Weston to prevent any further burglaries."

As the two detectives drove out of the parking lot, through the steamed-up windows of the police car, they saw several cruisers heading west to Etobicoke, where most of the emergency calls had originated.

Driving northwest, Thomson and Peersen encountered broken tree limbs strewn across the streets. Above the car, branches noisily slithered back and forth in the wind, like giant hands slashing through the rain-soaked night. On one avenue, they detoured around a tree that had fallen across the roadway.

On Weston Road, north of St. Clair, a crew was attempting to repair hydro lines that had been downed by falling branches. As they drove past them, Peersen felt the car tremble when a powerful gust of wind slammed into the left side of the auto, lifting the car. The streets were empty of people, creating excellent conditions for thieves who did not mind getting soaked to the skin.

It was well past one o'clock in the morning when they neared Lawrence Avenue and Weston Road. The wind was stripping the few remaining leaves from the tree branches and swirling them in tornado-shaped funnels, along with anything else in its path, including debris torn away from houses and sheds. A plank ripped from a backyard fence flew past the car, and several empty garbage tins crashed into its door. The rain was a wild torrent of water, visibility so limited that at times they felt as if they were driving blind.

Unknown to them, downtown at the precinct, distress calls were jamming the police switchboards. Many callers were unable to get through, the powerful winds and falling branches having cut telephone lines. Families were feeling isolated and helpless as the intensity of the storm increased with each passing minute.

In the town of Weston, Peersen and Thomson cruised slowly past the stores on Weston Road, peering through the misted car windows at the shops that lined the street. At the jewellery store, a cruiser had secured the scene, and the officers had arrested two young men. Peersen rolled down the window halfway and spoke to the arresting officer, grateful that it was not necessary that he get out of the car.

Thomson and Peersen continued their surveillance. They noticed that a tree branch had smashed a side window of Inches Drug Store, at the southeast corner of Weston Road and John Street, but the limb was hanging from the gaping hole, indicating that no one had broken in. The Squibb's Stationary Store, Kresge's, Reward and Agnew Surpass shoe stores, as well as the Loblaws, all seemed undamaged. They dreaded finding someone in the act of committing a crime, as apprehending the criminal would be a daunting task. Exposure to the elements for even a few seconds meant being thoroughly soaked.

As they drove cautiously along Weston Road, the radio in their car crackled.

A voice declared, "I've pulled a man from the river at the bridge … on Scarlett Road … I need a …" His stressed voice disappeared amid a sea of static

For the next several minutes, crackling noises dominated the airwaves.

Then, another voice screamed through the background sounds. "I've lost contact with my partner. I think he's somewhere along the river bank."

"Never mind him. Pull anyone from the river that … try to get as far as … try again to reach that other car. There're two people inside."

Messages were sporadic and difficult to follow, but they clearly communicated the chaos surrounding the city.

An officer's voice cried out, "Where's the car with Inspector James?"

Then they heard another frantic voice on the radio. "I see a house ... it's floating past me ... my God, there's a woman clinging to it ... I need a rope ... but I don't ... oh, shit."

"We're sending a car ... hold ..."

A voice interrupted. "Where's that car? I can't ..."

Another voice screamed, "What the hell happened to the TTC truck?"

"Shit, this is the worst I've ..."

"I need help. A family ... I think there are three kids ... they're trapped ... the water is rising fast ..."

Static!

"My God, they've been swept away."

For several moments, the radio went dead. Peersen and Thomson heard only the eerie noise of the wind howling around the car.

Then the radio resumed, and the haunting sound of the man's voice shouted, "Good God ... everything is giving way ... the children are now in the hands of ... I ..."

The frustration and grief in the voice left Thomson and Peersen speechless. They felt the sheer helplessness of those who were fighting to rescue families from the floodwaters.

Meanwhile, the rivers of rain continued to deluge the city.

On the radio, there was static, crackling, alternated by eerie silence. Communications had been severed. It was more ominous than the voices pleading for help, as each listener was left to his own thoughts and fears.

Within a few minutes, voices resumed their pleas.

"This is the dispatcher. Car number twenty-two is nearing. Two men are trapped in a house north of Weston. Do not launch any boats. I repeat, do not launch any boats. In this river, any boats would capsize ... enough dead already ... three bodies fished out ... near bridge ... Lawrence Avenue. Anyone who can assist, proceed to Lawrence Avenue Bridge."

Peersen and Thomson knew that communicating with the precinct was impossible, so they drove south on Weston Road and west on Lawrence Avenue. When they arrived at the bridge crossing the Humber, they noticed that all the streetlights were dark. A cruiser was blocking cars from crossing the bridge, the cruiser's flashing lights puncturing the black of the night.

Within seconds, a police constable informed them that the entire western half of the structure had collapsed. They were unable to see across the bridge, but the banks on the east side of the river were visible—swollen—almost engulfing the roadway. They watched in horror as large boulders and trees smashed into the remaining supports that held up the eastern section of the bridge. The remainder of the structure was clearly in danger of succumbing to the crushing forces assaulting its foundations.

The wind and water lashed their coats, blowing dirt and muddy water into their faces. Peersen approached the officer in charge. He appeared exhausted. Peersen recognized him. It was Paul Masters, whom Peersen knew had joined the force six years before. *He's wet behind the ears,* Peersen thought, which on this occasion seemed a redundant phrase. Peersen had observed the officer on prior occasions and was aware that he was brash, impulsive, and inclined to overreact when confronted with a difficult situation. Peersen wondered how well he would perform under fire, but on this occasion, he seemed to be all right.

"What's the situation, constable? We heard your team pulled out three bodies."

Masters bristled at being questioned by Peersen but hid his resentment.

"The count is now five, sir. They drove off the end of the bridge in the darkness, not knowing there was no bridge there. My partner, Mike Saunders, knows the area well and says there's a street downstream, Raymore Drive. He fears that all the houses have been swept away. Since we arrived a half-hour ago, the water has risen over twenty feet. Saunders says that the residents would never have had a chance to evacuate. This storm was supposed to have weakened before it reached us. I'd hate to see it if it was at full strength."

Peersen grimaced at the police officer's remark.

"Damn," Masters added, "there's another bloody driver trying to cross the bridge."

A car had approached the bridge from the east, and the driver was rolling down the window. PC Masters walked over and shouted angrily at the man, "Turn your bloody car around and get the hell out of here."

The distressed man explained, "My wife is alone, in our home on Scarlett Road and …"

Masters slammed his billy stick on the side of the car and ordered the man to leave. Frustrated, the helpless man placed the car in reverse gear and backed up.

Peersen understood the officer's forceful approach, as it was likely the hundredth car he had redirected. However, he disapproved of his handling of the situation. It was when civilians were severely upset that a police officer needed to be calm and reassuring. PC Masters worried him. He was about to reprimand Masters, when he saw Thomson motion for him to return to the car.

"I managed to get through to dispatch," Gerry told him. "They want us to go to Bloor Street. They need us to help control the traffic. The bridge has been closed."

Masters gritted his teeth as he observed the car with Peersen and Thomson disappearing into the driving rain, the wind lashing waves of water across his resentful face. He too longed to be in a warm car, ordering others about. He thought, *My time will come. An opportunity will arise when I can show them what kind of man I am.*

It required almost an hour for Thomson to drive to the Bloor Street Bridge, since on the streets numerous cars had collided because of the poor visibility. When they arrived on Bloor Street, they were informed that the Humber River had swollen because of the massive runoff from further up river, and there was danger that the structure might be sufficiently weakened to collapse into the river. No vehicle traffic was allowed. The Lakeshore and Dundas Street bridges were also closed, and they were told that the Old Mill Bridge had already caved in. The city was now sealed off, preventing anyone entering or leaving the city from the west.

News from the dispatcher continued. On Dee Avenue in Weston, three houses had been ripped from their foundations by the flooded Black Creek and were swept away. In Mount Dennis, hundreds of people had been evacuated from their homes and taken to emergency shelters. Highways surrounding Brampton had crumbled like soft mud, whole sections swept into the ditches.

Major portions of the Scarlett Road Bridge had fallen into the river, eaten away by the angry water slamming against it. The swollen river had carried large boulders and entire tree trunks, pounding them into the bridge's support structures. Some suburban streets were ten feet under water. Near Long Branch, homes had been swept into Lake Ontario, and the sheer force of the wind had torn one mother's infant son from her arms, sweeping the child into a watery grave.

Throughout the city, firefighters were frantic as downed hydro wires short-circuited, igniting countless fires. Crews were busy cutting the electric wires in flooded houses to prevent more flare-ups.

Unknown to those who were fighting the flooding in the west end of the city, similar conditions were occurring in the eastern areas, as the Don River and its tributaries had also poured over their banks. Bridges there were also in danger, although the threats were not as severe, as the bulk of the rain had hit the western sections, particularly the Humber Valley.

It was a night of despair that would never be forgotten by those who experienced the worst storm to descend on Toronto in its long history.

✧ ✧ ✧

The following morning, Saturday, the skies remained cloudy. The winds had abated, and an eerie calm engulfed the rain-soaked city. In the Hudson home, the oatmeal was bubbling on the stove and the coffee was perking when Tom's mother turned on the radio. As she placed the cereal bowls on the table, the aftermath of the previous night's storm came across the airwaves.

The announcer said, "As many as thirty people might be dead, and the search for bodies continues. It is impossible to estimate the extent of the property losses, but authorities are estimating that it will be in the millions.

"Fifteen military groups and eight army reserves, totalling over eight hundred men, are being called in to assist the city. The streets of Toronto are littered with debris and hundreds of homes have been flooded. Some remain under water. The city requests that residents remain off the streets to allow crews to clean up the debris.

The flooded river as seen on the morning after Hurricane Hazel swept through Toronto.

"Throughout today and tomorrow, the bridges on the west side of Toronto will remain closed. The east end of the city has not been as severely hit, as the clash between the remnants of Hurricane Hazel and the cold air from the west, collided to the northwest of the city, over Brampton, where the two storm systems spilled their massive water contents. The Humber Valley acted like a funnel, channelling the water southward through the city.

"Toronto has never suffered such devastation from a storm. It was unprepared for the fury of the onslaught of Hurricane Hazel."

On Sunday afternoon, Shorty, Harry, and Tom bicycled through the littered streets and travelled to the Humber Valley to gaze at the river. They approached the valley from the steep hill on East Drive. The disastrous water levels attained during the dark morning hours had receded, but the river remained swollen and angry. When they arrived at Scarlett Road, they gazed in awe at the high-water mark on the stucco walls of the Queensbury Hotel, located near the Scarlett Road Bridge. The mud caked on the walls indicated that during the night the water had reached as high as the second-storey windows, a distance of nearly fifteen feet.

They were amazed by the sight of the mature trees along the riverbank that had been uprooted and toppled, their massive roots exposed to the morning's gloomy light. As they approached the bridge, a police officer held them back.

A woman who was standing near them, looking down into the swirling water, began crying as she pointed to the debris trapped against the support pillars of the bridge. She said it contained the walls of her home, which had floated down the river during the night. A police officer tried to comfort her.

The boys stood beside the stream, still raging beyond anything they had ever seen, and imagined what it must have been like during the early hours of Saturday morning. A helicopter hovered above them, its pilot searching for bodies floating down the river. Along the riverbank, soldiers were combing through broken tree limbs and piles of debris, gathering the refuse into piles and igniting them with flame-throwers.

As they were watching, the roof of a house floated past and was snagged by militiamen in a boat and towed to shore. When they turned it over, a man's body floated to the surface.

Then they saw a dead pig, its bloated pink carcass bobbing in the current as it passed the small boat. One of the soldiers employed a pole with a hook to drag it ashore, where it could be burned in the refuse pile. While it was being pulled through the current, the pig turned over in the water. It was a young woman. The soldier gagged. The man beside him finished the gruesome task of pulling the corpse toward the river's bank where it could be retrieved.

Shorty, who was rarely lost for words, said nothing. Harry suggested that it was time to go home. Tom nodded in agreement. He was never to forget the sights that he witnessed on that October day in 1954. Hurricane Hazel would always be a part of his teenage memories.

On Monday morning, before leaving for school, Tom sat having his breakfast. He poured the milk over the hot oatmeal and sprinkled brown sugar over it. While he ate, the radio provided an update on the effects of Hurricane Hazel.

"On the night of the storm, the winds reached 110 miles per hour, and within less than twelve hours, almost eight inches of rain fell on a city ill-prepared for the flooding. It is feared that the death toll might reach a hundred. Many people remain missing. The damage will reach into the millions of dollars.

"At Holland Marsh, near Brantford, during the night the farms were under twenty feet of water. Only their roofs remained visible. This morning, the boulevard between the lanes on Highway 400, where it approaches Highway 401, is a rushing river of water. Throughout the city, it is feared that over four thousand people are homeless, their homes either having been swept away or too badly damaged to be habitable. On Raymore Drive, south of Lawrence Avenue, fourteen houses were washed away. The water rose so rapidly, that many had no chance to escape."

✧ ✧ ✧

When Tom and his friends arrived at school, they noticed that the flag on the front lawn was flying at half-mast. Recalling the day that King George VI had passed away, they knew that a death had occurred. They wondered if someone had drowned in the floodwaters created by the hurricane, but as no students lived near the Humber Valley, they thought it unlikely. Who had died?

Within minutes of entering the building, they heard that Joe Castle, the young head caretaker of the school, had drowned when the Humber River engulfed his home on Raymore Drive. He had lived alone in a modest bungalow, located at the end of the street, beside the wooded land along the west bank of the river.

Mr. Evanson announced that at the end of the week, the school would hold a service of remembrance in the auditorium to mourn, as he said on the PA system, "the passing of a devoted and hard-working member of the staff of York Collegiate."

At the end of the day, Tom was waiting for Shorty near the doorway at the front of the school. Shorty was at his locker collecting the books he intended to carry home. While Tom sat on the steps, three of the teachers departed the school. The teachers were engrossed in conversation and did not notice him. Tom overheard their conversation.

Miss Manson, the girls' PT teacher, said to Mr. Millford, her colleague in the department, "We'll certainly miss Joe. They didn't call him 'big' Joe for nothing."

Mr. Milford grinned as he replied, "Joe was well equipped for his main pursuit in life. The secretaries in the office called him 'Joe the Meat Man.'"

The third teacher present, Mr. Rogers, who had been Tom's homeroom teacher in grade nine, smiled as he said, "Joe's 'prime rib' will be dearly missed."

Tom gazed at the three teachers as they proceeded down the walkway and out of earshot. He gave little thought to their strange comments. As Shorty always said, "All teachers are a little weird."

✧ ✧ ✧

The same day they held the service of remembrance at YCI for Joe Castle, the newspapers contained a small obituary commemorating his life. They mentioned that during his twenties, Joe Castle had been a quarterback on the Balmy Beach Football Club.

However, the final death toll of the storm overshadowed the obituary. Eighty-one people lost their lives, most of them in Toronto. On Raymore Drive alone, thirty-six had perished. In all, the damages totalled $135 million. Many people lost everything and were never reimbursed by their insurance companies, due to a technicality in their policies. They were covered for "damages from wind, rain, and hail," but not for "high water overflow."

Many families never recovered from the financial loss.

Raymore Drive, the Eglinton Flats, and the floodplains of the Humber Valley were to become part of the Metropolitan Toronto Conservation

Authority. Never again would they allow homes to be constructed on land that was in danger of being flooded. Millions of dollars, as well as clothing and food supplies, were donated by residents of Toronto to assist those who had suffered losses.

Hurricane Hazel was a storm that was never to be equalled.

✧ ✧ ✧

November delivered more stormy days, but nothing like those during Hurricane Hazel. For people who had lost homes during the storm, the approaching yuletide season appeared bleak. The premier of the film *White Christmas* at the Imperial Theatre cheered some residents of the city. The sentimental movie starred Bing Crosby, Danny Kaye, and Rosemary Clooney. As the smooth voice of Bing crooned Irving Berlin's famous song "White Christmas," many tears were shed and warm emotions of nostalgia experienced.

When 31 December arrived, many were pleased to see the old year pass and to welcome the new year of 1955, despite the approach of the severe month of January.

✧ ✧ ✧

It was a frosty Monday morning in February, and the wind had increased since the break of dawn, holding the promise of another blustery day. Billowing dark clouds, laden with snow, tumbled across a leaden sky, while heavy snowflakes commenced descending across the barren landscape.

Father Malloy, the priest at St. Mary's, sat in the warmth of his study beside the fireplace, waiting for his housekeeper, Mrs. Saint, to bring him his morning coffee. Removing his eyeglasses, he gazed up when she entered the cozy room, observing her as she placed his coffee on the small table beside him. She also glanced at him, and because of the many years she had tended to his needs, knew that similar to the weather beyond the frosty windowpanes, he was troubled.

A second-generation Irishman, Father Malloy was the oldest child of a family of eight children. His brother Patrick was a police sergeant at the precinct where Detectives Thomson and Peersen worked. Sean was aware that the police referred to his brother Patrick as "Muscles Malloy." Father Malloy was also an imposing figure, his parishioners affectionately calling him "Mighty Sean." They had bestowed the nickname on him because of his *mighty* prayers and sermons, rather than his prodigious size.

Malloy was a good priest. For over twenty years, had been the guiding strength at St. Mary's, located on Vaughan Road. Easygoing and relaxed in his approach to life, he had never harboured any desires to be a bishop, much less a cardinal. All his life, he had only wanted to serve the needs of his flock. He loved his God with all his heart, as well as the Holy Mother Church and the people to whom he administered. In the confessional, he had always attempted to be as forgiving as he believed his Lord had been when on earth. He guided them to try to refrain from sinning but did not pass personal judgment. He placed their transgressions in the hands of God and gave them absolution.

On the blustery Monday morning, his thoughts were on one of the teenage boys of his parish, Patrick McCaul. The previous Saturday morning, in the confessional, the lad had confessed to a grievous sin. The boy had refused to specify the sin he had committed, but he said that he knew his soul was in danger. Father Malloy had urged him to confess his wrongdoing, pray to God, and cease whatever he was doing. The lad had replied that he could not openly confess the sin without betraying someone, and this he was unable to do. Despite the priest's urgent pleas, the boy would say no more.

After Patrick McCaul departed the confessional, Father Malloy prayed for the boy's soul and pleaded that God would open the lad's eyes to the error of his ways, enabling him confess his sins. He wished he knew what sin the boy had committed, so he might better guide and counsel him.

Saturday afternoon, after choir practice, Father Malloy was standing outside the coatroom door. He overheard the lads talking mischievously about Patrick, who was absent. The boys were joking about "Pansy Patrick" and saying that he had been screwing with another boy in the Amherst laneway. Father Malloy had now discovered Patrick's transgression. It was far worse than he had imagined. He burst in on the choirboys and chastised them for engaging in such sinful talk. The boys immediately fell silent, and without gazing at him, they silently departed.

On Sunday morning, Father Malloy confronted Patrick in the narthex and told Patrick that he knew the source of his troubles. He attempted to be as gentle as possible but pointed out that it was a great sin against God, and the Holy Mother Church. If Patrick were unable to confess and sin no more, he must deny him the sacrament of communion.

When the time arrived for Malloy to offer communion, Patrick was sitting in a pew with his mother, in the centre section of the nave. He did not attempt to approach the altar. Malloy was certain that Patrick's mother was puzzled about her son's behaviour. Following the service, a dejected Patrick disappeared among the many congregants departing from the church.

Now, on this cold Monday morning, Father Malloy was uneasy about his course of action the day before, as he felt that, in some respects, he had abandoned the boy. However, the teachings of the church were clear. Homosexuality was a great sin, and he was unable to condone it. He felt that God was testing his own faith, and he must not fail his beloved church and its infallible teachings.

Father Malloy thanked his housekeeper for bringing him his coffee.

"My dear Mrs. Saint, you are a saint by habit and a saint by name."

The elderly woman smiled, blushed, and told him to hush. No matter how many times he complimented her, she became embarrassed. Deep down, she loved his oft-repeated remark. It pleased her to tend the needs of such a devoted man.

After she departed the room, Father Malloy poured the rich cream into the dark liquid and swirled the mixture with a silver spoon from a set that a parishioner had given him. As he sipped, he again pondered his problem concerning Patrick McCaul. He thought about the parable of the lost sheep in the Book of Luke, and how there was more rejoicing over finding the lamb that had been lost than over the many that had never strayed. He felt that Patrick was a wandering lamb, and he had failed to draw him back into the safety of the fold.

He decided he would visit the lad's home the following day, as the boy's parents were certain to be upset that their son had not taken communion.

◆ ◆ ◆

On the same Monday morning that Father Malloy was pondering his dilemma, Detective Peersen had arrived late at the precinct. As he pulled out the chair at his desk, he saw Peckerman in the hallway, motioning for him to go upstairs to his office. It was past the hour of ten. Jim knew that he should have arrived earlier, as he was behind in his paperwork. Usually he was punctual in writing statements and filling in forms, but his surveillance activities had caused him to fall behind. Keeping an eye on the teachers at YCI was no small task, but he was determined to break their code of silence. Only one of them was a murderer, but the others were preventing the perpetrator from being brought to justice.

When Peersen walked inside the sergeant of detective's office, he noticed that his boss' expression was sullen and heard him sigh in exasperation as he said to Peersen, "This job never gets easier." He paused and then added, "I have an unpleasant task for you, Jim."

Peersen now realized that the mood of his boss had nothing to do with his tardiness.

"They've found the body of a teenage boy, apparently a suicide. The officers at the scene are requesting that someone from homicide go to the crime scene to confirm that it is in fact a suicide. Go take a look."

Peersen knew that to survive in police work, it was necessary to be emotionally detached from the victims, even though it was not always possible. Peckerman was aware of this too, but the suicide of a young boy had shaken him. The death of a child or a teenager always cast a quietness over the men in the station. Officers with children harboured fears that the dead teenager might have been their own child. The unmarried and the younger members of the force felt vulnerable, as it reinforced the truth that if a young person could be cut down like a weed, no one was safe, especially a police officer whose work was dangerous.

Peersen asked for details and Peckerman told him that they had discovered a body in a garage on the Amherst laneway. Peersen thought, *It's only a block from the home of Dinkman. Coincidence?*

Peersen drove to the scene. As they thought it was a suicide, it was not necessary for Thomson to accompany him. When he arrived, a police cruiser was parked in the laneway, which paralleled the Amherst Avenue, west of Oakwood Avenue. It was now near eleven o'clock, and the people who owned garages facing the laneway had long since departed for work. The man who owned the garage in question was retired, and when he opened his garage doors around nine-thirty to put away a snow shovel, he had discovered the body.

When Peersen entered the garage, he stared at the corpse. He thought he recognized the victim but was uncertain, as the face had distorted and drained of all colour. The slender teenager was hanging from a rope suspended over one of the thick beams that supported the roof of the garage, the boy's boots dangling several feet above the cement floor. Gravity had pulled the corded rope, which had squeezed the life from him, taunt around his neck, immediately below the chin. His ears and lips had turned blue, and his bulging eyes were red, due to the capillaries that had burst when the rope had tightened.

The body hung motionless, as there was no wind inside the garage, its stillness reinforcing that life had departed. His arms hung lifelessly, the white hands extending from the cuffs of the boy's blue winter jacket. The lad's red wool hat remained on his head, perhaps a sign that he had not struggled as the rope had strangled him. A tuft of the boy's blond hair protruded from beneath the rim of the cap, partially covering his forehead.

The coroner had already determined from the colour of the skin and the pooling of blood that the boy had been dead for approximately an hour.

Peersen turned away from the lifeless corpse and approached the coroner. He paused before he spoke to him, the sight of the boy having shaken him badly.

Struggling for words, Peersen addressed the coroner. "Nasty business.

It never gets easy, does it? Did the boy string himself up, or did he have help?"

"Don't know. When we get him to the morgue, we'll know for sure. But it appears suspicious. His hat is still on his head, which suggests that the body may have been posed."

"Any sign of a suicide note?"

"None."

"If he did commit suicide, the box he stood on is rather far from where it should have landed if he kicked it away. Any footprints in the snow outside to indicate that another person was present?"

"Impossible to tell, as there's been no fresh snow since yesterday, and the laneway is full of footprints and tire treads."

The assistant coroner examined the boy's hands, did a few other tests, and then reached into the victim's pocket to retrieve the lad's wallet. He handed it to Peersen.

He opened it and found a YCI student card with the victim's name printed in neat, careful letters: Patrick McCaul.

✧ ✧ ✧

When Tom and his friends learned of Patrick's death, they were devastated. The McCaul family was also in shock, compounded by knowing that there would be no funeral mass in the church, as Patrick had committed suicide. The newspapers reported that, although the police never found a suicide note, the coroner's office had ruled the cause of death as strangulation, resulting from suicide. There would be an inquest, but no further investigation unless the inquest ruled otherwise.

Two days later, they released Patrick's body. Sophie told Tom that Smith Brother's Funeral Parlour on Eglinton Avenue was where the family would hold the visitations. There would be a private ceremony in the chapel of the funeral home. Tom had not been inside its doors since his family had attended the funeral of Grumpy, the old man who had owned the house where Shorty now lived.

At school, Tom noticed that the teachers were shocked, although most of them had not known Patrick well. Miss Allyson was a noted exception and broke into tears when she heard the news. Patrick had not played on any sport's teams or distinguished himself academically. The classmates in Tom's homeroom were stunned, especially when they learned the details.

However, Tom overheard a few cruel remarks. One student said that "homos" always ended up at the end of a rope. Another said the "fairies" always flew off into hell. Besides, they reasoned, didn't everyone hate homos?

Tom and his friends privately experienced a collective guilt, convinced that they should have done more to have helped Patrick and be with him. They felt that they should have sensed his intentions and prevented it. If they had been with him that morning as he walked to school, perhaps he would still be alive. They were too young to realize that regrets, similar to wishes, are futile.

Death was not a concept that was easily understood at their ages. They still considered it something that happened to old people, not someone their age. Even the murder of Miss Stritch had not affected them personally, as she had been older, and they had never met her.

They were unable to accept that Patrick was gone from their lives forever. Never again would they attend the CNE with him or sit beside him at a movie at the Grant Theatre. The finality of death, they were unable to comprehend.

It was Harry who helped them in their grief. Somehow, his presence beside them supported them, and his inner strength sustained them. Tom realized that though Harry had never said much, even his silence possessed strength. However, when he did speak, his words contained the power of simple honesty. As well, when other students uttered cruel remarks, Harry made it clear that he was proud to have been Patrick's friend and was not afraid to voice his opinion. No one was stupid enough to engage Harry in a fistfight over the matter.

Tom always remembered the way Harry behaved during the days after Patrick died. He also recalled that when he had been a boy, in reference to Harry, people had said, "The man within the boy is visible." When Patrick died, Harry was a teenager of seventeen, but he possessed more inner strength than most adults acquire in a lifetime. Harry Heinz was a man among boys.

✧ ✧ ✧

In the late morning, two days before the funeral, Sophie called at Tom's house. She asked him if he would accompany her to confession at St. Mary's, because she did not wish to go alone. The church was located on Vaughan Road, west of Oakwood Avenue. She and Patrick had attended it ever since they had been toddlers. Patrick had sung in the choir.

A cold February wind cut the street as they walked north on Lauder Avenue toward the church. They trudged along in silence until they reached the top of the hill. In front of the church, Sophie turned and looked at Tom. Pain was etched into her face, and her eyes were red from crying. Tom's heart went out to her.

"Tom," she said, "have you heard the terrible things they're saying at school about Patrick?"

He nodded.

"Even in his casket, they won't leave him alone. They're saying he deserved what he got. They're calling him a pansy, a fruit, a fairy, a Thursday boy." It was a standard expression in Toronto that Thursday was "boys' night out," as on Friday night every guy went out with a girl. Those who preferred the company of other males were referred to as "Thursday boys."

Sophie continued. "Patrick was not queer."

Tom said nothing, as he placed his arm around her shoulder to comfort her. He felt guilty, because in the past, he too had questioned Patrick's manliness.

"I know for sure, Tom," she insisted.

Tom remained silent, and she offered no resistance as he held her close. Then out the blue, she confessed to something that was to change Tom's life.

"Tom, I have Patrick's baby inside me."

Tom was stunned.

She continued, her words interrupted by sobs. "He was so freaked out after what happened last March. While I was holding him in my arms trying to comfort him, before we knew it, we were making love. I didn't mean for it to happen. I knew it was a sin, but he needed comforting so badly, and besides, I loved him, and he loved me. I don't know what will happen when my parents discover that I'm pregnant, but I can't regret making love to him. It was so beautiful. I'm torn up inside, knowing that Patrick is gone forever. I don't know what I am going to do."

Tom retreated to a question that avoided his commenting on the fact that she was pregnant.

"Can you tell me what happened to him last March?"

"I swore never to tell, but now that he's gone, I guess my vow is meaningless. He was returning alone from a movie, and after getting off the Vaughan bus, he decided to walk home down the Amherst laneway. Three older boys from the high school grabbed him, pulled his wool cap down over his eyes, and threatened to kill him if he didn't let them do what they wanted. They pulled down his trousers and underwear, and two guys held him down, while the biggest kid entered him."

Recovering from his shock, Tom asked, "Did he know who it was that …?"

Sophie shook her head. "Because of the wool cap over his head, he wasn't able to see their faces."

Continuing, Sophie said, "He bled through his rectum for over a week. His mother discovered the stains on the bedsheets and confronted him. He refused to tell her why he was bleeding. His mom told his father, and he threatened to beat Patrick if he didn't say what had happened. Patrick refused, and his dad took his belt to him. He accepted the punishment, too humiliated to tell his parents what had happened in the laneway.

"However, his dad suspected that he had willingly done something unnatural. He had always felt that Patrick was not very manly. When Father Malloy refused Patrick the sacrament of communion, he felt that the church had abandoned him. His faith was really important to him. He had always believed that the church was his sanctuary.

"When he returned home after church, his parents demanded to know why he had not taken communion. He kept silent. His dad assumed the unnatural acts and not taking communion were related, and again, he beat him.

"Now, everyone at school and in the neighbourhood is spreading lies that Patrick was queer. He was gentle, kind, and more of a man than most. We loved each other and swore to marry one day."

"Did Patrick know that he was to be a father?"

"I never had a chance to tell him. I knew for sure only last week and was waiting for the right moment. Now, he's dead and will never know."

Tom kept his arm around Sophie and pulled her closer.

"Tom, like Patrick, I believe in the church's teachings. I also know that Patrick was beaten by his dad, tormented by the jerks at school, and at the worst moment in his life, the church denied him the sacrament of communion. He felt his life was beyond hope. My life is becoming the same. I need help. I must confess my sins to the priest and ask for forgiveness. Will you wait here for me until I come out of the church, and then walk me home?"

Tom nodded. She turned and entered the door.

✧ ✧ ✧

A tearful Sophie Cellini crept into the church. The pews were empty, the flickering candles located near the altar, the only motion evident in the tranquil interior. Entering the confessional, when Father Malloy pushed aside the wooden cover over the small aperture in the wall between the confessionals, it echoed in the silence of the confined space.

Sophie wanted to pour out her heart to the kindly priest, whom she had known since she was a child, when her family had emigrated from Italy. Her mother had taught her to faithfully confess her transgressions and plead for forgiveness. During the previous few months, she had been withholding information from the priest, and this had increased her guilt. It was time for her to confess.

"Father forgive me, I have sinned …"

She confessed to failing Patrick in his hour of need and told the priest about her pregnancy.

Father Malloy's heart sank as he realized that he had misunderstood Patrick's sins. He had completely misjudged the boy and accepted the cruel teasing of the choirboys as evidence of Patrick's guilt. He also noticed that Sophie did not ask for forgiveness for having disobeyed the church's teachings on chastity. However, he knew that the guilt of failing Patrick was eating her up inside. After she had finished unburdening her thoughts, she said, "Father, I seek forgiveness for my sin." She did not specify which sin she meant.

An awkward silence gripped the confessional. The priest was aware that she had said sin and not sins. He was hesitant to answer. Finally, he said, "God has forgiven you your sin of failing Patrick. Is there another sin, my child?"

"No, Father." She was unable to confess to the sin of loving Patrick. In her heart, she did not understand how it could be sinful, despite the church's teachings.

Father Malloy's failure to say anything about the sin of premarital sex caused guilt to flood over him. He thought, *Will God forgive me my sin of ignoring the girl's sin and also failing Patrick? The girl is with child. What should I do? She has committed a grave sin against the teachings of the church. I was dogmatic with Patrick, and the boy took his life.*

After a pause, Father Malloy continued. "My child, have you told your parents that you have Patrick's child within you?"

"No, Father. I fear my mother's anger. What am I to do?"

It was at that moment Father Malloy knew he was unable to deny her communion. If he did, her parents would know that she had done something sinful. He would be jeopardizing her future within the family. He would not make the same mistake that he had committed with Patrick. The matter had to be handled with great care.

"Go, my child. I will pray for you. Let me consider the matter, and I will help you when you tell your parents."

"Can I take communion on Sunday?"

"Yes, my child."

At Sophie departed, she was consoled, but still feared for the future.

✧ ✧ ✧

Outside the church, Tom was huddled in the doorway, his back to the wind. He felt it pressing against the collar of his coat and lifting his cap. He took Sophie's hand as they walked southward toward home, the wind blowing at their backs. Tom wondered if it were an omen, as he knew people said that the wind at your back was a sign of good luck. He also knew that Sophie would need all the luck the world had to offer if she were to survive the troubling days ahead.

By the time they arrived near home, Tom noticed that Sophie seemed somewhat comforted. After visiting the priest, Tom assumed that she felt the future was now in God's hands—as well as the hands of Father Malloy. He hoped that in some small way, his hand in hers had also reassured her.

✧ ✧ ✧

The elderly priest remained in the confessional long after Sophie departed, too dumbstruck to move. On this dreary February morning, he sat in silence, alone with his thoughts. In the solitude of the confessional, the sound of his breathing dominated the confined space. Confused thoughts troubled his mind

He thought, *I failed Patrick, my choirboy who served so faithfully at St. Mary's. I jumped to conclusions about his sins and denied him communion.*

Sophie also committed a grievous sin, and yet I failed to withhold communion from her. Which of my decisions was right? If I had I known the true nature of Patrick's sins, would I have acted differently? Was I less inclined to be understanding because I thought he had committed unnatural acts with another boy? I have always obeyed the teaching of the Holy Mother Church. However, I was unable to apply the teachings with wisdom. I have played a part in causing an innocent boy to take his life. Oh, God, in your great wisdom and mercy, reveal to me the path to follow.

Stumbling out of the confessional, he staggered across the north transept toward the altar, like a penitent approaching the throne of God on judgment day. Even though blinded by tears, he easily found his way, knowing the location of every stone on the floor and the position of each pew. Throughout the years, the church had been his sanctuary, as he had served at St. Mary's for twenty of the twenty-five years of his priesthood. Reaching the steps in front of the altar, he spread prostrate against the cold stones. At this most pivotal moment in his life, Father Malloy placed his all on God's altar.

Several minutes passed as he silently prayed. Then he pleadingly gazed upward at the life-size statue of the crucified Christ above the altar and poured aloud his lament and sorrow to his Lord.

"Oh, God," he cried, "how can I follow in your footsteps if I cannot even find the path? Should I have granted Patrick communion, even though I thought his sin was against the teachings of the church?"

Then, it was as if the air around him had coalesced into a voice. Later, he was not certain if the voice had been real, or if it was a sensation from within him that had taken on an existence of its own. It seemed to float on the tranquil air inside the church.

The voice spoke gently. "Why does the church consider the love that you thought Patrick had expressed to be a sin? When I was on earth, I said nothing about it being sinful."

"But your Holy Book states it is an abomination in Thy sight," the priest replied to the ethereal voice that now seemed to emanate from the life-size statue of Christ that gazed down at him.

The voice continued. "Those are the words of man, not God's words."

"But in the Bible, Paul of Tarsus was quoting the law, as written in Leviticus."

"Those were laws written by men. I came to earth to make known God's love."

As the voice continued, it seemed to drift from the statue and soar high above the altar, as though the enormous stones of the great domed ceiling had been infused with life and able to speak.

"No one is beyond the comfort and love of God. The sacraments allow the church to share God's love."

"But the church teaches that love between men is an abomination in

God's sight and a mortal sin. It is clearly stated in the scriptures. I have no right to ignore the church and the scriptures and decide what a sin is and what is not."

"Nothing written by man, even if the writer claims to be divinely inspired, is infallible as man habitually intrudes on the divine. Remember, in the past, the church not only condoned slavery but also sanctified it by employing the scriptures. As well, the church severed the left hands of sinners, stoned adulterous women to death, and burnt heretics in the flames, quoting the scriptures for these cruelties. Throughout the centuries, man has fought countless wars and slaughtered innocent people. These actions were sinful, yet they employed the scriptures to justify them all."

After a pause, the voice continued. "Your Heavenly Father gave you the gift of thought, and no man has the right to deprive you of that blessing. Faith accepted without careful thought is not meaningful faith. It is merely a repetition of someone else's faith. It implies that the faith was not of sufficient importance to deserve personal examination."

"I am carefully examining my faith at this very moment, but I am in a quandary," Father Malloy replied. "The church tells me that I must refuse the sacraments to those who disobey its important teachings. I am no longer certain what to think."

"If you refuse the sacraments to a child of mine, you place the child beyond my love. If you are ever in doubt concerning your actions, ask yourself if you followed the path of love. Your thoughts and actions toward others must reflect love. That is God's path."

Stubbornly Father Malloy reiterated, "I have no right to judge what is a sin and what is not. If everyone decided such matters for themselves, chaos would occur."

"That is why man has his own laws: to prevent chaos."

"But man's laws also state that unnatural love is a crime."

"I said that man has his own laws to prevent chaos, but I did not say that man's laws were always right in the eyes of God."

"Then how am I to decide to whom I deny the sacraments?"

"No priest, bishop, or layman has the right to deny the sacraments. The church merely administers the sacraments. It is God who bestows or rejects the love they contain. No institution created by man, even if it claims to be founded by your heavenly Father, must usurp the divine right. You must comfort and love all my flock, not just those with whom you agree."

"But cannot I love the sinner but condemn the sin?"

"This logic may apply in some circumstances, such as murderers, but not in this case. For centuries, many owners claimed that they loved their slaves but kept them in chains. Their only sin was being born black. Was this loving the sinner yet condemning the sin? To justify their cruel actions, for centuries they quoted the verses in the Bible pertaining to the obedience servants owe to their masters. They claimed that slavery was divinely ordained. This falsehood was perpetuated through quoting the Bible. Your heavenly father created all men and women equal.

"This is also true for all love that inflicts no hurt and does no harm. All love that is caring and respectful is created by God and equal in His eyes. No one has the right to judge such love as sinful. Judge not least you be judged and found wanting. When you stand before the throne of God, how will you justify rejecting what God has created? Murder, hate, cruelty, and violence are not His creations. These you may reject, as they are not founded in love."

Father Malloy remained confused. "But this means that at times my conscience will tell me one thing, and the Holy Mother Church another. What am I to do? How must I decide?"

"Set aside your ego. Question your faith, as well as the dictates of those in authority. Sometimes, they create edicts to maintain power, rather than serve God. Think, examine, allow love to enter your heart. Treat those you encounter on life's path as you wish your heavenly Father to treat you. Compassion and love are the natural outcomes of true faith, not dictatorial decrees."

"Guide me!"

The ethereal voice was silent.

Father Malloy gazed upward, pleading for the voice from on high to continue.

There was only silence. In supplication, the priest waited. He desperately needed to hear the voice of his Master, but there was only silence—ominous and deep.

Then, continuing to gaze upward at the ceiling of the nave, the humble priest stared at the shafts of light filtering through the Romanesque windows, splashing across the silent stones of the massive archways, high above the altar. In Father Malloy's rheumy eyes, he thought he saw wisps of vaporous air departing the church through the huge windows, as if the souls of those who had suffered were escaping into the abyss of endless perdition.

Father Malloy was determined that Patrick's soul would not be among them.

✧ ✧ ✧

Father Malloy had experienced an epiphany, and despite his moral confusion, he knew what God's love demanded of him. Shortly after 2:00 p.m., he was sitting in the bishop's office. He had known Bishop St. Clair for many years, and although he knew his superior was a man who usually adhered strictly to church policy, he was a cleric of great compassion.

Father Malloy unburdened his soul and explained the circumstances of Patrick's death to the bishop, sadly telling of the part that he had played in the tragedy. When he had finished, the bishop gazed at the elderly priest with profound sympathy.

"Your Excellency," Father Malloy continued pleadingly, "I feel compelled to offer Patrick's family the comfort and blessing of a funeral mass."

Bishop St. Clair breathed in sharply, and it was several minutes before he spoke. Choosing his words carefully, he replied. "Young Patrick took his own life, therein committing a sin against the Holy Ghost. He rejected the forgiveness of God."

"I am aware of this, and know the church's teaching. However, I believe the circumstances are exceedingly unusual. As God's servant, I failed the boy. My conscience will not allow me to fail him again. I must allow his soul to rest within the love of the church."

The discussion continued for another half hour, with many arguments presented, dismissed, and in some instances, agreed on. Finally, the bishop raised his hand to signify that the discussion was over.

After several minutes silence, Bishop St. Clair gazed at the elderly priest and declared in a soft voice, "Father Malloy, I understand your predicament. I cannot grant permission for a funeral mass for the boy. However, I will not oppose it. I know you feel compelled to act according to your conscience and faith. I will pray for you, and the soul of the young boy whom you obviously loved so much. God go with you."

Bishop St. Clair watched Father Malloy depart, and his heart wept for the elderly priest's soul.

✧ ✧ ✧

In the evening, Tom and his friends visited the undertakers together. After arriving at the funeral home, Tom stood close to Sophie, supporting her by simply being there, even if he spoke very few words. Harry had taught him this, though at the time he was unaware.

Patrick's mom was inconsolable, weeping quietly while seated in a high-backed chair, one of her sisters sitting on either side of her. On the opposite side of the room were Patrick's three sisters, none of whom Tom knew very well. Patrick's mom looked as if old age had suddenly gripped her. Her eyes were devoid of life, like those of a store window mannequin. One of her sisters placed her arm around her shoulders and was quietly consoling her.

Tom heard Mrs. McCaul say, "There's something wrong in life when the old must bury the young. Patrick was my first-born and only son." Her weeping now increased.

Another of Mrs. McCaul's sisters reached out and placed her hand over Mrs. McCaul's, which gripped a wet handkerchief among her tightly clasped fingers.

Mr. McCaul, dressed in a navy-blue suit and matching tie, stood beside the closed coffin and stoically shook hands with those who approached him. Tom was certain that the loss of Patrick weighed heavily on him. Mr. McCaul had been harsh with Patrick and demanded strict obedience. Remembering what Sophie had told him, Tom wondered if Mr. McCaul now knew the tragic story behind the blood on Patrick's bedsheets. Likely not!

Patrick had told Tom that during the last few years, life had been difficult for Mr. McCaul, and he realized the great stress the loss of his job had placed on him. Tom also knew that Patrick had suffered the brunt of his father's resentment. He noticed that throughout the evening, Mr. McCaul rarely glanced over at Mrs. McCaul. He greeted people as they approached the coffin, and although Tom thought their words of sympathy likely comforted him, he doubted they eased the pain that he was experiencing.

Shortly before it was time to depart from the funeral home, Father Malloy asked to talk privately with Patrick's parents. He placed his arms around Mrs. McCaul, embracing her firmly within his strong arms. He then explained that he wished to hold a funeral mass for Patrick.

Mr. McCaul asked in astonishment, "Father, how is this possible?"

Father Malloy smiled and held a finger in front of his mouth while creating a hushing sound. "The peace of God's love is to be extended to your son through the Holy Mother Church."

For the first time since she had learned of her son's death, the iron fist of sorrow eased its grip around the heart of Mrs. McCaul.

✧ ✧ ✧

The day of the funeral, the weather was bleak, the wind howling around the church, blowing gusts of snow inside the narthex each time someone opened the heavy oak doors. Quietly, the mourners filed into St. Mary's. People shook the dustings of white from their hats and brushed them from the shoulders of their winter coats. The stone floor of the entrance to the nave was wet and slippery by the time the pews were filled.

As the hour of eleven approached, people were standing at the back of the church, many unable to locate a seat. Everyone was aware that Patrick had committed suicide, a sin in the eyes of the church, and some had heard the rumours that he had engaged in unnatural acts. Some of those attending were undoubtedly curiosity seekers, who wondered how it was possible that Father Malloy would celebrate a mass for a suicide victim. However, most were genuine mourners and wished to support the McCaul family.

Then, as the funeral mass commenced, St. Mary's choir sang as the procession with the simple coffin slowly proceeded up the centre aisle. The hollow choral sounds of the boys' voices ascended to the vaulted ceiling, softly filling the nave, transepts, and sanctuary. The coffin came to rest near the altar, the foot of the coffin facing it. On the top of the pall, the cloth covering the coffin, Patrick's mother had placed a small white Bible.

When the final echo of the music for the processional died away, the congregation sang, "Joyful, Joyful, We Adore Thee," after which Father Malloy's rich voice floated over the church as he offered the opening prayer.

Then, gazing over the assembled crowd, Father Malloy commenced the Liturgy of the Word, his rich bass voice betraying a hint of his Irish ancestry. He read the scriptures and gave a brief homily, followed by the general intercession. Next, was the Liturgy of the Eucharist.

The preparation of the altar ensued, followed by the Eucharist Prayer and the communion rite. During the Final Commendation, Father Malloy gave an invitation to prayer, and the people sang the song of farewell as incense rose in the air, spreading outward from the thurible. The Prayer of Commendation ended the funeral mass.

Then Father Malloy decided to say a few additional words. Everyone was silent in anticipation, wondering what he would say. A few nervous coughs from the rear of the church broke the quietness within the sanctuary.

The priest, his face stricken with grief, gazed over his flock and hesitantly commenced his lament for the loss of Patrick's life.

"If ever there was a lad who was one of God's angels on earth, it was Patrick McCaul. The first time I realized that he was special was when he was a mere lad of eight, and I heard his clear soprano voice soaring above the others in the choir as he sang the beautiful words of 'Ave Verum.' I believe that God speaks to our hearts more through music than in any other manner. Indeed, God spoke eloquently through the voice of Patrick McCaul.

"Patrick's gentleness endeared him to my heart. It's strange that our world sometimes equates gentleness in a man with a lack of masculinity. Patrick, only sixteen when he went to be with God, was more of a man than some men will ever be in a lifetime.

"I have heard the rumours that are circulating in the parish. Some say that he committed sins against our Holy Mother Church. Christ said that that those among us who are without sin should throw the first stone. No person here today has the right to pass judgment on Patrick McCaul; not I and not the church. Patrick gave only love to those who reached out to him. I charge you, as you leave here today, to do likewise."

✧ ✧ ✧

When Father Malloy had delivered his final words, the congregation was hushed. Tom stared at the white Bible on the pall, unable to gaze at the coffin itself, knowing that it contained his friend, who had been taken so tragically from him. Then, as they slowly repositioned the coffin and moved it down the aisle toward the door, Harry, Shorty, and Tom, along with three of Patrick's cousins, followed behind as pallbearers. Descending the aisle, Tom gazed across the row where Sophie sat, but she had bowed her head, and he was unable to make eye contact.

Then, in the back row, Tom saw a pair of deep blue eyes. Their riveted gaze, staring at the coffin, seemed to pierce the dim light of the church. It was Detective Peersen, who had met Patrick on only a few occasions and yet had decided to pay respects to his memory.

Tom was unaware that Detective Peersen had been one of the policemen who had helped take down Patrick's lifeless body from its ignominious position in the garage on the Amherst laneway. He also did not know how profoundly the experience had affected him.

In the cemetery, the six of them lifted the coffin containing Patrick's lifeless body from the hearse to the graveside for the rite of committal. The raw winter winds stung their faces, the downy snowflakes melting as they mingled with the warm tears on their cheeks.

Tom listened as Father Malloy delivered the scripture verses and prayed, and then offered the committal and the intercession. His voice was choked with emotion. Mrs. McCaul cried quietly as they recited the Lord's Prayer. Mr. McCaul placed his arms around her and continued holding her closely as the concluding prayer was offered. Father Malloy ended the rites of committal with the prayer over the people.

When the staff from Smith's Funeral Home lowered the casket into the gaping grave, Tom was overwhelmed with the thought of Patrick being placed into the frozen ground. Blowing drifts swirled around the bleak opening in the earth and swept across the coffin, the howl of the wind a lament to nature's indifference. Tom's tears now became sobs, as his friend, with whom he had shared much laughter and mischief, was gone forever. He glanced over at Sophie, who was crying, and attempted to give her a small smile of encouragement but failed, since he was unable to stem his own tears. At that moment in his young life, Tom began the long journey to try to understand and accept the finality of death. It was a quest he was never to complete.

✧ ✧ ✧

Father Malloy's love for his church never faltered, but Patrick's death had taught him that it was his duty to question its teachings and filter all its edicts through the love of Christ. No longer would he accept arbitrary doctrines that destroyed lives.

He continued to preach to his congregation at St. Mary's, telling them that God had given them an intellect and conscience to guide them. He said that if their faith was truly of importance to them, they must examine it, scrutinize it, and compare their decisions with the teachings of Christ's love. The secular laws of man they had to obey, but the matters of conscience they had to consider carefully, as the ultimate decision was theirs. The church was a guide, he declared, not an absolute ruler.

Father Malloy's teachings eventually came to the attention of the bishop, and finally a cardinal in Rome. Church officials, who had not known Father Malloy personally, took a dim view of his teachings and were even more dismayed when they learned he had held a funeral mass for a suicide victim. They ordered Bishop St. Clair to remove him from pastoral care. Sadly, he placed him in an administrative position in a small parish in northern Ontario, where no congregation would hear his interpretation of God's love.

Years later, Father Malloy visited Toronto and had tea with Bishop St. Clair, who by now was His Eminence, Cardinal St. Clair. During the conversation, the cardinal mentioned the funeral mass Father Malloy had conducted for Patrick.

"Well, Father, after Vatican II, the church eased the restrictions on funeral rites for suicide victims, encouraging a more pastoral approach. Your beliefs were vindicated."

"Yes, Your Eminence. God does indeed answer prayer."

"Did you ever reconcile your struggle over the revelation you received that night in the church?"

"Yes, I believe I have."

"Would you share your insight with me?"

Hesitantly, Father Malloy began. "During the last ten years, although I had no duties in pastoral care, I attended mass faithfully. I became close friends with two men in the congregation who had been in a committed relationship, monogamous I might add, for over forty years. Visiting their home, I saw a love between them that was as gentle and pure as any I have ever witnessed. The deep feelings they shared blessed my heart.

"I also became friends with a couple that had been married by the church. Their marriage eventually contained such hate that it poisoned their lives and destroyed the happiness of their children. Yet because of the church's teaching, they remained together. I asked myself, which relationship had God blessed? I realized that I had no right to judge. If a love is pure and embraces the love of Christ, God blesses it. So, yes, I suppose I have reconciled my beliefs."

The cardinal was silent for a few moments, and finally replied, "St. Peter created the Holy Mother Church and Christ himself has blessed it. The church will adapt. It has altered its position on torturing heretics, slavery, and granting funeral masses for suicide victims. We must trust our beloved church."

"Yes, Your Eminence, but why are woman forbidden from serving God as priests, instead of in a subordinate capacity as a nun? When will the church cease its ban on contraception to alleviate the suffering of the poor? Only the rich can afford not to practise contraception. When will the church accept same-sex marriage and extend God's love equally to all?"

"We must leave that in His hands."

"Yes, Your Eminence. However, God has left it in our hands too. The church must always show compassion and love, and we, as servants of the church, must help the church to exhibit this love. It is God's way."

The potency of the words struck Bishop St. Clair forcefully, and deep within, he knew the priest was right. As Father Malloy departed, similar to many years before, Cardinal St. Clair watched the faithful priest depart. On the previous occasion, he had wept for the elderly man's soul. Now, he wept for his own.

✧ ✧ ✧

During the years ahead, Father Malloy remained comforted by the memory of the revelation he had experienced that night in the sanctuary of St. Mary's. However, he was saddened that the church continued to view as a sin the love that the ethereal voice had revealed was blessed by God.

When Father Malloy died within the embracing love of his church, he was happy that he never again had caused the destruction of life through blindly following the edicts of an unbending faith.

✧ ✧ ✧

Peersen was now dating Samantha regularly. He knew that she was the most special woman he had ever encountered, but he was aware that their relationship was not growing. As well, he realized it was his fault.

Was it his insecurities concerning her background? If so, it was not the entire problem. He remained uneasy when expressing his inner feelings with her. As well, he found it increasingly difficult to set aside his job and separate himself from the terrible crimes he investigated. Remembering the evening they had spent at the Savarin Tavern, he was no longer certain he had had been wise in discussing the Stritch investigation with her.

At a movie or when he was out for dinner with Samantha, he knew that he was often lost in thought, mulling over the details of a current case. She sensed his withdrawal and was tolerant, but not to the point, Peersen thought, that she wanted to share her life with someone who appeared incapable of communicating his inner thoughts with her.

Peersen realized that he had to clarify his feelings or risk losing her. Because they had made no commitments, he knew that she had the right to date other men and that he was powerless to object. He was seeing no woman other than Samantha, and though they had not yet made love, the petting and kissing were becoming increasingly difficult to control. In addition, he had not taken her to a social gathering of the police force. He was unsure how he would react when members of the morality squad began teasing him about dating "Spankie Anderson." Now Valentine's Day was approaching, and he felt that he needed to make a decision soon.

✧ ✧ ✧

Samantha had also been thinking about their relationship. Because Jim had made no commitment, she had not totally severed her ties with Frank Gnomes. Frank asked her out to dinner the second week of February, and as Jim Peersen was working around the clock on an investigation, she accepted his invitation. She still considered Frank a rogue, but a delightful one.

When he appeared at her apartment door, a dozen red roses in hand, his new black loafers shone in the reflected glow of the hallway lights. In his navy suit, he looked more appealing than when she had first met him. He was trim from his many hours in the gym at the club. His waist was narrower, and his stomach appeared flat and hard.

Frank's eyes sparkled as he handed her flowers. Possessing the assurance of a man who was on the way up the ladder of success, he had a cockiness about him, knowing that his job gave him access to the city's elite and those who were politically well connected. Samantha was aware that most women would consider him quite a catch.

They enjoyed a quiet dinner at a steak house on Church Street, where the chef cooked the meat exactly as requested. The heavy-bodied red Burgundy complemented the meal without overpowering the rich, meaty flavour of the steaks. After coffee and a cognac, Samantha was in a mellow mood as Frank drove up the driveway to her apartment. It would have been too cruel for her not to invite him inside for a nightcap. Inside her apartment, after only a few sips of their brandies, Samantha went into the bedroom to answer the phone. Frank followed in behind her and quietly closed the door.

✧ ✧ ✧

As the final days of February flew past, the winter weather continued unabated. The file on the Stritch investigation was now at the back of the drawer of Peersen's departmental filing cabinet. Occasionally, something happened that brought it back to mind. In the newspapers, he read that the YCI basketball team was in first place in their league, and that Forester Bernstein and Harry Heinz were the top scorers, followed by Horace Kramer. Peersen still wondered if the Kramer boy knew more than he had told them.

In March, Peersen read in the *Trib* that the YCI drama club had won the annual competitive drama festival, sponsored by the Eaton's department store. The plays had been performed in the auditorium in their College Street Store. The director of the play, Mr. James Rogers, had dedicated his students' win to the memory of Patrick McCaul. Though he had never been a member of the drama club, Mr. Rogers said that it was a fitting tribute to a fine boy who had once been a member of their student body.

Peersen threw the paper in the garbage. He had learned how the students at YCI had treated the McCaul boy and thought, *If the students and teachers had shown more consideration for him when he was alive, the boy might not have ended his days strung up from a wooden beam in a garage.*

✧ ✧ ✧

In mid-March, Peersen concluded that he had to make a decision about his relationship with Samantha. He knew he loved her, but was it sufficient to create a successful marriage? He knew he must find out. Because of the demands of a recent investigation, he had seen little of her for the past week, although he had talked to her daily on the phone. Sensing that she had been dating other men, he knew it was time for him to either declare his feelings or accept that their relationship would dwindle to a close.

Slowly, he had come to terms with Samantha's business activities and realized that he was ready to accept whatever teasing the guys at the precinct directed at him when they discovered he was dating her. He admitted that it had helped him to cope with her activities, knowing that she never allowed a customer to touch her. He smiled as he thought, *It's a hands-off, whips-on service.* He knew that if a customer did not respect her boundaries, she tossed him out on his ear, or rear, as the case might be.

Jim admitted that he remained puzzled as to Samantha's reasons for continuing in her chosen work. She was obviously well off financially. On a small table in the entranceway to her apartment, he had often seen envelopes, most of the senders familiar to him. The envelopes contained dividend cheques. They were mostly from blue-chip stocks: Bell Telephone, Dofasco, Imperial Oil, British American Oil. He suspected that she also held a sizeable portfolio of government bonds. Having accumulated such investments, why did she continue to engage in a risky business, serving customers who enjoyed having masochistic activities inflicted on them? Jim also knew that whatever her justifications, they were private.

The reason he needed to clarify his feelings at this particular time was that on the weekend of March 17–19, Peckerman had selected him as one of five detectives to represent the police department at a series of seminars in Montreal. The four other men attending the conference were bringing along their wives. Should he invite Samantha to accompany him?

If she accepted, he would not rush things. Ever cautious by nature, he would pay the surcharge to book a suite with two bedrooms. Being a policeman, and because of the tongue-wagging that would erupt over Samantha's presence, he did not wish to create further scandal by reserving a single room.

His decision made, he picked up the phone. A small band of sweat formed along his hairline as he dialled Samantha's number. She answered on the third ring. After the usual greetings and light banter, he explained about the trip.

"You're asking me to go to Montreal with a single man and stay in the same hotel suite with him?" she teased, amusement evident in her voice.

"Would you rather spend the weekend with a married man?"

"Well, yes, if I were married to him."

"Sorry, but for now, an invitation from a single guy is all that I can offer."

"Is it a two-bedroom suite?"

"Certainly."

"Well, that could be a problem. I wander in my sleep."

"As long as you wander into my room, it shouldn't be a problem."

Peersen now hesitated, fearing that he had perhaps gone too far.

"Well, I'm glad to hear that I would be welcome in your bedroom," she purred. "I was beginning to think I'd never hear you say such a thing."

"Then, it's a date?"

"You bet," she replied, laughing as she spoke.

"Great! I'll pick you up at eight o'clock Friday morning. I'll leave my car at your place, and we'll go to Union Station in a taxi."

"I'll have my suitcase ready. I won't pack too much, as it's only a weekend, and I intend to shop while you're at the conference." Then she teasingly added, "In case you're wondering, I'll leave my whips at home."

"Good idea," Peersen replied as he chuckled. "My rear end will likely be sore from sitting through the seminars, and I don't need anything adding to my woes."

Peersen had accepted the risk that cruel teasing might develop from the other police officers when they saw Samantha with him in Montreal. It was also possible that their reactions might hurt Samantha. He must start to integrate her into his life at some time. Why not now? "Faint heart ne'er won fair lady."

✧ ✧ ✧

Samantha smiled as she placed the phone back on the night table. *Thank goodness,* she thought, *the night that Frank Gnomes was here, I opened my bedroom door as fast as he closed it behind me. I thought Jim Peersen might be worth the wait, even though I still have doubts about having a serious relationship with a policeman.*

✧ ✧ ✧

On 17 March, the train with Jim Peersen and Samantha Anderson aboard was speeding eastward toward Montreal. It picked up passengers at Belleville and Kingston, and shortly after 3:00 p.m., the train pulled into Windsor Station.

The suite in the Hotel Cardinal Richelieu contained two spacious bedrooms, a generous-size sitting area, and a small kitchenette. Samantha was pleased with the accommodations. She walked over and parted the sheers that hung over the windows of the balcony doors, noticing that they faced east, overlooking the rooftops of old Montreal with its narrow streets and quaint courtyards. It was too early in the season for people to sit in the sidewalk cafés, the wind from the St. Lawrence River still cold.

Peersen embraced her as she stood gazing out the windows. His arms felt comforting, protective, and though all her adult life she had fended for herself, she enjoyed the feeling. She turned to face him, ran her fingers over the smooth contours of his handsome face, and kissed him gently. He responded eagerly.

Nothing more happened, as Jim had to leave for an afternoon seminar. Despite this, she now felt that a loving relationship with him was a distinct possibility. This was not something that she had experienced too often. The men she had met in Paris and Toronto only wanted to fulfill their own needs.

After Jim departed for the crime seminar, she went shopping. Later, they had a quick dinner in the hotel dining room, since he had an evening session. She had assumed that they would sleep together on the Friday night, but it failed to happen. Jim had arrived back at the hotel after midnight, and she had already gone to bed. She thought he might knock on the door, but he made no approach.

Saturday, while Jim attended more meetings, she continued shopping.

Before departing, he had assured her that he had booked a great restaurant for their Saturday evening meal and had a surprise for her after the meal.

Around 6:00 p.m., the maître d' of the elegant Le Petit Chateau on St. Catherine Street greeted them and showed them to a cozy table in a corner of the room, discretely private from the other diners.

"My, this is romantic," Samantha purred. "Was it your choice or that of the maître d'?"

"My choice. For the next hour, I want you all to myself."

"Hmm, *tres romantique, mon amour!*"

As the maître d' pulled out the chair for her, Peersen told her of the plans for the evening. "I have a surprise that I hope you'll like. I have great seats for tonight's hockey game. There will be a few fellow cops sitting near us. I hope you are okay with that. If you're not, we can forget about the game, have a drink in a bar, and go back to the hotel."

She smiled. "I'd love to see the game against Detroit."

Samantha thought that Peersen looked pleased with her response, and for knowing which team the Habs were playing. His smile resembled that of a young boy who had won first prize in a tournament.

"I think it will be a great game. You know that Montreal will be missing Rocket Richard from the lineup. Clarence Campbell suspended him last week, and he's out for the remainder of the season."

"Yes, I read about it."

The soft light from the candle on the table reflected from Samantha's glossy chestnut hair and flickered in the sparkle in her eyes. Her skirt was navy, her ample breasts showing beneath her robin's-egg-blue blouse. She looked classy, yet casual; perfect for sitting in the expensive seats of the Forum for a hockey game. She was glad she had placed a white angora sweater over her shoulders to ward away the chills. Despite their private location in the restaurant, she knew that several men in the room were watching her.

The waiter appeared and proffered the menus. He was dressed in a black tuxedo with a small bow tie. His shoulders were muscular, likely from exercising many hours in a gym. When the waiter left them alone, silence reigned for a few minutes as they perused the daily specials, as well as the appetizers and entrées.

When the waiter returned, they ordered drinks. Samantha requested a dry martini—extra dry, shaken, not stirred. Jim ordered a Johnny Walker, neat. When the waiter again departed from the table, Samantha observed that despite the young man's athletic build, he sashayed as he walked. She also knew that Peersen had noticed the young man's stride and mannerisms.

"I believe that our waiter is a little light in the shoes, a lover of pink tea," Peersen said.

"I had hoped you were beyond making such comments. It's none of your business, as long as he's a good waiter."

"True, but I couldn't help notice."

"Yes, and making a disparaging comment."

"Well, what I said is true."

"Perhaps."

Then she added, "There were many things I disliked about living in Paris, but I admired the way Parisian men kept their noses out of the bedrooms of other men. It's a habit that male Torontonians would do well to acquire."

Before Peersen was able to reply, Serge reappeared.

Samantha chatted with him amiably in French, acquired during her lengthy stay in Paris. He warmed to her instantly, even flirting as he leaned over to point out several items on the menu. They conversed for several moments, laughing conspiratorially several times.

Turning to Peersen, she said, "Jim, may I order for us? I'd like to surprise you."

"Be my guest," he responded.

A flow of French followed, along with several more bouts of laughter. When Serge disappeared, Peersen inquired about their amusement.

"Was the selection of dishes hilarious, or did you two arrange to meet later?"

"Well, actually, he commented on my taste in men and assured me that if I ever kicked you out of bed, he'd like to catch you. I told him that I had not yet been able to get you in bed, so his wishes were premature. He added that if I'd not yet managed to seduce you, then I'd not learned very much when I was in Paris." Samantha smiled impishly, her eyes sparkling as she teased.

Peersen blushed and laughed to hide his embarrassment.

✧ ✧ ✧

The dinner was superb, and Serge provided service that would have shamed the staff of the Le Cinq restaurant in the Hotel George V in Paris. He was attentive, intuitively anticipating their needs without ever intruding. He smiled admiringly at Samantha, and once or twice slipped Jim an admiring glance. Jim was uncomfortable with the waiter's attention, as well as Samantha's amusement, and was relieved when he had paid the bill and they had departed the restaurant.

Five or six minutes before eight o'clock, they took their seats in the hockey arena. Several of the wives of Jim's colleagues were seated in the same section. They smiled at him, and one of them winked. The women gazed at Samantha and inquired from their husbands about the attractive woman accompanying Jim Peersen.

Samantha ignored the reaction she had created and watched the referees and linemen, who were already skating around the ice surface in preparation for the game to begin. The seats Jim had acquired were excellent, and Samantha was glad that she had worn appropriate clothing—smartly casual, but warm—as seated around her were women with very expensive attire, several wearing mink coats, even though they were unnecessary in the heated arena.

Two rows in front of them, a flurry among the spectators indicated that someone of importance was entering the Forum. Samantha realized that it was Clarence Campbell, the president of the National Hockey League. Within a few moments, the crowds in the stands also recognized the VIP visitor, and great waves of booing and catcalls erupted.

The previous Sunday, in an NHL game in Boston, Montreal's star wingman, Maurice "Rocket" Richard, had engaged in a stick-swinging duel with Boston's Hal Laycoe, and in the melee, Richard had punched lineman Cliff Thompson in the face. Though both players were hospitalized, several days later Richard had appeared in Campbell's office, where he was to be disciplined for his participation in the brawl. The NHL president suspended him for the remainder of the season, including the playoffs. His ruling placed the Montreal team at a severe disadvantage, as their top scorer was missing from the lineup.

On this evening of Saturday, 18 March, Jim and Samantha were unaware that they were about to observe a momentous event in the history of the city's famous arena, the Montreal Forum.

At eight o'clock, the referee dropped the puck for the face-off to commence the first period of play. The Forum was electrified with action. Despite the foul mood of the crowds, resentful that Maurice Richard was absent from the lineup, the hockey game proceeded without incident. Each time Detroit scored, the displeasure of the fans increased. The boiling point occurred when the opposing team scored its fourth goal against the Habs, who only had one goal. A roaring chant from the upper sections of the arena floated down to the rows of seats below.

"We kill Campbell. We kill Campbell."

A few moments later, chunks of ice from the soft drinks pelted down on the section where Campbell sat, some of them landing on Jim and Samantha. Then, from out of nowhere, someone tossed a teargas bomb, and it exploded near Campbell. The spray from the canister, along with acrid smoke, spread instantly to those seated near the NHL president.

A mad rush to the exits of the arena ensued. People were choking, their eyes stinging from the biting fumes of the chemicals. Within seconds, the mobs started throwing everything possible in the direction of their hated foe—Clarence Campbell. Shoes, galoshes, rubber footwear, programs, and hats littered the lower rows of seats and the ice surface.

Peersen removed his suit jacket and placed it over Samantha's head as he steered her toward the nearest exit. Their eyes were watering profusely, and it was difficult to find their way, their problems compounded by the flood of debris reigning down on them. Something heavy hit Peersen on the back of the head, delivering a smack that almost caused him to lose consciousness. Next, several eggs hit him on the back of his shirt, their messy globs dribbling down over his pants and shoes. He heard Samantha whimper as a shoe struck her shoulder.

People on the far side of the arena were now also clambering toward the exits, as the smoke was quickly drifting across the ice surface toward them. An announcement blared over the PA system, clearly audible despite the noise of the throngs.

"Please depart from the arena as orderly as possible."

The next few words from the announcer added to the anger, increasing the level of pandemonium.

"The game has been cancelled, with Detroit declared the winner."

No further spark was needed to ignite the fans into a flaming frenzy. The crowds poured out of the Forum, their numbers adding to the masses outside the arena that were already rioting. Along St. Catherine Street, they smashed store windows and looted many of the shops. Everything not nailed down was either thrown or toppled. Bottles smashed against walls, lampposts, and street signs. Phone booths were pushed over and many set afire. A newsstand was sending flames high into the night sky. Wires were cut, and streetlights were shattered with rocks. The rioting crowds flowed along St. Catherine Street for a distance of almost twenty blocks. The scene resembled a war zone, the badly outnumbered police helpless to stop the invading army.

Jim guided Samantha cautiously along the street, careful not to trip over the debris that was strewn everywhere. As they passed the restaurant where they had dined earlier, in the doorway they saw Serge, the waiter, motioning them.

"Come inside, my lovelies," he said as he held the door for them.

While they rushed to safety, a burly rioter attempted to prevent their entry. The man's size did not deter Serge from decking the guy, leaving him flat on the sidewalk as he slammed the door shut.

During the next few hours, the police gradually restored order, although in a few of the laneways and alleys off St. Catherine Street, some of the fires burned until the early hours of the morning. Over a hundred rioters were detained by the police, and they laid formal charges against about sixty of them. The remainder melted into the darkness, some of them clutching stolen loot from the broken store windows.

By the time Jim managed to escort Samantha to the safety of their hotel suite, the possible horrors of the riot began to dawn on them. They might have been killed. They were fortunate that their injuries were minor.

Samantha shivered as she clung to Jim's warm body. The incident had left her badly shaken, and his presence was reassuring. She harboured deep feelings for him, unlike those she had felt for any other man she had met. Thinking back, she appreciated that he had courted her, like a hero in novels from bygone years, when they did not equate love with a quick roll in the hay. Never having been fully intimate with him, she was aware how much she was anticipating the moment.

Arms around each other, kissing, they edged toward the bedroom. As they embraced, her fingers instinctively unfastened the buttons of his soiled shirt. She ran her hand beneath his undershirt, her fingers gently caressing the muscles on his stomach. If he harboured any doubts about her willingness to be intimate, this simple action clarified her intentions.

He undid the buttons on her blouse and reached behind to unfasten her bra. His hand caressed her firm breasts, massaging her aroused nipples. With his other hand, he opened his belt buckle, allowing his pants to fall silently to the floor. As he removed his underwear, he watched her take down her skirt and panties and gazed in wonder at her. Then he took her in his arms, eagerly ran his hands over her slim body, and pulled her tight against his own. This was a totally new experience for him. He had petted heavily with women and kissed up a storm, but he had never gone all the way before. He was a virgin!

As they kissed, Peersen gently lowered her onto the bed, his tongue probing passionately. She eagerly responded and during the next few moments, as they explored each other's bodies, she guided him to heights of pleasure. When she cradled his manhood in her hand, she created within him a feeling beyond anything he had ever experienced. Although he would never admit to her that he was a virgin, she sensed his inexperience and gently continued to channel his lovemaking, moving her hands expertly over his hard body to guide him.

When their passion became too intense, she held him in check, and then within moments, brought him back to heights of pleasure. Finally, she allowed his desire to explode along with her own.

Lying in each other's arms, they were as one—alone in a universe where no one else existed. For Jim, the long wait for the right moment with the right woman had been worth it. It had been so glorious that he wished he had done it before.

✧ ✧ ✧

The following morning, they breakfasted in a small café not far from the train station. They conversed in quiet tones, like conspirators who had participated in an adventure and were now reliving the exciting moments in their memories. At times, they giggled like children, dissolving into helpless laughter.

They remembered Serge defending them, the eggs dripping from Jim's shirt, and of course, the previous night's passionate lovemaking. They pushed from their minds the violence of crazed fans reacting to their displeasure at a ruling over a hockey hero. They knew that real life was found in love, not in the hatred generated by sports or politics. Love was the balm that smoothed the difficulties of life. Love was indeed God's greatest gift, and it had now been placed in their hands.

The train pulled out of Windsor Station at 11:00 a.m., and shortly after, the western suburbs of Montreal flew past the coach windows. Samantha was dozing quietly, her head on Jim's shoulder. The train raced by Gananoque, rushing toward Kingston and the small towns huddled along the north shore of Lake Ontario. After arriving in Union Station, they travelled by taxi to Samantha's apartment. The sun was dropping heavily toward the horizon when they arrived. Again, they made love.

It was long after dark when Jim departed to drive home. He hummed quietly as he steered the car south toward Eglinton Avenue. It had been a wonderful sojourn in Montreal, and the welcome home event had been fantastic as well.

✧ ✧ ✧

Chapter Nine

Jim Peersen received considerable teasing at the precinct following the Montreal weekend, but nothing that he was unable to handle. He and Samantha were now constantly in each other's company, thoroughly enjoying their time together, as well as the lovemaking.

During April, they attended the University Theatre to see *East of Eden*, based on John Steinbeck's famous novel. The performances of the well-known stars Julie Harris and Raymond Massey delighted them, as well as the acting of Hollywood's latest heartthrob, James Dean. He played the role of a troubled youth yearning for the approval of his father.

Another evening, at the Royal Alexandra Theatre, the songs of the musical *Guys and Dolls* entranced them. After the performance, as Jim crooned, "I love you, a bushel and a peck," they went to the Colonial Tavern on Yonge Street to listen to Gerry Mulligan and the Chet Baker Quintet. They both sipped on beer while the jazz musicians wowed the adoring fans who packed the famous tavern.

During Jim's days off, they strolled along the leafy avenues of the Annex and occasionally enjoyed dinner at a favourite restaurant on Bloor Street. Samantha frequently slept over at Jim's apartment in the Annex.

On warm afternoons in May, they had cozy lunches on Jim's deck, where they were sheltered from the chilly spring winds. Jim continued to cuss at the annoying squirrels, while Samantha laughed at his foolish behaviour. In his defense, he told her that the previous year he had planted daffodil bulbs in large pots and wintered them in the landlord's basement.

When the weather became warmer, he had placed them outside on the deck. The squirrels had eaten all the plants before they had a chance to bloom. She sympathized with his story and teasingly quoted the line from Irvin Berlin's song in the musical *Annie Get Your Gun*: "The squirrels were doin' what comes naturally."

Jim smiled at her remark and then scowled at the furry little scoundrels scurrying among the trees, though he had to admit that they were cute scoundrels. Then one gray squirrel descended to the railing, where it sat and noisily scolded him. He shooed it away. It fled, its fluffy tail wagging furiously as it retreated into the limbs of a tree. Samantha and Jim laughed.

Gazing up as the squirrel disappeared among the foliage, Jim reflected on how happy he was. The small flowers on the maple trees heralded the new season, and he felt that he and Samantha were in the springtime of a romance that would endure throughout many seasons ahead. This thought remained with him as he drove Samantha home.

Two days later, dreaming about another romantic evening with Samantha, Jim dialed EM 8-1126 for a reservation at the Savarin Tavern. Later in the evening, as they enjoyed a fish dinner of broiled Winnipeg gold eye, he invited Samantha to accompany him to the Police Spring Dance. She accepted, and they clicked their wine glasses to toast their happiness. The shoals that might sink their relationship had not yet surfaced. This was soon to change.

The Police Spring Dance was on Saturday, 14 May. Jim was aware that taking Samantha to the dance involved a degree of risk. He knew that some of the men on the force would tease him, and that others would make crude jokes and offer snide remarks. He had weathered the comments after the Montreal weekend, and as he loved Samantha, he wanted to integrate her into his life. This was a necessary step if they were to build a relationship. The police force was important to him, and the sooner his colleagues knew Samantha, the better. She was terrific—intelligent, charming, and beautiful.

Samantha harboured mixed feelings about attending the dance. She was all too aware how cruel some of the police officers could be. Although she adored living in Toronto, as it was her home, when it came to diverse lifestyles, it was very different from Paris. Toronto remained parochial and suspicious of alternate ways of living. She wanted to share Jim's life, but she was not yet ready to retire from her questionable profession. Going to the dance with Jim might prove more awkward than he knew.

✧ ✧ ✧

The Savarin Tavern on Bay Street, between Richmond and Queen Streets. The Savarin is the building with the high-arched windows and the large sign hanging out over the sidewalk. The streetcars are the famous PCC cars. The Savarin was a favourite of Jim and Samantha's.

City of Toronto Archives, Series 381, id1264l-45

✧ ✧ ✧

On the evening of the dance, the sun was edging toward the western horizon when Jim parked his car in front of Samantha's apartment building. Within minutes, he arrived at her door. As he stepped inside, on the turntable of her new stereophonic record player he heard the recent rock and roll hit "Rock Around the Clock," with Bill Haley and the Comets. Despite the low volume of the music, the heavy rhythms vibrated the walnut cabinet of her stereo. Peersen knew that the song was from the MGM film *Blackboard Jungle*, starring Glenn Ford. It was presently at Loew's Downtown. They had advertised it as an "explosive drama of teenage horror." Jim wasn't certain if he liked rock and roll music, but the song was all the rage among the younger people of the city.

When Samantha entered the living room, there was no doubt in his mind about how he felt about her. The white strapless gown she was wearing was stunning. Her hair was neatly brushed in its usual June Allyson style, the small pearl necklace and tastefully applied makeup creating an appealing picture of elegance.

Arriving at the Royal York Hotel, they crossed the impressive lobby with its ornate columns and fancy plaster moulding. As they strolled toward the Imperial Room, two elderly men seated opposite the reception desk, relaxing in Windsor-back chairs, saw Samantha over the top of their newspapers. They dropped them to their laps to receive a better view. One of them sighed wistfully, as if recalling the days when he had been of the age to escort a beautiful young woman to a dance. The young clerk at the desk ceased sorting the mail and overtly ogled Samantha, making no effort to hide his admiration as she swept past the reception area. Peersen noticed the reactions to Samantha and felt proud to be her partner at the dance.

When they entered the spacious Imperial Room, a sea of tables confronted them. At the right-hand side, a band of mature musicians was playing a sedate version of "Rock Around the Clock." It was too stiff a rendition to capture the swinging rhythms of the rock and roll hit, but it seemed to please the crowds who were enjoying cocktails and chatting animatedly. They felt that the music was "hip," without having their ears assaulted with the real thing.

Peersen spied Gerry and his wife Ruth seated on the far side of the room. Gerry had raised his hand to signal the location of their table. Weaving their way among the throngs, they seated themselves. There were two empty chairs at the table, but before Peersen had an opportunity to introduce Samantha, Arnold Peckerman and his wife arrived. They offered introductions, and within a few minutes, they were all conversing amiably. Gerry knew who Samantha was, as Jim had told him about their relationship. He greeted Samantha warmly.

It was soon obvious that Peckerman was entranced with Samantha, but he had no idea who she was. He had overheard the gossip at the station about Jim's weekend in Montreal, but it never dawned on him that this sophisticated woman was the one who had caused the crude rumours.

As Peersen gazed around the room, he sensed that the men at the other tables were telling their wives and partners about Samantha. Unruffled, Jim remained confident that they were too mature to cause any problems. The men often joked and demeaned women whom they met in their investigations. He was confident that their coarse remarks would cease when they met her.

The dinner proceeded without incident. Numerous white-jacketed waiters criss-crossed the room carrying large trays containing plates of roast beef, French-style roast potatoes, and green beans almandine. The dinner was superb, the red wine accompanying the meal an overly sweet Niagara vintage. What it lacked in quality, it made up for in alcoholic content. The conversation soon flowed as easily and profusely as the wine, and as the meal progressed, the noise level became noticeably louder.

Peckerman, who had consumed more wine than the others, conversed at length to Samantha, pompously displaying his knowledge of crime and the methods he employed in difficult cases. Samantha listened intently, and teasingly expressed surprise when he declared that he was the chief of detectives.

"Didn't you suspect that I was well up in the department?" he said with a self-satisfied grin.

"Oh," she replied as she placed her hand on his arm teasingly, "I simply thought you were a bright boy." Everyone at the table smiled, and Peckerman beamed with pleasure.

After the waiters removed the dinner plates, there was a lull before they served the dessert. Peckerman excused himself from the table and weaved among the tables toward the men's room. Jim was unaware that Constable Paul Masters had seen Peckerman's departure and quickly followed his boss. Gerry noticed and was certain it was no coincidence.

When Peckerman returned to the table, he was agitated and his face was flushed. Gerry suspected that Masters had offered snide remarks in the washroom, and that the chief of detectives had overheard them, as it was obvious that Peckerman's attitude toward Samantha had changed. He now ignored her, and if she attempted to speak, he rudely interrupted her. The mood around the table became tense, and soon the conversation died. Pretending to listen to the music of the band, they turned their chairs toward the musicians.

When the band commenced playing the hit made famous by Toronto's own, the Four Lads, "Moments to Remember," Peersen invited Samantha to dance. They were the most striking couple on the dance floor, but the attention they garnered caused more of the guests to inquire who they were and for answers to be provided. They danced two more numbers, and then they returned to the table.

Gerry asked Samantha to favour him with a "swing around the floor." She smiled and accepted. Gerry was charming and chatted affably with her as they danced.

Jim and Samantha danced another set, which began with the song popularized by the McGuire Sisters, "Sincerely." He held her close as she rested her head on his shoulder, while they moved slowly across the floor. They were lost in the romance of the moment and were unaware that a beefy man and his bottle-blonde wife had edged close to them.

Suddenly, Jim and Samantha heard the man mumble the word "slut." When Jim gazed at them in surprise, the woman mouthed the word "prostitute." Jim flushed red with anger and noticed that the woman was with Paul Masters. He wanted to smash his fist into Master's sneering mouth. Samantha sensed what was about to happen and forcefully guided Jim back to the table.

As they seated themselves, Gerry realized that something was wrong. He did not ask what had happened, for fear of aggravating the situation. Jim and Samantha now sat in silence, Peckerman's dour expression adding to the deteriorating mood. Gerry attempted to revive the conversation but failed.

After they served coffee, Jim suggested to Samantha that they depart. The band was playing "Love Is a Many Splendored Thing" as they headed for the ballroom's exit. They went through the lobby and out to Jim's parked car.

On the way north up Mt. Pleasant Road, Jim thought of the words from "Love Is a Many Splendored Thing," by the Four Aces: "Love is nature's way of giving a reason to be living, the gentle crown that makes a man a king." At that moment, he did not feel like a king, but if he were an absolute monarch, he knew whose heads would roll.

✧ ✧ ✧

The first two weeks of July, Jim took his holidays, and Samantha cancelled her "sessions" in order to share the hot days of summer with him. On Monday, 4 July, the temperatures reached ninety degrees Fahrenheit, and the following day climbed to ninety-five degrees. The line ups at the Toronto Island ferry docks were lengthy. The St. Clair Ice Cream Shop on St. Clair, west of Dufferin Street, sold so many sundaes and scoops of ice cream that by Tuesday evening they had exhausted their supplies.

While Jim and Samantha were on holiday, following a leisurely lunch, they retreated to the shade of the deck. Reclining in soft chairs, cool drinks in hand, they watched the squirrels noisily quarrelling in the leafy branches above. In the backyard garden below, the dogwood and lilac bushes had long since dropped their fragrant blossoms, the flowerbeds displaying the deep greens and lush blossoms of early summer. The hosta plants that grew in the shade under the trees, protected from the afternoon sun, reached upward to kiss the summer heat.

Lost in thought, the ice cubes clinking against the sides of the glass, Jim drank his scotch slowly, appreciating the cool elixir as he picked up a copy of the *Toronto Tribune*. Samantha continued to sip on her glass of gin and tonic.

For two weeks, Jim did not have to go near the precinct. While they relaxed on the deck and chatted, the afternoon disappeared. Toward early evening, the leaves in the upper branches began to rustle gently in the breezes, a sign that the heat of the day was over. The air cooled slightly, aided by the sheltering verdant giants surrounding the deck. The shadows of evening lengthened while they discussed their plans for the forthcoming weekend. Later, after another leisurely drink, by candlelight they enjoyed a light dinner of green salad and pasta with shrimp. Then they entered the bedroom.

On Saturday, 9 July, Jim and Samantha set off early in the morning to attend the Stratford Festival of Canada. The Shakespearean festival had commenced two years earlier, held in an enormous tent beside the Avon River in Stratford, a two-hour drive west of Toronto. In its opening season in 1953, the big attraction had been Alec Guiness in *Richard III*. The following year, James Mason captivated the audiences in *Oedipus Rex*. In this year of 1955, the festival was featuring *Julius Caesar, Merchant of Venice*, and for the second year, Sophocles' *Oedipus Rex*.

Following their arrival in Stratford, Jim and Samantha enjoyed lunch, and strolled arm in arm toward the theatre tent, which the festival had purchased in Chicago. Jim had acquired tickets for an afternoon performance of *Julius Caesar*. Robert Christie was playing Caesar, Lorne Greene, a well-known radio announcer and actor, was cast in the role of Marcus Brutus, Douglas Campbell was Casca, and William Shatner was Lucius.

They had erected the tent on a hill overlooking the Avon River. Near the tent was the Stratford Teachers' College. When Samantha entered the tent, she was amazed at its enormous size. Its roof soared high above the seemingly endless rows of seats. The stage was surrounded on three sides by the tiered seats, thrust forward into the space normally occupied by the audience. It was the first thrust stage in North America.

Trumpets sounded as Jim and Samantha took their seats. The lights dimmed and darkness fell across the hushed throngs. Then, as the stage lights slowly rose in a visual crescendo, the actors magically appeared. Flavius Marcullus and several actors dressed as tradesmen faced an audience hushed with anticipation.

Samantha was fascinated from the moment the voice of Flavius echoed across the vast tent. The words painted an image, as if they were alive on the surface of an artist's canvas, each syllable like a brush stroke, clear and distinct.

> Hence! Home you idle creatures, get you home! Is this a holiday?
> What, you know not, being mechanical, you ought not walk upon
> a labouring day without the sign of your profession? Speak, what
> trade art thou?

The words had hidden meaning for Samantha. "What trade art thou?" The reply on stage had been "carpenter," but she felt as if Flavius had delivered the line to her and knew that her reply would be something quite different. She gazed at Jim, but he was absorbed in the production and had not sensed her personal interpretation of the words. The voice of the blonde at the dance remained in her brain: *What trade are you? Slut? Prostitute?*

During the intermission, among the crowds outside the tent, Jim saw Sam Millford, YCI's teacher of boys' PT, standing on the far side of the lawn. He was accompanied by a young man, perhaps eighteen or twenty years of age, with a handsome face and an athletic build. Before Jim and Samantha were able to approach him, a trumpet fanfare sounded to summon people inside the tent to resume the performance. After another fifty minutes of glorious drama, the play ended with the ringing words of Octavius: "So call the field to rest, and let's away, to part the glories of this happy day."

These words also contained a double meaning for Samantha. After the performance, Jim gazed around at the departing crowds but did not see Sam Millford and his companion. On the drive home, Jim was relaxed. Samantha wondered if perhaps he was relieved to have witnessed a murder that he was not required to solve. Despite her momentary brooding thoughts, it had indeed been a happy day for her as well. She thought, *All's well that ends well*; a truly Shakespearean sentiment.

✧ ✧ ✧

Samantha and Jim returned from Stratford to a city wrapped in the euphoria of summer. The Dominion Day weekend was past, and enthusiasm for long sweltering days was unblemished by cool mornings and early evening chills was increasing each day. The residents of the city revelled at the sight of the sandy beaches beside the lake, where an endless array of sun worshippers sprouted early each morning, toasting their bodies under the sun's hot rays, as they transformed winter's distasteful anemia to summer's golden tans.

Jim preferred to sunbathe on his deck, where his porcelain skin slowly bronzed. When standing beside the railing, he gazed with appreciation at the garden below. The rows of backyard vegetables and the front flowerbeds of Jim's neighbours in the Annex were pushing ever upward toward the sunlight. When he strolled around the neighbourhood, at the southwest corner of Bedford Road and Lowther Avenue, he observed the small children splashing noisily in the wading pool in Taddle Creek Park. Their protective mothers quietly chatted as they hovered in the background under the shade of the mature trees.

Jim had long since banished his wool garments to the rear of the closet. When he opened his cupboard door each morning, summer shirts greeted him, their white and pastel colours a welcome change from the somber tones of winter. The light colours contrasted magnificently with his deep tan.

He was anticipating sharing with Samantha leisurely picnics at the Islands, swimming at Sunnyside, baseball games at Maple Leaf Stadium, and lazy evenings on the deck with a glass of amber liquid. Whenever he heard the ice in his glass tinkle, which was quite often, he relished the thought that the only proper place for ice was in a cool drink, not on sidewalks and roadways.

Other changes had occurred in his dietary routines. Despite his love of scotch whiskey, white wine and cold beer became increasingly more attractive during the hot afternoons. Gone were the fussy meals of winter, and in their place he welcomed Toronto's traditional summer comfort foods: overcooked hamburgers, charred hot dogs, and potato salad swimming in creamy mayonnaise.

Cottage country held no allure for him. His back deck, with the kitchen and refrigerator adjacent to it, as well as the small restaurants on Bloor Street, were all within easy reach. He considered summer in the city far superior to long trips on the highways, mosquitoes, and open spaces. Jim was a true urbanite. The theatres, outdoor concerts, and strolls along the quiet leafy streets were all icing on the cake. Jim Peersen believed that nothing in the wide world was as glorious as the exhilaration he experienced each year as the city fully embraced July. It was Toronto's magical time. *Summer, glorious summer,* he thought. *And best of all, I'll share it with Samantha.*

Several evenings, Jim and Samantha went to Riverdale Terrace at Danforth and Broadview to dance under the stars. Every night, crowds packed the Northwest, Northeast, 400, Scarborough, and Dufferin drive-ins. Samantha and Jim did not attend any of the city's five drive-in theatres. They preferred the comfort of the double bed in Jim's apartment to the cramped front seat of an automobile.

On one occasion, they strolled down Yonge Street, the town's wondrous main drag, mingling with the crowds. Their meanderings ended at the Town Tavern at 16 Queen Street East, where Oscar Peterson Trio was wowing his fans. Another evening, they joined the lines of the pleasure-seekers at Pier 9 to board the SS *Cayuga* for the 9:45 p.m. dance cruise across the lake. On the return voyage, in the darkness, as the twinkling lights of Toronto's skyline became visible from the bow of the ship, the orchestra played "Stardust," the romantic Hoagy Carmichael hit of 1927: "when stars are bright, you are in my arms … my Stardust memory, the memory of love's refrain."

The following day, despite Jim's misgivings, they enjoyed the movie *Blackboard Jungle* at Loew's Downtown. They already were familiar with the hit song from it, "Rock Around the Clock." Rock and roll music was beginning to invade the music scene of the city.

The other film they liked was *Love Me or Leave Me* at Loew's Uptown, starring Doris Day and James Cagney. By contrast, it featured an old 1920s hit song "Love Me or Leave Me."

✧ ✧ ✧

On Lauder Avenue, days when Shorty and Tom were not working at the drug store, they played baseball in Fairbank Park, cycled the neighbourhood on their bikes, or journeyed on the streetcar to the swimming pool at Sunnyside. Ken and Tom slept out on the veranda several nights, since during the hot humid weather their bedroom did not cool until the early hours of the morning.

July quickly disappeared. August remained hot. One afternoon during the third week of the month, Tom and the gang decided to go downtown on the streetcar. Earlier in the day, there had been an enormous reception at city hall to welcome home eighteen-year-old swimmer Marilyn Bell, who the previous week had conquered the English Channel. The year before, she had been the first swimmer to cross the thirty-two-mile-wide Lake Ontario. She was now a Canadian hero, and the celebrations on her return to Toronto engulfed the streets of the downtown for hours. The following week, she was to appear on the *Ed Sullivan Show.*

Tom did not encounter the fans departing from the festivities, as he and his friends went to the University Theatre on Bloor Street, west of Bay Street. The film *We're No Angels*, starring Humphrey Bogart, Aldo Ray, and Peter Ustinov was immensely funny. After the movie, they visited Coles Bookstore on Yonge Street, south of Bloor Street. They eyed warily the sign in the store that advertised, "Texts and School Supplies Now Available."

✧ ✧ ✧

Similar to other years, the boys pushed thoughts of school from their minds by attending the glorious CNE. They visited it on Saturday, 27 August, the fair having opened the previous day.

Carol, Harry, Sophie, Jimmy and his girlfriend Paula, Shorty, and Tom entered the CNE grounds shortly before eleven o'clock. The first thing they did was visit the new Shell Tower, located at the west end of the newly named Avenue of the Provinces. The wide boulevard began under the Princes' Gates and extended westward to the new tower, passing alongside the Automotive Building.

Artist's drawing of the CNE Shell Tower, which opened in 1955.

The Shell Tower was a sleek 120-foot tower with soaring glass walls constructed by the Shell Oil Company. It contained an enormous clock at the top, and the tower was visible from any point within the CNE grounds. Prior to 1955, if a person became separated from their friends among the crowds, they usually arranged to reconnect by saying, "Meet me at the fountain," referring to the fountain near the Horticultural Building. Now, it became popular to say, "Meet me at the Shell Tower."

From the top of the magnificent structure, there was a bird's-eye view of the CNE grounds, and to the east, the buildings of the city's financial district. Except for Sophie, they all raced up the stairs and were breathless when they reached the observation deck, about twelve-storeys high. Later, they visited Canada's Sports Hall of Fame, another new feature at the 1955 exhibition.

The day soon disappeared, and in the evening, they attended the grandstand, which featured a variety show, "The Toast of the Town," with

Ed Sullivan as the master of ceremonies. The *Ed Sullivan Show* was one of the most popular programs on television, and fair-goers were anxious to see him on the enormous stage at the CNE. The show, produced by Jack Arthur, attracted huge crowds each evening during the run of the fair. They sat in the wooden seats and thrilled to the magic of show business.

Crowds at the CNE grounds, outside the now-demolished grandstand building.

✧ ✧ ✧

At the beginning of the Labour Day weekend, the stalker was no longer able to quell the need for blood. Three of the five previous kills had been on or near the Labour Day weekend, and there was the danger that the police might discover a pattern. The next kill had to be unusual and appear unrelated to any previous killings. It might even be necessary to resist the urge to violate the victim sexually, to throw the police off the trail.

On the Saturday of the holiday weekend, the weather forecast for the day was "hot, humid, light winds from the southwest, the high of the day eighty-six degrees Fahrenheit." The stalker donned a suitable outfit and headed for the ferry dock at the foot of Bay Street.

Shortly after four o'clock, the stalker was surveying the sun worshippers on the wide beach located on the south side of Centre Island. The sun beat unmercifully on the sand beside the lake, and some of the people were retreating into the shade of the bushes, a short distance from the shoreline.

✧ ✧ ✧

The stalker was not the only one who had listened to the forecast. Stevie Adams was seventeen-years-old and wanted to make the most of the last days of freedom before he entered grade twelve at YCI. A girl from school, Marion Bamford, was attending a family gathering at the Island and, despite her parents' warning that she should not see him, had arranged to meet him after sunset at the far end of the beach, not far from the lighthouse. Stevie thought it was great fun to defy his girlfriend's parents. Marion was an attractively slender, brown-eyed brunette who loved sex, even if it was in the bushes with sandy soil beneath her shapely rear end.

Stevie was intelligent but did not earn high grades at school. Rebellious by nature, he was more intent on having fun and flirting with the girls. His sandy hair, fair skin, and good looks made him highly attractive to the female sex. He had made enemies among the male students at YCI, as Stevie was competition to their own ambitions with the girls. Throughout the previous few years, he had stolen more than one boy's sweetheart.

No one would ever mistake him for a football player, as he was slender and slightly built, some of the boys saying that he was somewhat effeminate. It was one of the ways they extracted revenge for his ability to attract more than his share of the fairer sex. However, in the area where masculinity mattered, Stevie was 100 percent male. Even in a dark room, if a girl encountered him in close proximity, she was well aware of his manhood.

When Stevie departed from his home on Atlas Avenue, he was alone. He had always been a loner and enjoyed his own company. Arriving at Centre Island shortly after 6:00 p.m., Stevie was in an upbeat mood as he walked across the wide, steel gangplank of the Thomas Rennie Ferry. In his light-green shorts and white T-shirt, his tanned skin glistened with suntan oil as he strode purposefully from the ferry and strutted along the paved pathway toward the Venetian Bridge, which led to the southern beaches of the Island. A bulky portable radio in his hand noisily blared the harshly pulsating hit parade song popularized by Bill Haley and the Comets, "Rock Around the Clock." Several elderly ladies, wearing large-brimmed straw hats and knee-length sundresses, sneered in disgust at the racket emanating from the radio.

One of them solemnly declared, "Matilda, my dear, that boy is headed straight to hell. I know the devil's music when I hear it."

Matilda nodded in half-hearted agreement, as she thought, *The boy may be headed for hell, but his body and good looks are pure heaven.*

The heat of the day ended by the time Stevie snapped his towel to place it on the sand. It was nearing the hour of seven, and he was enjoying the warmth reflected from the sand as he observed the die-hard sunbathers who remained on the beach. Families with young children had long-since departed, and no one remained in the water, apart from a teenage couple frolicking in the shallow water not far from shore. Stevie was pleased that the crowds were thinning, as it would be easier for him to rendezvous with Marion Bamford. Stretching the full length of his six-foot body on the towel, he cupped his hands behind his head and relaxed as he envisioned having sex among the bushes.

By eight-thirty, the sun was slipping into the water of the lake, the darkness deepening among the bushes and tall grass that grew back from the shoreline. The tree trunks of the ancient willows were becoming black silhouettes, and the bushes that earlier in the day had sported shiny green foliage were now shrouded in shadows.

Stevie was pleased that the twilight was swiftly dying, as the hour was approaching when Marion had agreed to meet him. Her family was remaining on the Island after dark, since they had obtained a permit allowing them to build a campfire. Marion would slip away from the group when the "old folk" started warbling the sentimental songs they enjoyed: "I'd Like to Get You on a Slow Boat to China," "In the Good

Old Summertime," and "I'm Looking Over a Four-Leaf Clover." When these songs floated on the late-evening air across the flat grassy parklands of Centre Island, the participants in the singing truly believed that all was right with the world.

However, not all was right. In a secluded position near the beach, the stalker was observing Stevie Adams. When the teenager stood to pull on a shirt, his smooth body with its deep tan hinted at the fresh blood beneath his skin.

After Stevie pulled on his shirt, he relocated his towel to a position on the leeward side of a large clump of alder bushes, as the cool breezes were now blowing off the lake from the west. The place where he now set down his towel was more protected but was also more hidden from view. The stalker scanned the scene, and when convinced that no one was able to observe the boy, appeared out of nowhere, knelt down, and talked to him. Stevie was taken by surprise, as he was unaware that anyone was near. However, he was not alarmed, since he recognized the visitor.

The conversation lasted only a few minutes before Stevie felt strong hands seize him and push his face down into the soft sand. His muffled cries were inaudible above the sound of the waves and the wind from the lake. Taken by surprise, he was unable to struggle free before his air-deprived lungs stopped delivering oxygen to his brain.

When he was unconscious, the stalker dragged Stevie deeper into the bushes and sodomized him. Satisfied, the stalker now worked quickly to make the usual small cut in the boy's neck, and then, filled a glass container with his rich red blood. The task complete, Stevie was breathing but comatose. The stalker seized a thick tree branch and severely beat him. Several of the blows were to the right side of his neck, to hide the small incision where the stalker had withdrawn the blood. The blood flow was becoming a trickle as the stalker pushed his face once more into the sand. Within less than a minute, all signs of life ceased.

The boy's remains were then dragged further into the shrubbery, and a leafy tree branch was employed to wipe away telltale signs that the body had been relocated. The blood at the kill site was kicked over with sand.

Being on the staff at YCI, the stalker knew that the boy had many enemies among the students and that he had been in frequent fights with his schoolmates. It would appear as if the teenager had received a well-deserved beating.

On the journey back to the mainland, the stalker gazed from the oak railing of the ferry at the waves rippling outward from the rounded steel bow of the ferry. The stalker relaxed, listening to the throbbing engines that vibrated the timbers of the deck. Less than ten minutes later, when the boat thudded against the dock in front of the ferry terminal, the sky burst open and a torrential downpour descended. People raced from the ferry to the overhanging of the roof of the terminal.

The stalker smiled. The thundershower would further complicate the police investigation into the death of Stevie, since it would wash away any remaining traces of the killing, as well as any sign of the residual blood in the soft sand.

✧ ✧ ✧

On Tuesday, 6 September, the doors of YCI opened for another year. The news of the death of one of the grade-twelve students, Stevie Adams, caused numerous rumours to circulate around the school.

A grade-twelve girl said that that she had heard that Stevie had been buggered on a beach on Centre Island. Several senior boys repeated what she had said and added that they had always known that Stevie was a "fruit," and that he got what he deserved.

The comments caused Tom and his friends to remember the comments after the death of Patrick. It was as if some things in life never changed.

✧ ✧ ✧

Peckerman assigned the Adam's case to a pair of detectives other than Thomson and Peersen, since they were already investigating the killing of a wealthy socialite during the burglary of a home in Forest Hill. It was a high-priority case, and Peckerman did not want to distract his two star investigators.

The detectives handling the boy's murder at Centre Island had already decided there were three possibilities for the murder. A sex pervert had sodomized and severely beaten the teenager, or the boy had allowed a partner to sodomize him, and afterward had engaged in masochistic sex. The final theory was that one or more enemies he had made at school had sodomized him and beaten him as an act of revenge for something he had done. The latter two theories were the most likely, as the forensic team had determined that the teenager had likely known his attacker.

One thing was certain: the boy had no business being on the beach alone in an isolated location after dark. He had clearly been up to no good. Another aspect of the case was certain: a crime committed in an isolated place, with no witnesses, and almost no crime scene evidence other than the limb employed to beat him, was almost impossible to solve.

On the evening of the murder, Marion Bamford had been unable to understand why Stevie had not met her on the beach. When she learned of his death, she was too terrified to come forward and explain to the police why Stevie had been on the beach. For the remainder of her life, she wondered if her silence had assisted the killer in escaping justice.

✧ ✧ ✧

On the day after the news of Stevie Adam's murder hit the school, Tom and his friends journeyed downtown to Coles Bookstore to purchase their texts and supplies. They were cognizant that it was their grade-thirteen year, and that they were now the senior students of YCI.

It was to be the most important year in their young lives. The results of the grade-thirteen departmental examinations would greatly influence their lives during the years ahead.

✧ ✧ ✧

On Lauder Avenue, early on Wednesday morning, Sophie gazed out the front window of her home at the great oak tree, basking under the golden sun of early September. Acorns plunked to the sidewalk and scattered across the lawn, still damp from the early-morning dew. Young children crunched the acorns on the sidewalk under their shoes, while some lads picked them up and fired them at unsuspecting friends. The youthful miscreants chatted mischievously as they sauntered up the street toward their school, while teenage students walked in the opposite direction, south toward YCI.

For as long as Sophie could remember, she had always been in school during the first week of September. This year was different. Her parents had decided that she should not return for her final year of high school, as her baby was due in December, and it was becoming obvious that she was pregnant. She felt proud to be carrying Patrick's baby, but life had not been easy for her since her parents had learned that she was expecting.

Her father had been furious, but his anger had eventually softened as he accepted the inevitable. He loved his daughter and was now more worried about protecting her from the cruel gossip of the neighbours. Her mother had arranged for Sophie to travel to her aunt's home, in London, Ontario, on 9 September. Sophie would not return to Toronto until after the baby had stopped breast-feeding. Despite her objections, her mother had quietly asked her aunt to adopt the baby and raise it, safe from the turmoil that might erupt if the relatives and friends of the Cellini family knew of the true circumstances of the baby's birth.

Sophie had decided that when she returned to Toronto, she would take a secretarial course at Shaw's Business School to qualify for work in a downtown office. When financially able, she planned to move out of her parents' home and gain custody of her child, despite the stigma of being a single mother. She felt confident that she would succeed. Surely, her aunt would not prevent her from taking the baby. To be certain, she was determined not to sign any legal adoption papers, and be certain that the child's birth was properly registered, naming Patrick as the father.

The main obstacle to her plan was her mother. Sophie remembered the night that her mom had learned she was pregnant. She had been livid, even more than Sophie had expected. It soon turned to bitterness, and her mother was unable to talk to her civilly. Since then, her mother's attitude had not changed, and she made it clear that the sooner she departed for

London, the better. Sophie was deeply hurt, and though grateful for her father's understanding, felt abandoned.

A quiet tear trickled down her cheek as she gazed out across the roadway, watching the children happily skip along the sidewalk. Turning away from the window, she began clearing away the morning's breakfast dishes. As she placed them in the sink, she thought of her own days at school, when she had been happy in the classrooms at the Catholic school. High school had been difficult, but it too had created many fond memories. It seemed as if the joys of the previous years had now slipped beyond her grasp, buried beneath her reach.

✧ ✧ ✧

During the final days of September, Thomson and Peersen solved the murder of the wealthy Rosedale socialite. It was a neighbour, whose unwise investments in the stock market had ruined him financially. Though Gerry's colleagues were unaware, his little red pins had assisted him in solving the crime. The department promoted him to assistant chief of detectives. He shrugged off the promotion as if it were unimportant. They also raised Paul Masters to the rank of detective. Bulldog Masters lorded his promotion over the other constables, and he became even more disliked.

Jim Peersen and Gerry Thomson were too busy to care about Masters. They were already absorbed in another case, the brutal mugging and robbery of a woman in Queen's Park, behind the provincial legislative buildings. It had occurred in broad daylight, during the woman's lunch hour.

Over coffee at the precinct, Gerry informed Jim that the police officer, who lived on Holland Park Avenue, had mentioned that he had learned that Miss Taylor and Miss Allyson had both spent the summer in Vancouver. Later, as they entered the Savarin Tavern for its sixty-five-cent businessmen's luncheon, Gerry and Jim discussed this snippet of information.

"They went to Vancouver to be with Taylor's child," Thomson commented as he slowly drank his dark comforting cup of java. It was his fourth cup of the day, and he knew he had to cut down. He had eased his conscience by adding only two heaping teaspoons of sugar.

While they waited for the sirloin steaks, baked potato, and salad to arrive, Jim said to Gerry, "If Stritch knew about the baby, and if she knew who the father was, and if she threatened to reveal it to the school administration, Taylor would have lost her job."

"That's a lot of ifs."

"I know, but I've known lesser motives for murder. Maybe they argued, things got out of hand, and the murder happened during the heat of the argument."

"Do you really think that's what happened?"

Jim shook his head. "No, not really. I am just thinking aloud. The murder was too brutal, and I can't believe that Taylor wandered the valley at night. She lived with Stritch and would have had lots of opportunities to kill her."

Gerry nodded in agreement, placed his coffee cup down, and cut into his steak. "Do you have any ideas to help in our investigation of the robbery of the young woman in Queen's Park?"

"Not really. However, I've been thinking about the murder of the kid on Centre Island."

"That's not our case."

"I know, but when I learned about the details, something about the circumstances bothered me."

"Really?"

"There was something about it that reminded me of the Stritch case."

"I don't see any parallels."

In his spare time, which was rare, Peersen had been busy researching. He now retrieved sheets of folded papers from the inner pocket of his jacket, opened them, and placed them on the table. They were notes made from case reports, and certain words and key phrases had been underlined.

Jim continued. "On a hunch, I examined the crime scene notes and the autopsy reports on Steven Adams. The murder was violent, it occurred in an isolated location, and the body was relocated after the victim died. The autopsy report revealed that the killer had made a small cut in the boy's neck. I know it's a stretch, but I thought about Elaine Stritch. She also had a tiny incision in her neck, where she bled out. In both deaths, the cuts were directly into the carotid artery. The boy's murder and that of Elaine Stritch have distinct similarities."

"I think your theory is interesting but to link the deaths is far-fetched. A killer who rapes a young woman doesn't commit sodomy on a male."

"True, so I decided to examine the autopsy reports of other violent sex crimes that occurred in the years following the Stritch murder. The common denominator that I was looking for was neck wounds. The first one that I found was the murder of Shirley Hemmer in the Rosedale Ravine in 1953."

"I was suspicious of that case too," Gerry admitted. "The case they built against Tim O'Keefe for her murder was wrapped up too quickly."

"Right. At the time, we both felt that the evidence was circumstantial. And remember, O'Keefe cried innocent even as they dragged him away after the magistrate sentenced him."

Jim continued. "In Shirley Hemmer's murder, the autopsy report revealed that she had bled out through a slash in her neck."

"Come on! Her throat was cut from ear to ear. That's not the same as a small wound in the neck like in the murders of Stritch and Adams."

"True, but in all these crimes, the killer concentrated on the neck areas, and the autopsy reports revealed that the victims lost considerable blood that was not always accounted for. The missing blood is another common denominator."

Peersen turned to another page of notes. "There's more. In the 1951 death of Susan Holden in a parking lot on the Danforth, there was also a neck wound and a loss of blood. The coroner gave the small cut in the neck hardly a glance. If it had not been for the rape, they would have ruled it an accidental death. In 1952, Moira Peters was raped in a sleazy downtown hotel, her room on an isolated hallway. She died from supposedly self-inflicted multiple wounds to the neck. She was also raped. In the 1952 killing of Sandra Beaumont in High Park, her neck had been slashed by tree branches."

"I see your logic, but the cases are all different and the methods of killing are different—blunt force trauma with death due to hypovolemic shock, multiple neck slashes, asphyxia by forced drowning, throat cut, beaten to death."

"True, but all the murders are young females, except for the Adams boy. All were raped, including the Adams kid who was sodomized. The bodies were all found in secluded locations: isolated wooden ravines, a deserted parking lot, and a hotel room with a 'Do Not Disturb' sign on the door. All the victims bled out through the neck, often through tiny wounds, and in all the murders, the killer attempted to conceal the discovery of the bodies for at least twenty-four hours."

Gerry paused as he thought over the information, and then replied, "I suppose there are certain aspects of the crimes that are similar. But there are also many differences. You are theorizing that the common threads outweigh the many differences."

"Yeah, I guess."

"I'm not sure I buy your theory. It's true that in all the murders, the killer attempted to delay the bodies being found, but for the life of me, I can't see why it's important. The delay was not long enough to make much difference. The autopsy reports did not change much because of the time lapse."

"True. But the killer must have had a reason for the delay. It's just that we don't know what it is."

Gerry ended the discussion with his customary remark. "Now then, we'll just see about that."

Jim chewed silently on his steak as he observed his partner, who was lost in thought, mulling the ideas over in his mind. After several minutes, Gerry gave an almost inaudible sigh. Jim's theory was beyond the limits of his little red pins, and he was confused.

Finally, he replied, "You're suggesting we have a serial killer?"

"It's a possibly."

"I think it's a stretch."

"The key to all the murders is the Stritch killing."

"Why?"

"Okay, I'm theorizing again, but it's possible that the murder in the parking lot on the Danforth, the sleazy downtown hotel, the High Park, the Rosedale Ravine, and Centre Island involved victims that were selected randomly. The killer saw them and stalked them, then immobilized them, raped them, and finally killed them. Then he relocated the bodies to hide the murders. The Stritch case was different. It involved extreme rage. He likely targeted her well in advance, rather than randomly selecting her. Stritch may have discovered something incriminating about him, and it was necessary to silence her. Or perhaps the killer even had sex with her prior to the day of the murder, and it had been consensual. When she refused to continue, the murderer became enraged.

"I think Elaine Stritch was the killer's first kill, and it was an act of revenge. The murderer enjoyed the sadistic sex and was unable to stop from killing again, so murdered the other five victims to satisfy a craving for perverted sex. They were acts of compulsion, not rage. Despite the different methods employed in the actual killings, the modi operandi are similar."

Jim paused and gazed at his partner. "What do you think?"

Gerry hesitated. He was aware that Jim's thinking involved a world far beyond his little red pins. Gerry had always attacked crimes by fitting together the pieces of the puzzle, connecting dots, and finding relationships among his red pins. Peersen, on the other hand, pulled pieces of the crime from beyond the limits of the puzzles, coordinating unrelated pieces of information, and juggling them randomly until a pattern emerged. He realized that Jim's mind operated on a level that he did not fully comprehend. Was this to be the police work of the future?

Thomson finally replied, "I am not sure, Jim, but I suppose your theories are a possibility, and in a way, they make sense. Perhaps we should rethink all these murders."

✧ ✧ ✧

During the final week of September, Peersen purchased a spanking new 1955 Buick hardtop for the price of $2,895, including all options, and for the first time, a car with air-conditioning. He was proud of his new wheels. When he picked up Samantha at her apartment, she oohed and aahed at the car.

They drove down to Church and Charles Street East for an intimate dinner at the French restaurant, La Chaumiere. Samantha was particularly fond of the hors d'oeuvres cart, which contained at least twenty appetizers, including escargot heavy with garlic, trays of stuffed olives, stuffed mushrooms, wine-marinated anchovies, pureed cottage cheese with cognac and scallions, and quenelles of shrimp.

Samantha had allowed her hair to grow, and it now almost touched her shoulders. It made her lose her pixie look but added a degree of sophistication and elegance. Her pale-blue skirt and white satin blouse were chic, causing many an eye to admire her, both openly and surreptitiously. Jim did not realize that some of the glances were a result of his own appearance.

Samantha ordered the coq au vin and Jim the scallops Normandie. Over dinner, he told her about the teasing that the chief of detectives was receiving at the station. This was because the newspapers had reported that the Vancouver chief of police had been involved in a scandal over gifts he had given to a young female companion. They had included diamonds, liquor, and money, and they had been quietly slipped to her while the man was still the chief of police.

The men at the Toronto precinct teased Peckerman, wanting to know to whom he was slipping the goodies. Peckerman was not amused, Jim told Samantha. She laughed as Jim told her about the raunchy remarks.

"You had best be careful," Samantha warned. "When the guys see your new Buick, they may wonder if you have been slipping your goodies somewhere in exchange for cash."

Peersen grinned. He had indeed received teasing from the men at the precinct, but it was over his relationship with Samantha, and the comments were considerably crueler than those directed at Arnold Peckerman.

As they were leaving the restaurant, Jim noticed a couple sitting at a table in another room. They were partly obscured from view by an archway. The woman was wearing a bright red dress with a plunging neckline, and her hair was too blonde for her age. It was Wild Betty, a woman known to Jim from the police station, as they had arrested her many times for prostitution. Her companion, who was older, was cooing over her like a prize possession. Then Jim noticed that it was Richard

Dinkman. He said nothing to Samantha as he escorted her outside the restaurant.

✧ ✧ ✧

October was a busy month at the precinct. On days when Jim was not at the station, he and Samantha enjoyed several outings. On Friday, 21 October, they attended the preview of the David Milne Exhibition at the Art Gallery of Toronto (the Art Gallery of Ontario). Admission was free for the entire day.

The highlight of November was the Grey Cup Game in Vancouver on Saturday, the twenty-sixth of the month. Over thirty-nine thousand football fans gathered in Empire Stadium to watch the match between the Edmonton Eskimos and the Montreal Alouettes, the largest number ever to view a football game in Canada. Montreal was favoured to win by odds of seven to five.

The game was broadcast on ninety-two radio stations, and a special hookup through the United States allowed it to be seen on television. It was the largest communication network to have ever covered a Grey Cup game. Peersen and Thomson viewed the Grey Cup at Jim's apartment, with Thomson betting on the Alouettes. By a score of thirty-two to nineteen, the Montreal team lost.

✧ ✧ ✧

On Wednesday, 7 December, Sophie delivered a baby boy, Patrick Thomas Cellini. In the St. Joseph's Hospital in London, Ontario, on the birth certificate, she listed Patrick McCaul as the father. The nursing sisters were aware that she was an unmarried mother, but they treated her with sympathy and understanding.

The day the hospital discharged her and she was to return to her aunt's home on Commissioner's Road, her father arrived in London on the train. Sophie's eyes misted as her dad lifted his infant grandson into his arms and gently cradled him. Though he was obviously proud of the boy, the only words he spoke were, "I don't think your mother will be too happy about your choice of names."

✧ ✧ ✧

At her home on Lauder Avenue, Mrs. Cellini remained deeply troubled about Sophie's teenage pregnancy and the birth of her first grandchild. She knew that her husband, though at first upset, had come to terms with the situation. He was unable to deny her his support, as he loved her too much. Mrs. Cellini loved her daughter too, and thought it would have helped her if her husband had been able to talk about the situation, but he had remained silent.

Mrs. Cellini wanted to confess to her priest at St. Mary's, but since Father Malloy had departed from the parish, she had been unable to develop a sense of trust with his replacement. The new priest was an elderly man, near retirement, and she feared that he would judge her without the compassion that had been natural to Father Malloy. It made matters worse that in confessing her sin of being unable to forgive her daughter, she felt she must also confess that she too had been pregnant before she married. In her heart, she felt that she was responsible for Sophie's wanton ways.

She remembered the scriptures: "The sins of the father shall be visited on the sons." She knew now that this applied to mothers as well.

✧ ✧ ✧

Sophie returned to Toronto a week before Christmas. The baby had developed problems with breast-feeding, and the doctors had recommended that they put him on a bottle formula. Her aunt was anxious to take charge of the infant and was insistent that Sophie return home. It broke Sophie's heart to leave her newborn son in London with her aunt.

During the days after she arrived home, her mom's attitude toward her remained cool. She was adamant that she would never welcome the child into the family.

As Christmas drew nearer, the usual joy of the festive season was missing from the Cellini home, and the more Mrs. Cellini treated her daughter with indifference, the worse the situation became.

✧ ✧ ✧

Two days after Christmas, Tom called on Sophie and asked her to accompany him on a walk. They strolled down Amherst Boulevard toward Fairbank Park. The winter winds stung their cheeks and fluttered their scarves. Standing on the hill, on the east side of the park, they watched the youngsters sledding down the hills and the teenage boys playing hockey on the skating rink. The slap of the puck on the boards echoed in the cold air. They spoke of happier times, when they had been younger. In those days, their worst worry had been Kramer and his bullies, who appeared in the park to harass them.

"In a year or two, little Patrick will be old enough to go sledding," Sophie said, her voice choked with emotion. "I want him to be here with me. I want to hold him in my arms. Tom, I'm afraid my aunt in London will never give him up. That's what my mother hopes will happen. She's more afraid of scandal that simply loving her grandson."

Wishing to show that he was supportive, Tom placed an arm around Sophie and gave her a hug. She snuggled closer and leaned her head on his shoulder. Tom wondered if her response to him was more than friendship. He was confused but also pleased. Ever since Patrick's death, his feelings for Sophie had deepened. Throughout the days following the funeral, he had thought he was simply being protective, but now he knew that he harboured deeper feelings. Did he love her?

✧ ✧ ✧

January of 1956 crept into the world quietly at Tom's house, and as usual, his parents served a little port and sherry. This was the first year that he found the taste of the port somewhat pleasing. He knew that Sophie's family always purchased a sweet sparkling Italian wine to welcome in the New Year. Tom thought of her as he sipped the port and wished he was with her.

The final week of January, the school was holding the first dance of the year, the Winter Whirl. Tom intended to invite Sophie to accompany him. The other kids in his group, except for Carol, were unaware that Sophie was now a mother. Tom suggested that it was best if he and Sophie avoided talking about her extended visit with her aunt in London. They decided that if anyone asked her any questions, she should answer them as truthfully as possible, leaving out any mention of little Patrick.

To avoid any surprises on the evening of the dance, Tom told his friends of his intentions to ask Sophie as his date. They had all known Sophie for a long time and said that it would be great to see her. Tom became suspicious when he realized that Harry was silent.

Later, taking Tom aside, Harry said quietly, "Tom, I've known how you feel about Sophie longer than you probably have, and I think she has feelings for you as well. I know about her baby, and I'm happy for her. She'll need a lot of support, and you're the guy to give it. You can count on me too. I know the cruel comments people will make if they find out about the baby."

Harry placed his hand on Tom's shoulder, and for a few seconds he was too stunned to say anything. Recovering, he said, "Did Carol spill the beans about the baby?"

"No. I suspected Sophie was pregnant, so I asked Carol. She denied it. I know Carol well and could tell she was covering for her best friend. When Sophie said she was going to London for an extended visit, I wrote to a cousin who works as an orderly at the St. Joseph's Hospital. I figured that if Sophie were pregnant, she would likely be there as it's a Catholic hospital. I asked him to keep an eye out for a birth registered to a Sophie Cellini. He discovered the birth registration. When he told me the name of the child, Patrick Thomas Cellini, I knew who the father was, and it confirmed for me that she has feelings for you."

At first, Tom was resentful. "Why were you checking up on Sophie? It was none of your business."

"Sorry. It's true that it was none of my business. I did it because I feared that you might never tell me what happened, out of respect for Sophie. I wanted to help in any way I could. You know I won't tell anyone about it."

Slowly, Tom's anger subsided. He realized that he should have trusted Harry. However, he had been unable to say anything without Sophie's permission. It dawned on him that he had been lucky that Harry had not resented that he had not confided in him.

Tom admitted that it felt great to have Harry in his corner. Sophie and he were no longer alone. However, the conversation with Harry made him realize that he must tell Shorty, as he would be hurt if he found out later from someone else. Tom was confident that Shorty would understand. After all, Harry and Shorty knew better than anyone the terrible hurt created by people sitting in judgment on others. In addition, Tom knew that he must also inform his parents. He could not continue dating Sophie without explaining the situation to them.

✧ ✧ ✧

The following evening, Tom's mom was alone in the kitchen preparing dinner. Tom seized the opportunity to talk with her about Sophie and him. As he pulled out the kitchen chair to sit down, it scraped across the floor. His mom gave him a scolding look and said, "You can't lift a chair any better than when you were a child." Then she smiled, and Tom realized that she was teasing him. As she went over to the stove to place the scalloped potatoes in the oven, Tom commenced telling his mom about his relationship with Sophie.

After he had explained, his mom wiped her hands on her apron, pulled out a chair, and sat down across the table from him.

"I've known Sophie a long time. She's a fine girl. I know she's Catholic, and I admit that it crossed my mind that it might cause problems, but I figured your dating her was all right, as your relationship was not serious. From what you tell me now, things have changed. Sophie has a baby, and she intends to raise it on her own. If you love her and intend to marry her, Patrick's child will become your responsibility."

"I want to be a part of little Patrick's life. His father was one of my best friends, and when he needed me the most, I failed him. I should have been with him that morning, when he went into the garage on the laneway and …"

Tom was unable to finish the sentence. Then he added, "I will not fail his son, and I have no intentions of failing Sophie either."

"Are your feelings for Sophie born out of true love for her or guilt over Patrick?"

Tom had not considered this idea, and for a few moments, he remained silent. His mom reached across the table and placed her hand on Tom's. Their eyes met. He knew that his mom loved him and wanted what was best. The spell was broken when she went over to the stove to check on the potatoes, which were beginning to bubble over.

Mrs. Hudson remained silent as she commenced setting the table for supper. The clatter of the dishes and the clinking of the knives and forks absorbed the silence within the room. After a minute or two, she continued the conversation, and Tom heard the concern in her voice.

"Tom, I hate to see you begin your young adult life facing such a burden. Raising a child is no picnic. On the other hand, I have always tried to teach you to do the right thing and to think for yourself."

"Does it matter to you that Sophie is Catholic and has a baby?"

"Well, I admit there are problems, and yes, it does bother me. But on the other hand, although Catholics and Protestant may worship in different ways, we all serve the same God. I know that some members of our family will be shocked. A few of our Catholic neighbours will be against the marriage, as will some of the Protestants. Because the baby was conceived out of wedlock, this presents another problem."

Tom repeated his question. "Can *you* accept Sophie, knowing she's a Catholic and has a son?"

"I am not sure."

"But when I was a small kid, you said …"

"Yes, yes! I remember what I taught you. I guess there is a lesson here for me as well—there's a difference between preaching the right way to behave and actually doing it."

"I can't turn my back on Sophie."

"I understand that, Tom."

"What should I do?"

"Let me discuss it with your father."

◇ ◇ ◇

As January progressed, the situation did not become any easier for Tom. He continued dating Sophie, but her parents were cool to him, and at times, her mother was hostile. One or two of the neighbours, especially Old Windbag Klacker, gossiped cruelly about Tom Hudson dating a Catholic. They became Klacker's favourite topic of gossip in Marlton's Grocery Store. Whenever Tom called on Sophie, her parents never said anything other than, "I'll tell Sophie you're here."

On Saturday, 28 January, they went to YCI's Winter Whirl. Sophie looked terrific in her gray pleated skirt, white blouse, bobby socks, and saddle shoes. When they arrived, the sound-system was playing the hit by Fats Domino, "Blueberry Hill."

Within a few moments Tom was holding Sophie close on the dance floor, as they moved slowly to the song, "True Love," made popular by Bing Crosby and Grace Kelly. They continued dancing for two more songs, and then Tom went to the soda bar to get a couple of Cokes. It was then that he heard the whispering among a few of the students waiting to get drinks. He heard the word "slut" several times. Tom was aware they were watching him and was certain they were making the comments for his benefit. He ignored them. He wondered how they had learned about the baby.

When he returned to the corner of the gym where Sophie was with his friends, he gave her the Coke, and they continued to chat and laugh quietly. When they played the Elvis Presley hit, "Love Me Tender," he took Sophie's hand and they drifted out onto the dance floor again. Tom steered her close to the speakers, where the music was louder, to prevent her overhearing any gossiping tongues. He remained protective of her throughout the remainder of the evening, and they enjoyed the dancing thoroughly. The final number was Dean Martin's recording of "Memories Are Made of This."

Walking home in the cold night air, Tom thought that memories were indeed made of events such as this, but the cruel gossip was also a memory—one he would prefer to forget.

✧ ✧ ✧

Because the weather remained colder than usual, Samantha and Peersen spent many evenings indoors. On one occasion, they watched Mozart's opera *The Marriage of Figaro* on station CBLT. The topic of marriage reminded Samantha that she had read in the newspaper that the British press was already speculating on a possible wife for Prince Charles, who was only seven years old. She mentioned that they were predicting that nine-year-old Princess Anne of Denmark was a possibility.

"Charles is too young, and will not be eligible for at least fifteen years," Samantha said.

"I know that marriage requires considerable thought, but fifteen years is too much. How long are we going to take?" Peersen inquired with a grin.

"About fifteen years," she responded.

They both laughed.

"Actually," Peersen continued, "I made a decision today for our old age."

"What? Deciding not to grow old?"

Jim smiled. "Well, it will be for our future, when I'm older, and you will still be young. I purchased a building lot near the beach at St. Petersburg, Florida." The lot had cost him $295, and he had contracted a company to erect a beach house on it, at a cost of $4,990.

"If we never grow older, we can soak up a little sun during our mature-young years, on a winter vacation."

Samantha was pleased with his news.

Actually, Peersen hoped that the home would be erected by late spring. He did not mention that it would be great to visit somewhere far from Toronto, where no one knew them. At the precinct, the snide remarks and cruel jokes about his relationship with Samantha had not died away. As well, when he travelled around the city, because he was a detective on the police force, too many officers recognized him on sight.

The previous week, they had been at the Imperial Room at the Royal York Hotel, dancing to the music of Moxie Whitney and his orchestra. They had seen two other couples from the precinct, and Peersen had known from their smirks that they were telling their wives about Samantha. Even on the evening they had gone to Shea's Theatre to see Natalie Wood and James Dean in the film *Rebel Without a Cause*, they had bumped into a policeman in a coffee shop on Queen Street. The cop's reaction, and the way he leered at Samantha, clearly revealed his thoughts. Peersen was sick of it, but he did not intend to acknowledge their narrow-minded bigotry. *After all, it is the 1950s, not the Middle Ages*, he thought.

The temperatures continued below average during February. On the twenty-seventh of the month, Peersen was enjoying a coffee break at his desk, while he perused the front page of the *Toronto Trib*. An ad caught his eye. It was for an Easter weekend in New York City, which was $34.50, including train fare, two nights in a hotel, sightseeing, and transfers. If the workload at the precinct eased, a weekend away was an appealing thought. However, he would prefer to drive to New York in his new Buick.

✧ ✧ ✧

February also turned out to be a difficult month for Tom and Shorty at Greenberg's Pharmacy. The police had arrested Ruth for driving while intoxicated, and since it was her third offence, the judge had sentenced her to three weeks in the Don Jail. Without the availability of the truck, Shorty and Tom delivered all the orders on their bicycles, even the ones that were bulky and heavy. Sometimes it required two or three trips to complete a large order.

Following one particularly gruelling Saturday afternoon's work at the pharmacy, the boys met Sophie and Jane. Jane was a girl whom Shorty was dating. They all went to the Nortown Theatre at Bathurst and Eglinton. After the movie, Sophie told Tom that she had registered at Shaw's Business College to take a typing and secretarial course. It was the first step in her dream to become financially independent and regain control of her son.

The following week, Tom was studying hard, since it was important that he pass his grade-thirteen examinations in June. Throughout the remainder of February, Harry and Shorty were achieving great scoring averages on the basketball team, and it appeared that York had an excellent chance to make it into the semifinals.

After school, Harry spent more time in the gym perfecting his dribbling and shooting. If the team did not make it into the finals, he was determined that it would not be his fault.

One Wednesday afternoon after classes had ended for the day, Harry remained late in the gym to work out. Kramer was there as well. The other team members had long since gone to the showers. Harry and Kramer shot baskets at opposite ends of the gym and ignored each other. While they practised, the school became quiet, the day having ended, and the students gone home. Miss Allyson was the only member of staff who was in the building.

Shortly after five-thirty, Harry entered the showers. Kramer arrived a few minutes later. Harry ignored him. Old animosities ran deep. After a thorough soaping and rinsing, Harry sauntered toward his locker to get dressed. Only his towel around him, he fiddled with the combination lock for a few moments before it opened. Retrieving his underwear, he placed the towel on the bench. For a few seconds, he was naked in front of the locker. Suddenly, he became aware that someone was standing beside him. Looking up, he saw Kramer, wearing nothing except a silly grin on his face, the towel in his hand hanging down, touching the floor.

For a few seconds, Harry was too stunned to react. Despite the many times he had showered with Kramer, he had never really gazed at him. Now, Kramer was in the nude in front of him, his wet body glistening, water dripping from his hair. He had obviously departed the showers a few moments after Harry.

Kramer had carefully planned the encounter. He had come a long way since the days he had been a pimply, skinny kid. His skin was clear, and his shoulders were broad, though not as broad as Harry's. He was an inch shorter than Harry, but his waist was narrow, his stomach muscled and flat. Kramer's full head of dark hair, ruffled from the shower, fell over his forehead. Even his crooked nose, a result of Shorty having broken it in a fight when they were kids, did not detract from his good looks.

Kramer's smile, with its white, perfectly aligned teeth, was beguiling.

Their eyes met. Harry was unable to look away. Then without realizing it, Harry slowly dropped his eyes, allowing them to wander over Kramer's body. Harry felt a stirring in his groin. It was a sensation that he had never experienced before. Then he realized what was happening, recovered, and quickly turned his back on Kramer. He pulled on his underwear, praying that Kramer had not seen his arousal.

Kramer had noticed. Without a word, Kramer wrapped his towel around him, and flicked the water nonchalantly from his hair as he sauntered away.

✧ ✧ ✧

Carol sat in the gymnasium with a couple of her friends, watching the game that would determine which team proceeded to the semifinals of the basketball league. Students packed the gym, anxious to cheer the YCI team to victory. They were grateful that the game was on the home team's court, and it had not been necessary to travel to another school. The weather outside was cold and blustery. Though it was now the middle of March and spring was just a week away, winter had not lessened its grip on the city. The warmth inside the gym, accentuated by the heat created by the tension and emotions, held the cold weather outside at bay. This was an all-important game, and the spectators were confident that their school had the superior team.

Several of the girls that Carol was sitting with were more interested in the boys on the team than in the game, but they cheered and screamed every time YCI scored. They frequently passed comments on the two main scorers, Harry Heinz and Shorty Bernstein. Carol felt proud that the two basketball heroes of the school were her close friends.

Her ears perked up as she heard the girl on her left declare, "My God! That Bernstein is a doll."

Shorty was barreling down the court, dribbling expertly, controlling the ball. At midcourt, he passed the ball to Harry, who carried it closer to the basket, before throwing it laterally to Shorty. Within seconds, Shorty sunk it into the net. The crowd went wild.

Carol noticed that on the court, Harry moved with the assurance and speed of a professional player. His height and coordination added to this impression. He dominated the plays and could move the ball down the court in a manner that no player on the opposing team could effectively block. The students respected and admired his skills.

However, for the first time, Carol realized that the attitude of the crowd toward Shorty was different. Harry they respected, but Shorty they adored. As she observed Shorty, she realized that he was more like a ballet dancer than an athlete. His movements were fluid, and when he leaped to score a basket, he was graceful, his powerful leg muscles pushing his body effortlessly upward. Each time, after he had scored a basket, he gazed toward his shoes and self-consciously brushed his hair away from his forehead, too shy to acknowledge his achievement. It was an endearing quality, and the fans loved him for it.

Shorty had been a part of her life for as long as she could remember. She smiled as she remembered when they were about seven or eight, in the Amherst laneway, and she had tried to explain to the guys where babies came from. Shorty had shocked her by declaring that they came out of a vagina. In grade eight, he had been there when the guys had teased her about her lack of titties, because Sophie's had developed earlier than hers. As a kid, Shorty had been an irascible, cocky little brat. Now, he was a confident young man, and though he remained an imp in many ways, he knew how to be gentle and empathize with others.

She wondered, *When did he change?*

YCI won by a score of 108 to 98. The crowds applauded and whistled endlessly for their heroes. The team would now proceed to the finals.

The following day, Carol saw Shorty in the hallway between classroom periods, but he was listening to two girls, who were obviously admiring him. After school, she did not see him since he was in basketball practice. The next afternoon, when she went to her locker after school, he was standing there waiting for her. For the first time in her life, she blushed as she greeted him. It surprised her, as she had always taken him for granted and never thought much about him in that special boy–girl way.

"The gang is going downtown Saturday night to the Imperial Theatre to see the musical *Carousel*. Do you want to join us, or do you already have plans?" he inquired.

"Who's going?"

"Tom, Sophie, Jimmy, and Jane."

"Are you on your own?"

"I won't be if you go."

She knew that it was a sneaky way to ask her out, as he had used the same technique in the past. On these occasions, she had always made it clear that if she joined the gang, she was not his date. This time she said coyly, "Are you asking me as your date?"

"Anytime you want to be my date, I'd love it." He grinned.

"Well, I'd love it too."

Shorty's smile disappeared as he realized that she had accepted. He stammered as he told her that he was happy that she would go with him, grinned sheepishly, and awkwardly strolled away. Carol stood and watched him depart. She couldn't quite believe what had happened.

Slowly, she realized Shorty had not changed. It was her. The guy of her dreams had been right under her nose ever since she had been a small girl, and she had never noticed him.

Chapter Ten

The final week of March, Frank Gnomes was at his desk early in the morning, enjoying his coffee. He inhaled the delicious scent of the brew, thinking, *Coffee actually smells better than it tastes. Many things in life seem better before they are actually experienced. For me, marriage falls into this category. I wonder if the success I've achieved at my job will become another.*

Several stories were on his desk, and he knew his editor was growing impatient. The Canadian government had finally agreed to ship armaments to Israel, and the press and news stations were all commenting on this change in foreign policy. In addition, the editor had requested that he write a story about Khrushchev's claim that the dictator Joseph Stalin was murdered. Frank thought, *If that bastard Stalin was murdered, they should give the killer a medal.*

Frank was deciding upon the responses he would write when a colleague in the entertainment department of the *Trib* strolled by his desk. He inquired if Frank wanted two complimentary tickets for the following evening to hear Glen Gould, the new wonder-boy pianist, performing at Massey Hall. He was playing Bach and Beethoven concertos. It was a little highbrow for Frank's tastes, but it reminded him that he had not spoken to Samantha Anderson in several months. He accepted the tickets, thinking that he would call her.

Samantha was surprised when she heard his voice on the phone. She considered her relationship with him ended. After listening to his proposal, though polite, she explained to him that she had a partner and was not dating other men.

Typically, Frank responded in a smart-ass manner. "Do I have to get my ass spanked in order to see you?"

"I think you had best find someone else to kick your ass. I'm certain there will be a long line of associates who will happy to accommodate. Sorry, I'm not available."

"Pity. I still think you're the greatest."

"Thanks. If I need a reference, I'll call you."

"Anytime."

They were both laughing as they hung up the phone.

✧ ✧ ✧

Samantha was pleased that her relationship with Jim continued to develop. They had discussed no long-term arrangements, but they knew they loved each other.

When the time was ripe, she would relinquish her role in the sex trade, but she was not ready. Meanwhile, her job was not the only factor that was causing stress. It was becoming increasingly difficult to ignore the snide remarks from her neighbours in the apartment building, as well as Jim's neighbours in the Annex. The busybodies were well aware that they were sleeping together and were not married. In Toronto, similar to Paris, a person paid a high price to live a lifestyle not considered within the accepted boundaries that society tolerated, but in Paris, the boundaries were far wider.

Jim arrived at her door shortly before five o'clock. They had a drink and departed for the Seaway Hotel on the Lakeshore Road, just east of the bridge across the Humber River. They chatted intimately as they enjoyed a seafood platter: Long Island clams, filet of Dover Sole, and several whole lobsters. The price per person was three dollars.

Later, they attended the Royal Alexandra Theatre to see Maurice Chevalier on stage as he performed songs and impressions that had made him famous. They sat in the first row of the first balcony. The tickets had set Jim back four dollars each. The stock market had been good to him, and he knew he could well afford these extravagant evenings.

As Chevalier related amusing stories of Paris, Samantha remembered her initial enchantment with the French capital, and now wondered if the relaxed lifestyle of the city had influenced her to choose the wrong career.

Later, at Jim's apartment, she told him of her plans to move closer to the downtown, in a newly constructed, eleven-storey apartment tower on St. George Street, north of Bloor Street. A one-bedroom apartment was $125 a month, a steep price, but she considered it well worth it. She would be closer to Jim, and the apartment included a TV outlet. Jim wanted her to move in with him, but she declined.

"When the time is ripe, we'll live together," she told him. "In the meantime, enjoy your freedom," she said teasingly. "When I get you all to myself, I'll be a tough jailer."

"I look forward to it," he replied.

◇ ◇ ◇

On Saturday, 24 March, the Toronto Maple Leaf hockey team was to play the final game of the season in the Gardens, against the defending Stanley Cup champions, the Detroit Red Wings. The previous Wednesday, Kramer had skipped school and, early in the morning, stood in line at the Garden's box office to purchase two tickets. He knew who he was going to invite to the game.

Since the incident in the locker room, Kramer had attempted to talk to Harry and allay his fears that he might spread rumours about him, but other than during team practices, Harry avoided him. However, as the days passed, Harry became more relaxed, and one afternoon, when they had passed each other in the hall at school, their eyes met. Kramer said "Hi!" Harry smiled and nodded his head, although he never stopped to talk.

Finally, Kramer spied Harry alone in the lunchroom and approached him. Harry looked up, nodded his head in recognition, but continued eating his lunch. Though uninvited, Kramer sat down at the table. After a minute or two of small talk, he mentioned the forthcoming Leaf's game on Saturday night, and inquired if Harry had any interest in attending, as he was going to purchase tickets.

At first, Harry was amused at Kramer's intentions, knowing that tickets were almost non-existent, and that acquiring a pair was nearly impossible. Kramer persisted, and said that if he *did* succeed, would Harry accompany him to the game. Harry laughed, secure in the thought that Kramer would never get tickets.

"If you get tickets, let me know," Harry replied with a grin as he picked up his lunch tray and carried it back to the cafeteria counter.

Kramer interpreted Harry's response as an agreement to join him at the game and grinned smugly as he watched Harry deposit his lunch tray and depart for his next class. Harry was unaware that Kramer already had the tickets. The following day, when Kramer showed them to him, Harry was stunned. Kramer claimed that Harry had agreed to attend, but Harry insisted that he had made no such agreement. He thanked him for the offer and walked away.

Harry really wanted to see the game, and a strange feeling overcame him as he thought of the disappointed expression on Kramer's face. He was unable to explain why this bothered him, as he had never considered Kramer a friend.

During the afternoon classes, he mulled over Kramer's invitation. He was being offered an opportunity to view a much-anticipated game, and Kramer had obviously gone to considerable lengths to acquire the tickets. By the final period of the day, he was thoroughly confused. In the back of his mind, he feared that his turmoil had something to do with his reaction to Kramer's naked body. He sensed that in any dealings with Kramer, he was stepping into dangerous territory. As well, Shorty would view it as a betrayal of their friendship. Despite this, Harry felt unable to withdraw. After school, when he saw Kramer in the locker room, he reluctantly agreed to attend the game. As Harry walked home from school, he was deeply troubled. What had he done?

On Saturday evening, Harry and Kramer were in the Gardens. Harry had never attended a live game before, and the thrill of being in Toronto's hockey palace filled him with excitement. Even though they did not have seats, just standing room at the back of the grays, simply being at the game was exhilarating. Harry gazed down at the wide expanse of ice and the thousands of fans who were anticipating the arrival of their hockey heroes. Wild cheers erupted when the players skated onto the ice.

Harry gazed at Kramer, who was standing beside him as they leaned on the boards at the back of the grays, and realized that he was watching him. A strange feeling hit Harry in the gut, and he was unable to explain what it meant.

When the referee dropped the puck for the face-off, the crowds roared with anticipation, and the first period of play began. A new player, Frank Mahovlich, whom the coach had drafted from the minors to assist the Leafs, drew considerable attention. Playing left wing, he was a formidable player. His long, powerful legs propelled him down the ice effortlessly. Though this was only the fourth game he had played with the team, the press was speculating that he would be a regular in the lineup during the following season.

Several times during the first period, Kramer pressed his body against Harry, who immediately shifted away, as he felt that everyone around them knew what Kramer was doing. At the first intermission, Kramer went to the snack bar and purchased two cups of Vernors ginger ale and two bags of potato chips. During the second period, Kramer continued his antics, until Harry quietly told him to keep his distance. Kramer grinned and nodded sheepishly, but during the third period, he leaned against him more aggressively.

Finally, Harry said forcefully, "Piss off."

Although the Leafs had played well, they lost by a score of four to one. Ed Chadwick, the Leafs' goalie, had played a good game, but the Detroit offense had been too powerful, and the Leafs had not performed well defensively.

Despite the defeat of their heroes, Harry and Kramer were in a good mood as they exited the Gardens. Walking west along Carlton Street toward the subway, Kramer suggested they enjoy a cup of coffee before they returned home. Harry agreed. Instead of going to Fran's Restaurant, which was nearby, Kramer insisted they go to a coffee shop he knew, which was above a laundromat on Yonge Street.

Inside seated at a cozy booth, after Kramer ordered the coffee, Harry gazed around the room. It was dimly lit, but he could see the other booths, as well as the tables in the centre of the floor space. They were mostly occupied by young men—there was not a woman in the place. Kramer did not utter a word. After the coffee arrived, Kramer placed extra cream in his cup, stirred the liquid slowly, and sat back to watch Harry's reaction.

Ignoring his coffee, Harry continued sizing up the scene. Then, to his horror, he spied two men whose hands were extended across the table, fondly touching. Next, the right hand of one of the young men dropped under the table, and he groped his companion. They gazed into each other's eyes as if no one else in the world existed.

All of Harry's life, he had been able to size up a situation quickly. It terrified him that he had not understood sooner that Kramer had brought him to a coffee shop frequented by homosexuals. Every church denomination throughout Canada condemned homosexuality. Some offered prayer groups to change the homos to heterosexuals, thus healing them of their perversion. Psychiatrists classified it as a sickness that required extensive therapy. Newspapers said it was a violation against the decency of the nation and an affront to every moral citizen.

Ignoring the coffee on the table, Harry stood up to leave. He was about to curse Kramer for bringing him to such a vile place, when he saw the crushed look on Kramer's face. Harry had never witnessed such hurt. Unable to control his emotions, without saying a word, he tramped angrily out of the restaurant and down the stairs. He passed two handsome young men as he descended, who were laughing in a secretive manner, clearly displaying their shared intimacy. Stepping onto Yonge Street, Harry stumbled toward the College subway station, leaving Kramer behind.

When he arrived home, his dad was reading the newspaper, and he glanced up as his son entered the house. They exchanged a few words, talked briefly about the hockey game, and then Harry retired to his bedroom.

In the darkness, Harry lay in bed, his hands cupped behind his head, starring vacantly at the ceiling, visible in the dim light from the streetlights outside. He was angry and confused. As thoughts of the evening tumbled in his mind, he slowly realized that he was angry with himself, not Kramer.

It was early morning hours before he drifted off into a world of troubled dreams.

✧ ✧ ✧

As April arrived, spring weather finally unfolded across the city, and trees shed their winter dormancy. Shorty was pleased with the amount of money he had earned in tips during his evening shift at Greenberg's and intended to invite Carol to go with him to the Tivoli Theatre to see the Canadian premier engagement of the film version of Rodgers and Hammerstein's musical *Oklahoma!* They had filmed it in the new Todd-A-O process.

As Shorty cycled homeward, the warmth of the spring sunshine was losing its strength while the sun dropped in the western sky. Thoughts of Carol preoccupied him, and he ignored the chill, his jacket unzipped. After negotiating the left turn onto Oakwood Avenue, he pedalled southbound toward Clovelly Avenue. It was then that he noticed four players from the basketball team that YCI had defeated a week earlier to win the league championship.

In the final game, a player on the opposing team had fouled him, and in the foul shot, Shorty had scored an extra point. YCI won the game by thirteen points. Afterward, the player who had fouled Shorty instigated a brawl. Defending himself, Shorty delivered numerous brutal punches at several of the players before the referees and teachers stepped in and ended the fight. There had been hard feelings when the players departed the gym.

Now, on Oakwood Avenue, before Shorty had a chance to pass them by, one of the guys poked a hockey stick into the spokes of the front wheel of his bike, sending him tumbling to the ground. Dazed from the fall, without allowing him time to recover, the boys began kicking him. The teenager with the hockey stick grinned maliciously as he raised his improvised weapon to deliver a crushing blow.

Shorty covered his head with his arms to lessen the effects of the pending assault. It never came. The bully with the stick suddenly crumbled to the ground, struck from behind with a punishing thump. Someone had come to his rescue, and in the brief respite provided, Shorty struck back. Deciding it was no time to play by Queensberry rules, he kicked one of the other guys in the groin, and as he fell, he punched him in the stomach. Another kid fell to the ground, knocked down by a crack from the hockey stick, which was now in the hands of his rescuer. Shorty lashed out and kicked him hard in the shins. Within seconds, the four bullies fled, and Shorty was helped to his feet.

The shock he experienced was greater than the surprise he had felt when he fell from his bicycle. There, grinning at him, was Horace Kramer, his enemy ever since the days he had been a little kid. Lost for words and finding it difficult to say thanks, Shorty stared at his nemesis and said nothing.

"Are you all right?" Kramer asked nonchalantly.

"I ... think ... so," Shorty stammered.

"That's good. Those goons deserved a thumping. I guess they're getting used to losing battles with the boys of YCI."

"I guess."

Then as he turned to leave he said, "I defend anyone who is a good friend of Harry's."

Shorty watched Kramer as he casually walked southbound on Oakwood Avenue, crossing over to the east side, toward Bude Avenue.

What was all that about defending Harry's friends? he thought.

The following day at school, Shorty told Harry what had happened and repeated Kramer's odd remark. Harry told him how Kramer had offered him an extra ticket for the hockey game, and that he had gone to the Gardens with him.

Shorty stared at Harry in disbelief, as he heard him say, "Kramer's not so bad. He's played well during the basketball season, and I decided that it was time to let old grudges remain in the past. I enjoyed the hockey game, even though the Leafs lost to Detroit."

"Does this mean that Kramer is now a member of our group?"

"I can't make that decision. I'm not even certain that I'd ever accept another invitation from him to go anywhere. All I'm saying is that he's not such a bad guy, and it's time to let bygones be bygones."

Shorty gazed at his best friend. Harry had always been one to mend bridges. However, he knew that something was troubling Harry and sensed that it involved Kramer. He also realized it was no good prodding Harry. He would tell him in his own time.

Something else bothered Shorty. Carol had agreed to go to the Spring Frolic Dance with him, and he was uncertain how Harry would react. She had always been Harry's date, but he also knew that Harry had no romantic feelings toward her. Carol had finally realized that Harry loved her as a friend and that there would never be anything more. They had agreed that Carol would tell Harry about the forthcoming dance, and that she was going with Shorty. Shorty still felt guilty.

✧ ✧ ✧

The third week of April, Tom picked up Sophie to escort her to the dance. Shorty and Carol joined them as they walked to the school to attend the event. The flowering crab trees on the lawns were in full bloom, their colours muted by the shadows of evening.

Sophie was radiant. As they walked along the street, she gently caressed the corsage Tom had bought her. It was as if she could not believe it was real. Tom felt very proud. However, he felt it strange that Harry was not with them.

Growing older meant accepting changes. He had heard Gramps express the sentiment many times.

✧ ✧ ✧

Ignoring the cruel taunts at the precinct and the snide remarks of their neighbours, Jim Peersen and Samantha continued to explore the city's entertainment venues. One warm evening, they went to the all-you-can-eat buffet at the Town and Country Restaurant on Mutual Street. Afterwards, they attended the Crest Theatre to see Agatha Christie's play *Murder at the Vicarage*, and on another evening at the Crest, they enjoyed Noel Coward's *Present Laughter,* starring William Hutt. Another highlight of the month was motoring to Stratford to see a matinee performance of *Henry V,* and in the evening, *The Merry Wives of Windsor.* The festival had announced that it was to be the final season for the Stratford Festival under the big top.

It was late when they returned to Toronto, tired but happy. As Jim unlocked the door to the house, he saw the Saturday newspaper on the doorstep. On the front page was a picture of Queen Elizabeth II, who was celebrating her thirtieth birthday. The other photo was of Grace Kelly, who had recently married Prince Rainier III in St. Nicolas Cathedral in the tiny principality of Monaco. They were to honeymoon on the prince's private yacht on the Mediterranean. Samantha retrieved the newspaper and dumped it on the kitchen table. They would read it in the morning as they breakfasted on the patio deck.

In the third week of May, Jim and Samantha were returning from downtown, where they had attended Shea's Theatre to see Gregory Peck and Jennifer Jones in *The Man in the Gray Flannel Suit.* The phone was ringing in Jim's apartment as they unlocked the door. It was Gerry Thomson.

"Jim, I've been trying to reach you all evening. All hell's broken loose. Get down here to Earlscourt Park. A body has been found behind the change rooms. It's a staff member of YCI."

The phone went dead.

◇ ◇ ◇

It was past eleven o'clock when Peersen arrived at the scene. Despite the late hour, a small crowd had gathered. Showing his badge, Peersen ducked under the rope that cordoned off the crime scene and approached Gerry, who was standing beside the body, covered with a white coroner's sheet.

"About time you arrived. I've been here now for almost an hour, listening to old Doc Dicer bitch about having to work in the park at such an inconvenient hour. Of course, I really sympathized with his beefing," Gerry added sarcastically. "He didn't seem to notice that I was here too."

"Who's the victim?"

"Our good friend Richard Dinkman."

Peersen was stunned, but managed to reply, "Dinkman was a prime suspect, not a candidate for a murder. His murder has to be connected to the Stritch case. It's too much of a coincidence to be otherwise."

"Agreed. They both were employed at the same high school. And there are other similarities as well."

Jim knelt down and gingerly lifted the sheet. He grimaced as he saw the wide slash in Dinkman's throat, and noted that there was very little blood, either on the ground or on Dinkman's clothes. Jim dropped the sheet back into place. "How do you think this went down?" he asked his partner.

"The throat wound's deep. Looks like an act of rage, similar to the Stritch case. The killer also stabbed Dinkman several times in the back, likely post-mortem, as there's little blood around the wounds. Dinkman bled to death, but similar to the Stritch case, as you can see, there's almost no blood. There's blood smeared on the front of his trousers. I don't know what caused that. Perhaps the killer wiped the knife on them."

"Was Dinkman killed somewhere else and the body moved?"

"Yes. The guys working the scene say that Dinkman was killed over there, where it's dark and out of sight of people using the change rooms. The coroner says there's very little blood at the primary crime scene there as well. The killer moved the body to this location, away from the footpaths, further into the shadows. The body was found when a guy's dog made a hell of a racket, and the animal's owner investigated. This is the first time we've found the body shortly after the kill. The coroner says that the time of death was no more than two hours ago."

"Is the preliminary work complete?"

"Yes. Is there anything else you want to see before I tell them to remove the body?"

"Give me a few moments." Jim lifted the sheet again, carefully inspected the neck wound, and then examined the ground surrounding the body. After several minutes, he shook his head in frustration and nodded to Gerry, who in turn spoke to the medical attendants, instructing them to remove the body.

To Doc Dicer, Gerry said, "I want the autopsy performed ASAP—like yesterday."

"It'll be ready when it's ready," the chief coroner replied tersely.

"Now then, we'll just see about that."

As they transported the body to the coroner's van, Jim Peersen said quietly to Gerry, "I think the killer arranged to meet Dinkman in the park and killed him to silence him. I wonder what it was that Dinkman knew?"

✧ ✧ ✧

The following morning, shortly after ten o'clock, Thomson parked the car on the south side of Lombard Street. An ambulance and a hearse occupied the only two parking spots on the west side of the morgue. An elderly woman walking her dog eyed Thomson and Peersen warily as they approached the building, knowing that they were entering the realm of the dead. The two detectives ascended the six stone steps of the staircase that led to the impressive wooden front doors and entered the building.

Doc Dicer gazed at them as they walked into the autopsy room, grunted, and continued working. The chief coroner looked as if he had been run over by a truck, and it was not the result of the late-night call to Earlscourt Park. After arriving back at his downtown apartment on the night of the murder, he had consumed over half a bottle of whiskey.

"The autopsy is almost finished," he said. "Give me a few minutes, and I'll tell you what I've found."

When the few minutes became more than fifteen, the two detectives decided to go out into the hallway and sit down. As they waited, they got a coffee from a vending machine. It was even worse than the coffee at the machine at the precinct. It was another twenty minutes before the chief coroner summoned them into the autopsy room.

Doctor Dicer began without any preamble. "The killer is right-handed, as the throat was cut from left to right! The seven knife wounds in the back are post-mortem. I think the killer was enraged, to the point of being deranged. There's a particularly gruesome aspect to this murder. After the stabbings, post-mortem, the killer cut off the guy's dick, and then zipped up the victim's pants. Taking time to zip him up implies that he quickly got his anger under control. A psychopath, but a 'cool' one."

"No penis was found anywhere near the scene. Wonder what he did with it?" Gerry asked.

"Some killers take a souvenir, but a dick hardly fits that category," Dicer muttered. He was well known for his strange comments.

"What on earth are we dealing with here?" Thomson muttered under his breath as he exhaled between his teeth.

Peersen said, "Well, we know that in some way it's connected to Stritch's murder. It's too much of a coincidence to be unrelated."

"But this is a male victim. No rape was involved."

"True! But the removal of the penis, similar to a rape or sodomy, is the ultimate sexual violation of a body. The Stritch and Dinkman cases are the two bookends, with the other murders being acts of compulsion, metaphorically forming the volumes in between."

Thomson eyed his partner. "Metaphorically, you say?"

"Right."

Doc Dicer listened to the two detectives theorize and continued his examination. Silence now engulfed the room. To say it was deathly silence would have been hyperbolic.

The coroner now voiced his own concerns about the case. "At the site where the body was found, there was very little blood. At the actual murder scene, behind the change rooms, there was no blood splatter on the wall or in the immediate surroundings. We know the victim bled out, yet we have found almost no blood. Do you think he drank it? After all, he took the guy's cock, so perhaps he made a cocktail."

"That's a crude pun, even for you, Doc," Thomson replied.

"A dumb pun," Peersen added sarcastically, and then continued. "In the Stritch murder, as well as the other killings, there was very little blood."

Thomson nodded, recalling that the Stritch murder had also been particularly vicious.

"The killer's rage seems to be intensifying," Peersen said grimly. "This is the most brutal of all the murders."

As the two detectives departed from the morgue, leaving behind the acrid odour of death, Thomson muttered under his breath, "There're going to be many long days ahead. Better clear your schedule, Jim."

"Yes, and we can't let the details of the mutilations reach the press. We'll keep a lid on the autopsy report and only share it with Peckerman. Remember, we have a mole in the precinct that we haven't unearthed."

✧ ✧ ✧

News of Dinkman's murder hit YCI like an avalanche, as if a mountain had collapsed on the school. Everyone spoke in hushed voices, the usual chatter in the hallways muted. Few students were fond of the vice-principal, but no one had wanted to see him murdered. Even Jimmy said nothing, and he was one of the students who had suffered the most from Dinkman's petty rages.

The following week, Mr. Evanson announced that he had appointed Mr. William Matheson as acting vice-principal. Tension increased, as Matheson began harassing students in the hallways while they rotated between classes. He patrolled the school in a manner that made old Dinkman appear lax.

The tension in the hallways among the students matched the tension among the staff members. Detectives were again interviewing every teacher, asking them to account for their whereabouts on the night of the murder. For some it was easy, and for others it was difficult.

Many teachers openly expressed their fear that another murder was in the wings. Rumours spread, fuelled by the frequent visits of the same two detectives that had investigated the Stritch murder.

✧ ✧ ✧

The final week of May, after school, Shorty and Tom saw Harry and Kramer on Alameda Avenue, walking in the direction of Kramer's house. Puzzled, they looked at each other. They realized that Harry had always been the type to forgive and forget, but they thought that befriending

Kramer was going too far. Kramer had indeed performed well on the basketball team and displayed better sportsmanship than preceding years, but they remained suspicious.

✧ ✧ ✧

Since the evening that Harry and Kramer had attended the hockey game, the truce between them had slowly developed into an uneasy friendship. They had attended a few movies together, the latest being *Alexander the Great* at Loew's Uptown. After the movie, they went to the nearby Java House Restaurant on Yonge Street for coffee. Kramer made Harry laugh as he commented on the muscular soldiers in the movie. Harry had always known that Kramer viewed the world from a different perspective to his own, but he was beginning to realize that he shared more with him than just a love of sports.

One hot day, the type that teasingly appears during May, Kramer asked Harry to help him with his math homework. Harry agreed and suggested they go to the school library. Kramer said his math text was at home, so they walked along Alameda Avenue toward Kramer's house. They were unaware that Tom and his friends had seen them depart. When Harry and Kramer arrived at Kramer's house, they were alone, as Kramer's dad was at work and his stepmother was out shopping. They spread their books out on the kitchen table. The room was stuffy, so Kramer opened the window facing the back garden. The soft breeze from outside did little to cool the air. Harry pulled out a kitchen chair and sat down at the table.

Complaining about the heat, Kramer removed his shirt, and then stripped off his undershirt. The soft illumination entering the east window highlighted his well-muscled body, the contrasting light and shadows creating an image similar to those seen in art magazines.

Harry felt a stirring within that bothered him.

When Kramer sat down beside him, he pulled his chair close, their arms and legs touching. Harry moved away as he opened the books and commenced writing out the first algebra equation. Slowly he became aware that Kramer was gazing at him, not the math question. For a few seconds, their eyes met. Harry realized that he wanted to touch Kramer, and the thought scared the hell out of him.

To allow his feelings to dictate his actions was not an option. The Lutheran Church of his parents considered physical contact between men an abomination and believed that the fires of hell awaited anyone who engaged in such a gross sin. Some people hated Jews, Italians, Germans, or Chinese. Many hated blacks, while some Catholics despised Protestants, and some Protestants despised Catholics. Everyone hated homos.

Harry tried to ignore Kramer and concentrate on the algebra equations, but it quickly became impossible. There was a masculine scent to Kramer's body, and for a second or two, he averted his eyes from the books to take a forbidden look. It was then that Harry realized he was in serious trouble.

Fearing he might be unable to control himself, Harry abruptly scooped up his math books, and stood to exit the room. As he departed, he turned to look at Kramer, who was smiling.

Before Harry could utter a word, Kramer said softly, almost in a whisper, "Not now, Harry. But soon."

Harry now realized that he had been conned. Kramer had never intended to delve into any math. He wanted to delve into something quite different. Harry was confused, hurt, and angry. The thought that dominated his mind was, *How can Kramer live with the guilt of having such unnatural feelings?*

✧ ✧ ✧

In the days ahead, Harry avoided Kramer, but like a moth to the flame, he was drawn to him, unable to shut him out of his life. Harry refused to be lured to Kramer's house but met him a few times at a coffee shop on Oakwood Avenue.

By mid-June, the classes at YCI had finished for the year, and the departmental grade-thirteen examinations commenced. Whenever they met, the sexual tension between them was like an elephant in the room. Harry refused to talk about it but was unable to resist seeing him. When Harry was alone, to avoid thinking about Kramer, he concentrated on his studies.

One evening, after completing the final cramming for his French examination, Harry prepared for sleep. He switched off his bedroom lamp and, in the dark, stretched out on his bed. As usual, his hands were cupped behind his head. He tried to relax. From the open window, he felt the warm breezes blow across his naked body. They triggered thoughts of the afternoon in Kramer's kitchen.

Images of Kramer's masculine body floated before his inner eye. He wondered how looking at anything so beautiful could be a sin. He had not intended to feel this way about Kramer. It had come from somewhere inside him, as if the feeling had been created at birth. Did God really condemn a feeling that came from the essence of his being? He had been taught that God created all things good. How could his feelings toward Kramer not be good? He knew that hatred and bigotry were evil. He had experienced them many times and seen the evil they generated.

Though confused, he began to understand that his self-loathing had been created by the world around him, a world that often ignored bigotry and hatred, yet despised the type of feelings that had grown inside him.

Then, the unthinkable happened. He imagined what it would be like to hold Kramer in his arms. It did not seem evil, as he sensed it would be an act of love. His manhood was aroused, a rare experience for him. Slowly, his hands crept toward his privates, and for the first time, he successfully pleasured himself.

When calm returned, he knew that life had cheated him. He was experiencing what other boys had experienced since they were ten or twelve years of age. A tear ran down his cheek as he gazed up at the darkened ceiling and cried to his creator, "Oh God! What am I to do?"

✧ ✧ ✧

Harry's final examination was on Wednesday, 20 June. It was chemistry. He met Kramer after school at their usual coffee shop. Had anyone observed them closely, they would have realized that this was not the meeting of two friends. They smiled and laughed as they joked and teased each other.

In the few days since Harry had admitted to himself how he felt about

Kramer, it was as if God had heard his prayer of anguish. His self-loathing had lessened to the degree that he was able to gaze at Harry directly in the eyes and derive pleasure from the feelings that stirred within him. Kramer sensed the change and responded readily.

Though guarded at first, slowly, they talked about their feelings. Kramer admitted to Harry that when he had been a kid, he had been attracted to him. Sometimes, the reason his gang had stalked Harry's friends was so he could observe him.

He admitted that his hatred of Shorty began when Shorty had punched him in the nose on that long-ago Halloween night. However, during their latter years of high school, it was because he had been jealous of Shorty's close friendship with Harry. Finally, he had understood his feeling for Harry, even though he had known that he was aroused by his own sex ever since he had been a young boy. He had recently put aside his dislike of Shorty, because he realized that he wanted to share Harry's life, and Shorty was an important part of it.

Harry admitted that he had never liked Kramer, and the change in his attitude toward him had been confusing and surprising. He said he had a long way to go before he was completely comfortable with his feelings, and that he needed time. Kramer told him not to worry. They would keep everything a secret. In due time, something special would happen between them.

Harry blanched and dropped his eyes, saying nothing further.

As neither of them would begin their summer jobs for another week, they met regularly during the next few days. They exchanged more confidences and shared ideas.

One afternoon, they talked about the murders of the members of the staff at YCI. During this discussion, Kramer confessed that some evenings he used to visit the walking trails of the Humber Valley to meet other guys. The liaisons were casual and certainly dangerous, but it was the only place he knew where guys could meet for this purpose. As the valley was far from his neighbourhood, he felt that no one would recognize him.

"I had not counted on seeing a few of the teachers of YCI in the valley, near Raymore Drive. I knew who they were, as my public school had given an induction program the previous June, and we had visited YCI. Besides, I rarely forget a face."

Kramer paused and then continued. "I saw old Matheson. Then I noticed other teachers arriving too. The following week, I followed Matheson and saw him go inside a house on Raymore Drive. I also saw Matheson on the east side of the valley, the same day that Stritch was murdered."

"Did you ever tell the police?"

"I told them about seeing Matheson, but not about the other occasions when I observed Millford, Hitch, and Miss Manson near the valley."

"You must tell them," Harry said forcefully.

"I admit that I would like to see detective Peersen again. That guy is gorgeous. I couldn't take my eyes off him from the first time I saw him. But if I tell them what I saw, they might question me more about why I was in the valley so often. It would expose me."

"Agreed. But if you don't tell the police, a murderer will remain free."

"Sorry, no way."

"All right, here's what we'll do. We'll go to the police station together. We'll say we were going to meet there to ride our bicycles. We had become friends, but because our buddies thought we were enemies, we chose a place far away from the neighbourhood. We knew they would make fun of us if they saw us, and as we were all starting high school at YCI after the Labour Day weekend, we kept quiet about it. We saw several adults in the valley. You can explain how you rarely forget a face, as you put it, and when we met them the following week in the classrooms at school, we discovered they were teachers and learned their names. Afterward, we were too afraid to admit we had seen them, as one of them might be the murderer."

"They'd never believe such a cock-and-bull story. Besides, how do we account for our coming forth at this late date?"

"Dinkman's murder. We'll tell them that it took us a long time to work up the courage, but we're now frightened as the murderer has killed for a second time and has not been caught. We'll go to the police station together and back up each other's story about who we saw in the valley."

"It's too risky."

"Kramer, this is something we need to do. We can't ignore the murders. We must help the police."

Kramer was not convinced, but he agreed to think it over.

✧ ✧ ✧

By the end of the week, Kramer realized that his refusal to do the right thing would seriously damage his relationship with Harry. At the police station, it was Peersen who interviewed them and took their statements. Peersen questioned them thoroughly, and though he thought their story sounded rehearsed and unlikely, he had no proof that it was false. It still bothered him that Kramer stared at him in an odd way. He wasn't certain what it meant, but it made him uncomfortable.

After the interview, Peersen spoke with Thomson, and they agreed that the following day they would bring down to the station the teachers whose names the boys had given. Bill Matheson they would leave alone for now, as they already knew that he had been in the valley.

✧ ✧ ✧

In the evening, after Jim had met with the two teenagers at the station, he and Samantha dined at the Sign of the Steer, a restaurant at Davenport and Dupont roads. On the wall of the restaurant that faced Davenport Road was a huge, green neon sign, its outline in the shape of a steer, its arched body and enormous horns pointing upward. Jim and Samantha approached the restaurant from the west side and entered through the enormous wooden doors.

During the salad course, Jim told Samantha about the recent development in the case, and by the time the steaks arrived and the waiter had poured the red wine in the large fat glasses, Samantha was well informed.

**The Sign of the Steer Restaurant at
Davenport Road and Dupont Street.**

As usual, Jim ignored the fact that he was not supposed to discuss police business with her. After a brief update, she agreed that the Stritch and Dinkman murders were linked, as well as the other rape/murders, as the profile of the killer was the same in all the cases.

"The killer is psychotic," she said. "He is highly attracted to women, but subconsciously hates them. After the first murder, he realized that the power created by a rape was a deep-rooted thrill, and he learned that the kill added to his excitement. I agree that the first and most recent murders were acts of rage—revenge killings. The other murders were more clinically executed. The victims were stalked, raped, and killed in a dispassionate manner. You are looking for a killer who is likely charming and sociable, his hatred well hidden from those he meets in daily life. Only when he's threatened or humiliated does his rage surface. He is extremely dangerous, and when he feels it is safe to continue, the rapes will begin again. He is a psychopath."

"Is it possible that the killer is a woman?" Peersen inquired.

"It's possible, if the woman were exceptionally strong, and in her childhood she learned to associate a male figure with extreme violence or developed a hatred of them. However, I think it unlikely, as women rarely slit a victim's throat."

Jim nodded in agreement.

Apologizing for discussing his work with Samantha, Jim now changed the subject. He talked about the ninety-seventh running of the Queen's Plate on 16 June, at the new Woodbine Race Track. The total purse had been $3,500. Governor General Vincent Massey had presented the cup to the owner of the winning three-year-old, Canadian Champ. Jim told Samantha that he had won twenty-five dollars at the track by betting on the favourite.

As they chatted, Peersen gazed around the restaurant, a habit that had been acquired since his early days on the force. In a secluded corner, he noticed Miss Taylor and Miss Allyson, engaged in an intimate conversation as they shared a meal. In a conspiratorial manner, Taylor leaned over the table to chat with Allyson. Peersen thought, *I wonder what those two are up to?*

✧ ✧ ✧

The next morning, Thomson and Peersen questioned the teachers whom Kramer had seen in the Humber Valley. Manson, Hitch, and Millford all insisted that they had not been to the valley. However, Hitch, more nervous than the others, admitted that she sometimes visited a friend who lived on Raymore Drive. She said that if anyone had seen her in the area, it was because she had been at her friend's house. The friend drowned when Hurricane Hazel swept away his house. However, she insisted that she had not been in the valley the night of the murder of Elaine Stritch.

"What was your friend's name?" Gerry inquired.

"Joe Castle. I kept quiet about the visits, as I knew that the other teachers would talk if they knew I went to the home of a caretaker."

After she departed, Thomson said, "I wonder if any of the other teachers ever visited the handsome Joe Castle?"

"If they did, it might explain why the female teachers, who were close friends of Miss Stritch, concocted alibis that covered for each other."

"It explains the actions of the female teachers, but what about the men?" Thomson pondered aloud.

"The activities in the house may have involved the men as well. What if it was a sex club?"

"That's a stretch of the imagination. These people are teachers, not exactly the downtown party type."

"True, but stranger things have happened. Besides, do you remember the background check we did on Joe Castle? As a teenager, he was arrested for 'weenie wagging' in High Park. Despite his youthful indiscretion, Dinkman recommended that they promote him to head caretaker. Also, remember that Dinkman hired all the teachers who had dubious pasts, and that they always involved some sort of sexual misconduct."

"It makes you wonder what it was that Dinkman knew, and if it was what got him killed."

In light of the new information, Peersen and Thomson realized that the pieces of the puzzle were slowly fitting together, even though the identity of the murderer remained elusive. Something was missing, and they were unable to place their fingers on it. Then, another illuminating piece of information came their way.

Miss Taylor arrived at the station. She revealed that she suspected Stritch had known something about Gregory Baldwin that had upset her. Taylor speculated that Stritch had discovered that Baldwin was having sex with the students. She also said that she thought that Mr. Dinkman knew about the "diddlings," as Miss Taylor referred to the sexual antics, and had threatened Baldwin with exposure.

After Miss Taylor departed, the detectives were not certain how to proceed. The key word in the new information was "suspected." Miss Taylor had no proof, only her suspicions. Without proof, it was all hearsay evidence.

The case had now become so convoluted and involved that Peersen and Thomson needed time to decide their next move. On the following day, Jim was attending a conference in Hamilton. They decided not to proceed further with the case until Jim returned to Toronto.

✧ ✧ ✧

On Tuesday, 26 June, Peersen arrived back at the precinct later than usual. Because of his overnight stay in Hamilton, he had not been in touch with the station during his absence, and thus had not spoken to Samantha since early the previous evening. He had driven from his hotel in the steel city directly to the police station.

When he entered the precinct door, he was aware that the officers on duty were whispering and gazing at him suspiciously. Some were smirking. When he reached his desk, Gerry Thomson suggested that they go outside for coffee. Gerry said he wanted to talk to him about something that had recently occurred.

Thomson began hesitantly. "Jim, Samantha was arrested late last night. She was charged with keeping a common bawdy house. Detective Paul Masters made the arrest."

Jim exclaimed forcefully, "This is bullshit!"

"I know. I think it's an attempt to discredit you. Masters claims that Samantha propositioned him in the Gymnasium Club last night, and that they drove back to her apartment. After their arrival, she offered him a drink and proceeded to remove her clothes as she told him that for forty dollars she was all his. When she began to undress, he identified himself as a police officer and attempted to place handcuffs on her. She resisted, and he was forced to subdue her. Her lip was split in the struggle."

Jim was furious, and Gerry tried to calm him by assuring him that Samantha was okay. As Jim got control of himself, Gerry explained that Samantha had phoned one of the best lawyers in the city, William Broda. He had already arranged for her to appear before a judge, who released her after her lawyer posted a hefty bail bond. Samantha was already at home, and arrangements had been made for a hearing before a judge the following morning to set a date for trial. Having connections had indeed been helpful.

Jim immediately rushed to his desk and phoned Samantha, who answered on the fourth ring. She was relieved to hear from him and assured him that she was all right. She told him that the legal work had already been arranged.

"Stop worrying, Jim," she said. "And don't be anywhere near me when

I see the judge tomorrow. It might be construed as interference in the case of another officer."

"I'll come up to your apartment right now."

"No. Finish your day, and I'll see you tonight. Honest, I'm fine."

Ignoring her advice, he departed from the precinct immediately and drove to her apartment. He encountered two of Samantha's neighbours as he entered the building. They gazed sternly at him and clucked their tongues in disapproval. They reminded him of two old hens, upset that the rooster had nailed a younger hen while they received nothing. Their demeanor demonstrated that they knew about the arrest. Nasty rumours always travelled faster than the news of a good deed.

That night Jim dozed fitfully, while Samantha slept comfortably. When dawn arrived, he was a wreck and felt that only a gallon of hot coffee would save him from self-destructing. Samantha dressed in a green wool dress with a stylish black leather belt and walked confidently out of the building.

✧ ✧ ✧

Inside the courtroom, Samantha and her lawyer, William Broda, waited in the hallway outside Courtroom Six. Broda was a short balding man, impeccably attired in a navy-blue suit. He and Samantha sat on a wooden bench as Broda explained his strategy. Everything had been arranged, Broda assured her. A few minutes later, they were summoned by a court clerk, and they entered the courtroom of Judge Anthony Nerroni.

Judge Nerroni was an imposing man, in both physical size and professional status. His large head and chiseled features resembled Zeus more than a mere mortal. Young lawyers feared him, and those who were more experienced had learned to be leery of his alert mind and quick temper. His enormous bulk and personality completely dominated his courtroom.

It was after ten-thirty when Judge Nerroni granted Broda permission to approach the bench. The prosecuting attorney also stepped forward. Broda placed several affidavits in the judge's hands and requested to present extenuating information in Judge Nerroni's chambers. The judge scanned the documents Broda had handed to him, and then passed them to the crown attorney, who blanched as he read them.

After a few moments, Judge Nerroni banged his gavel on the bench to recess the court. Rising from his chair, he waved his beefy hand to indicate that the lawyers should follow him to his chambers. With a dramatic flurry of his billowing black robes, the judge disappeared through the oak-trimmed doorway, and after the others had entered, the heavy door thudded shut.

Judge Nerroni seated himself heavily into his chair and continued to peruse the documents Broda had provided. After several minutes, he placed his glasses on his desk. He gazed up, his bushy eyebrows arched, and requested that the bailiff summon Detective Masters to appear in his chambers. As they waited for Masters to arrive, the creaking of the judge's chair, straining under the weight, was the only sound disturbing the silence.

After Masters arrived, the judge instructed him to recount the details of the arrest, as stated in the charges. Masters recited from memory. When Nerroni had finished, he inquired if Masters had any details to add from his notes. Masters removed his black logbook from his jacket pocket, thumbed through it, and after several minutes officiously stated, "No, Your Honour. The incident occurred exactly as I stated."

"Of course, you know you will be required to restate them, under oath, in my courtroom, when the trial occurs."

"Yes, Your Honour."

"Very well. Mr. Broda, will you ask the bailiff to bring in the tape recorder that you say you have provided."

Silence again gripped the room, and Paul Masters wondered what was occurring. For the first time, his smug look faltered. He knew that something important was happening but was unable to determine what it was.

When the play button on the recorder was pressed, the sound of someone knocking on a door was heard. Next, recorded voices filled the judge's chambers.

"Police. I have a warrant. Open the door."

There was a long pause, more rapping noises, and then a woman's voice said, "Hold your badge and warrant up to the peephole."

Another pause followed, and they heard the sound of a lock being turned and a door opening.

Then a man's voice said, "Guess what, Spankie old dear? I don't have a warrant. I think it's time for you to service me. Get your clothes off. I'm horny as hell."

It was the voice of Paul Masters, and everyone recognized it.

The woman's voice was obviously Samantha's, and she was heard responding, "If you want sex, you're in the wrong apartment. There's an elderly woman down the hallway who might want you, but I certainly don't. There's also a young man on the floor below me, if that's what you prefer."

There was the sound of a slap and a crashing sound, as if someone had fallen to the floor.

"Don't fool around with me. You're a cheap whore. Well, not cheap in the dollar sense, but cheap nevertheless. Service me or I'll arrest you."

"What charge?"

"Operating a common bawdy house."

"I'll never have sex with you, and no amount of money could ever make it happen."

There was the sound of another slap and a struggle. After a brief pause, the apartment door banged shut. Broda switched off the tape recorder.

An ominous quiet descended over the room. Judge Nerroni's bulk shifted in his chair as he gazed intently at Masters, and then in a threatening tone he snarled, "Detective, do you wish to revise any of your statements?"

The blood drained from Master's face.

"Detective, are you aware of the seriousness of making a false arrest, fabricating evidence, and uttering false testimony?" Nerroni inquired.

Masters said nothing but continued to stare in disbelief. Like a weasel in a hunter's snare, he was trapped.

"Bailiff, escort the good detective to a private room in the Chateau de Jail. See that he has the finest gourmet bread and water. When a representative from the police association arrives to assist him, notify me. And get Chief of Detectives Peckerman on the phone. I want the department to begin the process to relieve the detective of his duties, permanently."

Turning to William Broda, the judged thanked him for bringing the case to a swift close so that the court's time was not wasted.

◇ ◇ ◇

Later that evening, at Basel's Restaurant at Yonge and Gould Streets, Jim and Samantha celebrated over a quiet dinner. She explained that one of her clients was a sound engineer at the CBC. He had convinced her of the danger of entertaining men in her apartment and had offered to wire her apartment for sound, placing microphones in every room. At the end of each two-week period, she erased the tapes. In this instance, it had been her salvation.

Next, she informed Jim that she was retiring from the business. She had acquired sufficient money to establish a trust fund to finance a halfway house for women who wanted to escape working on the streets. William Broda had assisted her in the legal work, and with the help of an investment broker, the earnings would keep the establishment operating in perpetuity. She said she had enough money remaining for her to live comfortably.

As they strolled north on Yonge Street toward Jim's car, they passed the Imperial Theatre. *The Sixth of June,* the story of D-Day, was playing. Jim felt that with Samantha's release from all court charges, and her retirement from her risky business, was as great a victory as that of the soldiers that had landed on the beaches of Normandy. *Sometime in the future, I will have my revenge on Paul Masters,* he thought.

The view is looking north up Yonge Street from Front Street in 1958. The bank building on the left is now the Hockey Hall of Fame, and the attractive building on the right has been demolished. In the foreground on the right, behind the fencing, the O'Keefe Centre (now the Sony Centre) is under construction

✧ ✧ ✧

On a Saturday afternoon, Kramer and Harry journeyed downtown to Varsity Arena on Bloor Street to attend a charity fundraiser, sponsored by the Maple Leaf Hockey Team. George Armstrong gave Harry his autograph. Afterward, Shorty and Harry went to a restaurant that had opened just two years earlier, the Swiss Chalet, at 234 Bloor Street, across the street from Varsity Stadium. It was the first of what was eventually to become a successful chain of over two hundred eateries throughout Canada and the United States.

Sitting in a booth near the rear of the restaurant, they chatted and enjoyed the barbequed chicken. Kramer informed Harry that he had something he wanted to tell him, something that had bothered him for a long time.

"I vowed I'd never tell anyone what I am about to tell you, but I guess it's time I told you about Patrick McCaul."

Harry tensed.

"Patrick was raped in the Amherst laneway."

"What are you talking about?"

"That's why Patrick committed suicide. They tore off his pants, and while two guys held him down, the third guy buggered him."

"How do you know this?"

"Because the guy who did it, bragged about it. He said that he told me because he knew that in the past I had also ridiculed Patrick. I didn't tell anyone, as I was afraid what might happen to me if he ever discovered I told. Besides, he might find out about me."

"Seems to me that you've been afraid to tell a lot of things in order to protect yourself," Harry responded scornfully. Then he added, "Your attitude toward Patrick was despicable. It was one of the reasons that I used to despise you."

"I know I deserve that," Kramer replied and averted his eyes, unable to look at Harry.

"Why did you torment Patrick so mercilessly? You accused him of being what you actually were."

"I don't know. I can't explain it. I've lived with the regret every day since he committed suicide."

"Who did it to Patrick?"

"Tim Wilkinson—Wilkie."

"That jerk made Patrick's life miserable ever since that day in the shower room. I never knew about the rape. My God, how Patrick must have suffered."

"I know I cannot right the wrong that I did, but I think it's time we did something to avenge Patrick," Kramer said determinedly.

Harry gazed at Kramer, now diminished in his sight. He admitted that he did indeed want revenge for the suffering Patrick had endured.

"You're right," Harry answered. "The school year is over, and we don't know where Wilkie lives, but we know that he'll be at the dance at Casa Loma. Let me talk to Shorty and see if we can come up with a plan."

As they walked away from the Swiss Chalet, Harry thought, *Kramer's treatment of Patrick will always be a cloud that that hangs over our relationship.*

✧ ✧ ✧

The evening of the dance at Casa Loma, Kramer and Harry, along with their dates, joined Carol and Shorty, Jimmy and Paula, and Sophie and Tom. Jimmy's dad drove them in his pickup truck. Sophie and Carol were in the cab, while everyone else piled into the back. Mr. Frampton dropped them off two blocks from the castle, so their friends would not see them getting out of the truck. They wanted to appear at the iron gate like sophisticated adults. Passing under the great stone archway that surrounded the huge doorway, they entered Henry Pellet's palatial home, with its fancy turrets and towers.

The band was playing "The Theme from Picnic" as Sophie and Tom stepped onto the dance floor. Sophie was beautiful, her dark hair pinned up, the curls on her head reflecting the soft glow from the ornate sconces lighting the room. Tom thought she had never been lovelier. He kissed her cute little nose, and as she smiled up at him with her smoldering brown eyes, he knew that she was the girl he wanted to be with for the rest of his life.

Gazing around the dance floor, Tom recognized many of the students from his grade-thirteen year. He nodded to a few of them, while he and Sophie moved around the floor. The students looked mature in their formal attire, and Tom imagined that if Sir Henry Pellet could gaze over the assembled crowd, he would have thought it as grand as any group that ever visited the castle during the days when his home was the most sought-after venue for the elite of Toronto.

Songs such as "The Great Pretender" and "You've Got the Magic Touch," both made popular by The Platters, were well received, but the hits that brought the teenagers to life were Elvis Presley's "Hound Dog" and "Don't Be Cruel." While Tom and Sophie were dancing to the latter, they passed by Tim Wilkinson and his girlfriend. Tom ignored him. He had never liked him since the day he had been so cruel to Patrick. Besides, of all the guys at the school, he considered him the crudest. He had once heard a girl in his class mutter under her breath, "Wilkie is as sophisticated as a turd in a punch bowl."

The evening passed quickly, like all good times, and before they knew it, the bandleader was announcing the titles for the final set of songs for the evening. Sophie and Tom were too absorbed in each other to notice Wilkie leaving the ballroom to go to the washroom. Later, Tom learned that Wilkie had hidden a small bottle of vodka in the tank of one of the toilets, and throughout the evening, he made numerous visits to the washroom to sneak gulps from it.

✧ ✧ ✧

When Wilkie opened the washroom door, he was too preoccupied with finding his elicit alcohol to notice Shorty, Harry, and Kramer walking in behind him. When he entered the washroom stall, as he was lifting the lid on the toilet tank, they grabbed him from behind and overpowered him.

Before Wilkie was able to catch a glimpse of the avengers, his head was shoved in the toilet. Each time they pulled him to the surface for air, a voice snarled, "Remember Patrick McCaul? We know what you did in the laneway."

Then they blindfolded him, stripped him of everything except his socks and underwear, and tied his hands behind his back with his shirt. They marched him out of the washroom, still blindfolded, so he was unable to see where they were taking him. Within a few seconds, he was standing in the doorway that led to the dance floor. They pushed him into the ballroom, at the same instant removing the shirt tied around his hands. Then they slammed the door shut so he was unable to retreat. Wilkie now tore off the blindfold.

The laughter that followed echoed off the walls of the old castle. Kramer and Harry continued to hold firmly shut the door leading to the hallway where the washroom was located. Wilkie had no way to escape other than the main entranceway. To reach it, he had to cross the entire dance floor. Many of the girls watching his marathon run shrieked with laughter, while the guys joined in the catcalls and offered crude remarks.

"Hey, Wilkie, take it all off!" a guy shouted.

"Hey, cute buns," a girl screamed.

"Why not show your whole self?" another girl yelled, the way she said the word "whole" displaying her real meaning.

When Wilkie reached the entranceway, blocking his path was Mr. Matheson, and standing beside him was the august Mr. Tyrone Evanson. Matheson, wishing to impress his boss, decided that as acting vice-principal, he should establish his authority and take charge of the situation. He grabbed Wilkie by the arm and roughly pushed him back into a small alcove inside the doorway.

"Cover yourself, you idiot," Matheson demanded. "No one needs to see the sight of your ugly butt."

"They dunked me ... they dunked me," Wilkie sputtered.

"I don't care what they did. If you had not interfered in things that were none of your business, this likely wouldn't have happened. Cover yourself and get the hell out of here."

"I need to get my pants and find out who dunked me."

"There's no way you're going back on that dance floor," Matheson screamed and shoved Wilkie unceremoniously through the outer doorway.

By now, Wilkie was almost hysterical, and in his desperation, he forcefully pushed Matheson out of his way. Caught by surprise, Matheson stumbled backward and crumbled to the floor. Suddenly, Wilkie was standing in front of Mr. Evanson, who bellowed at him to leave the scene. Wilkie turned and fled outside into the castle's courtyard. Helplessly, he stood on the brick paving stones and pleaded for someone to go into the washroom and retrieve his pants.

Inside, lying on the floor in the hallway, the dazed Matheson looked up and saw Evanson towering over him, a fierce expression on his face.

"Matheson, it sounds as if you know what caused the boys to perform this prank?"

"Wilkinson is a corn-holer. He buggered the McCaul boy," he blurted out without thinking. "He and two other boys ..." Then he stopped, realizing what he had admitted.

Evanson's eyes narrowed in disgust. He sputtered accusingly, "You knew what he did and said nothing?"

Defensively Matheson stammered, "I overheard Wilkinson bragging about it, along with two other boys. They were outside the door of the science lab. Of course, I did nothing. It wasn't my responsibility to police the activities of queers."

"But the McCaul boy committed suicide. Didn't it occur to you that their actions had something to do with him hanging himself?"

Frustrated, he shot back, "Sure, but I considered it none of my business."

"You are an irresponsible son of a bitch," Evanson spat in disgust. "I'll see you in my office tomorrow morning."

Matheson gazed at his boss as he strutted imperiously from the scene. Matheson knew that his job as temporary vice-principal had likely arrived at an abrupt end. Standing up, he rubbed the back of his head, as he realized that he had hit it against the stones of the wall when he had fallen backward.

◇ ◇ ◇

While Matheson staggered away from the scene, the band was playing the Elvis Presley hit, "Love Me Tender." Sophie and Tom were on the dance floor enjoying the final song of the evening.

After the dance, Jimmy's dad picked them up at the pre-arranged spot, not far from the castle, to drive them home. While they were travelling along St. Clair Avenue, Harry and Shorty told Tom what they had done to Wilkie and the reason for their actions. Tom now learned what Wilkie had done to Patrick. He was horrified and felt pleased that Wilkie had suffered such a humiliation. Tom resented that they had not included him in their plans to avenge Patrick. In addition, he was surprised that Harry had participated in such a wild scheme, as it seemed out of character for him. Tom was unaware that Kramer had planned the strategy.

✧ ✧ ✧

The following morning at YCI, Matheson's footsteps echoed in the empty halls of the school as he approached the office. The students had departed for the year, enjoying their holidays, and he was marching to his dismal fate. He thought, *Evanson is such an old pussy. Damn it, it's not my job to interfere with the criminal acts of queers. Rape was too good for that wimpy McCaul kid. He got what he deserved. Being raped isn't the worst fate in the world.*

When he entered the office, he saw the dour face of Mrs. Applecrust peering at him. He was certain that she knew what had happened to Patrick McCaul. Slowly, it began to dawn on Matheson how much trouble he was in.

The old secretary said nothing, but thought, *Being an asshole must be a prerequisite for the job of vice-principal. With Dinkman gone, and Matheson on his way out, I guess they'll place an ad saying, 'Asshole wanted.'* As usual, she would never have uttered such foul language aloud, but she still considered a few bad words not too great a sin, if they were self-contained.

Entering the chambers of Tyrone Evanson, Matheson was greeted by the sight of Detectives Thomson and Peersen, seated in chairs opposite the principal's desk. They listened as Matheson tried to excuse his behaviour. The more Peersen heard, the more enraged he became. He remembered the sight of young Patrick's body hanging from the rafters of a garage on that dismal gray February morning, something that would haunt him until the day he died. Yet, here was a man who had known about the rape of the lad and said nothing.

Although Peersen was seething within, he remained quiet as his partner explained to Matheson the seriousness of his actions.

Then Gerry stood to his feet as he said, "William Matheson, I am arresting you for criminal indifference."

As they departed the office, Matheson in handcuffs, Peersen wondered if Matheson was capable of worse crimes, since he obviously considered rape a matter of no importance to the victim. It crossed his mind that the charge of criminal indifference might be difficult to sustain but not an indictment for murder.

✧ ✧ ✧

Frank's editor at the *Toronto Trib* requested that he write an article about the aftermath of Hurricane Hazel. As it was June, Frank thought it odd to be writing it as this time. He would have preferred to write it in October, the month the disaster occurred. Apparently, a flood in India had inspired the editor to want a flood article at this time. Frank would rather have pursued a political story, either international or national, but he could not ignore a direct request from his boss.

He decided to locate a survivor from Raymore Drive, the street where the floodwaters had swept away all the houses. After an hour's research, he located the address of a woman, who now lived on Edenbridge Drive. She agreed to the interview. She had been in her house when the swirling waters had hit.

Looking north on Yonge Street toward Yonge and Queen Streets in 1958. The Simpson's Store (now The Bay) is on the left.

✧ ✧ ✧

The interview was not what Frank expected. The woman was overweight, in her late-sixties, and seedy in appearance. Her teeth were yellowed by many years of heavy smoking. Frank began by asking her about her life following the terrible tragedy. Then he asked her about the night of the storm. The elderly widow told her story in detail. Time had not dimmed her memory.

She told him that she and her husband had been in the house, and described her terror as the force of the water ripped her home off its foundations and swept it downstream. When the wreckage lodged against a group of trees, a fireman extended a ladder to her. She grabbed hold, held on, and eventually her rescuer pulled her to safety. Her husband drowned.

Two hours later, her son found her. She told Frank that the son had been away for the evening with three of his friends, buddies from York Collegiate Institute, which he used to attend.

"Your son attended YCI?" he asked.

"Oh, yes. We used to live on Atlas Avenue, before we moved to Raymore Drive. My son, Sammy, played on the basketball team. Coach Millford thought the world of my son," she said proudly. "I used to see Mr. Millford often, as he and other teachers from the school frequently visited the house next door to us on Raymore Drive, in the late hours of the evening." Then she hesitated, unsure whether to say anything further.

Frank urged her to tell him more about Mr. Millford and the teachers.

A gossip at heart, she complied. "I hate to say it, but those teachers were up to no good," she whispered conspiratorially. "The man, who owned the house where they visited, was a real looker, the Rudolph Valentino type. You know what I mean? His name was Joe Castle. He was the head caretaker at the high school where the teachers taught. Some evenings, the noise at his house lasted until the wee hours of the morning. I often heard the shrieks and screams. They were the kind of noises that mean only one thing … if you get my drift."

Frank decided to be direct, so there was no misunderstanding what she was implying. "Do you think the teachers were having sex at the house?" Frank stated bluntly.

"Well, if they weren't, then I'm a virgin."

"Do you remember if they had a soirée a few nights prior to the Labour Day weekend in 1951?"

"A what?"

"A soirée—a wild party."

"Why don't you speak English? Do I look foreign to you?"

Clearly irritated, she finally continued. "Well, it's a long time ago, but I can remember it quite well. My nephew and his wife had a baby boy that August, just before the holiday weekend. On that particular evening, they phoned to tell me the news. I had to shut the window to keep out the damn noise from next door, so I could hear what my nephew was saying. Yes, it was the thirty-first of August in 1951. I send a gift to the brat every year, and they never so much as send a thank-you card. You know, the younger generation is going to hell in a handbasket," she added, smacking her lips with satisfaction.

When Frank departed the house on Edenbridge Drive, he had a good story about Hurricane Hazel, and its effects on those that the storm had directly affected. However, the information on the teachers at YCI was a greater story. The teachers had been visiting a house on Raymore Drive on the night that Stritch was murdered. This opened up a can of worms. The teachers had lied about their whereabouts, and now he knew why their stories all covered for each other.

Frank thought, *I doubt that the cops know about this. Should I tell them, or should I work the angle by myself?*

✧ ✧ ✧

Peersen was catching up on his paperwork as Sergeant Malloy approached and informed him that Miss Taylor was at the outside desk and asking to see him. This was her second visit during the last few days, and Peersen wondered what had brought her back to the station. A few moments later, Peersen and Thomson escorted her to an interview room and Peersen pulled out a chair for her to sit down.

"What can we do for you Miss Taylor?" Jim inquired politely.

"Well," she began hesitantly, "last night I had a conversation in the Dominion Store, on Oakwood Avenue, with Debbie, whom, as you know, was Mr. Dinkman's wife. She said that the grocery prices were becoming too expensive for her, and she was having problems making ends meet. She said that she had decided to sell the house on Ashbury Avenue, as she was unable to afford the expenses, even though she had no mortgage."

"Why is this important to our investigation?"

"Well, last night, after I went to bed, I thought about her words. I remembered that the night Dinkman came over to my place, he bragged, after a few drinks, that he had a safety deposit box full of cash. He implied that it was for his personal use after he got rid of Debbie. I ignored his remark, as I certainly did not intend to share his miserable life, even if he were a free man and rich. It occurred to me that Debbie must remain unaware of the safety deposit box or else she would not be so short of money. In the box in the bank, there might be proof of what Dinkman knew about Baldwin. Perhaps Baldwin committed an indiscretion that Dinkman knew about. I know that Baldwin hated Dinkman with a passion that bordered on murderous hate."

After she finished, she stopped and gazed at Peersen and Thomson. They asked her a few more questions, and after another several minutes, they thanked her, and she departed.

After Miss Taylor left, Peersen discussed with Thomson the information she had provided. They agreed that Baldwin was too light in his shoes—fairy light, as Peersen liked to say—to have raped the women. However, one never knew. Baldwin might be bisexual, and it would explain him buggering the Adams boy. They also reasoned that a guy like Baldwin might enjoy cutting off a man's penis.

"All the murders were committed after Baldwin returned to Toronto following his vacations in France," Peersen said. "Several of the kills were on the Labour day weekend."

It also occurred to Jim that perhaps his theory of the murders had been wrong. There was no serial killer. The Dinkman and Stritch murders were unrelated to the others. Was it possible that someone had killed Dinkman and Stritch to silence them?

They knew that they could not ignore Miss Taylor's information. They were also aware that it would require time to find the bank where Dinkman rented a safety deposit box, as well as time to obtain a court order to have it opened. It could be weeks before they had sufficient proof to approach Baldwin with a warrant in hand.

They decided that the following day they would visit Baldwin and unofficially ask a few preliminary questions to rattle his cage, hoping that it might cause him to make a mistake. They would assess his reactions and decide if there was sufficient cause to apply for an arrest warrant. If they charged him, they could keep him in custody until they were able to locate the safety deposit box. However, if it turned out that Baldwin had murdered Dinkman, they remained unsure if they had a suspect for the other murders.

As they were leaving the precinct for the day, they noticed that at the front desk, Frank Gnomes, the *Trib*'s infamous reporter, was haranguing Sergeant Malloy, who was clearly not amused with the rough teasing he was receiving. When Gnomes spied Peersen coming along the hallway, he turned away from Malloy. Frank had known Peersen since his university days.

"Well, Jimmy boy, how's my favourite detective at the station?"

Peersen grimaced, as he was aware that Frank's words might cause the other men to suspect that he was the mole at the precinct.

"I doubt I'm your favourite anything, Frankie boy. What does a fink like you want with me?" Peersen responded with a half-hearted grin.

"I thought it was time we shared a little information."

"Your idea of sharing is usually getting something and giving nothing in return."

"My, my, but we're cynical today."

After a minute of two of bantering, Peersen said, "Cut the crap, Frank. Do you have anything worth sharing?"

Frank nodded.

Peersen motioned for him to follow him to an interview room, where Frank told him about the sexual activities of the teachers of YCI and their visits to Raymore Drive. Thomson and Peersen now had their suspicions confirmed as to why the teachers had banded together.

"Thanks for the heads-up, Frank," Peersen said. "If you get anything new, call me," he added as a casual brush-off.

"Do I get any brownie points for this little visit?"

"As my partner likes to say, 'Now then, we'll just see about that.' If anything happens that's newsworthy, I'll try to give you a heads-up."

"Is that a promise?"

"No, but for old time's sake, I'll do my best."

As Frank exited the station, he gave Malloy another dig. The sergeant almost leaped from behind his desk in anger as Frank Gnomes waltzed out the door. Peersen shook his head in amusement as he watched Frank disappear. Despite the reporter's outrageous antics and flippant manner, he had to admit that he respected his tenacity and analytical abilities. He also knew that he was likely the only one at the precinct who did.

✧ ✧ ✧

The following morning, Peersen and Thomson drove out of the parking lot of the police station to visit Baldy Baldwin. They proceeded to Gerrard Street. It was a clear and sunny day, and they hoped that the good weather was a sign that they would accomplish their objective.

They parked illegally on Bay Street, walked the short distance to Baldwin's second-floor apartment in a Victorian bay-and-gable house, and rang the doorbell. Several minutes later, Baldwin appeared at the door. It was past eleven o'clock, but he was still dressed in his housecoat. He smiled flirtatiously at Peersen, but his grin disappeared as he looked at Thomson.

Baldwin inquired curtly, "What do you two want?"

The slight whistling in his speech and lisping voice made him sound more effeminate than usual.

"Is it convenient for us to come in and talk?" Thomson replied.

"Do you have a warrant?"

"No."

"Then it's not convenient."

"Okay, we'll wait until you get dressed, and we'll talk at the station."

Baldwin looked at them intently as he assessed the situation, remaining composed and in control as he mulled over their request.

"Do I need a lawyer?"

"We're not arresting you. We simply want to ask a few questions."

"Okay, wait here while I get dressed."

He left the door open a crack as he ascended the stairs.

Peersen and Thomson waited impatiently. It was almost ten minutes before Baldwin shouted from the top of the stairs for them to go up.

Baldwin had donned a charcoal gray suit, neatly pressed as if it had just arrived from the dry cleaners. The burgundy tie and well-starched white shirt added to his carefully chosen outfit. Despite the early hour, he walked over to the teacart containing liquor bottles and poured three fingers of scotch.

A man who drinks this early in the day is not a man to be trusted, Thomson thought, ignoring Baldwin's antics as he proceeded directly to the reason for their visit.

"Mr. Baldwin, I know this is an inconvenience, but we have questions that we need answered. As you will soon be leaving for France for the summer, we thought it best to interview you immediately."

"What do you want?"

"We have learned new information."

Baldwin placed his drink on an end table. "What information?"

"You were having sexual relationships with the students. Dinkman discovered your little perversion and blackmailed you, and that's why you killed him."

Gerry did not state the accusations as speculative or say they thought he might be, but stated them as if they were known facts. He hoped to frighten him into a confession or at least making a slip.

Baldwin stretched out his arm and admired his gold cufflinks, and then, he calmly raised his drink again to his lips. Cool as a cucumber he stated, "The accusation is ridiculous."

Peersen continued to bluff Baldwin into thinking they knew more than they really did.

"We know that you were in Earlscourt Park the night of the murder."

Then he provocatively asked, as he smirked knowingly, "You cut a souvenir from Dinkman's body. What did you do with the guy's dick? Shove it up your ass?"

Baldwin's facial expression changed instantly. It was as if a switch had flipped. His condescension disappeared like a mast thrown to the stage floor, and in its place, pure hatred and rage enveloped him. In one swift movement, he threw the glass of whiskey toward Peersen, the liquid spilling over the expensive rug. Deftly, he snatched a revolver from behind the liquor bottles on the teacart, and before Peersen or Thomson were able to react, he was pointing the gun directly at them. Peersen noticed that Baldwin had already removed the safety catch.

The bastard was well prepared, Peersen thought.

Gone was the polished, well-educated French teacher with the prissy manners. Standing before them was an enraged killer. Peersen knew he was gazing into the same horrifying eyes that Baldwin's victims had seen during the final seconds prior to their death. Chills shot up his back.

"Who are you to judge me?" Baldwin snarled viciously, his voice as hard as steel and equally as cold. Thomson and Peersen found it difficult to believe he was the same man they had interviewed on previous occasions.

Keeping the gun pointed at them, Baldwin shouted toward the bedroom hallway. "Come out here and help me to play a little game."

Then he turned to his captives and explained. "I was having an intimate session with a student when you arrived at my door. You should know better than to disturb a man during playtime."

As they waited, from the end of the hallway, they heard a bedroom door open. Peersen wondered if it were one of the boys on the basketball team. Perverts like Baldwin usually preferred teenagers with well-developed muscles. The footsteps, though catlike, were clearly audible as they approached the living room.

To their astonishments, a scantily clad girl, about fifteen or sixteen, with a pretty face and slim, immature body, appeared in the doorway. It was now obvious that Baldwin had faked his effeminate manner to avoid any suspicion that he was sexually involved with his female students. The teenager smiled at Peersen as she gazed at Baldwin holding the gun. Her expression was of amusement, as if she were observing a game.

"Cuff the two of them with their handcuffs," Baldwin ordered her. "You'll find them behind their backs, attached to their belts."

"We're policeman," Gerry said forcefully.

"Oh, that's part of the game," Baldwin told the girl. "You handcuff them, and we can all have a wild time."

The young girl smiled, anticipating the antics that would occur once she had handcuffed the two men. Meanwhile, Baldwin held the gun steady, ensuring that if he fired the revolver, he would not miss. When the handcuffs were in place, he instructed the girl to fetch three blankets from his bedroom cupboard. It was several minutes before she returned, the blankets cradled in her arms. Peersen recognized the striped pattern on them. They were thick Hudson's Bay blankets. Baldwin told her to wrap one around each of the men and one around herself. As she placed the blankets around them, Baldwin held the gun steady to ensure compliance.

Thomson warned, "You'll never get away with this."

Baldwin grinned at the girl, as if Thomson's remarks were also part of the game. Then his smile changed to a sadistic smirk, and the deafening sound of gunfire echoed through the room. The girl slump to the floor, a bullet through her chest. Peersen was certain that she was dead before she hit the floor. The odour of cordite filled the room. Thomson now realized that Baldwin was completely insane.

"Notice," Baldwin explained dispassionately, "how the blanket absorbs the blood oozing from the wound. No blood-spatter either. She will join you tonight in the lake with the little fishies. It's a pity, but leaving a witness alive is extremely foolish."

"Blood seems to fascinate you," Thomson said, trying not to show any fear in his voice.

"The flow of blood is always fascinating," Baldwin replied in a calm, cold voice.

Peersen said, "That gunshot will soon bring the police here."

"I don't think so. No one will arrive here for many hours. You didn't have a warrant, so you have no backup. No one will think anything of the gunfire. The Chin Family, who lives below me, is in Hong Kong. A loud noise is par for the course in this busy neighbourhood. Cars backfire all the time. As for the bodies, they will not be found for a few days, as they will be in the lake. They'll drift to shore eventually."

Baldwin laughed malevolently, his back toward the door, to facilitate an easy escape. His hand remained steady as he aimed the gun at his two captives. He continued to keep his distance from them. If either detective attempted to hurl himself at him, he would be able to shoot him first.

Peersen knew he was going to die, but unlike in the movies, his past life did not flash before him. He thought of the future he would never have. His life with Samantha had been regrettably short. His hopes disappeared that someday he and Samantha might marry, have children, and grow old together. If the fates blessed them, they might even have had grandchildren. Now, it was just a faded dream. A sudden death was all that waited him.

✧ ✧ ✧

Earlier the same day, Miss Bettina Taylor had finished her morning coffee and cereal, and was sitting in her housecoat out on the second-storey veranda that overlooked Holland Park Avenue. Mary Allyson was still asleep. Finishing her coffee, Bettina glanced at her wristwatch. She had an appointment with revenge, and it was time to get dressed. As she opened her clothes closet door, she thought of Gregory Baldwin. She was pleased with her decision to have visited the police the day before. Now, she had to discover if the police had acted on her information.

She had not always despised Baldwin. Her first year on staff at YCI, she had found him charming and amusing. When she and Elaine Stritch became roommates, she was aware that Gregory and Elaine were close friends, but also knew that they were not lovers. One Saturday afternoon, Elaine had suggested that she join her and Greg for coffee. This was how she became acquainted with Greg in her out-of-school hours.

Elaine did not object when Gregory and Bettina became lovers. Elaine was the only teacher on staff who knew about their relationship. She was certain that if the other staff members discovered their secret, they would shun them. They were such prudes.

At first, when she and Greg were together, he was kind and considerate. She had not minded sneaking around to make love; she thought that it added to the adventure. Bettina remembered the evening they had dined at La Chaumiere. He had ordered the entire meal in French and talked romantically to her.

Slowly, his attitude toward her changed. The more sex he had, the more he wanted. He seemed unable to control his compulsions. Then his behaviour altered further. He became increasingly moody, irritable, and prone to fits of sudden anger when denied sex. One evening, he attempted to initiate masochistic sex into their lovemaking. She refused, and he dumped her.

After their relationship ended, when they were at school, he remained debonair and charming toward her—a cosmopolitan man of the world. However, she knew that he despised her. She was also aware that several members of staff were ambivalent toward Gregory. Some of the teachers considered him not masculine enough for their tastes.

Others, such as Elaine Stritch, adored him. Though Taylor knew that Baldwin was not Mister Macho, he was masculine where it counted. Besides, he was great to be with. A cup of coffee with Gregory was always interesting, and accompanying him to dinner a treat, as he was familiar with the best restaurants in the city, ones that others were unable to afford. In addition, he could discuss theatre as if he had been on the stage during the performance.

Then a month after Greg ended the affair, to her horror, she missed her period. The child was Greg's. She discovered the hard way that he had not always taken precautions. When she told Gregory about her predicament, he laughed and told her to go to a back alley and get an abortion.

"That's what a whore always does," he had cruelly taunted.

Her doctor, whose office was on St. Clair near Avenue Road, sympathized with her situation. Most doctors treated unmarried women who were pregnant scornfully, as if they were the scourge of society. She would never forget his kindness. He provided her with a certificate declaring that she required time off school for health reasons. Before her pregnancy was obvious to others, she left for Vancouver to stay with her sister. The final week of July, she gave birth to a boy. He was two months premature. At first, it had appeared doubtful that he would survive. The doctor placed him on a special bottle formula, rather than having him breast-feed.

Labour Day was on the first day of September that year, so she left the second week of August to return on the train to Toronto to begin the new fall term. It was a tiring journey. Her heart ached to be with her infant son, but she was well aware that she was unable to afford to give up her teaching job. Each month, she had to send money to support him.

Her sister wired her twice a week to report on the progress of the child. By the final week of September, he was out of danger. She smiled as she remembered the telegram that simply said, "All's well. Growing like a weed." The boy was now a healthy four-year-old.

Bettina and Mary Allyson, the school librarian, were friends. Taylor had learned to ignore Mary's weepy ways, and although Mary was interminably shy with most people, she seemed comfortable with Bettina. Mary was older than she was and nearing retirement. When Bettina had confided in her that she had a son, Mary Allyson sat in the coffee shop and cried with joy. Amid the tears, she declared that if Bettina required assistance to raise the boy, she would love to help.

Finally, Bettina and Mary decided to live together. Mary told her that she would take early retirement in two years' time, and then they could bring the boy to Toronto. They would raise the child as a couple, the lad having two mothers. Bettina smiled as she remembered the day they had agreed on the plan.

Going to the police station had been the first steps Bettina had taken to extract revenge on Gregory Baldwin.

On this sun-filled morning in June, the school year had ended, and apart from some grade-eleven exam papers to mark and a couple of staff meetings, her time was her own. There remained one last thing she wanted to do.

✧ ✧ ✧

Peersen continued to stare at Baldwin. He knew that the only reason that he had not pulled the trigger was that he wished to toy with his prey a little longer. Levelling the gun directly at Peersen's chest, Baldwin clarified which of his victims would die first. His laughter was high-pitched as he taunted them.

The delay saved Jim's life.

Baldwin's back was to the door, and he was unable to see it silently open. Its well-oiled hinges, the product of a meticulous mind that disliked anything being out of order, made no sound. A hand appeared through the opening and reached for one of the solid mahogany sculptures, located on the end table beside the door. As the door swung open further, the heavy object thudded into the centre of Baldwin's back. The gun dropped to the floor.

As Baldwin fell, he raised his arm to defend himself against another blow, but the mahogany weapon struck his uplifted arm, and the sickening sound of breaking bones was heard. Baldwin crumpled to the carpet, whimpering as he defensively held up his other arm. The third blow hit the arm, and the fourth blow struck him violently on the head. The sound of crunching bones sent shivers up Peersen's spine. Baldwin did not move.

Emotionless, Bettina Taylor gazed at the lifeless shape on the living room floor. Her revenge was complete. Her foe was vanquished.

Bettina located the handcuff keys and freed the two detectives. Peersen immediately bent down and felt for Baldwin's pulse. It was weak, and his breathing was almost non-existent.

Thomson immediately phoned for an ambulance. Then he called the precinct. Within minutes, they heard the wail of a siren as an ambulance approached. The nearby Toronto General Hospital had dispatched it to the scene.

Peersen, Thomson, and Bettina watched as the medics examined Baldwin. The young medic shook his head and said, "I'm sorry, but the man's gone."

Bettina muttered under her breath, "The bastard's gone to hell, where he belongs."

❖ ❖ ❖

Later, Taylor told the police that she had arrived downtown earlier in the morning and maintained surveillance on Baldwin's apartment. She had hoped that she might see the detectives drag him out in handcuffs. The detectives were already inside when she arrived on the scene. When she heard the gunshot, she went into the house to see what had happened. After listening outside the door, she crept inside and managed to rescue the detectives.

Later, when the police scoured the crime scene, they discovered Dinkman's penis in a small plastic container. At the bottom of a clothes hamper in the bedroom, they found a cloth bag containing seven bottles of blood, each one labelled with the names of Baldwin's victims, including Stritch and Dinkman.

The following day, Peckerman held a conference, and with more pomp than a coronation, smugly announced to the press that his police department, under his expert guidance, had solved seven crimes. He then explained that Baldwin had been a serial killer, provided details of the various murders, and ended with announcing that the killer was dead.

Peckerman did not mention that his department had arrested the wrong person for the Rosedale Valley murder.

✧ ✧ ✧

In the Following Days

Shorty and Tom were sitting on the veranda of the Hudson home, chatting about recent events. Their high school days were behind them, June was coming to an end, and the summer lay ahead. They saw Jimmy crossing the road, in his hand a copy of the *Trib*. Something important must have happened, as it was rare to see Jimmy with a newspaper.

As he approached the veranda, he held up the front page. On it were pictures of Mr. Baldwin and Miss Taylor, as well as a house on Gerrard Street. They knew that the photos of their former teachers were from the school's yearbook. There was also a photo of a teenage girl. The caption said that she was a student at YCI. They recognized her face but did not know her personally.

As they eagerly scanned the paper, they were shocked to read that Mr. Baldwin was dead, and that he had killed Mr. Dinkman and Miss Stritch. In addition, the police confirmed that Baldwin had committed five other murders.

Stunned into silence, the three boys huddled around the newspaper. They had always considered Baldy Baldwin a bit of a joke and thought his worst crime was butchering the French language, not to mention how he had slaughtered the English tongue. Sitting in his classes for the past five years, declining the verb and memorizing vocabulary, they had never considered that he might be a serial murderer. Though he had strutted like an ostrich, he had been a raptor in disguise.

As they read the front-page article, they recognized the names Peersen and Thomson, the detectives whom Mr. Baldwin had held at gunpoint. They smiled nervously at Frank Gnomes' description of Miss Bettina Taylor, who had apparently killed Mr. Baldwin.

The article began by saying, "Similar to Sampson in the Book of Judges, who slew a thousand men with the jaw bone of an ass, with a mighty blow, Bettina Taylor felled the killer with a mahogany statue..."

Aware of Miss Taylor's strength, they remembered how she had ruled her math classes with an iron hand, but felling a killer was not a deed that they had thought within her abilities. The article also stated that though Miss Taylor had killed Mr. Baldwin, the police considered it had been necessary to save the lives of the two detectives.

✧ ✧ ✧

As they were discussing the turn of events, they saw Mrs. Klacker coming up the street. They ignored her. Her nose was high in the air while she imperiously strutted along the sidewalk. She was sporting a new spring outfit that she had purchased from the Holt Renfrew department store.

The outfit was a total departure from her usual attire. The skirt was robin's-egg blue, the frilly blouse a pale shade of yellow. Her skirt matched her broad-brimmed hat, a fancy white ribbon trailing down at the back of it. The outfit seemed more appropriate for attending a formal garden party than visiting a grocery store. Despite wearing new clothes, she had not discarded her clunky, brown heavy oxford shoes. She sailed up the street like a cumbersome battle cruiser with colourful sails, but a battle cruiser nonetheless.

Tom remembered his mom telling him that during the war years, Klacker had employed her vicious tongue against those of German, Japanese, and Italian heritage. Now, she considered herself the moral guardian of York Township. Neighbours who employed foul language, drank alcohol, or failed to attend church regularly, she grouped together with the "heathens" who attended synagogues and temples. Her greatest moments of glory were when she discovered that someone had engaged in "illicit coupling," as she referred to it. Another highlight of her existence was learning that a couple was "cohabitating in sin." She loved her "hundred-dollar words" and never missed an opportunity to employ them. Her fancy vocabulary extended to individuals whom she said were "beneath her station in life." Jimmy was one of them.

Of all the boys on Lauder Avenue, she had singled him out. Because Jimmy was short, skinny, and freckled-faced, in her eyes he was odd. She said that if he survived his teenage years he was "destined to be an incorrigible criminal." Whenever she saw Jimmy on the street, she told him that he was "bound for incarceration."

Jimmy watched her strutting along the sidewalk and said, "I've suffered her bullshit for years. She's a mean bitch."

Tom thought about Jimmy's words. When he had been younger, he had ridiculed Mrs. Klacker, but she was now more of a threat than a joke, as she might discover that Sophie had an illegitimate child. He knew the woman did not like Sophie, as she was Catholic and Italian. Klacker had often seen him in the company of Sophie, and they had not escaped her vicious tongue, but the abuse had been mild compared to what she would hurl if she found out about Sophie's baby.

The boys continued reading the newspaper and digesting the information about Miss Taylor and how she had rescued the detectives. As they turned over the front page, to where the article continued on the second page, Tom noticed that Jimmy was watching Klacker as she approached Mr. Marlton's Store.

Jimmy left the veranda and stealthily walked over to the side of the store, where a rope was hanging down. Tom had not noticed it before. Unknown to him, early in the morning Jimmy had climbed to the roof of the store and positioned a pail of water above the door. The bucket was not visible, as it was on a ledge above the second floor. Old Klacker opened the door, anxious to display her Holt Renfrew outfit to the neighbours inside the store.

Jimmy yanked on the rope. He had timed it perfectly.

The cascade was like pent-up waterfalls. Klacker was directly under the full stream of the downpour. It plummeted from two storeys above, flattening her hat, which now resembled a huge soggy pancake drooping over her head. Her blouse and skirt were sodden, clinging to her body. Not that anyone would have cared, but her brassier was visible through the wet material. Streams of water dripped from her skirt, forming an ever-enlarging puddle at her feet.

Thoroughly shocked, gasping for breath, and sputtering, she wiped the water from her face with the back of her hand and removed her soggy hat. Then she spied Jimmy peering around the corner of the store, and although she had no idea how he had done the deed, his grin told her that he was the creator of her misfortune.

"You criminal miscreant and foul-mouthed little shithead," she screamed. Then she stood in shock as she realized she had said a cuss word. From the veranda, Shorty and Tom shook with laughter. Old Klacker realized that her superior vocabulary had deserted her, and this added to her rage. As the boys were no longer small kids whom she could browbeat, she retreated.

Klacker never turned around. Walking away, her back toward Jimmy, when she heard his laughter, she raised her hand in the air and gave him the finger. This unseemly gesture increased his laughter, and it continued until she reached her house and went inside.

The women in the store never received the supreme thrill of viewing a genuine forty-dollar, Holt Renfrew outfit. News of the prank soon spread, and Klacker was now the subject of the petty gossip, rather than the source.

✧ ✧ ✧

The following evening, Tom was returning home after attending a movie with Sophie. He was tired, as he had worked the morning and afternoon shifts at Greenberg's Pharmacy. Tom had delivered many heavy orders, since Ruth remained in jail. She had been caught in the back of the van having sex with a customer. When the police caught them, Ruth was enraged and resisted arrest. The officer's partner arrived on the scene, and it required the two of them to subdue her. Mr. Greenberg finally decided that it was time to hire another driver, but he had not yet found one.

Arriving near home, despite the darkness, Tom saw that Nan and Gramps were sitting on the veranda. The night was unusually hot for the end of June. His grandparents were quietly observing the street scene as they waited for their bedroom on the second floor to cool.

As he approached the steps that led to the veranda, Tom saw Mrs. Martha Klacker approaching from the other direction. Within seconds, she was blocking his path. She knew he was one of the teenagers who had witnessed her humiliation, and she gave him a look that would have curdled cream. He excused himself as he passed in front of her to walk up to the veranda.

"I'll never excuse you, young man. Your behaviour is despicable."

Tom assumed she meant his laughing at her predicament the previous day. Her rant continued. "It's bad enough that you're hanging around with a Catholic girl, but she's not even Canadian."

Tom was stunned.

"What's the matter? Is your own kind not good enough for you?" she added sarcastically.

From the veranda, Nan and Gramps could hear her. Gramps stood up from his chair to step down to the sidewalk. Without a word spoken, Nan placed her hand on his shoulder to motion for him to sit down again. Before Tom knew it, Nan was standing on the sidewalk beside him, facing the enraged Martha Klacker.

Nan appeared small and insignificant beside the bulky Mrs. Klacker. However, Nan remained calm, stared at Klacker, and said, "God gave you two ears and one large mouth. You should listen twice as much as you talk. If you listened more in church on a Sunday morning, that foul tongue of yours might learn a little kindness. Now, off with you, old woman, before I get my broom and swat you like a broody hen in a cloth bag on a clothesline."

"Mind your own business," Klacker responded indignantly.

"If you'd mind your own business instead of everyone else's, I wouldn't need to be here on the sidewalk speaking with you."

Nan motioned for Tom to go up on the veranda. They walked away from Klacker, who stood rooted to the spot in disbelief. Tom heard her mutter, "This used to be such a nice neighbourhood."

As Tom reached the safety of the veranda, Gramps said to him, "I married quite a gal, don't you think?"

Tom grinned as Nan sat down again in her favourite chair. He gazed toward the sidewalk, but Klacker had slunk away into the shadows.

✧ ✧ ✧

Gerry Thomson was relaxing in his favourite chair in the backyard, nursing a half-empty bottle of Molson's. He had pulled back under the lilac bushes, the foliage shading him from the hot afternoon sun. On the grass beside him was a novel he had been trying to read. He had placed it down. His mind was elsewhere. Finally, he pulled his old straw hat over his eyes and retreated into his world of thoughts.

Ruth's voice disturbed his reverie. She was standing beside his chair, gazing down at him.

"What's the matter, dear? You haven't been the same since the incident on Gerrard Street. It's been a week now. I thought that having the past few days off work might do you some good, but you seem to be brooding. What's troubling you?"

"I feel old."

"What's brought that on?"

"I should have spotted the similarities in the murder cases. It never dawned on me that we were dealing with a serial killer. My little red pins failed me. I'm the senior detective. I've more experience. I should have seen the connections. I think I'm too old for this business."

"No one could logically have seen the connections."

"Jim did! He's younger and more up-to-date."

"You did your best."

"Yes, but it wasn't good enough. Besides, I helped send an innocent man to prison for the murder of the girl in the Rosedale Ravine."

"I know that troubles you. However, it wasn't your case, or he would never have gone to jail in the first place. Come on, what else is bothering you?"

Gerry removed his old hat, wiped the sweat on his brow, and gazed up at her. Ruth knew him better than he knew himself. Yes, there was something else.

"I kept placing suspects into pigeon holes where I thought they fitted, instead of carefully following the evidence."

"I think you're being too hard on yourself." Then she thought for a few minutes and continued. "Times are changing, and so are police methods. You can adapt."

"I'm not certain I can. The city I knew so well is disappearing. People from all over the world are coming to Toronto, bringing with them strange ideas and their own set of prejudices and values. Neighbourhoods that remained the same for decades are now changing overnight. People are moving to the suburbs, and immigrants are flocking to the downtown area. My little red pins can no longer keep track of suspects. People live in Scarborough or Etobicoke and work in the inner city. Everything is expanding. Suspects live miles apart, and connections are impossible to trace."

"You'll cope."

"I wonder."

As Ruth returned inside the house, Gerry pulled his hat over his face again. He wasn't certain that he could function in the new world facing him.

✧ ✧ ✧

The first day back at the precinct, Chief of Detectives Arnold Peckerman summoned Jim to his office. Peckerman congratulated him on a successful conclusion to the Dinkman murder and the Stritch case, as well as the five other homicides. Then Peckerman rose from his chair, came out from behind the desk, and sat on the corner of it, gazing down at Peersen who remained seated.

"Jim," he began in a fatherly tone, "I have great respect for your abilities. The department thinks highly of you too. The chief believes you have the qualities that would make for a future chief of detectives, and someday, perhaps the chief of police. You have the finest mind of any detective on the force."

Jim sensed that a "however" was coming.

"However, there is one thing that bothers the chief, and I admit that it's a problem for me too. Your relationship with Miss Anderson. Her lifestyle is highly questionable. As well, the department frowns on its officers living with women unless they're married. Everyone knows that you and that woman are sleeping together. A police officer's life must be beyond reproach, able to stand the test of public scrutiny, especially if he is in a senior position. Are you aware of the station gossip?"

"Very aware. It's cruel, petty, and none of their business."

"Well, it's my business. I run this precinct, and I want all my officers to tow the line."

Peersen gazed at his boss for a few moments. Then, without saying a word, he stood to his feet, opened the door, and walked out.

Peckerman gazed after him. He was shocked that one of his men had walked out on him but felt pleased that he had placed his cards on the table. *Sometimes,* he thought, *it is best to be blunt with young officers. Peersen has a brilliant career ahead of him. Why should an indiscreet affair with a hooker ruin his chances of promotion?*

The next morning, Jim walked into Peckerman's office, having opened the door without knocking. Peersen placed an envelope on Peckerman's desk and again walked out without saying a word. Peckerman opened the envelope—it was Jim's resignation. It would become effective at the end of the month.

The resignation shook Peckerman profoundly. He had never had an officer defy him in such a manner. He knew there would be hell to pay. The best detective on the force, perhaps in the entire city, was now lost to the department. Just as Peckerman was considering what course of action to take, he saw Gerry Thomson entering his office, also without knocking on the door.

"It is true?" he inquired. "Has Jim really resigned?"

Peckerman's stunned silence provided Gerry with all the confirmation he required.

"So, it's true. Jim's leaving the department. He told me that he wanted to start his own detective agency. He's done it! What a shot up the rear end that will give the department. That guy will solve crimes while you guys sit around picking your noses."

"Quiet, Thomson, or you'll join him out the door."

"Damn right I'll join him. I'm giving you my resignation too. I'll be leaving at the end of October, when I have served sufficient time to receive a class-B pension. I'm taking early retirement and intend to be Jim's partner in his new venture, if he'll have me."

"You're kidding me!"

Gerry's final words were, "So long, Peckerhead. Fire me if you want. Before you'll be able to build a case against me with the police board, I'll be retired."

✧ ✧ ✧

That evening, Jim was already sitting out on the deck enjoying his first drink when he heard Samantha unlock the apartment door with her key. He placed his glass of scotch aside and walked inside to greet her. Their lips met, as he held her tightly against him.

Despite the turmoil of the past week, Samantha sensed that Jim was relaxed. Smiling, she accepted a glass of white wine, and they strolled out onto the deck. Jim mumbled an expletive as one of the squirrels raced across the deck railing and leaped to an overhanging branch. "Silly little bugger," he exclaimed as the squirrel gazed saucily back at him, eyeing him safely from its perch on the tree.

"Life's full of silly little buggers," Samantha responded.

"True," he responded as he grinned. "However, today I flushed a few of them down the drain."

He then told Samantha about the resignation he had given Peckerman. Before she had a chance to inquire about his future plans, he explained that he intended to apply for a private detective's license and that Gerry wanted to join him as a partner. In the meantime, his earnings from his investments would support him until his new enterprise flourished.

At first, Samantha was too surprised to react.

In the intervening silence, Jim raised his glass. "Here's to all the silly little buggers of the world," he declared.

Their glasses clinked in unison, the sound reverberating softly in the warm evening air. Jim smiled, sat down, and slouched in the chair as he extended his legs up onto the wooden railing. He gazed impishly at her and smiled over the rim of his glass as he sipped, clearly pleased with himself. He was also pleased that he had not allowed Peckerman to push him around. He did not tell Samantha about the demands that his police boss had delivered the previous day.

After a second drink, he said, "It's hot. I don't feel like cooking dinner, and I don't want you fussing with it either. Let's have another drink and then walk down to the Swiss Chalet on Bloor Street. I just want a half chicken and salad."

"Fine. I'll have a chicken salad."

It was after eight o'clock when they strolled down the tree-lined streets of the Annex toward the restaurant. When they arrived at the Swiss Chalet, there was a line up. The weather had induced many others to skip preparing a meal and to dine out. After fifteen minutes, the hostess escorted them to a booth near the rear on the right-hand side. As they sat down, a waitress was clearing a table opposite them to accommodate two more diners. Two teenagers arrived and occupied the table.

Samantha and Jim did not bother with the menu, as they already knew what they wanted. While Jim considered his choice of salad dressing, Samantha gazed at the teenagers that had just arrived and noticed that they were both broad-shouldered like football players. Then she thought, *They're certainly a handsome pair.*

Jim and Samantha gave the waitress their orders, and then chatted about Jim's new venture. Surreptitiously, Samantha gazed at the teenagers again. The young men were clearly enjoying each other's company, and though there was nothing overt, she sensed that they were a couple. There seemed to be an intimacy between them. They leaned close toward each other as they conversed, as if in a private world of their own. Then, one of them reached out and touched the other's hand. It was a small gesture, but the body language that accompanied it confirmed her thoughts.

A few minutes later, one of the teenagers turned his head and, for the first time, noticed Jim. The lad quietly whispered something to his partner. The other boy turned and looked at Jim. Sensing that the lads were watching him, Jim glanced sideways and for the first time, looked directly at them. One of the lads stared back at him and smiled.

Jim realized it was Horace Kramer. He now sensed there was something different about the lad. The sulking, reticent teenager of former years had disappeared. Jim was now gazing at a confident young man. Then he noticed that the teenager sitting beside Kramer was Harry Heinz, whom he remembered well, as the boy had always impressed him.

Jim spoke to the teenagers, and they responded in a friendly but wary manner. The conversation continued, and Samantha sensed that there some sort of bond between Jim and Harry. She was unaware that the suicide victim that Jim had cut down from the garage in the Amherst laneway had been a close friend of Harry's.

Within a few minutes, the lads were at ease, and as they continued conversing, the usual light banter that develops among males bubbled to the surface. They lamented that the Leafs had not made it to the play-offs and speculated on the Argonaut's line-up for the forthcoming football season.

The mood of the conversation changed when Harry said, "Detective, I never told you how much it meant to my friends and me that you were at Patrick's funeral. It was a long time ago, but we still remember."

Jim dropped his eyes. The suicide of the McCaul boy remained a festering wound within him. After learning that the Wilkinson boy had brutally raped him, the cruelty of the deed had added to his deep feelings of anger over such a young life having been lost. He would have arrested Wilkinson if he had any proof that he had committed the crime against Patrick in the laneway. As Harry continued to speak, Samantha asked the boys to share their booth with them. They were reluctant, but Jim motioned to them, and they complied.

Jim changed the subject by enquiring about the teenager's plans for the summer. Harry informed him that he was going to work in a law firm. In the fall, he would enter the faculty of arts and science at the University of Toronto. He eventually intended to enter law school, and when he was able, open his own practice.

Kramer said that he was taking a job as the assistant manager of the

U-Clean Laundromat on Yonge Street, as well as the coffee shop above it, and planned to attend night school to take business courses.

He grinned as he said, "I expect to be a millionaire by the time I'm thirty." Then he added, "I'm trying to convince Harry to share an apartment with me in the downtown area, where he will be able to walk to classes."

Harry smiled, but said nothing about Kramer's suggestion.

"Detective, I guess you'll spend your summer solving crimes," Harry said, changing the subject.

"Strange that you should mention my plans for the summer," Jim responded. "I resigned from the police force today. I intend to spend the next few months obtaining a license to operate as a private detective. My partner, Detective Thomson, has expressed an interest in joining me. I think he's crazy to give up his job at the precinct, but he says he wants to take early retirement."

"After I pass my bar exams and set up my own practice," Harry said, "if clients require an investigator to help with their defense, I hope I can recommend you and your partner."

"That's a long time off, but stranger things have happened."

Their meals arrived, and the conversation rolled easily as they enjoyed the food. After they finished eating, the small bowls of lemon water arrived for them to rinse the chicken grease off their fingers. When the cheque arrived, Jim insisted on paying the bill. Harry and Horace objected but finally accepted and thanked him for treating them.

Outside the restaurant, they shook hands, said goodbye, and wished each other a safe and happy summer. Samantha was surprised when Kramer gave her a hug and told her she was one of the most beautiful women in the entire city. She was delighted with the compliment and kissed him on the cheek.

"I think you really will be a millionaire by the time you're thirty," she said.

They parted. As Samantha walked away with Jim, she turned and gazed back at the two handsome teenagers. She noticed that Horace had his arm draped over Harry's shoulder, and it was obvious to her that she had been correct. There was an intimacy between them that hinted at more than just friendship.

Turning to Jim, she said, "We've not seen the last of those two. They're remarkable young men."

Jim said nothing, but thought, *I bet Harry Heinz will do amazing things with his life. He's an extraordinary lad.*

✧ ✧ ✧

On the evening of Saturday, 30 June, Shorty and Carol went to the St. Clair Theatre. On their way home, they took a shortcut through a narrow laneway that connected Northcliffe Boulevard and Lauder Avenue. The film at the theatre had been a love story, and as they walked through the darkened laneway, the warm summer air seemed ripe with romance.

In a secluded spot, where the night shadows were deep, they stopped and embraced. They wrapped their arms around each other, their bodies pressed together. Their lips were eager, their tongues probing deeply. Carol felt Shorty's arousal, but she was unable to retreat from his embrace, as her back was against a garden fence. Besides, she did not wish him to stop.

During the next few minutes, Shorty forgot the vow he had made to Tom not to be intimate with Carol before they married. It was as if fate was programming their destiny, and it was beyond their control. The kissing became more fervent, their hands exploring intimately. Their passions and desires overwhelmed them, and within moments, though in a standing position, they removed sufficient clothing to be open to each other.

Then, as Shorty fully accepted her nearly naked body, Carol uttered a muffled cry while pain shot through her, but when it died away, ecstasy replaced it. Shorty created heights of arousal she had never before experienced. Though passionate, he was gentle, sensing that it was her first time going all the way. Their lovemaking became more intense as they enjoyed the intimacy and passion. Each time they almost reached fulfillment, Shorty held back, and then deepened the lovemaking once more, creating feelings of excitement that were beyond description.

When they had reached total satisfaction, the intensity subsided. They held each other as if the world was ending and some unseen force might tear them apart. Life could never recreate such a moment again. The beauty of young love had triumphed.

As Carol was fastening the buttons on her blouse, she glanced away. Shorty placed his hand under her chin, turned her head toward him, and gently raised her face to his own. Despite the darkness, in his eyes she sensed the depth of his love. A warm tear trickled down Carol's cheek as she returned his gaze. Before he was able to speak, she said, "Oh, Shorty, it was wonderful. I love you so much. I never dreamed that our first time would be like this."

Then she hesitated before adding, "I never wanted our first experience to be against a backyard fence in an alley."

"I didn't either. But whether it was against a wooden fence or in the royal suite at the Royal York Hotel, I could never love you more. It was the first time that you were truly mine, and I was truly yours. The location was not as important as the love we felt for each other."

The absurdity of the location of their first lovemaking suddenly caused them both to grin. The grins slowly turned into conspiratorial giggling and then to laughter.

Shorty's usual mischievous ways surfaced as he said, "Carol, in the future, we may be the only couple in all of Toronto that is sexually aroused by the sight of a backyard fence." He grinned impishly.

Carol smiled. "We should have a wonderful sex life then, as everywhere we go in the city we'll see a fence. Perhaps we will have to live our lives indoors."

She then tenderly gazed at him and caressed his cheek. "Let's get out of this laneway," Shorty said.

As they strolled up Lauder Avenue, he said, "It's time to stop calling me Shorty. My high-school days are over. I'm entering the adult world, and I want to be called Bernie. With the horrible name that my mom and dad gave me, I think that Bernie Bernstein is the best compromise. Agreed?"

"Agreed."

Continuing up the street, arms around each other, Shorty earnestly poured out his feeling to the girl that he had loved for as long as he could remember.

"I wanted to make love to you so much that I ached," he confessed. "You are the only girl I ever wanted. I want to marry you. A long time ago, I vowed that our wedding night would be special. It still will be, even if I have to drag a wooden fence into the honeymoon suite."

"On that night," she said, as she giggled at the thought of a fence in the honeymoon suite, "it will be the first time for us as man and wife, and that will be special too."

Shorty regretted that he had not been a virgin before the encounter in the laneway. He also knew it was best to leave the past in the past. Ruth had been his teacher in the techniques of having sex, but she had been unable to teach him anything about the art of love. This had come from within him.

During the summer ahead, Shorty would be working for a construction company to help pay his tuition fees at the University of Toronto. Then he was facing at least three years of university studies. He intended to enter the Ontario Education College and qualify as a high school teacher. He wanted to teach PT. To receive his certificate would require another year after graduating from university. It might be five or six years before he would be financially able to marry Carol.

Carol was also thinking of the years ahead and gripped his arm tighter as they proceeded up the street. She told Shorty, "In the fall, I'm enrolling at Shaw's Business College to earn a secretarial diploma. Money will be tight, and I know it will take a few years before we can marry, but it will be worth the wait.

"However, there is something else. My parents are not too happy that I'm dating you. They'll be really angry when they find out that we intend to marry. My parents don't want me to marry a Jewish person, but I think they would change their minds about you if you converted to Christianity. How do your mom and dad feel about you marrying a gentile?"

"The decision will be mine. My parents will allow me to choose my own religion and my bride. I have already chosen to accept the Jewish faith, and I cannot give it up. It's not just my heritage, it's who I am."

They walked on in silence. The optimism of youth allowed them to believe that somehow a path would open for them. They knew that the older generation had difficulty accepting diverse lifestyles. Where others had failed, they felt they would succeed, finding a way to overcome the hurdles that would arise during the years ahead. Perhaps they were right. After all, it is often those who refuse to accept the unacceptable that change the world.

✧ ✧ ✧

Tom's parents went to bed early on the final Saturday in June, and as usual, within minutes Mr. Hudson was asleep. After his wife nudged him with her elbow, he drowsily opened his eyes.

"Thomas," she said urgently, "we need to talk."

"About what?"

"Tom and Sophie."

"Oh, well, yes, I've been thinking about them too," he replied sleepily.

"What do you think of Sophie?"

"I don't know her all that well, even though she has lived on the street for many years, but from what I've seen, I like her."

"I like her too. I'm proud of the way Tom has behaved toward her. We've always tried to teach him not to judge the quality of a person by the church they attend or their nationality. He loves Sophie as he knows she's a good person."

"I think she'd be a good wife for Tom," Mr. Hudson responded. "I'm glad that he finally told us about her son. Tom will be a good father to the boy, especially knowing that his father was his friend Patrick."

"Tom would be a good father to the boy no matter who his father was."

"True. However, I think we need to talk with the Cellini's and see how they feel about Tom and Sophie eventually marrying. I have a feeling they will be against it. Because I'm Tom's father, perhaps I should talk to them. It's important to Italians that the man of the house makes the decisions."

"How little you know. Mrs. Cellini rules the roost in that house. We must convince her to give Tom and Sophia a chance. We'll go to see them together."

"I guess you're right. I'll talk to Mr. Cellini and see if there's an agreeable time."

"Good. Now you can go to sleep."

"No more elbows?"

"You're safe, unless I think of something else."

✧ ✧ ✧

After breakfast the following day, Tom watched as his mom and Nan prepared to go to church. He did not intend to go with them. During the last year and a half, they had been attending an evangelical congregation on Oakwood Avenue, as his grandmother had been finding it difficult to travel the distance to attend The Salvation Army, which had been her place of worship for decades. During the past few years, she had often sighed wistfully as she declared that growing older had its share of problems. For her, changing churches had been one of the most difficult.

The events of this particular morning became a part of the folklore of the Hudson family. After they returned from the service, Tom's mom informed Gramps what had transpired, and he told Tom. Everyone in his family is still familiar with the tale.

This is what happened.

✧ ✧ ✧

It was a cloudless morning. The streets were quiet as Tom's mom and Nan ambled along at a leisurely pace. They arrived at the church on Oakwood Avenue a few minutes before the eleven o'clock hour. They sat down in a pew just as the choir was entering the church.

As the service commenced, the singing was spirited, and the congregation clapped their hands when they sang words of the lively chorus of the hymn: "In the blood, in the blood, are you washed in the blood of the lamb?" The sermon was long, and although Tom's mom was uncomfortable with its simplistic viewpoint, she approved of the young Pastor Jones' sincerity. She was also impressed with his knowledge of the Bible. He was able to recite numerous verses from memory.

After the sermon, the prayer service commenced. The congregation softly sang well-known choruses and silently prayed for sinners to repent and return to the Shepherd's fold. Sometimes, the pastor and other well-meaning members of the church mingled among the congregation and talked with selected people, urging them "to decide for Christ." They referred to the custom as "fishing for souls." Tom's mom was silently praying, her eyes closed, when she felt a hand on her shoulder. Looking up, she saw it was Pastor Jones.

"My dear Mrs. Hudson, have you anything for which you wish to repent?"

Startled, Tom's mom gazed up at him.

He continued. "I understand you have allowed your son, Tom, to date a girl who is not a born-again Christian, and that they intend to marry. In the book of John, it states that only those who are 'born again' can enter heaven. We must all live our lives according to the teachings of the Bible. Do you wish your son to be condemned by God?"

Tom's mom hesitated, unsure what to say. She was shocked that a minister of the gospel could be so narrow-minded and judgmental. Finally, she said to him, "Pastor, do you live *your* life according to the teachings of the Bible?"

"Of course, my dear."

"Then why aren't you in jail?"

"What on earth do you mean?" he replied, the shock evident in his voice.

"The Bible says we must stone to death those who work on the Sabbath. In Deuteronomy, it states that we should stone to death our children if they believe in the wrong gods. If you ever did such a thing, you would be imprisoned. The scriptures also say that if you touch the skin of a dead pig, you are unclean. I saw you playing football at the church picnic last summer. Didn't you touch the leather ball? Are you unclean? According to the Bible, you are. Then, there are the verses that demand that you do not plant more than one kind of seed in the same field or wear clothes made of more than one type of material? As well, according to the Bible, it is okay for you to own a slave or two, if they are not from your own tribe. I guess that means you can't have a Canadian slave, but is okay to own a Mexican."

"Mrs. Hudson, you are being disrespectful."

"No, pastor, I'm simply applying your own logic. You are arbitrarily choosing the verses in the Bible you wish to obey, the ones you wish to interpret literally, and the ones you have decided to ignore. Like the Pharisees of old, you have great knowledge of the word of God, but very little insight into their meaning. Worst of all, you fail to grasp the love of Christ, which is the most important message of the Bible. You have no right to sit in judgment of others. The Bible says that we should not judge others or He will judge us. You have no right to judge my son Tom or his girlfriend."

The pastor stared at Tom's mom as if he were gazing at the worst moral criminal he had ever encountered.

"If your faith means anything to you," Tom's mother continued, "then think about it. Examine it and use the brain that God gave you. Stop accepting teachings simply because the church and other clergy have always taught them. Think about them. Probe. You might find the exercise enlightening."

"Mrs. Hudson, you have committed the grave sin of arrogance."

Tom's grandmother had heard the entire exchange of words, and at this point, she looked up and met the preacher's gaze. Reaching out her hand, she rested it gently on the pastor's arm.

"Young man," she began in a soft but firm voice, "I'm afraid that your sin is far worse than arrogance. You have committed the sin of extreme ignorance. When you have lived as long as I have, you might learn that ignorance within the church does more harm than all the atheists in the world could ever do. They breed bigotry and prejudice that ruins lives, and worst of all, they hide behind the Bible to excuse their inexcusable actions."

The pastor was stunned. He was not accustomed to having his teachings challenged. Regaining his composure, he replied, "My dear woman, you're talking to your pastor."

"Yes, and I'm talking to a pastor who is wet behind the ears." Then Nan quoted the words from the first book of Corinthians (chapter 13, verse 11). "'When I was a child, I spake as a child, I understood as a child, I thought as a child: but when I became a man, I put away childish things.'"

Then she added, "Sonny, it's time for you to grow up."

Lost for words, the pastor stammered for a moment or two and then retreated up the aisle, having lost his zeal to convert sinners. He had no wish to battle verbally any further with Grandmother Hudson. He had found her tongue sharper than the sword of Gideon.

As Tom's mom and Nan departed the church, Nan said, "I hope the young pastor prays about what I told him. If his prayers are answered, he'll be a wiser man when he steps into the lions' den again."

Tom's mom chuckled as she said, "Never mind the lions' den. You were quite a pussycat yourself."

◇ ◇ ◇

It was late, and the china clock on the mantle in Jim Peersen's apartment had finished striking a single resonant chime to denote the early morning hour. Jim was in his bathrobe, a brandy snifter in hand, mulling over the events of the day. Absentmindedly, he thumbed through the morning's mail, hardly noticing the envelopes, even those that contained dividend cheques.

His thoughts wandered back to when he and Gerry had discussed Gregory Baldwin's autopsy with Doc Dicer. The chief coroner had summed it up by saying, "It's rare to examine a corpse that has had such extreme violence inflicted on it, especially by a woman. Every place where Baldwin was struck, the bones and tissue looked as if they had been hit by a truck. I guess dead men tell no tales."

The coroner's final statement remained with Peersen: "Dead men tell no tales."

On this evening, the statement still bothered him. Had Miss Taylor's rage been from past hurts, or an attempt to silence Baldwin? Peersen had always known that Taylor was physically strong. She was also a clever woman.

Then he remembered that Miss Taylor had supplied the information that had implicated Baldwin. Many other thoughts now tumbled in Jim's brain. As he strolled down the hallway to his bedroom, he thought, *I think the Taylor woman deserves closer examination, and I'd best do it before my resignation becomes effective.*

✧ ✧ ✧

Peersen decided that he should visit Miss Taylor again, on the excuse of a routine follow-up, and see if he could push her buttons a little and provoke a reaction. The following day, he arrived unannounced at Taylor's flat on Holland Park Avenue. She had just returned home from school minutes before. Taylor was cool toward him but accepted his reason for visiting. Shortly after the interview began, Miss Allyson entered the flat. It was unusual for her to arrive home at such an early hour, and she became flustered when she saw that Peersen was with her roommate.

While Peersen explained to Miss Taylor the follow-up details of the case, he inquired if she had suffered any nightmares due to the horrific events in Baldwin's flat. She said it had been difficult, but she had managed, and gave Jim a forced smile to demonstrate her appreciation of his concern.

Gazing across the room, Jim noticed that Miss Allyson had picked up a small photograph of a young boy. It had been in a silver frame on the mantle. Allyson gazed fondly at the picture, almost cooing as she looked at the picture.

Taylor stomped across the room and grabbed the photograph from Miss Allyson's hand. Peersen was surprised at the depth of the rage and had no idea why Allyson's actions had provoked such anger. Within seconds, Taylor contained her fury and assumed her usual demeanor. The incident confirmed Jim's thoughts concerning Miss Taylor.

Leaving the flat, Jim thought, *Beneath Taylor's professional façade lurks deep anger.* Peersen decided it was time to discuss his ideas with Thomson. As usual, Gerry retreated to his little red pins and said that he could see no discrepancies in Taylor's original alibi. However, because of his newly found respect for Jim's theories, he suggested that they recheck every aspect of her statement.

After checking and rechecking, they discovered no discrepancies. Next, they revisited the man who owned a variety store on Oakwood

Avenue. In the original investigation in 1951, he was one of the persons whom they had questioned about seeing teachers in the neighbourhood on the evening of the murder. He had stated that he did not see any of them on that particular night. This was not unusual, as it was impossible for him to notice everyone that passed in front of his store.

However, on this occasion he said that he had recently learned something new from the son of one of his neighbours. In 1951, the boy had been a student at YCI. The shopkeeper suggested that they interview the young man, as he had recently said that he had seen one of the teachers on the evening in question.

After receiving his name and address, they visited the young man, who confirmed that he had seen Miss Taylor the night of the murder. He said that he remembered, because she had been his math teacher that year. "I saw her boarding a Rogers Road streetcar at the corner of Oakwood Avenue and Rogers Road."

"What time was it?"

"Shortly after nine. Even though it happened a long time ago, I remember the time as the variety store was closing."

"What direction was the streetcar headed?"

"The streetcar was westbound, travelling toward Bicknell Avenue."

Thomson was aware that at the end of the streetcar line, it was possible to board a Weston Road bus, which would give access to the Humber Valley.

Peersen said to Thomson as they departed the young man's home, "Taylor was not at home the evening Stritch was murdered. She lied. She and Dinkman covered for each other. Heaven only knows where Dinkman really was, likely with the hooker Wild Betty. I believe we have grounds for a search warrant of Taylor's flat."

They had no problem convincing a judge for a warrant. When they searched Taylor's flat, they discovered jars of blood in a padlocked cupboard in the pantry. On them, Taylor had placed handwritten labels with the victims' names. The jars were not full. Taylor had filled the small containers found in Baldwin's apartment from these larger jars. Then she had typed the labels she placed on the smaller jars and wiped the jars clean of fingerprints.

Peersen wondered how Miss Taylor had been able to hide the containers of blood in Baldwin's apartment. He remembered that while Gerry was calling an ambulance, they had both been distracted. Perhaps when she went down the hallway to use the washroom, in the confusion, she retrieved the bottles of blood from her oversized purse and slipped the decoy jars into the laundry hamper. It was a good theory, but unless she confessed, they would never be certain if this was how she had accomplished it.

It now remained only to make the arrest. The evidence was solid.

While they were placing the sealer jars in a box to deliver them to the evidence room at the precinct, Taylor arrived home. The next few minutes passed too quickly for anyone to intervene or prevent a tragedy from happening.

Taylor flew into a rage when she saw that they had found her trophy jars of blood. Grabbing a knife from the kitchen counter, she flew at Peersen, whom she viewed as her archenemy. Thomson attempted to block her but failed. She continued her rush toward Peersen, but before she was able to reach him, one of the officers drew his gun, aimed it at her, and shouted for her to drop the knife and surrender.

Realizing that they had trapped her, she quickly turned around and dashed toward the doors that led to the large veranda across the second-floor level of the house. Without pausing, she leaped headfirst over the railing, crashing to the cement walkway below.

Jim was the first to arrive outside on the veranda. He gazed over the pine railing. A pool of blood was draining slowly from Miss Taylor's head. Peersen was certain she was dead.

✧ ✧ ✧

In the days following Miss Taylor's demise, Jim and Gerry fit together some of the pieces of the puzzle, but they realized that they would never know the entire story.

Peersen learned from one of the teachers that during a house party, shortly before the Labour Day weekend of 1951, Elaine Stritch had overheard a drunken staff member mention a sex club on Raymore Drive and hint that Matheson had attended it. It explained why Stritch went to the Humber Valley. She likely wanted to see if the club did in fact exist. Learning that it did, she feared that it was true that Matheson had attended, and became extremely upset. This explained why her eyes had been red from crying.

One of the grade-thirteen female students at YCI, at the urging of her parents, finally came forward and informed the police that several weeks before the Labour Day weekend in 1951, Miss Stritch had caught her and Miss Taylor in an "embarrassing situation," as the girl had worded it. The girl claimed it was not consensual. They now had the motive for Stritch's murder. Taylor had killed Stritch to prevent her from telling anyone. Taylor knew that Stritch was going to the Humber Valley and was familiar with the trail where Elaine would be walking.

When they found a bloody penis-shaped object in Taylor's apartment flat, they realized that she had employed it to violate her victims. She had likely also sodomized the teenage boy on Centre Island with it. In all the murders, there had never been any semen found.

Peersen suspected that Taylor had relocated the bodies to delay their discovery for at least twenty-four hours. He theorized that she had mistakenly hoped that the passage of time would degrade the evidence sufficiently to account for the lack of semen, as she feared that they might not believe that the killer had always employed a condom.

When Dinkman's safety deposit box was finally located and a court order secured to open it, Peersen and Thomson assembled more pieces of the puzzle. It contained personal papers and large amounts of cash. Among the papers was a handwritten note revealing that the vice-principal had discovered that Baldwin sexually molested several of his grade-thirteen female students. Dinkman had learned about it on a tip from Mr. Meagan, the Latin teacher. It was now obvious that Dinkman had confronted Baldwin and demanded money for his silence. As Baldwin had sufficient funds, he succumbed to the blackmail.

Peersen learned from one of the teachers that Dinkman had inadvertently allowed it to slip that a teacher on staff was having an affair with a student. However, they now knew that Dinkman had been referring to Baldwin, not Taylor. Taylor had no way of knowing this, and decided it was necessary to kill Dinkman. The police would never know what excuse she fabricated to lure him to Earlscourt Park.

When Miss Taylor went to the precinct and hinted to the police that Baldwin was having affairs with his students, she did not realize that she had inadvertently hit on the truth. Her motive had likely been revenge, because he had rejected her. However, it was also possible that she wondered if Elaine had told Baldwin about her own affair with a student. It was better to be safe than sorry. She decided to frame Baldwin, but when the opportunity presented itself, instead of allowing the police to arrest Baldwin, she killed him. "Dead men tell no tales."

As far as Peersen could determine, Baldwin had never revealed to anyone what Stritch had told him about Taylor. Peersen suspected the reason he kept quiet was that he feared that if the police investigated Taylor's sexual activities and interviewed the students at YCI, they might uncover his own crimes.

When Thomson and Peersen interviewed Taylor's elderly foster parents, they stated that many years after their son died in the strange knife accident, they discovered that one of their son's best friends said that their son had bragged about molesting Bettina. Because of the recent events, they now wondered if Bettina had murdered their son to escape the molestations.

✧ ✧ ✧

Jim discussed the events with Samantha, and she expressed the opinion that Bettina was a psychopath and did not feel that society's conventions applied to her. Taylor murdered to satisfy her own needs. In her cruel world of fantasy, she was simply doing what she thought necessary, and then discovered it was pleasurable.

Samantha speculated, "I think that when Taylor killed Stritch, it unleashed feelings inside her that she had not known existed. It aroused within her the pleasure she had felt when she had killed her brother. She had likely sexually violated Stritch simply as an act of revenge and preplanned to retrieve her roommate's blood as a trophy. However, she found that watching the blood drain from the unconscious Stritch fascinated her even more than when she had killed her brother. From that time forward, Taylor was unable to control the urge to indulge in the pleasure again."

Peersen listened carefully as Samantha continued. "Taylor's compulsive need to store the blood from her victims was how she relived the gratification of the kills. For her, blood and violence were a substitute for the sex act."

Peersen asked Samantha, "Do you think Taylor was a lesbian?"

"No."

"But she had an affair with a female student."

"True. I can't really explain Taylor's motives. It's possible that when her stepbrother sexually molested her, she was both repulsed and fascinated. She may have molested the female student in imitation of her stepbrother. But I'm convinced that in her way, she loved Gregory Baldwin, even though she hated him for ending their relationship. Such dichotomous feelings are common in persons who are as mentally disturbed as Miss Taylor was. I think Taylor had a pathological hatred of women, perhaps caused by the self-hatred she endured because she had not spoken out when her stepbrother molested her. I'm speculating," Samantha said, "but I think she sodomized the boy on Centre Island in revenge for the abuse she had received from her stepbrother. It's all very complicated," Samantha added. "No one truly understands the intricacies of the human mind."

"I believe that qualifies as the understatement of all time."

Jim now explained to Samantha that when the teachers at YCI were confronted with irrefutable evidence, they had finally confessed to their participation in the sex club in the home of Joe Castle on Raymore Drive. One of the teachers, who knew Dinkman well, said that Dinkman had told him that it began when Dinkman was soliciting a prostitute on Jarvis Street and inadvertently observed Joe engaged in the same activity. They met the following week, and Dinkman blackmailed Joe into allowing Dinkman to take his prostitutes to Joe's house, where he could perform his sexual acts in private. Soon, to reduce the risk for Dinkman, he coerced Joe into procuring the hookers for Dinkman. They both had many evenings in Joe's home, sometimes sharing the same girl.

Next, Dinkman pressured Joe into allowing him to invite a few carefully selected friends to Joe's house to enjoy prostitutes. This went on for many months. Finally, Debbie Dinkman became suspicious. She followed her husband one night and discovered what was happening in the house on Raymore Drive. She threatened to phone the police unless they allowed her to join the group.

Joe was handsome and well endowed in the way Debbie liked, but he was unable to satisfy her, so they recruited a few male prostitutes to attend the private sessions. Eventually, more people, male and female, were permitted to visit the house on Raymore Drive, for a price, of course. In the basement, Joe built a sex dungeon where members with kinky tastes could indulge their fantasies unobserved. They said that Miss Taylor frequented the dungeon.

The only rule the club observed was that all sex must be consensual and that they pay Joe and Dinkman in advance for allowing them to attend. Joe's share of the money was to buy his silence and continued participation. They also agreed that the sex club, as they now referred to it, should meet only one night a month. If it were more frequent, it might arouse the suspicions of the neighbours. They were unaware that one neighbour had already noticed.

Friends whom Dinkman knew from schools where he had previously taught were among those he invited. They all had overactive sex drives. Dinkman then conceived the idea that if these teachers were on the staff of YCI, he would be able to communicate with them better, as well as control them, ensuring that no outsiders ever found out about the club. Dinkman never revealed to Evanson the background of the teachers he hired.

The entire deck of cards tumbled out of their hands when Elaine Stritch was murdered. Any investigation into their lives could reveal their participation in the club. The teachers closed ranks to prevent the police from discovering the truth. The teachers were convinced that there was no harm in this course of action, as they were certain that no member of the club had committed the murder. After all, Elaine Stritch had not been involved with the club.

Jim discovered that Anthony Bowler, Jim Rogers, and Gayle Manson had all been members, along with Bill Matheson, Sam Millford, Bettina Taylor, and Greg Baldwin.

Next, Jim said, "I don't think Miss Allyson knew anything about the sex club, and she certainly knew nothing about the murders."

"I agree," Samantha said. "She has an introverted personality, was drawn to Taylor's forceful character, and saw the possibility of having a dream fulfilled by helping raise Taylor's young son. However, her lies about the whereabouts of Taylor on the night of the murder prevented suspicion from falling on Taylor."

Then she inquired, "Are the police going to lay charges against Miss Allyson for giving false evidence?"

"I believe they will have to, but I pity the judge who presides over the case. I hope he owns a pair of water wings or a row boat."

✧ ✧ ✧

In the days ahead, the police decided that details of the sex club were never to be released to the press. Toronto of the 1950s was too virginal a town to cope with such knowledge. It would have destroyed the public's faith in teachers. As well, it would have ended forever the self-proclaimed image of "Toronto the Good."

A few of the "gutter press" tabloids wrote articles based on rumours, but few people paid any attention. It was too outlandish to be believed.

✧ ✧ ✧

The Valley Vampire was no more. With the solving of the Stritch case, as well as the Dinkman murder, five other murder investigations were closed. The bottles of stored blood were conclusive evidence. This time they were certain that they had the original bottles, clearly labelled in Taylor's handwriting, and with her fingerprints on them.

Peersen gave Frank Gnomes an exclusive on the parts of the story that the police could release. He wrote a series of articles that earned much money and increased circulation for the *Trib*. In gratitude for the tip that

Peersen had given him, much to Peersen's annoyance, Frank's stories made Jim the most famous detective in Toronto. Frank relegated Gerry Thomson to the background, and Gerry was grateful.

The wrath of hell descended on the head of Chief of Detectives Peckerman when the chief of police summoned him to his office and demanded that he explain why the promising young detective, Jim Peersen, had resigned from the police force. Peckerman was stunned when at the end of the interview, the chief shouted, "You're a bloody incompetent asshole."

Peckerman was not certain if he was more stunned at the accusation or the intemperate language.

✧ ✧ ✧

On Monday, 2 July, Tom sat alone on the veranda steps watching the occasional car passing on the street and observing those who were out for a stroll before retiring for the night. The stillness of the warm air magnified the happy voices on the surrounding verandas. He thought about the months ahead and realized that, unlike previous years, the summer would not be his own. He had found employment as a file clerk at the Canada Life Building on University Avenue, where he would work until he had saved enough funds to go to university. After he graduated, he intended to apply to the Toronto Teachers' College. Few aspiring teachers attended teachers' college after university, so it would give him an advantage at hiring time.

Lost in thought, he did not hear the screen door open. Gramps came out on the veranda and sat quietly in his favourite chair.

After a few minutes, he said to Tom, "Well, me boy, you're off to work on Tuesday morning. How does it feel to be a working man?"

Tom turned and smiled at him. "I am not certain."

"Don't worry about the days ahead," he said. "They have a way of taking care of themselves. Many a stormy night on the Grand Banks, I wondered if the schooner would ever drop anchor in a safe harbour, but here I am today, talking to you."

"Gramps, my job is not what worries me. I don't think you ever had anyone telling you that you shouldn't marry Nan."

"I see. It's your girlfriend Sophie who worries you."

"She's more than my girlfriend. I want to marry her."

"I think you had best place some faith in your mom. The pastor at the church gave her a rough time, but your mom had no problems fending him off. And heaven help any of the relatives who try to criticize Sophie in front of your grandmother. She likes her. Me? I think she is pretty, intelligent, and has a real mind of her own." After pausing, as if reflecting, he added, "She reminds me of your grandmother."

Tom smiled at his last remark, and they sat in comfortable silence.

Tom finally rose from where he was sitting on the veranda steps and sat beside his grandfather. "Gramps," Tom began in a quiet voice. "I want to tell you something, and I want you to promise that you will never tell a single soul."

Gramps replied with his usual silly remark about secrets. "I can keep a secret. It's the damn fools I tell them to that can't keep their mouths shut."

"Seriously, Gramps, I want you to promise."

"Okay. My mouth will be as tight as a cod's tongue in a frying pan."

"I've told Sophie that I want to marry her. She told me that because of the objections of her parents, and other problems, it would be too difficult. We have agreed that as soon as we can earn enough money, we are going to live together, unmarried. We'll let the future unfold as it will."

Gramps looked at Tom, his eyes narrowed, and a frown creased his brow. He decided not to offer any advice. "I'll respect your secret, Tom. I'll not tell a soul."

However, Gramps feared for the days ahead as they unfolded in his young grandson's life.

On the veranda, on that warm June evening, after a few moments of silence, Gramps quietly began to hum his favourite hymn: "Abide with me; fast falls the eventide; the darkness deepens, Lord with me abide ..." Whenever Gramps was troubled, he retreated into the world of faith that had guided him on the stormy seas of the Grand Banks.

Tom remained quiet, grateful that despite the changes the future would bring, Gramps would always be there to share his secrets. Life on Lauder Avenue was secure.

Deep in his heart, Tom was also convinced that no matter which path he followed, he would share it with Sophie. He also hoped that Old Prune-Faced Klacker would not be treading the same path.

Author's Notes

Many people assert that all novels are autobiographical. This is not true in this instance, as the story is clearly fictional. However, some of the incidents I based on my own high school days, and the locale of the story is my childhood neighbourhood. I also admit that I borrowed some details from the background of my parents and grandparents and transplanted them onto the Hudson family. However, the personalities of Tom's family members, their conversations, and actions are certainly not those of my own family. Other than the historical personages mentioned, the characters are fictional, and any similarity to real persons is coincidental.

York Collegiate Institute is fictional, and not to be confused with York Memorial Collegiate, located at Eglinton Avenue West and Keele Street. I intentionally placed the fictional YCI near Oakwood and Rogers Road, within the boundaries of my old neighbourhood. The teachers mentioned in the book were invented, and any resemblance to my real high-school teachers is coincidental. In some ways, it is a shame that Miss Hitch, Mr. Bowler, Miss Allyson, Miss Taylor, or Coach Millford never existed. Such characters might have made school reunions worthwhile.

I have portrayed the 1950s as a decade that I remember fondly. They were wonderful years to have lived in Toronto. Despite its perceived inhibitions and blandness, I remember the city as being gloriously diverse, colourful, and fascinating. It was not a gastronomic wasteland or cultural desert, as later decades were to view it. Its downtown restaurants, theatres, and nightlife were wonderful, and its forested residential neighbourhoods were livable, akin to small villages. They were the years that the city was establishing the institutions that allowed the city to become the cultural centre that it is today.

However, like many cities of the era, there was a downside. In writing this narrative, I could not ignore the prejudices and intolerance of the decade. I have raised issues that in the 1950s they never would have discussed. The benefits of hindsight and the freedom of the modern era allow me to include such controversial subjects.

Today, it may be difficult to contemplate Toronto as a city where Catholics and Protestants did not readily socialize, and where anti-Semitism was common. In the 1950s, homosexuality was against the law, and ethnic and racial jokes were for the most part sociably acceptable. The advancement of women in the work force was not equal to that of men. Couples that lived together before marrying, single mothers, and divorced women were often the subject of cruel gossip. Not all this bigotry has disappeared in the modern era.

Weather reports, sporting events, and political happenings are accurate. All information about the CNE and the Stratford Festival is a matter of record. The prices mentioned for automobiles and other articles are accurate, as well as the names of the restaurants, their menus, phone numbers, and prices. The restaurant and the hotel in Montreal are the exceptions. Real estate prices, including those for Florida and New York City, are also accurate.

During the 1950s, the movie houses of Toronto dominated the social scene. The performances mentioned at the Royal Alexandra Theatre are real, as are the prices that Jim Peersen paid for the tickets. All movies in the narrative are listed in the correct month, and in the theatres in which they actually appeared.

It was an era when most families attended a place of worship. However, Toronto was a hockey town that valued the sport almost as highly as its churches. Maple Leaf Gardens was the cathedral of hockey. In some respects, hockey was the religion of the masses, alongside the films of Hollywood. The hockey game that Kramer and Harry attended was an actual game and occurred on the date mentioned. Even the scores are true. However, their attendance at the game is obviously fictional.

The Montreal hockey riot was a real event and occurred on the date mentioned, although the reader views it through the eyes of the fictional Jim Peersen and Samantha Anderson. The happenings surrounding Hurricane Hazel are also accurate, and we experience them through the actions of the two imaginary detectives.

Events surrounding the 1951 royal tour of Princess Elizabeth and Prince Philip are mostly true. The death of George VI and the coronation of Queen Elizabeth II are as reported in the history books, but of course, the comments of Gramps during the coronation ceremony are fiction. A few readers may think it a pity that they did not hire Gramps to be a broadcaster for the CBC or the narrator for the official coronation film. Had they employed him, the film would now likely be considered a classic.

In this book, the invented narrative and characters serve as a medium to relate the history, cultural events, sports' scene, and social attitudes of 1950s Toronto, and place them within in an intriguing story. Readers will judge if I have succeeded.

Readers may wish to speculate on which character in the story was the inspiration for the title of the book. Several could ably fulfill the role, including Harry. Even though he did not engage in an intimate act with Kramer, he reluctantly cast aside his innocence to accept an idea that had formerly been repugnant to him. However, none of the characters is the reluctant virgin. The city of Toronto claims the title.

At the beginning of the 1950s, the city continued to cling to its traditional values and prejudices, which had survived despite the upheavals of the war years. However, as the post-war years progressed, despite its struggle to resist, Toronto succumbed to the decadent pleasures that the modern era presented. By the end of the decade, there was little doubt that the city's virginal innocence had disappeared. Whether this was good or bad is a value judgment. To paraphrase the words of Samuel Fletcher—nothing is so dainty sweet as lovely decadence. Some would argue that the decadence was simply the development of the city's collective freedom. After all, Toronto survived the transition and emerged as a vibrant, cosmopolitan, tolerant city, even though in the eyes of many, it had lost its virtues.

The serial killer is an exaggerated metaphor that extends through the story, representing the transition from traditional values to abandonment. Year by year, similar to the city, the stalker's inner needs and impulses determined the course of daily life.

We can only wonder what Tom's grandmother Hudson would have thought of the following decade, the decadent 1960s, when the city was definitely "a virgin no more."

Coming Soon

A Virgin No More
Toronto Trilogy, Book Three

In the years after graduating from high school, Tom Hudson labours for four years to earn sufficient funds to enter university and eventually attend teachers' college. His friend Shorty—Forester (Bernie) Bernstein—drops out of university and becomes involved in the drug culture in Toronto's infamous Yorkville area of the 1960s. Tom's relationship with Sophie is not without problems, as are those of Tom's high school pals, Harry Heinz and Horace Kramer.

On the Saturday evening of the Labour Day weekend in 1965, prior to beginning his new career in the classroom, Tom and his sweetheart, Sophie, witness a seemingly random murder on the Yonge Street subway.

Chief of Detectives Arnold Peckerman assigns the murder case to Detective Paul Masters. Private detectives Jim Peersen and Gerry Thomson are drawn into the investigation. Harry Heinz, who is now a young attorney, also becomes involved in the case.

Disaster then strikes again, when the killer murders one of Tom's friends. The murder investigations lead to the corridors of power at Queen's Park and eventually to Ottawa, where they threaten to bring down members of the federal cabinet.

The third book in the Toronto Trilogy relates the struggles of Tom, Harry, and their friends, as well as detectives Peersen and Thomson, to solve the crimes. Frank Gnomes, a reporter at the *Toronto Tribune* is attracted to the case and begins an investigation of his own.

The story provides an intriguing insight into life in Toronto during the 1960s, a decade in which decadence prevailed. The narrative explores the lives of Tom and his friends, as they build their careers and mature in their relationships. All this occurs while a murderer casts an ominous shadow that threatens their survival.

The background of the story is the metropolis of Toronto, as it sheds the traditions and values of its past. *A Virgin No More* is a story of the city during a decade when it is evolving into an urban centre that embraces the worldliness of the modern world.